SOUTHERN STORM

CAPE REFUGE SERIES

SOUTHERN STORM

BOOK TWO

Terri Blackstock

ZONDERVAN™

GRAND RAPIDS, MICHIGAN 49530 USA

Southern Storm
Copyright © 2003 by Terri Blackstock

Requests for information should be addressed to:
Zondervan, *Grand Rapids, Michigan 49530*

Library of Congress Cataloging-in-Publication Data

Blackstock, Terri, 1957–
    Southern storm / Terri Blackstock.
        p.   cm. — (Cape refuge series ; bk. 2)
    ISBN 0-310-23593-6
    1. Missing persons—Fiction.   2. Police chiefs—Fiction.   3. Kidnapping—
Fiction.   4. Georgia—Fiction.   I. Title.
    PS3552.L34285S68 2003
    813'.54—dc21

                                                      2002156134

Published in association with the literary agency of Alive Communications, Inc., 7680 Goddard Street, Suite 200, Colorado Springs, CO 80920.

Interior design by Beth Shagene

Printed in the United States of America

03 04 05 06 07 08 09 10 /❖ DC/ 10 9 8 7 6 5 4 3 2 1

*This book is lovingly
dedicated to the Nazarene.*

ACKNOWLEDGMENTS

I've been writing professionally for over twenty years now and long ago realized that it never gets easier. The truth is, each book is more difficult than the one before it. Fortunately, I have people in my life who help me. I'd like to thank some of them now.

Thanks to my dear friends (and family) of ChiLibris, a group of Christian writers who hold me accountable and constantly challenge me to grow as a writer and as a person. Writing can be a solitary life, but ChiLibris keeps me connected to others with the same passions. I also owe a debt of gratitude to James Scott Bell, lawyer-turned-writer, for answering all of my legal questions with such patience. And again I thank Dr. Harry Kraus Jr., surgeon-turned-writer, for choreographing medical emergencies with me and helping me figure out how to write my way out of them.

A special thank-you to those at Zondervan for their excellent work in getting my books into the stores. I owe more to Dave Lambert, Sue Brower, Lori VandenBosch, Bob Hudson, and the others on the fiction team than I can say.

Thanks also to Greg Johnson, my agent, whom God seemed to drop out of the sky for me eight years ago. He is evidence to me that when I follow God's direction, I can't go wrong.

And finally, thank you to my husband, Ken, for brainstorming with me, encouraging me, and rooting me on when the deadline looms near and my creativity seems dried up. I appreciate your constant reminders that I panic on every book, and it still usually turns out all right.

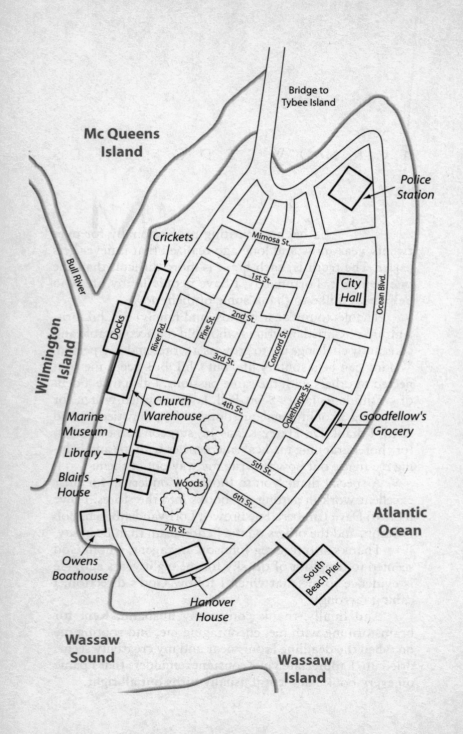

SOUTHERN STORM

CHAPTER

1

*T*he Georgia Weather Bureau's prophecy
of fifty-mile-per-hour winds had been fulfilled and sur-
passed, much to Matthew Cade's chagrin. As chief of the
small Cape Refuge police force, Cade could do little about
the ravages of the storm as it beat across the island toward
Savannah. But the safety of the residents was always his
concern.

Though it was two in the afternoon, the sky looked
as dark as nightfall.

Lightning bolted overhead in a panoramic display of
white-hot fingers, grounding on the island and splaying
across the angry Atlantic. The thunder cracked in rapid
crashes, and rain slatted down at an angle that made
umbrellas useless and flooded some of the streets.

Cade strained to see through the windshield of his
squad car. The rain pounding on his roof and his wipers
slashing across his windshield made it difficult for him
to hear the radio crackling on his dashboard. He turned
it up.

Fender benders had been reported at three locations on Cape Refuge, and a power line was down near the condos lining the north beach.

If everyone would just stay inside, maybe they could avoid any more problems. But that never happened. On days like this, residents insisted on driving through the storm at the same speeds they used on dry, sunny days. Tornado watchers stood out on their front porches, watching the sky for funnel clouds. And the most reckless among the residents would brave the lightning and drag their surfboards out to the waves, hoping to catch a thrill in the tempest.

Cade and his police force were left to clean up the messes and head off new disasters.

The dispatcher's voice crackled across the radio, and he picked up the mike. "Go ahead, Sal."

"Chief, there's another power line down on a road over at the dock. Somebody's going to get hurt unless you detour that traffic."

Cade sighed. "All right, I'm on my way."

He set the mike back in its holder and turned on his blue lights. Making a U-turn, he headed back around the southern tip of the island, then northbound toward the dock. He couldn't have residents driving over live power lines. He hoped the power company would hurry up and get its trucks out here.

The wipers swiped across his windshield, but the rain pounded too hard to give him much visibility. He strained to see.

Most cars pulled to the side of the road to let him pass. He turned on his siren to alert the others, but three or four kept their course in the lane in front of him.

"Get out of the way!" he yelled, pulling so close to the car in front of him that he knew one touch of its brakes would put him in the front seat with the driver.

Fortunately, the man pulled over. The other cars ahead of him still hadn't heard or seen him, so he moved up behind the next one, his siren still blaring. A block ahead, Cade saw a man standing on the opposite side of the road, seemingly oblivious to the rain pounding down on him. Passing traffic sprayed walls of water up over him, but he just stood there, watching the traffic pass.

The car in front of Cade still didn't move, so he punched his horn. The southbound lane with traffic coming toward him had cleared as drivers pulled off to the shoulder of Ocean Boulevard. He pulled around the car in front of him into the southbound lane and gently accelerated.

The man on the side of the road still stood there, drenched and undaunted. Cade knew that, as he passed, his tires in the water would spray him. Why didn't the man move?

He kept his siren blaring and pushed his horn again as he drove northbound in the southbound lane. He pulled even with the car that had refused to move out of the way and looked across at the driver. The driver looked back, panic evident on his face— a teenager, probably a new driver with no idea how to react. The kid slammed on his brakes.

Cade stepped on his accelerator and turned his eyes ahead again—just in time to see the pedestrian step out in front of him.

Cade yelled and slammed on his brakes. His car slid straight toward the man. . . .

Thunder cracked at the same instant as the impact. The man flew up over the hood and smashed into Cade's windshield, shattering it . . . then, as if he'd bounced, he flew out in front of the car and landed in a heap in the middle of the road. Cade couldn't move for a few seconds, then fumbled for the door handle and managed to get out. The rain flooded over him, and the wind almost knocked him back into the car. He rushed toward the man.

Oh, dear God, what have I done?

He heard yelling and doors slamming as other drivers got out and splashed toward him.

Reaching the man first, Cade knelt in three inches of water. The victim's eyes fluttered open, and his lips moved without sound. Cade grabbed the radio on his shoulder. "Sal, I need an ambulance just half a mile north of the Pier!" He yelled the words to make sure he was heard. "I need it right now! I just ran over a pedestrian!"

"Right away, Chief."

Cade touched the man's head, careful not to move it. Warm blood soaked his hand, but the pelting rain quickly washed it away.

"Can you hear me, buddy?"

The man tried to speak, but Cade couldn't hear him. Thunder crashed again.

He touched the man's throat; his pulse was weak, erratic.

"Hang on! You're gonna be all right. Just hang on." He had to stop the bleeding, so he pressed against the wound at the back of the man's head. But there was so much blood . . . too much . . .

The man tried to rise up, and this time Cade heard his raspy voice. "You have to . . . please . . . out of control . . ."

"Don't move!" What did one do for an open head wound?

He heard sirens blaring, voices calling. Someone opened an umbrella over them in a feeble attempt to shelter the victim from the storm, but the wind turned it inside out. Someone else threw a raincoat over the man. . . .

Lightning flashed, thunder bolted. . . .

"Cade," someone said, "he just ran right out in front of you!"

The blood was coming so fast. The man's pulse weakened. Where was that ambulance?

"I saw him. It was like he was in a trance or something."

"Is he dead, Cade?"

The siren grew closer, and he prayed that people would stay off the road and leave the ambulance a path. It stopped short, and he heard feet running toward him. Paramedics knelt beside the body, and Cade moved back. "Head injury," he yelled over the storm. "He bounced off my windshield."

As the medics worked, Cade backed farther away, his mind racing with the facts.

I've hit a man . . . an innocent man. . . .

He started to whisper rapid-fire prayers for a miracle. The man couldn't die. That was all there was to it. Police cars were meant to keep people from danger, not kill them.

"Call for a Medi-Vac, Cade!" one of the medics cried. "And clear us a path. He's running out of time."

"The helicopter can't fly in this! You'll have to drive him." He helped the paramedics get the man into the ambulance and then directed traffic as the ambulance headed out.

He shook his head, trying to pull himself together. Somebody had to be in charge here. But what did the chief of police do when he was the one who had almost killed a man?

He turned and saw some of his uniformed officers coming toward him.

"J.J., detour traffic," he yelled. "Keep it off of this block until we finish here. Jim, get over to the downed power lines out in front of the dock and divert traffic there. Alex, you take pictures and work the accident. . . ."

"But Cade, are you sure you don't want to work it?"

"I've got to get to the hospital and see if he's all right." His voice broke. "Just write the report and treat me like any other driver who hit a pedestrian. Call my cell phone if you have questions. It should get a signal by the time I reach Savannah." He walked back to his car and got in.

Through the shattered windshield, he saw Alex looking back at him as if he wasn't sure what to do. Then he turned away and began questioning witnesses.

Cade closed his eyes and lowered his head to the steering wheel. *That man could die.*

Why had he stepped out into traffic? He must have seen Cade coming. The squad car lights had been flashing and his siren was on. Even people in cars with radios blaring and air conditioners humming had heard him and gotten out of the way. How could this man have stepped into the path of a speeding police car?

He felt as if a fist had punched a hole in his lungs. He found it hard to breathe, and his head had begun to throb.

He reached for the keys hanging in the ignition, then realized that he couldn't move this car until they'd finished working the scene. Besides, he couldn't drive with a busted windshield.

He got out of the car and started walking through the rain.

"Where are you going, Chief?" Alex asked him.

"To find a ride back to the station so I can get my truck."

"I'll take you, Cade!" Melba Jefferson, a little round woman who attended his church and made it her business to comfort those in need, stood nearby, fighting her umbrella with a distraught look on her face.

"Okay, Melba," he said. "Let's go."

She led him to her car parked on the side of the road. He got into it, and she slid her round body into the driver's side. "Honey, are you all right?"

He shook his head. "It's not about me, Melba. There's a man dying."

She reached into the backseat and got a box of tissue. "Sweetie, your hand's all bloody."

Cade looked at it. The man's blood had stained it, though the rain had begun to wash it away. He pulled out several tissues and wiped the rest of it off.

Melba pulled out onto the street, and Alex directed her so that she could turn around and head back to the station. When they were on their way, she stayed quiet, which Cade appreciated. Clearly, Melba knew when words were appropriate and when they weren't.

She drove him up to the station, pulled into the parking lot. "I'll get some people praying, Cade," she said.

He nodded. "You do that. Thanks for the ride, Melba."

Cade jogged across the gravel parking lot to his truck, jumped inside, and was pulling out onto the street before Melba could get her car turned around.

CHAPTER

*I*s this some kind of April Fool's joke?"
Blair Owens leaned on the small conference table in the
cramped library and tapped her pencil on her palm.
"Because if it is, I need to get back to work."

"It ain't no April Fool's joke," Morris Ambrose told
her. "That woulda been last Thursday."

She laughed. "You people can't seriously want me to
run for mayor. That's insane. It's ludicrous. And I wouldn't
go around saying it out loud, Morris, or you might lose
your seat on the city council. Folks will start thinking
you're showing signs of dementia."

Morris was undaunted. So were the other three who
had come with him—Jerry Ann Shepp who ran the Cape
Refuge Racquet Club; Matt Pearl, proprietor of the most
expensive restaurant in town; and Gerald Madison, who
owned Madison Boat Shop.

"Blair, think about it for a minute," Gerald said, wiping the beads of perspiration from above his lip. "The
mayor's seat is empty since Fred got thrown in jail. Some

real lowlifes are running. Sam Sullivan doesn't have the brains of a shrimp, and Ben Jackson hates big business."

Blair grinned and shook her head. "Gerald, Cape Refuge doesn't have any big business."

"You know what he means!" Jerry Ann piped in. "Blair, he's an electrician and thinks he needs to stick it to every business owner in town. We need somebody with a clear head and a back-bone. Somebody honest. Somebody who can't be pushed around."

"Oh, brother." Blair felt the scars on the right side of her face burning. It always happened when she was surprised or embar-rassed or, in this case, amazed. She got up and went to the pot of coffee she had brewed for this Sunday afternoon mystery meet-ing. Glancing out the door into the room stacked with books, she saw that Gray Foster was still studying at one of the reading tables, his nose buried in a book.

She turned back to the group. "This is crazy. Just crazy. I'm not the political type. I hate that kind of stuff. I'd much rather *fight* city hall than *run* it. Besides that, I'm not all that committed to living here since my parents died. One day I might pick up and move. You don't want a mayor who'd do that, do you?"

Matt Pearl, dressed in a designer suit with a black T-shirt underneath, crossed his sockless foot over his knee. "We know you, Blair. If you were elected mayor, you'd stay."

She poured her coffee and took a sip. "See, that's just it, Matt. I couldn't get elected. I've insulted ninety percent of the res-idents of Cape Refuge at one time or another. No, you've got to find yourself another patsy."

The four of them looked at each other with brooding eyes. "Well, who then? We've got to come up with our own candidate so some rube doesn't take the mayor's seat."

Jerry Ann began to rub her temples. "It's awful, you know. For our town to be without a judge, a mayor, and a newspaper all in one fell swoop."

"That's the way it goes." Blair came back to her seat. "But I'm not the one."

The phone rang, and she excused herself and dashed out into the book room and across to her office to answer it. "Cape Refuge Public Library, may I help you?"

"Blair, it's Morgan."

"Let me call you back, Sis. I've got people here."

"It's important. Did you hear about Cade?"

Blair stiffened. "No, what about him?"

"He hit a pedestrian. The man might die."

Blair caught her breath. "You're kidding."

"Melba Jefferson saw the whole thing. Cade's on his way to the hospital."

Blair shoved her blonde hair back. "Is Cade hurt?"

"I don't think so. Melba didn't mention it. She just said he's pretty torn up about it."

"Okay, I'm closing shop and going to the hospital."

"Come by and get me," Morgan said. "I'll go too."

"Five minutes. Be ready." Blair reached for her keys hanging on a hook on the wall. She hung up and ran back into the conference room. "Meeting's over, guys. Thanks for coming by. I have to run to Savannah."

She herded the four out of the library and turned back to the college student. "Gray, you have to go."

"Let me stay, Blair," he said. "Come on, I'm right in the middle of something. I'll lock up when I leave."

She didn't have time to argue, so she gave in. "All right. But don't leave me a mess to clean up."

"I won't."

She hurried out to her car, hoping the streets weren't too flooded to get through.

Cade was hurting, and she didn't want him to be alone.

Morgan set the phone back in its cradle and took off her apron. At twenty-eight, she was responsible for Hanover House, a bed-and-breakfast that served as a halfway house for the down-and-out instead of a haven for tourists. In an attempt to foster a family atmosphere for the tenants, she cooked a full meal each night and expected everyone to eat together. But tonight, Cade, her husband's best friend, was in trouble. She wished she could reach Jonathan to tell him, but he'd gone to Savannah for his Sunday Bible study at the county jail.

"Sadie, can you watch Seth and get dinner out when it's done? I've got everything in the oven. It should be ready at six."

Her seventeen-year-old foster daughter bounced baby Seth on her hip. "Sure, no problem."

Morgan smiled at the young girl she had found hiding in her boathouse just a few months ago. She'd had a broken arm and was desperately hiding from the man who had beaten her. Only later had Morgan learned about Seth, Sadie's baby brother, still in the man's possession.

Thank goodness that was behind them and Sadie's mother had given Morgan and Jonathan legal guardianship over both of them while she served her prison term. Sadie was more help than responsibility, and seventeen-month-old Seth was pure joy.

Morgan heard Blair's horn outside, and she pressed a kiss on Seth's cheek, then Sadie's. "Don't forget dinner. And when Jonathan gets home tell him I went to the hospital with Blair."

"I didn't think we had a hospital on Cape Refuge," Sadie said.

"We don't. They took the man to Savannah." She pulled on her raincoat, grabbed an umbrella, and dashed out the door.

The umbrella did little good. By the time she'd climbed inside Blair's old Volvo, her long hair was soaked. "Look at me," she said with disgust.

"Yeah, look at you." Blair put the car into reverse and, wrenching her neck around, backed out. "You're the only one I know whose hair can take a rainstorm."

Morgan didn't answer. She'd always hated her curls; Blair had always coveted them. "Hey, you might want to cut through the island, since Ocean Boulevard is blocked off at the South Beach Pier."

"I'm on it," Blair said and pulled her car out of the driveway.

CHAPTER

The tempest still raged in Savannah as the tropical storm pushed inland. Trees bent like bows in the wind, their leaves and branches reaching west. Water rose on some of the streets, making them impassable, but Blair navigated her way through the detours and reached Seventy-third Street and Candler Hospital at last.

The white building with its black windows loomed up in front of them, and she drove around to the emergency room and pulled up to the door. "Here, I'll let you out and park."

Morgan looked relieved. "Thanks. I'll find Cade. Use my umbrella."

Blair watched as Morgan rushed in. Pulling out of the covered drive, she found a parking place not far from the door. Normally, she wouldn't have used the umbrella, but she didn't like the idea of looking like a wet puppy in front of Cade.

The moment that thought flashed through her mind, she rebuked herself. This wasn't a fashion show, for heaven's sake. She had come to support Cade, not impress him.

Still, she used the umbrella and made a run for it. She made it inside without too much damage, and shaking out the umbrella, she looked around for Morgan or Cade.

Morgan stood at the reception desk. Blair joined her. "What's the story?"

"The man's still alive," Morgan said. "They said Cade is back there, that we could go to him."

Blair followed Morgan through the doors and into the wide antiseptic hall. She saw Cade farther down, sitting outside an examining room, his chair tipped back on two legs. His head leaned back against the wall, and he stared into space with reflective brown eyes. She could see he was troubled.

Something in her chest tightened.

Blair slowed her step as they approached. "Cade?"

Cade turned and dropped the front two legs of his chair. Surprise registered on his face as he got to his feet. "Blair . . . Morgan. What are you doing here?"

Morgan went to hug him. It was natural for her, the Earth Mother. Who *wouldn't* want a hug from her? Blair hung back.

"We heard what happened," Morgan said. "How is he?"

"I don't know. He's in surgery." He looked at Blair and offered a half-smile. "You're wet."

She smiled. "So are you."

He looked down at his wet uniform, then regarded her again. "I can't believe you came here in this storm."

She shrugged. "We couldn't let you go through this alone." Blair sat down in the chair beside him, and he dropped back into his own. His dark hair was still damp and disheveled, and the lines around his eyes gave him the look of a man much older than thirty-three. Those lines were part sun, part laughter, part stress. Today's accident had added at least another ten years.

"Cade, are you all right?" Morgan asked. "Were you hurt at all?"

"No, not me. But this guy's in really bad shape."

His chair went back on two legs again. Blair saw clearly that he was not all right. "I can't believe this happened."

"How *did* it happen, Cade?" Blair asked.

He swallowed and crossed his arms over his chest. "I was trying to hurry over to a downed power line, and I saw him standing on the side of the road, looking straight at me. And then he just stepped out in front of me. I slammed on my brakes, but the car skidded because the road was too wet. . . ." His voice broke off, and she saw the slight tremor in the muscles of his chin.

Blair wished she had a little Earth Mother in her. "Who is he?"

Cade shook his head again. "That's just it. I don't know. He was trying to speak, but he didn't make any sense. The paramedics said he had no identification on him. None. Not even a wallet. Not a penny in his pocket."

"Well, that's not so unusual on Cape Refuge," Blair said. "Tourists leave their stuff in hotel rooms or glove compartments all the time while they go to the beach or sightsee."

Cade's eyes glistened as he stared straight ahead. "He just stood there. People spraying him as they went by. *Why* did he step in front of me?"

"Maybe he was drunk," Blair offered.

"Who knows?" He rubbed his eyes. "I can't notify anybody until we find out who he is. They need consent forms signed, insurance. I don't even know who to call."

His nostrils flared with the effort of holding back tears.

Cade was tough, but he had a sensitive heart. She knew what this was costing him. She wanted to touch his hand, but that kind of gesture didn't come as naturally for her as it did for Morgan.

She looked away, hoping to make him feel less vulnerable.

A door opened near them, and a doctor came out in green scrubs with his mask pulled below his chin. Cade got up and looked at him hopefully.

"Chief Cade?"

Cade nodded. "I've got my men trying to figure out who he is, so we can notify the family and get the insurance—"

"I'm sorry, Chief." The doctor's words cut Cade off, and the rest of his sentence hung in the air. "He didn't make it."

Cade's mouth dropped open, and he looked as though he hadn't heard right. Then understanding dawned. "Oh, no," he whispered.

"We did what we could," the surgeon said, "but he had multiple injuries. A very serious head injury, and the gunshot wound through his torso."

Cade stared at him blankly for a moment. "No, there was no gunshot. Just the impact of the car. He was walking and he came out in front of me—"

The surgeon shook his head. "He was shot, all right. Maybe that's why he stumbled out in front of you."

Blair looked up at Cade and saw the confusion on his face. "You mean, he was already shot, trying to wave down help? And I came along and ran him over?"

The surgeon took off his surgical cap and wadded it in his hand. "I'm sure you tried to avoid it, Chief. But yes, there was probably already an injury. It looks like he was shot at very close range. Possibly a suicide attempt. Maybe he lost his nerve and went for help."

Blair saw the color draining from Cade's face, and for a minute she thought he might just hit the ground. "He might have lived," Cade said. "I might have gotten him help."

Blair forgot her inhibitions and pulled Cade into a hug, and he slumped over her. She felt his body shaking, his breath catching as he tried to calm himself. She touched his damp hair.

"I killed a man . . . a perfectly innocent man whose name I don't even know."

Blair knew he had killed men before in the line of duty, men with guns who were trying to use them, men who were intent on murder.

But this was different. "Cade, it's not your fault."

"Why didn't I stop sooner? Why wasn't I going slower? A man standing there bleeding to death in the rain, and I didn't even see that he was in distress."

"How could you have known?" She would have pulled back then, but he clung so tightly that she kept holding him. Morgan began to rub his back.

The surgeon looked as if he didn't know whether to stay or go. "Chief, given the gunshot, how would you like us to proceed?"

Cade straightened and looked back at him, clearly trying to think. "Well, the gunshot changes everything. I'll call the medical examiner. I'll need to see the body, take pictures, examine his clothes for evidence." He paused, his eyes moving back and forth as he thought through the proper steps. "Just give me a minute, Doc."

Cade watched the doctor head back to the operating rooms. Morgan had tears in her eyes as she touched Cade's face. "Look at me, Cade," she whispered.

Cade looked down at her.

"You know you didn't do it on purpose," she said. "The man was already dying. You can't blame yourself."

Cade raked his hands through his wet black hair. "I killed a man who was in trouble. How are we going to notify his family? There could be a wife, children . . . ?"

Blair wished she knew what to do. "We'll figure out who he is, Cade."

Cade started to pace. "I need to call the station, tell them to change it from an accident scene to a possible crime scene. We have to figure out where he was walking from, so we can determine if it was suicide or homicide. His car's probably parked at the South Beach Pier, since he seemed to be coming from there. It's raining, so the parking lot wouldn't be full. Maybe we can figure out which car it is and find the weapon. . . ."

Blair wished she could help. "Cade, what can I do?"

"Nothing," he said. "I just need to get busy. Thanks, you two, for coming."

Blair watched him head down the hall.

"Well, I don't guess there's anything else we can do here," Morgan said. "We might as well go."

But Blair just stared in the direction he had gone. "I think I'll stay. Take my car and go on home."

"Why?"

"Because I think after he examines the body he's going to need some support. I want to be here. I'll ride home with him."

Morgan just looked at her for a moment. "Are you sure? It could be hours."

"That's fine. I can wait."

"What about the library?"

"Gray Foster said he'd lock up."

Morgan sighed. "Well, all right. If it goes too long, call me and I'll come back to get you."

As Morgan left her, Blair took the seat Cade had abandoned, and waited.

Two hours later, she watched as the Medical Examiner and some orderlies wheeled the body out to an ambulance for transport to the morgue. Cade and Joe McCormick, his detective who had rushed to the hospital as soon as Cade had called with news of the shooting, walked out behind them.

Blair got up, and as Cade turned around, she saw that he looked pale and defeated. Surprise registered on his face at the sight of her. "You're still here."

She felt a little silly. "I figured you might want some company for the ride home. Morgan took my car."

His eyes softened as he gazed down at her. "I appreciate that, Blair."

The scars on her face felt hot, and she knew they were flaming. She turned her face away and glanced toward where Joe and the medical examiner stood at the exit. "So what do you think? Homicide or suicide?"

"Hard to say," Cade muttered. "All I know is the impact of my car did more damage than the gun shot. He might have made it if—"

"If he hadn't walked out in front of you?" Cade was going to try to shoulder the whole burden of guilt. She couldn't let that happen.

He raked his hands through his rain-styled hair. "Guess we'd better hit the road. I have a ton of work when I get back."

She fell into step beside him. "Have they identified the man yet?"

"No, but we should have something soon. Joe's running his prints through AFIS."

"AFIS?"

"Automated Fingerprint Identification Systems. If the guy's ever been fingerprinted before, we should find a match pretty quickly. But they still haven't found a car or apartment or hotel room yet. The rain isn't helping. His tracks were washed away, so they haven't been able to determine where he came from."

They went through the ER to the overhang just outside the door, and stood there for a moment as Cade stared out at the storm. Blair saw in his eyes that he wasn't hanging back because of the weather. He was still working through the facts, dealing with that dead body he'd just had to examine, trying to make some logical sense of it all.

"I could go get the truck," she said. "Bring it up for you."

Still staring at the rain, he shook his head. "I'm okay. I won't have you getting drenched to keep me from it. I'll get the car and come get you."

"No way." She grabbed his keys out of his hand and started for the truck. But he launched out behind her, reached it before she did, and unlocked her side. She slipped in, soaking wet.

Cade got in on the other side, slammed the door shut, and set his hands on the steering wheel. For a moment he stared out through the blurred windshield, as if gathering his strength for the drive home. The sound of the rain against the roof was punctuated by the thunder cracking at unexpected intervals. "You didn't have to stay all this time, Blair."

She stared straight ahead at the raindrops making quarter-sized circles on the windshield. "I know."

"How'd you hear about the whole thing?"

"Melba's prayer chain."

Cade's face twisted. Blair knew he was thinking that she wasn't a praying woman. "She called you to pray?"

"Of course not. She called Morgan, who told me."

"Oh." Disappointment slackened his face.

Blair knew her lack of faith in the things he believed was like a wall between them, but she refused to masquerade as a believer when she wasn't one.

He backed out of his spot and pulled out into traffic on the busy street beside the hospital. "Maybe I can brainstorm with you on the way back," Blair said, "and help you figure out how to find out the man's identity, in case there's not a match for the prints. You gotta admit I'm a pretty good problem solver."

He considered that a moment. "Guess there's no better person to help me figure it out." He sighed. "You should be a cop."

"Yeah, that'll be the day. I look awful in black."

He smiled then, and Blair felt a small sense of victory.

For a while, he drove through the storm, concentrating on the roads rather than trying to make conversation. He drove too carefully, as if certain that another pedestrian-in-distress would jump out in front of him.

The steady *whish-whish* of the wipers worked itself into Blair's brain as she tried to think of solutions. Finding the man's identity wouldn't make Cade feel any better about what had happened, but at least he wouldn't feel so helpless.

"I'm thinking that you could give a picture of the man to the media and let them get it on the ten o'clock news. By midnight you're sure to have somebody calling with information."

"Where are we going to get a picture, Blair? We can't very well flash shots of the man's dead body on the television screen. I don't want his family to find out that way."

"Yeah, you're right." She thought about that for a moment. "Maybe just a physical description of what he was wearing and what he looked like. Weight, height, eye color . . ."

He blew out a long breath. "Maybe someone's already missed him. Maybe they'd call in. Then I could go to their residence and explain what happened."

She shot him a look. "Yourself?"

"Who else?"

"Well, I don't know, but Cade, don't you think you should send someone else?"

She saw the muscles of his jaw flexing. "No. I'm the one who should go."

Silence again. Blair knew there was no use trying to talk Cade out of that. As difficult as it would be for him, he would never ask anyone else to do it.

"It's weird how suddenly life can spin out of control," he said.

She let her eyes settle on him. "Isn't it, though? I've been there, Cade."

His face softened and he looked over at her. "Yeah, I know you have."

She didn't have to say it. The day her parents were murdered had been the worst day of her life. One minute she was standing in a city council meeting with her sleeves rolled up, ready to fight for Hanover House to stay open, and the next she was standing in the room with her parents' dead bodies. Cade had been right there beside her.

"I felt helpless that day too," Cade whispered, as if he'd read her mind.

"You weren't, though. And you're not now."

They drove across the Island Expressway to Tybee Island, wound their way to the mouth of the Savannah River, then crossed the island bridge to Cape Refuge. "My cell phone doesn't work on the island. Let me just stop by the station and see how far they've gotten," he said, "and then I'll take you home."

"Take your time," she said. "In fact, just don't worry about me. I'll call Morgan to pick me up when she gets home."

They rounded Ocean Boulevard at the northern tip of the island, and as they approached the small police station, they saw that the parking lot was full of television vans.

The media had already heard.

Cade groaned. "I don't believe this."

"Keep driving, Cade," Blair said. "Give yourself a minute to think."

Cade passed the station and headed down the island. "They must have heard the police scanner. This is all I need. Now it'll be broadcast all over the airwaves."

"But they don't know who the man is, right? So it won't matter."

Cade breathed a laugh. "Right. They'll just tell how the Cape Refuge police chief ran some injured man down. And every family in town whose father isn't home will think it's him."

"Maybe the newscasts will lead someone to identifying the body."

Cade reached the South Beach Pier, where the accident had occurred. The road was clear now. It didn't look as if anything significant had happened here . . . like a man dying for no good reason. The blood had all washed away.

He drove past Hanover House and headed to Blair's house, next to the library. He pulled onto the gravel parking lot in a grove of pine trees and mimosas, and stopped the truck.

She didn't get out. "Cade, are you going to be all right?"

He didn't answer for a moment—just stared through his windshield to the trees beyond her house. "Yeah. Thanks for coming. I really appreciate it."

She was quiet for a moment, racking her brain for the right thing to say.

"Cade, if you need some company when you go tell the family, I'll go with you. I'm not known to be the most sensitive soul in the world, but I know what it feels like to get horrible news about someone you love."

He patted her hand. "Thanks for the offer. I'll let you know."

"And for what it's worth, when you told me about my parents . . ."

He met her eyes, waiting for her to go on.

"Well, you did it right. You'll do this right too."

"Thanks," he said.

She got out and ran through the rain to her front door, but she didn't go in until Cade was out of sight.

CHAPTER

*T*he moment Cade pulled into the parking lot of the police station, reporters surrounded him with microphones aimed like grenade launchers.

"Chief Cade, is it true the man you hit is dead?" someone asked him as he got out of the truck.

He slammed the door and didn't answer. Maybe they didn't yet know about the gunshot.

"Did you know the man you killed?"

He trudged through them, wanting to just get inside and get dry. They seemed ravenous, standing out in the lightning and rain, waiting for a morsel of news. "I'm not ready to make a statement yet," he said.

At the front door of the station, which had once been a laundromat, some of the reporters pushed closer to follow him in. "Please wait out here!" He barely had room inside for all the officers on duty. Storm or not, there wasn't room for all these reporters.

"Chief Cade, don't you feel any compulsion to speak to the people about what you did?"

He turned back to the reporter whose face he saw each night at six and eleven. There was something gratifying about seeing him sopping wet now. "No, James, I told you I'm not ready to make a statement."

He went in and stood on the mat just inside the door. Man, he was wet. He'd give anything for a change of clothes. He should have gone by his house and gotten something before coming here.

J.J. Clyde sat at one of the desks talking into a phone, and Cade pointed at the door. "Don't let any of them in, you hear?"

J.J. put his hand over the phone. "I hear, Chief. Any word on who the man is?"

"None," Cade said. "Where's Joe?"

"On the phone in your office. It's been ringing off the hook, people asking questions."

Cade shot a look through the storefront window to the crowd of reporters standing in the elements. He imagined they were just as interested in the storm pummeling the coast as they were in the death. He almost wished for a tornado to get their mind off him.

He went into his office and found Joe, Cade's second-in-command and the town's only detective, sitting in a folding chair near Cade's desk, the phone cord stretched taut. "No, ma'am, I can't comment on the investigation. Yes, ma'am."

Cade saw that Joe, too, was wet. No doubt he'd been out in the storm with the others, looking for the man's car.

"No, no one was in jeopardy at any time. Yes. All right."

He hung up the phone and got to his feet. "It's been a madhouse. Rumors flying all over town. J.J. said we had a few calls speculating on who the man was. Somebody said he was a Hollywood producer renting a cottage over in Eastgate, but they checked and that man is alive and well. Somebody else claimed he was the sprinkler guy putting in a new system over at the Catholic church. But the sprinkler guy is accounted for." He looked at the puddle gathering under Cade's feet. "You really ought to change clothes, Cade."

"Later." Cade ran his hand through his wet hair. "So what are your thoughts on the gunshot?"

"Sure raises the stakes, doesn't it? If it wasn't suicide, then we've got a killer out there."

Cade dropped into his chair. "We can't speculate until we have some evidence. There's got to be a car somewhere. An apartment he was occupying. A condo or hotel room. Something."

"Alex checked the condos in that area," Joe said. "He wasn't a tenant. I was thinking about sending men around to all the hotels on the island, to see if any guests are unaccounted for. It'll take a while."

"Better get started."

"Will do." Joe started for the door. "What about the press?"

"Ignore them. They know about as much as we do right now. Soon they'll be scurrying off to meet deadlines."

"I hear some of them did live remotes for their six o'clock broadcast."

Cade dropped into his chair. "You're kidding."

"Nope. Sorry, Chief. Two birds with one stone, you know. The storm and the accident both in one place. How lucky can they get?"

Cade rubbed his face and watched as Joe disappeared. Could this day get any worse?

When he heard a knock on the door, he looked up with dread. Jonathan Cleary—Morgan's husband and Cade's best friend—stood in the doorway. "Hey, buddy. You okay?"

Cade just looked at him.

"Man, you need a change of clothes."

"Tell me about it."

Jonathan came in and turned the folding chair toward Cade's desk. He sat down. "Morgan told me what happened. Want to talk?"

"I don't even know what to say." Cade slapped his hands on the desk and made himself straighten. "You don't happen to have any new tenants at Hanover House, do you?"

"Not this month, no. And we checked. Everyone's there."

He sat back, rubbing his mouth. "There are hundreds of tourists on the island this time of year. Maybe I need to do what Blair suggested and make a statement to the press, to give them a physical description."

"Morgan told me about the gunshot," Jonathan said. "You gonna tell them?"

Cade looked down at the wood grain on his desk and wondered how long it would be before the press learned of that. Doctors and nurses from the hospital knew, and he'd notified his men as soon as he'd heard. Morgan had told Jonathan. . . . Someone would leak it, and the town would panic.

Cade rubbed his eyes. "I can't believe this happened. A man's life . . ." He sighed. "Jonathan, I know I didn't run the man over on purpose, but maybe I was driving faster than I needed to. Maybe I was negligent by not stopping in time. I saw him standing there. If he was bleeding, I should have seen it."

"From a distance, in a driving rain? Cade, you didn't do anything wrong. You were trying to save lives."

"And I took one instead."

Jonathan shook his head. "No, you didn't, man. The guy stepped out in front of you. I talked to Melba Jefferson myself after Morgan told me. She said she saw the whole thing and that you didn't do anything wrong. The man walked right out in front of you, almost like he meant to. And she didn't know about the gunshot wound, but she would have said if she'd seen him bleeding. It was pouring rain, Cade."

Cade got up and paced across the room, his shoes squeaking on the floor. "He's dead, Jonathan. The man is dead and I killed him." He stepped into the doorway and, through the glass, saw that the press corps was not going away.

He turned back to Jonathan. "I have to go make a statement," he said. "I have to give them a description of the man so they can put it on the news. If I don't, they'll start making up facts."

Jonathan got up. "They're going to attack you with all kinds of questions. Why don't you let someone else do it? Joe McCormick or somebody."

"I don't believe in passing the buck. I can take it." He walked to the door, took in a deep breath.

"Don't you want to put on a dry shirt and comb your hair?" Jonathan asked. "I could go to your house and get you a change of clothes."

"What's the point? I'm going outside anyway."

Jonathan grunted. "Let them in, man. You don't have to do this out in the storm."

"They're not coming in here and disrupting my whole operation. There's not room."

Jonathan groaned. "At least take my umbrella."

Cade took the umbrella and Jonathan touched his shoulder. "What about the gunshot?"

Cade thought that over for a moment. They were going to find out anyway, but if he could hold off just a while longer, maybe he'd find the man's identity and be able to determine whether it was suicide or murder. There was no point in creating a panic about some killer still at large when there might not be any foul play involved. "Think I'll wait," he said. "There's too much we still don't know."

Jonathan opened the door for him, and Cade stepped out and opened the umbrella. The winds had died somewhat. The umbrella might hold, after all.

The press swarmed and Cade took immediate control. "I'd like to make a statement," he yelled over the voices. "Please get back. I have a statement to make."

The reporters got quiet, but they didn't step back. Microphones loomed so close to his face that he felt he might emerge bruised. He hoped the rain didn't electrocute any of them. Trying to ignore them, he spoke.

"This afternoon at 2:00 P.M., a pedestrian was killed on Ocean Boulevard near the South Beach Pier. The man had no identification. I'd like to give you his physical description in hopes that someone who recognizes it can identify him.

"The man was wearing a red plaid short-sleeved shirt, khaki pants, and a pair of Dockers deck shoes. He had blondish-brown hair and brown eyes, was approximately 220 pounds, approximately thirty-five years old, and about six feet tall. If anyone listening to this can identify this man, we would appreciate your calling 555-8327. Thank you."

"Chief Cade, did the impact kill him instantly?"

"No, it didn't," Cade said. "He was alive and speaking right after he was hit and did make it to Candler Hospital in Savannah alive. He died shortly thereafter."

The reporters began shouting out questions, but Cade headed back inside, blocking out the noise. Jonathan ducked back in with him and took the umbrella out of his hands. "Good job, Cade."

Cade sighed and looked back out at them. "Maybe it'll do some good. We've got to get a name."

"We'll be praying for you, man."

Cade stared at his friend for a long moment. "'Preciate it, man. You have no idea how bad I need it."

CHAPTER

Cade looked weary and tired when Blair found him at the police station at eleven that night, and from the defeated look on his somber face, she knew he still hadn't been able to identify the man.

"Hey," she said from the doorway of his office, and he looked up at her and smiled.

"Hey. What are you doing out so late?"

"I thought I'd come by and watch the news with you. Jonathan told me you'd made a statement to the press. I see most of them are still out there."

He glanced at his watch. "Yeah, they're doing live broadcasts. Guess it's time, isn't it?"

He had finally changed clothes, and instead of his uniform, he wore a pair of khaki pants and a blue dress shirt with the sleeves rolled up. His face was gray with end-of-day stubble, and his hair seemed to have been unattended since he'd been drenched that afternoon. She felt the urge to push it back off of his forehead.

He got up, stretched, and turned on the television that sat on top of a file cabinet. Turning a chair around for her, he said, "So you think they know about the gunshot yet?"

She sat down and pulled her feet up to the seat. "Probably. But they'd find out sooner or later, Cade."

"I thought we'd have found something by now. But the man seems to have come out of thin air. No match on his fingerprints. No car, no nothing."

"There's something somewhere. Just give it time."

He dropped back down in his own chair, and she saw his fatigue as he leaned his head back. The theme song for the *Channel 3 News* came on, and she glanced back at him. His face had tightened, and she knew he dreaded the report. The camera zoomed in on the anchor who had stood out in front of the station just a short time ago. Covered with makeup and hair mousse, one would never know he'd been standing in torrential rains for most of the night.

"Our top story tonight, another baby kidnapped from a hospital in the southeast."

Blair smiled at Cade. "Well, at least you're not the headliner."

Cade didn't seem comforted by that.

"According to a spokesperson for the Woman's Hospital in Hilton Head, South Carolina, the day-old baby of Sarah and Jack Branning was kidnapped at 1:00 P.M. today. The kidnapper has been identified as a woman dressed as a nurse, with curly blonde hair and black-framed glasses."

"Want something to drink?" he asked, as if trying to divert his own attention.

"We might need vodka." She grinned at him. Cade didn't drink, and the thought that he'd have some sitting around his office was absurd. She'd hoped to get a smile out of him, but his eyes had drifted back to the set.

"This disappearance makes the fifth in as many weeks. The others were taken from hospitals in Florida and Southern Georgia.

"And in other news . . ."

Cade's picture flashed up on the screen. "There it is."

"*The Cape Refuge chief of police is in the hot seat for running down an injured man on Ocean Boulevard at 3:30 P.M. today.*"

"Okay," Cade said, "they know he was shot."

"*Sources say that Chief Matthew Cade was on his way to direct traffic around a downed power line when he hit an unidentified pedestrian who was bleeding from a gunshot wound to the abdomen. The man was rushed to Candler Hospital in Savannah but later died. Police don't yet know how the man was shot and have been unable to identify him.*"

The anchor paused, and the video of Cade's press conference filled the screen. "*The man was wearing a red plaid short-sleeved shirt, khaki pants, and a pair of Dockers deck shoes. He had blondish-brown hair and brown eyes, was approximately 220 pounds, approximately thirty-five years old, and about six feet tall . . .*"

As he spoke, another picture flashed on the screen—a sketch of the dead man's face.

Cade sprang up. "What in the name of—?"

"*Our WSAV-TV News sketch artist was able to make this drawing of the man who was killed. If you know him, please contact us here at Channel 3, or you can call the Cape Refuge Police Department at 555-8327. Chief Cade refused to comment on his part in the man's death, though he did say that the man spoke to him before he died.*"

Blair dropped her feet. "Cade, is that what the man really looked like?"

"Exactly. What did that reporter do? Go to the morgue to draw the man's face? What if his family sees that? What if they're sitting in the living room wondering why Dad's not home and all of a sudden that stupid sketch pops up on the screen?"

It was just the kind of thing she'd expected from the press. Blair got up and grabbed the phone. "I'll get to the bottom of this right now."

"Who are you calling?"

"A friend at Channel 3. I'm going to find out how they got the picture and how they knew about the gunshot."

Cade changed the channel and watched the tail end of another station's coverage of his impromptu press conference. Relieved, he saw that there was no picture there, but they too had the information about the gunshot. He switched to the third local channel. Again, no picture, but the gunshot dominated the piece.

Blair got the station's recorded greeting, then navigated her way to her friend who worked in the newsroom. She'd worked with him several times when he'd needed research done for a report he was working on. He'd hired her, knowing that she had an uncanny gift for finding facts that no one else could find.

The man answered quickly. "Jason Geddis."

"Yeah, Jason, hi. Blair Owens."

"Yeah, Blair. How's it going?"

"Great. And you?"

"Can't complain."

She met Cade's eyes. He looked as if he wanted to jerk the phone out of her hand and interrogate him himself. "Listen, I was just watching the news and saw the sketch you guys had of the man who died on Cape Refuge . . ."

"Yeah. Pretty good reporting, huh?"

She didn't comment. "The police didn't release a sketch of the man, and there were no media at the scene of the accident, so really, Jason, how did you guys get that?"

Jason laughed. "Well, I'm not saying this was the right thing to do or anything, but our artist went to the morgue. He told them he was sent there to do a sketch of the man to help police identify the body. So they let him in."

Cade turned the volume down on the set and looked over at her, waiting.

"You're kidding me. And they *believed* him?"

"Sure they did. Let him right in. Ethics aside, it was an exclusive, and it might help identify the guy."

Cade set his hands on his hips and stared down at her, waiting.

"So that would be how he knew about the gunshot too, huh?"

"Yep. The person helping him mentioned it."

Blair breathed out a bitter laugh. "Amazing. How do you guys sleep at night?"

He muttered something about sleeping just fine, and she quickly said good-bye. She knew the scar on her face was crimson.

Cade's face was red too. "Tell me, Blair."

She sighed. "He led them to think he was with the police department, and this rube let him right in, gave him access to the body, and listed the injuries."

Cade dropped back into his chair. "Unbelievable."

She watched him for a moment as he leaned his head back and stared at the ceiling. "Cade, maybe it's for the best," she said. "You've got his face out there now. Somebody's bound to call in soon."

"And what if they call Channel 3 instead of me? Is the press going to rush to the family's home and ask them for a statement?"

Blair tried to think of something that would comfort him, but the phone rang, and J.J. rushed into the doorway. "Chief, we've got a lead."

"Already?"

The phone began to buzz again. The viewers were already responding.

Cade picked up the phone. "Chief Cade."

Blair sat and listened as one after another television viewer called in to ask questions or provide leads.

It was going to be a busy night.

CHAPTER

*I*t was after midnight when the phone calls with empty leads stopped coming. Blair still sat in a chair in Cade's office, her feet propped on his desk. Cade's eyes were dry and weary, but fatigue had not drained him of worry. He wished it would.

"I'm going home." Blair dropped her feet and got up. "You ought to do the same. Get some sleep, Cade."

For a moment he just looked at her, his finger rubbing gently across his lips. She was pretty; he'd always thought so. The scars on her face marred only her self-image, as far as he was concerned. They were part of her, the part that spoke of pain behind her tough shell, the part that reminded him how vulnerable she could be.

He wished she was a believer, so that God could heal the inner reaches of those scars.

He wished it for selfish reasons, too.

"I'll go home soon," he said. "Thanks for being here during this. I appreciate your support."

"No problem." She got up and started out.

Cade followed her. He mentally kicked himself for sounding dismissive or impersonal. He really did appreciate it. She had been there at the hospital when he'd needed someone, and tonight as the saga continued, she'd helped so patiently and compassionately.

Yet it always ended so coolly with them, as though some line existed between them that neither would cross.

It had finally stopped raining. He walked her to her car, opened her door, and stood there as she got in. "Be careful," he said.

She smiled up at him. "You too. Go home, Cade."

"I will."

Closing her door, he stepped back and watched her drive away.

The wind was muggy and angry, and he looked at the night sky, wondering how in the world this day had taken such a horrible turn. He slid his hands into his pockets and crossed the quiet street to the beach. His feet left the pavement and began to rock through the sand as he walked to the edge of the water.

The morning sun had come today as it always did, and the tide had risen and fallen. Waves still beat against the shore as if everything was the same. How could he have known when he got up this morning that he was going to kill a man today?

Or would the man have died anyway, from his wound?

He went to the lifeguard's stand, climbed up, and sat in the chair that looked out over the water. The night stars twinkled bright and abundant tonight, reminding him of God's majesty, but he couldn't help questioning God's purpose. He leaned his head back against the wooden slats of the chair. How did one repent for something he had not meant to do? His heart had cried out in contrition ever since the accident occurred. God knew he was sorry, but it didn't make anything right. For all he knew right now, there was a family grieving because they had seen their father and husband's face flashed on the television screen, a poor sketch of a dead man rendered by someone who'd never seen him alive. By morning he expected to know who the man was. But what then?

As he sat in the lifeguard's chair staring up at the sky, he tried to pray. But his supplications to God were a jumble of incoherent fears, concerns, and self-indictments.

He should pray for the wife, the family, if there was one. He should pray for the friends and loved ones who would grieve over this missing man. He should pray that, if it wasn't a suicidal gunshot, the shooter would be found. But he couldn't manage it.

He climbed down to the soft sand and walked down the beach. The surf rumbled loud tonight, hitting hard against the shore. Tourists clamored for rooms in beachfront hotels, but on days like this, when a storm had come and gone and the ocean was restless, they often had trouble sleeping with the roar of the Atlantic in their ears. Tonight the commotion of the waves only mirrored the noise of the voices inside his head—voices that questioned, taunted . . .

Oh, how he wished that his mentor, Wayne Owens, were here to talk to. Blair reminded him a lot of her father. She had his matter-of-fact ways, but without his passion for Christ. She had much advice to give, but few answers. Still, she'd been a comfort to him, and he had to admit that there was no one he'd rather have had by his side tonight.

He turned around and started back to the police station, where his night staff fielded phone calls and chased down leads. He stopped beside the lifeguard's stand again, leaned against it, and looked out over the water.

"Lord, help me." It was the only thing he could manage to pray tonight. Maybe what he had done today had put up a wall between him and God. He hoped not. He could not stand the thought of being isolated like that.

Maybe he just needed to rest.

He went back to the station, got his keys, and headed back out to his truck. Quietly he drove home, hoping that the day would shed some light on the things he needed to know and, thus, change everything.

CHAPTER

7

*B*lair had not slept well, and when dawn began to break across the sky and turn the darkness in her room to gray, she got up and decided to check on Cade. She called his house first and waited as the phone rang four times. Finally, his voicemail picked up.

"Hi. You've reached Cade. I'm not at home right now but if you'll leave a message, I'll call you back."

The phone beeped and Blair cleared her throat. "Hey, Cade, it's Blair. I was just checking on you, hoping you're all right. I'll try you at the station." She hung up and dialed the number of the police station.

"Cape Refuge Police Department." The voice was dry and clipped. She recognized it to be Alex's.

"Alex, this is Blair Owens. Can Cade come to the phone?"

"Cade isn't in," Alex said. "He doesn't usually come in until eight."

"Yeah, well, I thought he might have gotten started earlier today. He must have gone to Cricket's."

"Yeah, you'll probably catch him there."

Blair decided that instead of calling, she would just get in her car and drive over to the dock. The little restaurant called Cricket's sat back from the water. It was where fishermen and sailors and those who worked along the beach often had breakfast in the mornings. As she pulled into the parking lot, she saw that Cade's truck was parked there.

She left her car and went inside the structure that looked as if a strong wind might blow it over. One whole wall was made of screens, which let in the ocean breeze, along with the sea air and the rank odor of fish from the boats docked nearby. She stepped in, letting the screen door bounce shut behind her, and looked around at the usual faces. Her parents used to be among them. They had come here each morning for years in hopes of ministering to seamen who were passing through. Their little church was housed in the warehouse just a few yards away.

Blair walked up to the bar and waited for Charlie to notice her.

"Well, if it ain't Marian the Librarian."

"Hey, Charlie. What's going on?"

"Not much," he said. "Same old same-old." He poured her a cup of coffee, shoved it into her hands.

"Have you seen Cade this morning?" she asked.

"Yeah, he was in earlier."

"Where is he? His truck is still here."

"I don't know," he said. "Musta left."

Blair took her coffee and stepped out of the restaurant. She looked up and down the dock, wondering if Cade was nearby. By now, most of the shrimp boats had already gone out, but some of the late-goers were still preparing their rigs for the day's work.

She walked up the dock, saw her brother-in-law, Jonathan, getting his tourist boat ready to take passengers out for a day of saltwater fishing. His nineteen-year-old deckhand helped the passengers board while Jonathan busied himself on the deck.

She waved and called out, "Jonathan, you seen Cade?"

He turned. "I saw him a little while ago coming out of Cricket's," he yelled back. "I figured he was headed to work."

"He's not there and his truck's still parked at Cricket's," she said.

He shrugged. "Then I don't know where he went. Sorry."

As she kept walking, she saw Toothless Joe chomping on his cigar as he prepared for his dolphin tour. Up ahead was Mill Malone, loading his cargo for a trek up the coast. Cade was nowhere to be found.

Giving up, she went back to her car and headed back to the station. Maybe his truck had died in its parking spot, and he had hitched a ride or walked to the station.

But when he still wasn't there, she began to get concerned.

"Where could he be?" she asked Alex. "I mean, if he was out working, wouldn't he have let you know?"

"Usually," Alex said. "But he'll come along shortly. He's a big boy."

"I know he's a big boy," Blair said, "but I'm worried about his state of mind. He's really beating himself up about what happened yesterday."

"Maybe he headed over to Savannah looking for the family."

Now, there was a possibility. "Do you think he knows who it is yet?"

"I don't see how. We got a few calls through the night but they were all lame leads. Didn't take us anywhere."

Blair checked her watch. It was past time for her to open the library. She supposed Cade would turn up eventually, with or without her help. Trying to put him out of her mind, she headed home.

Five hours later, when Blair checked on Cade again, he had still not been in to the police station. No one had heard from him. Several important matters had come up and they had tried to contact him, but he had not answered the cell phone that he used when he went into Savannah. His truck still sat at Cricket's, and no one in town seemed to know where he was.

By that evening, when there was still no trace of him, Blair began to fight a growing sense of dread. Something had happened.

He would not have just disappeared without a trace. She went over to Hanover House and found everyone sitting around the table—the whole brood of them. Mrs. Hern sat with that blank Alzheimer's stare, a dribble of mashed potatoes on her chin. Gus Hampton scarfed down a pork chop with the urgency of a starving man, his elbows digging into the table. Felicia, the big woman who'd just been there a few weeks, seemed to be the only one among them who had any manners, though Blair couldn't imagine where she'd gotten them. She'd been in jail for ten years before coming here, and Blair doubted they emphasized etiquette in the prison cafeteria.

Sadie seemed preoccupied with her baby brother, Seth, who sat in a high chair between Morgan and Jonathan.

"His truck's been at Cricket's all day long," Blair said, standing over the table.

"Sit down, Blair," Morgan said. "I made plenty."

Blair waved her off. "Not hungry. Jonathan, they haven't even heard from him at the police station."

"At least have a glass of tea," Morgan insisted.

"I don't *want* a glass of tea. Did you even hear what I said, Morgan? Cade is missing!"

Jonathan slid his chair back, and took his plate to the sink. "Calm down, Blair. He's not missing." He rinsed the plate off, then wiped his hands on a towel. "He was just really upset about what happened yesterday. Maybe he just went off by himself to think."

"No way," Blair said. "It's not like him to buck his responsibilities. He would have been out pounding the pavement today trying to find out who this guy was."

Seth got restless and started trying to stand up in his high chair.

"No, Seth," Sadie told him across the table. "Sit down. Eat your peas."

When Seth managed to turn around and got up on his knees, Morgan pulled him out of his high chair. "Well, maybe that's what he's doing. Maybe he just went to find some leads on the man."

"But don't you think it's strange that he wouldn't share those leads with anybody at the police department?" Blair asked. "They haven't heard from him all day long. He hasn't even called to see if they've learned anything."

That got Jonathan's attention. "Weird," he said. "Makes me wonder about that woman."

"What woman?"

He shrugged. "Well, I don't know. He was talking to some woman at Cricket's this morning. It wasn't anybody I knew. I saw him coming out with her."

Cade with a woman? Blair was silent for just a moment. She knew her scars were reddening. "What did she look like, Jonathan?"

"I don't know, mid-thirties, long, big brown hair, kind of petite-looking."

Blair hated petite women, especially the ones with big hair. She wasn't exactly an Amazon herself at five-feet-five, but those tiny little women really got on her nerves. Men loved them, though. She supposed Cade would be no exception. "Why didn't you tell me this when I asked you this morning? I asked you *point-blank* if you had seen Cade."

"And I told you point-blank that I had seen him coming out of Cricket's."

She grunted. "You didn't say anything about a woman."

"Well, I didn't think it was relevant at the time."

Baby laughter came from the living room, then a ball rolled into the kitchen and Seth came running after it. Jonathan laughed and scooped the ball up, then rolled it back across the floor. Seth screamed in delight, and Morgan followed him.

But Blair's eyes pinned Jonathan. What was wrong with them? Didn't they understand how serious this was? "I need more specifics, Jonathan. Did he look like he was just talking to her in passing or did she look like somebody he knew? Were they deep in conversation? Were they headed out to *her* car or *his*?"

He rolled his eyes. "Come on, Blair. You know me. I was busy, and I don't have time to sit around watching the movements of every guy that comes out of Cricket's. I had passengers on my boat."

"He's your best friend, Jonathan. Don't tell me you wouldn't be interested if you saw him with a woman."

"Then I guess that means I didn't consider her to be any kind of love interest. He just looked like he was talking to her. He had a real serious look on his face. I saw them walk around Cricket's, but I didn't see what car they got into."

She sighed and turned to Morgan, who had caught Seth and was handing him a cookie. "We've got to find out who that woman was," she said.

Morgan put the toddler down. "I think so," she agreed. "Someone must know."

Blair grabbed up her keys. "I'm outta here. I'll let you know what I find out."

As Blair went back to her car and pulled away from the family home that had become everyone else's family home, she thought of some petite, big-haired woman with Cade. Had he gone off with her? Did she have anything to do with his disappearance? Frustrated beyond measure, she drove back to Cricket's. His truck still hadn't been moved.

That night, Blair had trouble sleeping again. She tossed and turned, and twice she got up and called Cade's voicemail again. He still was not answering. She lay in bed, wondering what on earth could have happened to him. Who was the woman Jonathan had seen him with? If he was seeing a woman, Blair would have known it. He wouldn't have kept it secret.

Maybe this woman did have something to do with the case. But why would he just vanish like that after meeting with her? Had he been a victim of some kind of foul play?

Did it have anything to do with the man he'd hit?

By morning she called the station again. There'd still been no word from him, and they admitted their concern. She drove over to Cricket's, noting the irony that today the sky was cloudless and blue, and the sun shone so brightly that the water glistened like a bed of diamonds. It felt like it should be storming until Cade turned up.

Cade's truck still sat in the parking lot. She almost ran into her brother-in-law as he came out of the rickety restaurant. "Jonathan!"

"Still looking for Cade?" he asked.

She grabbed his flannel shirt. "Jonathan, he hasn't been heard from since yesterday morning when he was here at Cricket's. Where do you think he could be?"

Jonathan's eyes squinted in the morning sun. "I don't know, but I'm getting a little worried myself."

That was all Blair needed. "Jonathan, let's go to his house. We have to get inside somehow and see if there's a clue."

"We can't break into his house! He's the chief of police. You don't think he'd arrest us? I have firsthand knowledge that Cade puts the law over friendship."

"It wouldn't be like breaking in," she said. "I just want to see if there's anything wrong. He could be dead in there, for all we know."

Jonathon jerked his arm back. "Come on, Blair. He's not dead."

"Well, how do you know? It's not like him to do this. Something has happened!"

Jonathan looked out at his boat. So far no tourists had shown up for his tour, and his deckhand sat in a rusty folded chair, looking like he'd rather be in bed.

He turned back to Blair. "I'll tell you what. I know where Cade keeps a key. We'll go in and see if everything is all right. But we're not going to snoop around through his stuff. He deserves his privacy."

"Fine! That's good enough for me."

He told his deckhand to board any passengers who showed up, then Blair drove him over to Cade's house. She followed Jonathan around to the backyard and waited as he went into a utility room to look for Cade's extra key.

She stood in Cade's backyard and noted that the grass needed cutting. She crossed it and went to his patio, where a green iron table stood with four chairs. One of the chairs sat back away from the table, and a pair of mud-caked work boots stood in it.

She sat down and leaned forward, her eyes scanning the crepe myrtles that weren't yet in bloom, the azalea bushes that were, and the hodgepodge of untended and unidentifiable plants.

Something at her feet startled her, and she looked down to see Cade's big black cat. It looked up at her and let out an urgent meow. "Hey, kitty." She reached down and picked it up. "Come here." Cradling the cat, she began to stroke it.

Jonathan came back out. "Found it."

Blair looked up at him. "I didn't know Cade had a cat."

"Oh, yeah. His name's Oswald."

"After the assassin?"

Jonathan grinned. "No, after the theologian, Oswald Chambers."

The cat purred as she stroked it, then meowed again and jumped down, rushed to the door as Jonathan went toward it.

Jonathan opened the door, revealing the small laundry room, and the cat darted inside and headed straight to his empty bowls on the floor beside the dryer.

"He's hungry," Blair said. "See there? Cade wouldn't leave his cat to starve."

Jonathan scooped some food out of the Cat Chow bag and dropped it into the bowl, and the cat devoured it.

"See? That cat hasn't eaten today."

Jonathan seemed to turn that over in his mind.

As he got the cat some water, Blair stepped into the small kitchen, with its round little table and four chairs, and looked beyond it to the living room she had never been in before. All these years she had considered Cade a close friend. It seemed strange now that she'd never had cause to be in his house.

Jonathan went in and turned the light on. It looked different than she would have imagined, had she ever given Cade's living quarters a thought. The couch and love seat were brown leather, and a beige recliner sat opposite the love seat. A big beige ottoman served as a coffee table and footrest.

The decorating style spoke of masculine comfort, but it was neat.

She walked through the kitchen, saw that nothing seemed out of place. A lone coffee cup sat inside the dishwasher. The coffee pot sat half full and cold.

"Bed's made up," Jonathan called.

Blair went to the bedroom, saw the queen-size bed draped over with a gold and brown comforter that matched the curtains. There was no way to tell if he'd been home since yesterday.

"Man, he's neat," Jonathan said. "We used to really butt heads when we roomed together in college. I don't remember a day when he didn't make up his bed. I went weeks without making up mine. Drove him crazy."

Blair crossed Cade's room and went to the walk-in closet. She turned on the light and stepped inside, trying to determine whether he had packed or left in a hurry. Three suitcases lay on the top shelf.

"Do you think a bachelor would have more than three suitcases?" she asked.

He followed her in. "I doubt it."

"So he didn't pack."

Jonathan shook his head. "No, I wouldn't think so, either. As neat as he is, it seems like there'd be a space on the shelf for a missing suitcase if he'd taken one."

Blair turned back to him. "Okay, so what does that tell us?"

"Well, it tells us that he didn't plan to be going on a long trip. And the fact that he left his truck at Cricket's would sure be an indication that whatever happened wasn't planned."

She turned off the closet light and walked around his bedroom, saw the Bible and another book open on his bed table. It was just like Cade, she thought. In the midst of his worrying— probably after a sleepless night—he had gotten up and read his Bible.

Jonathan picked it up. "Oh, man. Numbers 35. He was reading about the cities of refuge."

"What are those?"

He put the Bible back down. "They were a provision God made for someone who had accidentally killed. There was a death sentence for taking someone's life. The family of the person you killed had the right and obligation to kill you."

"Obligation? Legally?"

"Yes, because God said that bloodguilt polluted the land. But in case the death was an accident, the Lord set up six cities of refuge. Every city in Israel was less than thirty miles from one, and the roads were smooth and well maintained, so someone who'd accidentally killed could get there within hours before the avenger could overtake him. The family of the dead man couldn't avenge the death if he was in a city of refuge. He was safe there until he could stand trial before the congregation."

She looked down at the Numbers passage. "Does Cade consider himself to have bloodguilt?"

"Probably," Jonathan said. "You know Cade. He doesn't let himself off the hook for anything."

"But none of this applies today. That was Old Testament stuff."

"Everything in the Old Testament is a picture of something in the New. Cade knows that. And besides, the city of refuge probably gave him comfort. It probably reminded him that God makes provision for accidents."

"What did he do? Run off to some modern city of refuge?"

Jonathan frowned. "Cape Refuge was practically named for that whole concept. No, Cade wouldn't go off looking for that city. He knows where his real refuge is found."

Jonathan looked at the other book, *My Utmost for His Highest,* and pointed to the author's name at the top of the page it was opened to. "Oswald's namesake."

Blair took the book, careful not to lose Cade's place. Keeping her finger there, she looked just inside the cover. "I thought so." She showed Jonathan the inscription there. "Pop gave him this."

Jonathan swallowed. "I remember."

She opened to the page he'd been reading from. "It's yesterday's reading. Which means he hasn't been home to read today's."

"Not necessarily. But it sure doesn't look like he has." With troubled eyes, he looked around the room and sighed. "Well, I can't say that breaking into his house has enlightened us any."

She went up the hall, looked into the second bedroom where Cade had a desk and computer. It was turned off.

Going back into the living room, she looked down at the phone, saw the light blinking. "He has voice mail. Do you know how to get it?"

"Of course not," Jonathan said. "Besides, it's probably us. I've left at least three messages myself."

She looked down at the caller ID and clicked the arrow key to scroll through his calls. Her own number came up several times, along with that of the police station, Hanover House, and several of the television stations in the area. She scrolled through until she came to a name she didn't recognize.

"William Clark. Do you know who that is?"

Jonathan shook his head. "It's a Savannah number. Probably a reporter."

Frustrated, she abandoned the caller ID. "Where could he be? I can't imagine him vanishing unless something happened."

"Me either," Jonathan said, "but let's not jump to conclusions. There might be a perfectly good explanation for where he is."

"I sure wish he'd let us in on it."

Satisfied that there were no clues here, they took the cat outside, along with its bowls, and locked the door. Blair went back to Cricket's, hoping to get some more information about what Cade had done in there yesterday, whom he had been talking to, where he had gone. She finally hit pay dirt when Creflo King, who owned most of the parking lots in town, told her he had seen Cade talking to a pretty woman yesterday.

Again, Blair bristled. "Who was she, do you know?"

Creflo sucked on the toothpick in his mouth and leaned on the counter. "Never seen her before. Nobody from around here, and she wasn't dressed like a tourist. She had on a dress like she was going to church. I just figured she might have been kin to that man Cade killed, they were talking so serious and all, and Cade had this whipped look on his face like he was about to bust into tears or something."

Now they were getting somewhere. Blair turned that over in her mind. He must have had someone come forward about the body.

"Did he leave here with her?" she asked.

"Oh, yeah, sure did." Creflo took off his cap and scratched at the bald spot on his scraggly head. "In fact, I walked out behind them. He got into a blue PT Cruiser with her and they took off."

Her eyebrows shot up. "He got into her car?"

"That's right."

"You didn't see the license tag, did you?"

"Of course not. It did have a Hertz sticker, though, so the car might have been rented. I didn't see no reason to be suspicious. Cade's a cop. He knows what he's doin'. And he has the right to go off with any woman he wants."

Blair wasn't sure why that statement stung her.

When she realized she had gotten all the information she was going to get out of him, she headed to the police station, and found Joe McCormick sitting at Cade's desk with a pile of reports in front of him. He looked up at her with weary eyes and ran his hand across his closely shaved head. "What you got, Blair?"

"Joe, I talked to Creflo King at Cricket's and he said that he saw Cade getting into a blue PT Cruiser with a woman yesterday morning before he disappeared."

"Yeah, what else is new?" He went back to writing. "I found that out yesterday."

Her mouth fell open. "Well, why didn't you tell me?"

He grunted. "Why should I tell you? You're not a member of this police department. I don't have to share classified information with you."

"Well, why is it classified?" she asked. "Come on! For heaven's sake, I was calling all over the place yesterday trying to find him."

"Well, we didn't know where he was," Joe said, "and we still don't. We don't know who the woman is, and we don't know anything about the blue PT Cruiser or where they went." He dropped his pencil and leaned back, rubbing his eyes. "I'm beginning to get concerned, Blair."

She sat down in front of him, her eyes locked on his face. "Define 'concerned.'"

Joe gave her a smirk. "Concerned, meaning that something's not right. Besides his wanting to find out who he ran over, we might have a murder case on our hands—that man had been shot. Cade would be here working on this case. I mean, it's possible that Cade just took off with a girlfriend, but I just can't see that happening."

"No, me either. Besides, Cade doesn't have a girlfriend."

Joe got up, went to the window. "He was too worried about the identity of the man. He had us all hopping the day of the accident. He wouldn't just vanish the next day."

"So who is the woman?"

"We're trying to find out." He turned back to her. "But there are a lot of unknowns right now. If we could determine the identity of the dead man, then maybe we could figure out who she was."

"Then you think she was connected to the man who was killed?"

"It's just a guess, but it's as good as any other."

When Blair left the station, she sat behind the wheel of her Volvo, trying to think. Joe's concerns only validated her own. Something had, indeed, happened to Cade.

Fear churned in the pit of her stomach. What if he wasn't all right?

She drove home, pulled into the parking lot between her house and the library. She didn't feel like working today, but she supposed she had no choice. She went to the library next door and unlocked it. It felt cold and barren in here today, even though outside it was nearing eighty degrees already.

She thought of the petite woman with the blue PT Cruiser. Was it even possible that she was Cade's girlfriend? That he'd been so traumatized over killing the man, that he'd gone off with her without telling anyone?

No, it wasn't possible, she told herself. That was ludicrous and completely out of character for Cade. She was thinking like Creflo King, not like an intelligent woman who knew Cade well.

Cade was in trouble. But she didn't have a clue how to help him.

CHAPTER

At three o'clock that afternoon, Blair's restlessness overcame her, and she decided to go back to the police station to see if there had been any news. As she pulled into the parking lot, she saw Joe burst out of the police station and head to his car.

"Joe," she called through her car window. "Has anything happened?"

He glanced back at her as he got into his unmarked car. "Somebody just reported finding an abandoned car."

"Where?"

"In the woods over by Hampton's Place." He slammed his door and started his car.

Hampton's Place was a condominium complex about a half mile from South Beach, where the man had been killed. Was it his car they had found? Would it have his identification? Would it provide any clues about Cade? Blair turned her car around and followed him.

When they got to the parking lot of Hampton's Place, Joe got out of his car and stalked toward her. "Are you crazy?" He flung her door open. "Following me like that! I'm on police business, Blair. I ought to ticket you."

"After we see the car." Blair got out of her Volvo and, with an air of authority, started toward the man and the other cops waiting for Joe at the edge of the woods.

Joe grabbed her arm. "Blair, I don't want to arrest the town librarian for interfering with an investigation."

Blair looked up at him. "Come on, Joe. Please let me go. I just want to see the car. I won't get in the way."

"You're already in the way!" He turned to the cops who had been the first responders and ordered them to tape off the area before anyone else went near the car. Turning back to Blair, he said, "Don't you cross that tape, Blair Owens. There could be footprints or other evidence and we don't want it trampled."

She didn't answer, just waited until they had taped it off, then walked the perimeter until she could see the car.

Harris James—the man who'd found it—stood under the shade of a pine tree in a wooded area. Blair had known him for years. He was a Cape Refuge native, and he and his family had owned the property on the southern tip of the island for generations.

The red-haired man looked excited as he led them through the trees to the car that had been abandoned there. It was a gray four-wheel drive Passport.

"I was just walking through the woods," he said, "and I ran across this SUV with the driver's door wide open. Look here, there's blood and a gun on the seat. I figured I'd better call the police."

Blair wanted more than anything to duck under the yellow tape and examine the car for herself, but she hung back, listening.

Joe radioed in the tag number, then checked the outside of the door and window for prints, took a few pictures. Blair could see that there was blood on the outer edge of the seat, and splattered on the door.

But if it was suicide, wouldn't he have shot himself in the head? Why would he put the gun to his abdomen? And if he wanted to die and had the energy to walk to the street, he could have just shot himself a second time.

On the other hand, maybe someone had shot him and left him for dead. Maybe they hadn't expected him to be able to go for help.

Blair straightened and looked around, scanning the ground for footprints. The car had been here for two days, and the rain had washed any prints away.

Joe opened the glove box and pulled out the registration. "Car's owned by a William Clark."

William Clark. Where had she heard that before? Blair racked her brain, trying to think. William Clark, William Clark. *The caller ID!* She caught her breath and called out across the tape. "William Clark's name came up on Cade's caller ID this morning."

He pulled back out of the car and regarded her. "What do you mean, it came up?"

She realized she had just incriminated herself, and shrank back. "Well, I sort of used his key. I know where he hides it." *Okay, it was a lie,* she thought. Jonathan had been the one who knew where he had hidden it, but she didn't want to drag him into this. "I just went in to make sure he wasn't lying dead in the house, and I looked at his caller ID, and the one person I didn't recognize was William Clark."

Joe came toward her. "Then someone from the dead man's family must have called him. Only, Cade's number is unlisted. How would they have gotten the number?" He looked back at the vehicle, then turned back to Blair. "What time was that call?"

She shook her head. "I didn't think to get the exact time. I didn't realize the call was significant."

Joe went back to searching the car, and Blair watched. They dusted for prints, took pictures, bagged the floor mats, vacuumed for trace evidence, chalked the location of the gun, all before having a tow truck come get the car to take it to a secure location where they could examine it more thoroughly.

As the tow truck took the vehicle away, Joe looked at Blair. "All right, I've got to go over to Cade's house," he said. "Blair, you come show me where the key is."

Blair was glad she had watched Jonathan put the key back. She followed him over to Cade's house.

Oswald, Cade's cat, nuzzled up to her feet as soon as they got to the backyard, and Blair leaned down and stroked his back.

She got the key out of the utility room, and Joe took them and went in. "Don't touch anything, Blair. I don't know if a crime's even been committed, but just in case, we don't need to disturb any evidence."

She realized with a pang of guilt that she had disturbed quite a bit that morning. So had Jonathan.

She led him straight to the caller ID. He flipped through the callers and came to William Clark.

Joe nodded, his forehead still pleated. "Okay, the call came at five-thirty yesterday morning."

"Five-thirty," she whispered. "What a time to call somebody, especially if you don't know them."

"And if they didn't know him, how did they get his number? Cade's not listed. Most cops aren't."

"Maybe someone at the police station gave it to her."

"No way," he said. "That would never happen. Besides, I checked on the drive over, and no one from that number called the station. In fact, we didn't get any calls after 2:00 A.M. Not until 7:00 this morning."

"So it was someone who already had his number, then," Blair said. "Someone who knows him socially, maybe?"

Joe didn't commit to an answer. "I've ordered a copy of William Clark's driver's license. That'll have his picture. Once we have that, we can decide for sure if he's the man Cade hit, and we can go from there."

She waited as Joe made a search of Cade's home, then finally, he let her put the key back and headed back to the station. Blair followed him as if she belonged there, and when they arrived, Joe didn't stop her. Preoccupied, he hurried into the small building and went straight to the fax machine. Blair stood at the door, waiting to see the DMV photo for herself.

Joe jerked it out of the machine and started to nod. "That's him, all right."

Blair looked at the picture and saw the similarities to the sketch that the artist had drawn. She looked up at Joe. "So what have we got? A man who was shot in his own car, someone from his house calling Cade, Cade disappearing with some woman in a PT Cruiser . . ."

He rubbed his temple. "Maybe the woman in the Cruiser was the one who called Cade from Clark's house." He sighed. "Well, it won't be hard to find out. I have to go there and notify the family."

"I'm coming with you."

Joe looked at her like she was crazy. "Think again. Police business, Blair. You're not a cop. Why do I have to keep reminding you of that?"

"Show me in the police manual where it says that only officers can notify families of tragedies."

Joe shook his head. "Blair—"

"You can't, can you, Joe? You can't because it's not in there. Cade was going to let me go with him because he knew that I could relate to how this family felt getting this kind of news."

Again, a little white lie. Cade had never really committed to letting her go with him. But she knew she could have talked him into it.

"You don't know *what's* in our manual. It sure doesn't say to take the town librarian with us!"

"Come on, Joe. You know you don't want to go by yourself. Maybe if I come it'll soften things up a little. Maybe I can give his wife a hug or help her in some way."

He almost laughed. "No offense, Blair, but that's not your thing."

She threw her chin up. "It could be my thing," she said. "I watched my parents and Morgan do it enough. I can hug, Joe. Come on, I want to see this woman. I want to see what she drives, and I want to see if she has big brown hair and is petite, and I want to ask her if she's the one that came here yesterday to see Cade and if she knows what happened to him."

"And what if she's not?" he yelled. "What if she's just a woman who doesn't know her husband is dead? And we go and tell her and break her heart? Are you prepared for that, Blair? You gonna interrogate her then?"

"I can handle it. Take me with you, Joe!"

He sighed and got up, strolled to the window and looked out. Finally he turned back around. "All right, Blair, but only because I have the feeling I couldn't get rid of you if I wanted to. And Cade thinks a lot of you and trusts your instincts. But you let me do the talking unless you have something worthwhile to add. And when I say it's time to go, we're going. Got that?"

She almost hugged him just to prove she could. "Yep, I got it. You're the boss."

"That'll be the day," he muttered as he started out of Cade's office. "Blair Owens doesn't have a boss."

CHAPTER

They rode in silence to Savannah and found the address of the man who had died. The house was situated in one of the town squares set up by James Edward Oglethorpe when he'd laid out the city of Savannah in the eighteenth century. It was an old house across the street from Washington Park, though it looked as if attempts had been made to preserve and restore it. The Savannah Historical Society had declared the entire downtown area a historical landmark so that it couldn't be bulldozed and made into parking lots. Some of the homes still needed transformation from eyesores to historical beauties.

The Clark house was painted pink, with white lacy trim and wrought-iron railing, but parts of the house were in stages of decay and disrepair. As they pulled into the driveway of the modest structure, Blair had the feeling that William Clark may have been working on restoring the house completely but hadn't quite finished.

Something about that saddened her. She looked up at the front door, and wondered if someone was already grieving behind it, or if she and Joe would be breaking the news. She recalled sitting out in Cade's police car the day her parents were murdered, trying to push through the shock. The worst news of her life had attacked her with no warning.

Joe pulled far enough into the driveway to see that the garage attached to the back of the house was closed. Clearly, the update on the house had included the more modern garage than some in the area had.

"I was hoping to see if there was a PT Cruiser here," he said.

Blair just looked at the garage. There was a window there, but she knew she couldn't get away with going to look in it.

Joe started to get out. "Now I'm telling you, I do the talking, you hear?"

"Fine, sure." Blair got out and looked up at the front porch. "Don't worry about me."

They walked up to the front porch, and Blair hung back as Joe raised his hand to knock. "Now, Blair, I mean it," he said in a low voice. "Nothing about Cade or her being in Cape Refuge, at least not until I've had the chance to break the news about her husband."

"And if she already knows?"

His eyes pierced her. "Then you let me do the questioning. Got that?"

She agreed, but only because she had no choice. He knocked again.

She heard footsteps coming to the door, a fumbling with the lock as if it hadn't been opened in some time, and then a woman peaked out from the darkness. She was a blonde instead of the brunette Blair had expected, but she did qualify as "petite."

"Yes? May I help you?" she asked.

"Mrs. Clark?" Joe asked.

"Yes," she said.

"Are you the wife of William Clark?"

"Yes." She opened the door wider. "Do you know where my husband is?"

He shot Blair a look. "Ma'am, I'm Joe McCormick with the Cape Refuge Police Department, and this is Blair Owens."

She half expected him to introduce her as the town librarian, as if that had any bearing at all on anything. But he left it at her name.

"Could we come in for a moment and talk to you?"

The woman studied his badge, then looked up at him with pleading eyes. "You have bad news, don't you?"

When he hesitated, she stepped back from the door and let them in, watching their faces with glistening eyes. Blair's heart ached for the woman. She remembered Cade walking into the City Council meeting on the day of her parents' murder, asking Morgan and her to come outside. She had known there was bad news, though she could never have imagined how bad it was.

They stepped into the dark house that smelled of age. When the woman had closed the door, she turned back to them. "Has something happened to my husband?"

"Ma'am, if we could just sit down for a moment."

The woman ushered them into a parlorlike room and turned on a light. Suddenly Blair was able to see her fully. Her eyes were a light green, and her skin was pale like porcelain, untouched by the sun.

Blair took a seat on a sofa, and Joe sat down next to her.

The woman remained standing. "Willie killed himself, didn't he?"

Joe looked up at her, stricken. "Why would you ask that?"

"Because he said he was going to when he left here that day. We'd had an argument—a stupid, silly argument—and he said he was going to kill himself. He hasn't been home in two days. . . ."

Blair looked at Joe, waiting for him to go on. He set his elbows on his knees and looked down at his hands. "Your husband is dead, Mrs. Clark," he said. "I'm so sorry to be the one to tell you."

She seemed to deflate with the news, and wilted into the chair across from them. Her face twisted as tears reddened her eyes. "I didn't think he'd do it. He'd threatened it before, but he always came back home. We always made up."

Joe swallowed and went on. "Mrs. Clark, Sunday afternoon, during the storm, your husband walked out in front of a police car. He was struck. He died shortly after being taken to the hospital. But they discovered that before the accident he had been shot. We found his car today. The gun was still on the seat."

"Oh, Willie!" Her cry carried over the house, and she fell back with both hands over her face.

"We would have notified you sooner, but we weren't able to identify him until we found the car today."

Blair knew she had to do something to ease the woman's anguish. She got up and went to her. Stooping on the floor in front of her, she pulled the woman into her arms, as Morgan would have done. The woman's body shook with sobs. "I'm so sorry," she whispered. "I know this must be a shock."

"I'd been calling around," she said through her sobs. "Looking everywhere. I even called the hospitals, but they didn't have anyone by his name." She drew in a breath. "Where . . . where is he?"

"He's at the Chatham County Morgue," Joe said in a low voice. "We need for you to go identify the body."

Blair felt the pain of that finality racking through the woman's bones. All her questions about Cade vanished from her mind as Blair felt her grief.

Mrs. Clark pulled back. "I want to go now. I want to see him. Maybe it's not really him."

Blair looked back at Joe.

"All right," he said. "I'll take you over there right now."

"No, I'll drive my own car. I want to be alone."

"But are you sure you're up to driving?" Blair asked gently.

"Yes." She got up and looked around helplessly. "My purse. I'll get my purse."

"We'll follow you over there," Joe said. "I'll go in with you. Be sure to bring some identification."

She looked off, her eyes fixed on a spot on the wall. "It was just a little fight. Nothing to kill yourself over. I thought he was just taking a breather, putting some space between us." She pressed her hand over her mouth. "I'll back my car out and you can follow me over."

Blair followed Joe out, feeling as helpless as she'd ever felt. When they got back into Joe's car, she looked over at him. "Should I go in with her?"

"No. You'll need to wait in the car. I'll go."

"But she may need some comfort. Some support."

"Blair, I really need for you to wait in the car." He started the car and watched the garage door come open. A white Buick Regal pulled out.

"Not a PT Cruiser," he said. "And she wasn't a brunette."

Blair nodded. "But you still need to ask her if she was in Cape Refuge yesterday, or if she called Cade."

The woman pulled out, and Joe led her to the County Morgue.

Joe had been inside the morgue for over half an hour, when Blair finally saw him coming back out. His face looked pale and grim. He got into the car, set his hands on the steering wheel, and stared down at the dashboard.

"It was her husband, all right."

"Is she going to be okay?"

"I guess so. I hope she has some kind of support system."

Blair looked toward the door. "Where is she?"

"She's filling out paperwork. She didn't want me to stay with her." He started his car, and pulled out into traffic.

"So did you ask her about the phone call?"

"Yep. She claims she didn't call him and says she's never been to Cape Refuge in her life."

Blair frowned. "Then how does she explain the phone call?"

He shook his head. "She couldn't. And I checked. No one else lives in that house, and there wasn't anyone there besides her yesterday."

Blair leaned her head back on the headrest. "Weird. That just doesn't add up." She narrowed her eyes, trying to think. "I would have believed her about not being on Cape Refuge, since she doesn't really fit the description, but to lie about the phone call."

"Yeah, it worries me too. She swears up and down that she didn't know about her husband until we told her. That she wouldn't have had any reason to call Cade."

Blair shook her head. "We need a picture of her. We need to show it to the ones who saw the woman yesterday. We have to find out if she was the one they saw with Cade. She could have changed her hair, or had on a wig or something."

"That should be easy enough," Joe said. "I can get a copy of her driver's license when we get back."

CHAPTER

*W*hen they were back on Cape Refuge, Blair went into the station with Joe and waited as he ordered the license. While they waited for the picture to be faxed, she stepped into Cade's office.

His chair sat empty—a comfortable executive chair that he'd gotten when the city council had allocated thousands of dollars for themselves rather than fixing the potholes on Ocean Boulevard. Cade was probably the only one who really deserved it.

On his wall hung a matted and framed copy of a newspaper article that had come out about him when he'd solved her parents' murder. Melba Jefferson had given the framed account to him as a gift. Ordinarily, Cade would not have been vain or insensitive enough to put it up, but Melba had brought a hammer and hung it herself. He'd explained it to Blair with sincere apologies, and she'd understood why he'd left it hanging.

His desk held several stacks of files and papers, with a couple of gaudy paperweights on top, which had probably been passed through several of his predecessors.

"Picture's here," Joe said from behind her. "I made you a copy."

She took it and looked down at the image of Ann Clark. Her hair in the picture was just the way she'd worn it today—blonde, thin, and shoulder-length. "I'll take it to show Jonathan."

"I'll take it to Creflo King and the others who saw her," Joe said. "Let me know what Jonathan says."

She hurried over to Hanover House, hoping Jonathan had made it home already. She found him in the kitchen on his back under the sink, working on fixing a leak. He smelled of sweat, saltwater, and fish. He had just come in and hadn't had time to shower or change yet before Morgan had hit him up with the leak.

Blair knelt beside him and thrust the picture at him. "Jonathan, look at this picture. Could this be the woman Cade was with the other day?"

He slid out from under the cabinet and studied the picture. "Well, no. The woman had brown hair, kind of big and frizzy."

"Okay, picture this woman with that hair. It could have been a wig or something."

He looked up at her. "Who is she?"

"She's the wife of the man Cade ran over."

"No kidding?" He got to his feet and leaned back against the counter. "Cade was talking to the wife of the man he killed?"

"I'm asking you," she said. "It may not be her at all. But look at her face, her eyes."

"She had on sunglasses," Jonathan said. "But she did look really pale. I hadn't really thought about it until now, but yeah, it could have been her. You think she had something to do with Cade's disappearance?"

She sighed. "I really don't know. But yes, it's possible." She went to the phone on the kitchen wall and dialed the police station. Alex answered again. "Let me speak to Joe McCormick, please." She waited as Joe picked up.

"McCormick."

"Yeah, Joe? Jonathan says she could be the same woman, only with different hair. What did you find from Creflo?"

"He's here right now," he said. "He remembers her being real pale. Says she had on sunglasses, so he didn't get a good look at her face."

"Sounds like a disguise, like she might not want to be identified later," Blair said. "But could all that crying back at her house have been an act? Could she have known all along about her husband?"

"Maybe. I'm checking rental car places in Savannah, trying to see if any of them has a Cruiser and whether it was rented out yesterday. If she came here with evil intentions against Cade and went to all the trouble of a disguise, then she probably wouldn't have wanted to be seen in her own car. And Creflo mentioned a Hertz sticker."

Blair sat down, clutching the phone. "Evil intentions?"

"Hey, I don't know what happened to Cade, but he's still not here. She's the last person he was seen with."

Morgan came into the room, and Blair looked up at her, then at Jonathan. "I think Cade is in danger, don't you, Joe?" she said into the phone.

"Could be."

"Go search her house. See if there's any clue."

"I was thinking the same thing," he said. "Only I have to convince a judge to give me a search warrant, and there's no clear evidence of a crime being committed."

"Explain to them that the chief of police of Cape Refuge has disappeared. Don't you guys have a brotherhood or something? When a cop is shot, the whole force goes after the perpetrator. Shouldn't it be the same thing for one who's vanished?"

"We'll see," Joe said.

Frustrated, Blair hung up, and she turned to her sister and brother-in-law, who stood staring at her.

"He thinks it was her?" Jonathan asked.

"Sure does."

"What could this woman have done to him?" Jonathan asked. "She's what, five-foot-two, a hundred pounds? It's not like she could overpower him."

Blair felt sick. "Depends on what kind of weapon she had."

"Well, did Joe question her?"

"Not really." Her eyes ached with tears. "It was kind of a touchy thing, you know. I mean, how do you interrogate a woman who's just been told she's a widow?"

"But if she's a suspect in Cade's disappearance," Morgan said, "wouldn't it be appropriate to question her?"

"Well, sure, but we still don't know for sure she is the same woman. Different hair, different car . . ."

Jonathan pushed off from the counter and started toward the stairs. "I'm going to shower and head for the police station."

"What for?" Blair asked.

"I don't know," Jonathan said. "I just want to talk to Joe. Make sure he understands the urgency. Cade's time might be running out."

Blair watched him leave, and Morgan came up behind her and began massaging her shoulders. "Your shoulder muscles are like bricks, Sis."

Blair wasn't listening. "If she lied to us, what could it mean?"

"I hate to think," Morgan whispered.

Blair turned around and looked at her sister. "If anything happens to him . . ." The statement trailed off. If anything happened . . . what? Would she die? Destroy something? Implode?

She thought of that city of refuge passage he'd been reading in his Bible. It was her last clue about where his head had been before he disappeared. What did it mean?

She needed more information.

"Morgan, I need to borrow a Bible."

The delight on Morgan's face almost made her angry. "A Bible? Sure."

"Don't get excited. I just want to do some research on the passage Cade was reading before he vanished. And I need to borrow a concordance."

Megan quickly led her into the office, as if she feared she would change her mind if she lingered. "Here," she said, thrusting a Bible at her. "It's Pop's Bible. It has his notes."

Blair's throat tightened as she looked down at it.

"And here's the concordance." She dropped it on top of the Bible. "And here, take these commentaries." She pulled three dictionary-sized books out of the shelves and dropped them on the stack.

"We might be getting a little carried away here," Blair said.

Morgan turned around, still a little too happy at the request. "I just want to make sure you have everything you need. You know what you always say, about knowledge being power."

"You're getting your hopes up, Morgan. You think my research is going to lead me to some dramatic conversion. It won't. I just want to get inside Cade's head."

"I know. Just information. That's fine."

But as Morgan pulled out more books, Blair began to wish she'd never asked.

CHAPTER

*B*lair curled up on her couch that night with her father's Bible and read the passage that Cade had been reading the morning he disappeared. Though she'd spent most of her childhood in church and had endured endless hours of Bible teaching from both parents, she couldn't remember ever hearing about the cities of refuge until today.

One would think that it would have been incorporated into some of the town's celebrations, or at least explained in Cape Refuge's written history, since someone who had a part in naming the island clearly had known about Numbers 35. But this wasn't the case.

She tried to imagine what Cade had been thinking when he'd turned to that passage. Had he considered himself guilty of manslaughter, even though the man might have died, anyway, from the gunshot? Was he thinking he had bloodguilt on his hands? That he needed refuge from some unseen Avenger?

She began to read about the Levitical cities and how six were to be set apart.

> Then the LORD said to Moses: "Speak to the Israelites and say to them: 'When you cross the Jordan into Canaan, select some towns to be your cities of refuge, to which a person who has killed someone accidentally may flee. They will be places of refuge from the avenger, so that a person accused of murder may not die before he stands trial before the assembly. These six towns you give will be your cities of refuge. Give three on the side of the Jordan and three in Canaan as cities of refuge. These six towns will be a place of refuge for Israelites, aliens and any other people living among them, so that anyone who has killed another accidentally can flee there."

It was interesting, she thought, but had no application to Cade's life today. Even Cape Refuge wasn't a shelter from the legal system. People came there, specifically to Hanover House, to take refuge from their own trials.

She read on, about the distinction between manslaughter and murder. If the killing was proven to be intentional homicide, the avenger—someone from the dead person's family—would have the responsibility of putting him to death.

No death row. No government executioner. Up-close-and-personal revenge. That was what was called for.

But if it was an accident, then the congregation was to let him live in the city of refuge until the death of the high priest.

No complete acquittal. His life was altered for years. She wondered if he had to leave his family, his friends, or if they came with him. Did he have to stay in that place alone, eking out a living among priests and other manslayers?

And what did the high priest's death have to do with anything?

She read further.

"Do not pollute the land where you are. Bloodshed pollutes the land, and atonement cannot be made for the land on which blood has been shed, except by the blood of the one who shed it. Do not defile the land where you live and where I dwell, for I, the LORD, dwell among the Israelites."

Did Cade think he had somehow defiled the land? Or had he already gotten that call before he turned to that passage?

Could it be that he'd heard from Ann Clark and wondered why she wanted to meet with him? Maybe he sensed revenge in her voice.

The passage gave Blair no peace—just more questions that kept her from sleeping.

She rose feeling achy and frustrated the next morning. She headed over to Cricket's and saw that Cade's truck was still there.

Wearily, she went into the place and took a table where someone had left a copy of the *Savannah Morning News*. She picked it up as Charlie brought her a cup of coffee.

"Thanks, Charlie," she said, taking a sip.

He nodded. "Terrible about Cade, ain't it?"

She looked up at him. "What do you mean?"

"The article in the paper," he said. "Don't look good."

She looked down at the front page, and gasped. Her coffee sloshed and spilled.

CAPE REFUGE POLICE CHIEF UNDER SUSPICION.

Charlie grabbed a napkin and blotted up the coffee as Blair began to read.

The disappearance of Cape Refuge's Police Chief Matthew Cade, after running down a pedestrian on Monday, has cast him under a cloud of suspicion, sources said Monday. The dead man, who had been shot before walking into the street, was identified as William Clark yesterday. Chief Cade disappeared after

being seen having breakfast with Ann Clark, the wife
of the dead man.

Blair almost choked. How could they have put this in the
paper? They weren't even sure it was her, and here it was in print
for everyone to see?

Creflo King, who breakfasts each morning at a small
island diner called Cricket's, said he saw Cade there getting into the car with Clark's wife the morning after he
killed Clark. "I didn't know who she was then," King
said, "but later the police showed me a picture of her
and said that was who she was. Her hair was different,
but it was the same woman I saw, all right."

Chief Cade has not been seen or heard from since.
Savannah Morning News tried to contact Ann Clark,
but she did not return our calls.

"Makes you wonder if William Clark's death was an
accident, after all," King said. "Sure makes you wonder if this ain't something staged just so they could be
together."

Blair screamed and flung the paper across the room. "How
could he say that?"

She saw Creflo King sitting at the bar, looking back at her
over his shoulder.

"How dare you!" she screamed across the crowd. Everyone
got silent, and all eyes turned to her as she erupted out of her seat.
"Creflo King, how *dare* you say those things about Cade!"

Creflo shrugged. "Just told the truth."

She picked up the paper she had thrown and waved it in the
air. "It was your fifteen minutes of fame, wasn't it? You must feel
like a big man now."

Creflo got up. "All I did was answer the questions, Blair."

"You've ruined Cade's reputation," she shouted. "You've
made people think he was an adulterer and a murderer! How
could you do that to him?"

She started toward him across the wooden floor, and Charlie stepped into her way. "Come on, Blair. Calm down."

"I will not calm down!" She looked around at the astonished faces, most of whom she knew well. "Everybody in this place knows that Cade is a decent, upstanding Christian man. If any of you knew him at all, you'd know how upset he was over the accident that happened the other day. He was beating himself up over it. There's no way he did that on purpose!"

She got to Creflo and grabbed his red plaid collar. Through gritted teeth, she said, "You call that paper right now, and you take back what you said."

"I can't, Blair," he told her. "I told them the truth. I did see him leaving with that woman. Joe told me hisself that it might be William Clark's wife. And he ain't turned up since, so you tell me, where is he?"

"I don't know where he is," she said, "but I can guarantee you he's not in some lover's arms, snickering about how he got her husband out of the way." She shoved him, and he stumbled back against the counter. "You make me sick, you know that? We don't even know for sure if that was Ann Clark, but if it was, she has time to hide all the evidence before the police can search her place. But you got your stinking name in the paper! I could just kill you."

"You hear that, everybody?" Creflo yelled. "Blair Owens just threatened me right in front of God and everybody."

She knew her scar was flaming just the way she hated it, and she slapped her hair back from her face and pointed at him.

"Don't doubt me for a minute, Creflo," she said. "If you open your mouth and even speak the name of Matthew Cade, I will personally come back and deliver on my threat." With that, she stormed out of Cricket's, leaving the gossip and speculation to go on behind her.

CHAPTER

Joe McCormick cut through the squad room at the Third Precinct in Savannah. The officer at the front desk had pointed him to the offices in the back, Sergeant Tim Hull's domain. Joe had worked with the detective on a number of overlapping cases in the past and figured he wouldn't have any trouble getting his help now.

But Hull wasn't in his office. Joe stood in the doorway, surveying the clutter of weeks-old coffee cups and empty Diet Coke cans, wadded fast-food bags and ashtrays overflowing with cigarette butts. From the looks of things, one would have thought the occupant of this office was a stuffy old Lou Grant type, but that wasn't true. Hull looked more like Don Johnson from old *Miami Vice* reruns, with his sandy hair and darkly tanned skin, his two-day growth of stubble, his neutral-colored blazers, and his sockless ankles.

He would have fit right in on Cape Refuge, though he looked more like one of the lifeguards on the police department payroll than the cops who protected the island.

Joe looked toward what Hull often called "the war room" and saw the detective standing over a fax machine with a cigarette hanging from his mouth. "Hull!" he called, and the man turned.

Taking the cigarette out and stubbing it in a nearby ashtray, Hull blew out smoke and grinned at his island counterpart. "Well, if it isn't the big man from the small town." He reached out to shake.

"I need to talk to you," Joe said. "It's about our police chief."

Hull pulled a pack of cigarettes out of his pocket and lit another one. "Can't talk now. I'm on my way to the hospital. Another stolen baby, this time right here in Savannah. It hasn't been missing more than an hour. I've got to get over there if this fax machine will hurry up and print out what I need."

Joe regarded the paper rolling through the machine at its own pace, and finally Hull jerked it out. He took his cigarette out and studied the page for a moment. Then he seemed to remember Joe was there. "Walk with me. I'm in a hurry."

Joe matched his step. "I'm trying to get a warrant to question a woman and search a house over at Washington Square. Since it's on your turf, I thought you might want to be involved."

Hull took his cigarette out again and squinted at him through the smoke. "What for?"

"The wife of the pedestrian Cade ran over the other day lives there."

Hull shook his head. "I heard about his disappearance. Is this a lead on where he is?"

Joe nodded. "We think she was the last one seen with Cade the morning he disappeared. And if so, then her weird behavior might implicate her in her husband's shooting. I need to question her and search the house and see if there are any clues as to where Cade might be."

They burst out the front doors of the precinct, and Hull dropped his cigarette and stepped on it. "Good luck trying to convince a judge to give you a warrant to search a bereaved woman's

house, when you can't even be sure a crime has been committed."
He reached his car and unlocked it. "Your chief could have gone
fishing, for all you know. There's no evidence of foul play, if the
papers are right, and he hasn't been gone that long. That's a hard
sell to a judge. And you say she *may* have been the last one seen
with him? You don't know for sure?"

"She called his phone that morning," Joe said. "Witnesses
are pretty sure she's the same woman he was with. And the car
they got into was a rental car that was checked out at the airport
the night before, and returned the next day."

Hull reached his car but didn't get in. "Was she the one who
rented it?"

"Whoever it was apparently used a fake name and ID. We
can't trace it. I'm thinking there might be some revenge involved,
Hull. I know you don't know Cade that well, but he wouldn't up
and disappear like this. I don't want to do any kind of intense
search. I just want to walk through her house, check the bedrooms, the basement, her car. I want to scare her a little in hopes
of her spilling her guts."

Hull put his hands on the roof of his car and shook his head.
"Maybe she did go talk to him, just to look into the eye of the
man who killed her husband."

"She said she didn't. Said she'd never been to Cape Refuge."

"Maybe she chewed him out and wasn't proud of it, so she
lied. That doesn't mean she had anything to do with Cade's disappearance or her husband's shooting."

"All of those things could be true," Joe said. "But I want to
know for sure. If I can get the warrant to search her place, do you
want to go along or not?"

Hull looked across the roof of the car, thinking. Finally, he
opened the car door. "I've got to go, Joe. I have to see about this
missing baby. A woman walks into the mother's hospital room in
a nursing uniform and tells her she needs to take the baby because
the doctor is on the floor and needs to examine it. Half an hour
passes before the mother inquires about when the baby will be
brought back. Turns out the woman who took the baby isn't

employed there. Baby's gone. Now that's a crime, Joe. A real-live, bona fide crime. I realize you don't see many of those on Cape Refuge, so you go looking for crimes where they haven't happened."

Joe just looked at him. "We had a double homicide just a few months ago, Hull. You know that."

"Well, you and I both know that's not what this is. Chief Cade will mosey in in a day or so, claiming to be depressed about running a guy down, with a song and dance about how he needed to get away. Your famous yet amusing city council will be in an uproar, and there will be hearings and meetings for months on whether or not to fire him. You might even get the job."

He got into his car, closed the door, and rolled the window down.

Joe leaned in.

"When I get the warrant, Hull, do you want to search the house with me or not? I can do it alone, but I thought I'd offer you the chance since it's your territory."

Hull sighed and started his car. "Missing baby, Joe. First things first."

Joe stepped back as the car pulled away, and watched the man drive out of sight.

*H*ull had been right about the judge's reaction to Joe's request for a warrant. He'd claimed there was no proof of a crime even being committed in Cade's case. His only option now was to question her and ask permission for a walk-through of her house. If she didn't grant it, he was out of luck.

Joe had half hoped that Hull would pass on sharing the questioning with him now that there wasn't a warrant, but the truth was that he needed another pair of eyes. He could have brought any of the officers from Cape Refuge with him, but none of them were trained detectives. He didn't have time to give them a cram session on this kind of search.

Hull had agreed to come a little more easily than Joe had expected, but he had known the Savannah detective wouldn't want to be left out. Since the FBI had taken over the baby-kidnapping case, he'd had no reason not to come. He would meet Joe at the house at noon, he said.

Joe pulled up to the front curb of the house at 11:55 in his own unmarked car. The house he'd visited just days ago looked unchanged. Nothing seemed out of the ordinary.

Another unmarked car pulled up behind him, and Joe got out and closed his door quietly. Hull was dressed just as he'd been earlier, in a faded navy blue T-shirt under a tweed sport coat that looked like it had seen better days, a pair of khakis with a dirty hem, and deck shoes with no socks.

"Thanks for coming," Joe said.

"Sure you want to do this, Joe?" Hull took the cigarette out of his mouth and dropped it on the sidewalk.

"I know it'll be unpleasant," Joe said, "but it has to be done."

Joe led him up the front steps to the door and knocked hard. After a moment they heard footsteps again, then Ann Clark opened the door and peeked out.

"Mrs. Clark, I'm Detective McCormick from the Cape Refuge Police Department. I was here yesterday?"

She touched her throat. "Yes?"

"This is Detective Hull from the Savannah PD."

"Nice to meet you," she said.

Her eyes looked swollen and red, as if she'd been crying for days. Joe felt an instant pang of guilt. He hoped he wasn't making a mistake.

"I'm kind of busy right now," she said.

Joe pressed on. "Ma'am, we need to ask you a few questions. Do you mind if we come in?"

By the look on her face, it was clear that she did mind, but she stepped back from the door. She led them to the same parlor where he had broken the news yesterday. Joe took the same sofa, and she sat across from him.

Hull remained standing, looking around as if he was already involved in a search of the place.

Joe looked up at her. "Ma'am, I just had a few questions to ask you."

"I read the article in the paper today." Her voice wavered. "The things they said about me, they weren't even true. I don't know your police chief, Detective. I've never seen him in my life."

"I'm sorry about that article," he said. "It was irresponsible reporting. But witnesses believe it was you they saw on Cape Refuge, and we know for sure that a call was made from this house to Chief Cade's house on Tuesday morning." He leaned his elbows on his knees. "Mrs. Clark, you seemed surprised when we told you your husband had died. Were you?"

She cleared her throat. "Well, it was a shock, as you can imagine."

"But did you know about it already?"

She fidgeted, got up, walked near Detective Hull as if guarding her things from him. "I had seen it on the news the night before."

Joe stared at her. "You saw it on the news? Then why didn't you call us to let us know who he was?"

"I wasn't thinking clearly," she said. "I don't know."

Now Joe was sure she was involved. Why else would she have lied? He got to his feet, and faced her. "Why did you let us think you were hearing it for the first time, Mrs. Clark? Why the act?"

Ann Clark came back to the chair she had been sitting in and stood behind it, fingering the cord across the top seam. "I told you, I wasn't thinking clearly. I heard about it on the news the night before, and I was kind of in denial, hoping you were coming to tell me it was all a mistake, that he was all right. In the hospital maybe, but that he wasn't dead." Her voice broke then, and she crumpled over the chair, bringing her elbows close up to her chest and covering her face with her wrists. "Willie is dead. He shot himself to get away from me. What did you want me to do?"

Hull turned around, and Joe just looked at her. He hated it when women cried. He never knew what to do. Shoving his hands into his pockets, he looked down at his feet. "Mrs. Clark, we're not certain it was suicide. Do you know of any enemies your husband had?"

Her face went crimson. "I told you he'd threatened suicide. Even told me how he would do it! He had a gun and said he was going to shoot himself. He was his own worst enemy."

Joe shot Hull a look. "Mrs. Clark, why didn't you call the police when he threatened suicide?"

She pressed her hand against her forehead. "I told you. I was in denial. I wanted to think it was just another threat. But now that it's done, I see that I should have called someone to stop him." She broke off and muffled her mouth.

Joe decided to switch gears.

"Ma'am, witnesses saw Chief Cade talking to you that morning, then getting into a car with you, and now Chief Cade is missing. Are you sure you don't know anything about that?"

She stiffened again and looked at him, her wet face raging red. "Of course not. I don't know who they saw your police chief with, but it was *not* me."

"We just thought that since Chief Cade was involved in the accident, you might have had reason to want to see him."

Anger tightened her face, and her hand trembled as she touched her throat again. "I've already told you, I've never been to Cape Refuge in my life."

"Ma'am, we have your number on Chief Cade's caller ID. We know someone from this house called him the morning he disappeared."

She seemed to struggle with her answer, then finally, she let out a rough sigh. "I'm sorry, my brain is just so muddled with all this ... I can't think ... I did try to call him. But I didn't speak to him. There was no answer."

Joe was silent for a moment. Her story wasn't adding up. "Why did you try to call him?"

"Because I had seen the news report the night before, and I spent all night just a wreck, not knowing what to do. I didn't sleep at all. I was pacing the floor and praying. And finally, early the next morning, I decided I needed to call him. I don't know what I was hoping, but it didn't matter because I let it ring twice and then I hung up."

"How did you get his number? It's unlisted."

The woman fidgeted again. "I have a friend who works for the phone company."

Joe got out a notepad and pen. "What's that friend's name?"

She seemed cornered. "I don't want to get her in trouble. What does it matter, anyway? I didn't reach him."

Detective Hull finally spoke. "Ma'am, we were wondering if you'd give us permission to walk through your house."

Her face twisted. "Walk through? For what?"

"As I told you," Joe said, "Chief Cade is missing and the witnesses thought they saw him with you."

"And you think he's here?"

For a moment he thought he saw fright cross over her face, and she looked toward the door leading into the dark hall. Something was up, he thought.

Hull clearly noticed it too. "Ma'am, if you don't give us permission, we'll have to get a warrant. In that event, it won't be a walk-through, but a full search of the premises."

She stared up at him, visibly shaken. Joe hoped she didn't know enough law to realize they didn't yet have probable cause for a warrant.

Hull's bluff worked. "Well, go ahead," she said. "I have nothing to hide...."

Hull headed out of the parlor and into the hall. Joe followed. "You take the upstairs," Hull said in a low voice. "I'll take this floor and the basement."

Joe nodded and went upstairs. He began checking the bedrooms, every bathroom, an extra study that he found near the back of the house. He looked in closets, drawers, trash cans, but the garbage bags all looked freshly changed.

He came downstairs and saw Ann standing in the hallway at the bottom of the stairs, looking up at him with worried eyes. "I told you you wouldn't find anything there."

He saw the open basement door. Hull trudged up the steps and stepped back into the hall.

"Nothing there," he said. "Just a lot of dust and mold."

"Of course there's nothing," she said. "What do you think? That I have some man hidden in my house somewhere?"

Joe went into the kitchen, noting how clean the place was. Nothing seemed out of place, and it smelled of Lysol. Wouldn't a woman in mourning at least leave a glass out? How many people would scrub with Lysol until the house reeked of it, when going through something like this?

Not many, unless things just weren't what they seemed.

When they had finally left the house, Hull said I-told-you-so, then headed back to his precinct. Joe went back out to his car and sat behind the wheel for a moment. He hated to go back empty-handed or to tell the rest of the force—or Blair and Jonathan, for that matter—that they had not found anything concerning Cade. Where could he be? The fact that he hadn't found evidence against Ann Clark certainly did not take her off the suspect list. She could have put a bullet through Cade's head and dragged him off to some remote grave in the middle of the woods, though he didn't think she looked strong enough to do such a thing. But one never knew.

A chill went up his spine at the thought that something like that could have happened to Cade. He didn't know what his next move would be, but somehow, he had to find his friend before it was too late.

CHAPTER

*S*craping, rattling, darkness ...

Cade slid out from under a black quicksand sleep and struggled to orient himself. He could not see a thing in the opaque darkness. His head felt as if it had been cracked through the skull. He reached up to touch it and felt a sticky, painful wound. What in the world had happened?

The scraping sounded again, and he tried to sit up. A crack opened in the darkness. Dim light shown through as the silhouette of a woman stepped into the doorway.

He frowned. "Who are you?"

She turned on the light and it flooded the room, blinding him. He squinted and turned his face away from it, then he forced himself to look back at her. The face was familiar, but he couldn't place her.

"Headache?" Her eyes were hard, piercing. "You're lucky you're alive."

"Who are you?" He tried to sit up again, but the pain in his head pulled him back down.

"Think. It'll come back to you."

He tried to think. There had been an accident . . . a man killed . . . a phone call at home . . .

He squinted his eyes at her. Was she the woman he'd met at Cricket's? She looked different, yet the same. Her hair had changed . . .

"Mrs. Clark?" he asked.

She didn't answer him, and he watched as she brought a two-liter bottle and set it down beside his cot.

He raised up as much as he could and looked down at himself. Blood had dried all over the front of his shirt. He touched his head again, found the gash that had bled. "Was I in an accident? I don't remember—"

"No accident," she said, moving back to the door. "It was quite deliberate."

Confused, he tried to focus. He was in a small room, with nothing but the cot he lay on and a commode. It wasn't a hospital—the walls were studs and tarpaper, like in a basement. And he couldn't imagine why he would be here with her.

She had wanted to talk alone and had suggested that they go for a ride in her car so he could show her where the accident happened. He had obliged, recognizing her grief.

That was the last thing he remembered.

"I want to know what he told you," she said.

He looked at her. "What who told me?"

"My husband, before he died. You said in your press conference that he spoke to you. What did he tell you?"

"Nothing . . . I don't know . . . I could barely hear him. He was bleeding to death."

Her teeth came together, and she spoke through them. "The gunshot. What did he say about the gunshot?"

Her curiosity implicated her, and he realized he was in danger. He tried to rise up again. "What did you do, knock me in the head with something?"

"I asked you a question!"

Her face was harder than he remembered, and her eyes were cold. She'd been wearing sunglasses at Cricket's.

"I didn't even know about the gunshot until after he was dead." He tried to get up again. What had happened to his head? "I need to use your phone," he said. "Please . . . I need to call the station . . ."

She laughed then, a brittle, frigid sound. "You're not calling anyone, and you're not going anywhere. You're staying right here where I put you."

Finally he managed to sit up. "Why? What purpose could that serve?"

"Many purposes."

With great effort, he got up and started toward her.

She took a pistol out of her pocket and leveled it on him. He froze and recognized it to be his own firearm.

"Get back on that bed before I blow your head off."

He knew she meant it. It was clear in her eyes. "Why? What do you want? Is it revenge?"

"Shut up and get back on the cot."

He backed to the bed and slowly lowered himself down. "What are you keeping me here for?"

She didn't answer. She just kept that gun on him as she backed out of the door. He saw that he was in a room inside a basement, and across the room outside his door stood wooden stairs, probably going into her house. She closed the door behind her. He heard it lock and then heard scraping noises as if she pushed furniture against the door. He wondered if anyone was looking for him. Surely people had seen him leaving Cricket's with her. Surely *someone* saw him getting into her car.

But how could she have gotten him here? She wasn't big enough to carry him. He wondered if she had drugged him at Cricket's. He did remember feeling very tired as he'd gotten into her car, but he hadn't slept that well the night before.

His throat felt blistered and parched, and he wondered how much time had passed. He looked down at the water bottle she had brought him, grabbed it, and drank down the water. It went down smooth, wetting the tissue in his throat, hydrating his mouth.

He looked at his watch, squinted to focus on the date. It was April 7. He'd been missing for three whole days?

He felt a lethargy washing over him, making him weak, sleepy, heavy again. He lay back and searched his brain for a plan of escape.

But he was so tired . . .

Then he heard voices. Distant, muffled voices coming from the vent over his head. Somewhere in another room of the house, their voices carried.

Sleep tried to pull him under into a swampy haze, but he fought to stay awake.

". . . told you I should have killed him . . . never wanted to bring him here . . ." It was Ann Clark's angry voice. "He didn't tell him. . . ."

". . . stupid phone call . . . why didn't you think?" a man's voice said. "We can use him. . . ."

". . . too dangerous . . . ," he heard Ann say. "What if they do search again . . . ?"

The sounds became more muddled, confused, and the words blurred and flattened in his head as he drifted deeper. . . .

Just before he went entirely under, he thought he heard a baby cry.

"Lord . . . please . . ." No clearer plea would form in his mind. He couldn't make his thoughts evolve into words, and soon his brain released those thoughts as blackness overtook him again.

CHAPTER

*B*lair sat on the porch at Hanover House, watching Joe McCormick's car pull away. He had come to update them about the search, and his news—or lack thereof—had left her numb.

She'd had such hopes that the search of Ann Clark's house would lead them to Cade.

Morgan sat down in the rocking chair next to Blair, but didn't rock. Silently, they both stared out at the ocean lapping against the beach across the street.

"He'll be all right," Morgan said. "He has to."

Blair couldn't answer. He wasn't all right. It was a knowledge that came from the deepest part of her heart. Cade was in trouble, and no one was able to help him.

"I have to feed Oswald," she whispered.

Morgan looked over at her. "Cade's cat?"

"Yes," she said, "someone has to feed him."

Morgan touched her arm. "I don't want you over there alone. It could be dangerous. I don't want whatever happened to Cade to happen to you too."

"I'm not going in," she said. "I'll just feed him outside."

"Well, I'll come with you then."

Blair was glad Morgan had offered. As she waited for her to go tell Jonathon, Blair walked to her car and leaned against it, looking out at the beach. How many mornings had she seen Cade out there in his kayak, rowing as the sun shone down on him?

She wondered if, perhaps, he had done that the morning of his disappearance. Maybe he'd gone kayaking again, and had an accident in the water. Maybe he'd drowned . . .

Panic rose inside her, and she tried to think whether she'd seen his kayak in his utility room either time she'd gone in for the key. She couldn't remember.

"I'm ready." Morgan hurried down the steps and got into the car.

As they drove across the island to Cade's house, Blair was pensive. The thoughts of all the things that could have happened to Cade stirred new grief in her soul. She hadn't entirely gotten through the grief over her parents; she couldn't imagine dealing with Cade's death too.

He couldn't be dead. He just couldn't.

A tear rolled down her scarred cheek, and she wiped it away.

Morgan noticed. "Jonathan's getting a prayer chain activated," she said quietly. "They'll all be praying for him."

Blair nodded. "Good."

Morgan smiled. "I expected you to come back with something cryptic about sending empty wishes up to the sky."

Blair swallowed. "I have to at least consider the possibility that I could be wrong about prayer. If there's any chance at all that it works, then I want it done for Cade."

Another tear. She smeared it away.

They pulled into Cade's driveway. His truck still wasn't home. It sat where he'd left it.

She got the bag of Cat Chow she'd bought and the jug of water and went around to the backyard. Before looking for the cat, she stepped into the utility room. The kayak hung in its place on the opposite wall.

She wilted with relief. "The kayak's there. I had started to think that maybe he took it out and drowned."

"I hadn't thought of that," Morgan whispered.

The cat meowed and came toward her. Blair bent over and picked him up. "Hey, there, Lee Harvey. How're you doing?"

"Lee Harvey?" Morgan asked with a smile. "I think he named him after Oswald Chambers."

"Whatever." Her relief quickly turned to sorrow, and she realized that this abandoned cat was a symbol of Cade's vanishing. He might not be dead in the ocean, but he could be dead *somewhere*. She felt her mouth trembling, and those tears spilled over again. Slowly, she went to one of the patio chairs and sat down.

Morgan sat down beside her. "Honey, are you all right?"

"No, not really." Blair buried her face in the cat's fur. She could feel Morgan's soft gaze.

"Your interest in Cade is deeper than friendship, isn't it?" she asked softly.

Blair looked up at her. "Why would you ask that?"

"Just a sense I have. I've always thought he was interested in you."

Blair caught her breath. "Interested in me? How do you figure that?"

Morgan took the bag of cat food and tore the top open. "The way he looks at you. You know it and I know it, Blair. You two have gotten close over the last few months, whether you want to admit it or not."

"We've become good *friends*, Morgan. That's all. I'd feel this way if any of my friends suddenly disappeared, so you don't have to make more of it than there is, okay?"

Morgan shrugged. "Okay."

Blair put the cat down, filled his bowls, then sat back down and watched as he ate. "I don't get God."

Morgan just looked at her. "I didn't think you believed in God."

Blair shook her head. "Sometimes I do, sometimes I don't. But if there is one, I don't get why he would let this happen."

"We don't know what happened, Blair. Maybe nothing. Maybe it's all just a misunderstanding. Maybe Cade will come riding back into town with some perfectly good explanation."

Blair shook her head. "You and I both know that's not going to happen."

"Well, don't blame God before you even know what to blame him for. God's the only one who knows for sure where Cade is."

"God and that Clark woman," Blair said.

"You still think she was involved?"

"Joe said she admitted that she called him." Blair closed the cat food and put it into the storage room. "All she had to do was slap on a wig and sunglasses, and show up here intent on doing Cade in."

"But why would she want revenge if it's clear her husband tried to kill himself first? She couldn't blame Cade."

"Maybe she's really the one who shot him. Maybe she thought Cade knew. Or even if it was a suicide, maybe she just needed to blame somebody." Blair knew that was why she'd entertained the possibility of God existing. It was handy, when she needed someone to take the blame for Cade's disappearance.

Pulling herself together, she got up and wiped her tears on her sleeve. "Well, let's go," she said. "I have some computer work to do at the library. I'm going to find out everything I can about Ann Clark today."

CHAPTER

*S*lowly, gradually, Cade emerged from the mire of his unconsciousness and realized that he still lay in the dark basement room. The two-liter bottle he had drunk from earlier lay empty on the concrete floor.

He didn't remember finishing it off. He remembered drinking it while he'd racked his brain for a plan to escape, and then he'd grown so sleepy that he'd hardly been able to think. Had the woman drugged his water?

He squinted up in the direction of that small vent above his head. He'd heard voices coming from it. A man's and a woman's. . . .

He forced himself to sit up and looked around in the darkness. He got up and stumbled drunkenly to the door. He felt a light switch next to it and turned it on.

The bulb at the center of the ceiling cast the place in a yellow glow, revealing exposed studs and tar paper, like a room that had never quite been finished.

He tested the doorknob and found that it was locked. It was a metal door, not something he'd be able to kick through. He banged on it with his fist. He had to get out of here.

But the door would not budge.

Giving up, he leaned back against the wall and tried to think. The room had no windows through which to escape. The vent in the ceiling over his cot was no more than six by eight inches.

He turned to the wall and wondered if he could kick or beat his way through the Sheetrock. He peeled back the tarpaper but saw only cement beneath it.

There was no way to break through.

Weary, he went back to his cot and sank down. It was hot, sweltering, and he was thirsty again. His stomach burned with hunger.

He wondered where his cell phone was. He'd been wearing it the morning he'd met with this woman, even though he couldn't get a signal on the island. He had planned to drive in to Savannah that day to confer with the Savannah police about possible missing person reports.

She must have taken it, along with his gun.

He spotted the tank on the toilet lid and stumbled toward it, lifted it, and slipped it between the cot and the wall. Maybe if she came back, he could use it to knock her off guard, and somehow get the gun out of her hands.

He heard the scraping sound again and knew his banging had alerted her that he was awake.

He waited, every muscle in his body poised in readiness.

Her face was hard as she stepped into the room. She held the gun in one hand and a box of Kentucky Fried Chicken in the other. In her apron pocket, she carried another bottle of water.

"Just so you know," she said, "if you try to escape, I'll kill you."

His fingers closed over the tank lid. "What do you want from me?"

She didn't answer, just thrust the box at him and set the bottled water down on the floor beside the door.

"Go ahead and eat while I'm feeling generous. I don't want you dead just yet."

He needed her to come farther into the room. Just a little closer. . . . "Look, if you think you're going to get ransom for me or something, you're sadly mistaken. I don't even know anybody with money. Not anybody who'd put a dime out for me. Most of my family members are broke."

"It's not ransom we want."

We? Of course. He'd heard another voice through the vent.

"Then what do you want?" he asked. "Revenge?"

He had heard vengeance in her voice that morning she'd called. The idea of meeting with her had worried him, which was why he'd picked a public place.

He had gone to Numbers 35 to read of the cities of refuge, then had prayed that God would be his emotional refuge from a bitter, grieving widow who blamed him for her husband's death. He'd prayed for words to comfort her in her suffering.

But she must have drugged him and brought him here.

"You're our scapegoat," she said. "A distraction."

"Scapegoat? For what?"

She didn't answer, only smiled coldly at him. His hand slid over the toilet lid. He had to make her come closer. Softening his voice, he said, "Look, you seem like a decent person who was motivated by grief and shock when you abducted me. It may have seemed like a good idea at the time. Revenge and all that. Maybe you even planned to kill me. But surely now reality has set in, and you must see that this is crazy."

From some distant part of the house, he thought he heard a baby crying again. She and William must have been new parents. Now the husband and father was dead. No wonder she had snapped.

She stared at him then, her eyes dull and unmoving, as she seemed to process his words. Blocking the tank lid with his body, he started to slide it out of its hiding place.

"I think I have a fever," he said. "I've been having chills, and my head is splitting."

"Your head hurts because you fell down the basement stairs."

"Fell?" he asked. "How?"

"We dropped you."

She said it so coldly that he wondered for a moment if she was a psychopath.

"We?"

"You're making me tired, Chief Cade. I didn't come here for an interrogation. You're the prisoner, remember?"

She wasn't going to come closer. He was going to have to go to her. Pulling the lid behind his back, he scooted to the end of the cot and opened the box of chicken. She still held his gun on him, but he knew that one carefully aimed swing with the tank lid would be enough to knock it out of her hand.

He feigned interest in the chicken, judging her distance from the corner of his eye. If he didn't still feel drugged, he'd be more certain of his chances. But he had no choice but to act now.

She pulled a writing pad and pen from the pocket that had held the bottle and tossed it to his cot. "Here, take that. I want you to write a letter."

"A letter?" he repeated.

"Yes. Address it to Joe, your second-in-command at the Cape Refuge Police Department."

He glared up at her. "What do you want it to say?"

"Copy what I've written on the second page of the pad."

That gun was still on him, but he realized that if he did as she wanted, when he handed it to her, he might have the chance to get the gun.

And just in case his attempt to escape failed, maybe he could plant clues in the letter.

"Write it word for word. No tricks, Chief. I'm warning you. Don't change a thing. Make it look natural."

He read the letter.

Joe,

   Just wanted to touch base with you guys and let you know that I haven't dropped off the face of the earth. I was just a little depressed after the accident, so I decided

*to take some time off. The truth is, I'd been seeing a girl
from Savannah, and we decided to get married.*

*I know it sounds crazy, and I'm going to have a lot
of explaining to do when I get back, but I've never been
happier. Let everyone know that for me, will you?*

*I'll call as soon as I know when I'm coming back.
Meanwhile, I know Cape Refuge is in your good hands.*

He closed his eyes. "They're never gonna believe I got married."

"I've done my homework, Chief. You're an eligible bachelor
in your town. Very quiet about your private life. There's a lot of
speculation about you. They'll believe it."

Cade wasn't going to argue. If they didn't believe it, maybe
they'd realize the letter was fake. The more unbelievable it was,
the better.

He started to print.

"No, that won't do," she said. "That's not how you write."

He looked up at her. "How do you know how I write?"

"I've seen your handwriting," she said.

"On what?"

"I told you, I've done my homework." She raised the gun.
"Do it right, Chief. Do it right or lose that hand."

He knew she meant it, this desperate, crazy woman. He tore
off the paper, and started on the next sheet. *Think. Think!*

He changed his *d*s, looped them bigger than he normally did.

"Try again." She was getting angry now, holding that gun
aimed at his forehead. "I'm warning you! I know how you write.
This is your last chance, Chief. You're just as good to me dead as
alive."

He wiped the sweat dripping into his eyes and tore off the
top sheet, and began to write again. He wrote it just as she'd typed
it, in his regular handwriting, conscious of that gun pointed at his
forehead. It wouldn't be mailed anyway, he thought. He was going
to get out of here any minute now.

But just in case, he signed it "Matt Cade." Joe would realize
it was a fake as soon as he saw the signature. Cade had never gone
by Matt in his life.

He handed the pad back to her, hoping she'd move one step closer. She still hadn't seen the tank lid at his back.

She read over the letter. "Good. That one should do."

He turned the lid sideways, brought it to his side, watched her stick the letter into her pocket. Slowly, he stood up . . .

. . . and swung.

The lid knocked the gun from her hands and sent her reeling back. She screamed as he grabbed her arms and flung her around, picked up the gun, and jabbed it into her ribs.

"Let go of me!" she screamed. "I'm not alone in this house! Let go of me!"

He threw his hand over her mouth and pulled her small body back against him. Keeping the gun in her ribs, he walked her through the door, out into the larger part of the basement. He looked around, saw the empty bookshelves that had been in front of the door. That was the scraping he had heard. Each time she left, she slid them back, so that if anyone came down here they wouldn't know a door was behind them.

He shoved her toward the stairs and forced her up. He still felt dizzy, weak, drugged, but he could do this, he thought. As long as he had the gun. . . .

They were halfway up the stairs . . . when the door at the top creaked open.

Ann flung herself out of his grasp, and Cade raised his gun.

A gunshot blasted him back. Pain cracked through his leg, hurling him back down the stairs, smashing him on the concrete floor. Another shot . . . his body jolted . . .

Voices . . . a man's yelling . . . Ann Clark hysterical . . .

Agony in his leg . . . his side . . .

He felt his arms being lifted over his head, his body being dragged . . . a door closing . . . that scraping sound.

He thought of the wall being bricked up with Edgar Allen Poe evil, someone discovering him forty years from now, nothing but a skeleton in a dark hole.

Blood loss drew him into its mire, and finally, he succumbed to the dark.

CHAPTER 17

The air conditioner hummed from the large vent overhead, and Sadie shivered and tried to get comfortable in her desk. Her English teacher waxed poetic about the lessons one could learn from Shakespeare, but Sadie's gaze drifted across the room to a cluster of girls, busily engaged in note writing—not on the merits of Shakespeare, but probably on something much more important, like what Sadie had worn to school today.

Never the recipient of those notes, she'd been the subject of a few. She knew that because, after registering their whispers and stolen looks across the room, Sadie had occasionally waited for the class to empty and dug them out of the trash.

The first one that had her name had knocked the wind from her like a shovel swung across her stomach. *Whack!*

It had criticized the shoes she wore, the way she wore her hair, whether it was really blonde or bleached that way. Another gossiped that she was seventeen, two years older than the other tenth graders.

The final blow had come when she'd found one in which they had called her the "tramp daughter of a jailbird."

Whack! Whack!

She had read others, where they'd called her stupid and suggested that she needed to be put back into seventh grade instead of tenth, because she had the education and the brains of a manatee.

She knew they were right. She didn't have a strong background in school. For most of her life, she had yawned through classes and had trouble focusing, since she'd gotten so little sleep at night. Most nights she spent avoiding the men her mother brought home and all the other "friends" who came and went through all hours of the night, vile foulmouthed people with selfish motives, coming to buy drugs and sell them and sometimes even to make them.

School had been a sanctuary to her, but she couldn't say that she'd been able to learn all that much. She had street smarts, her mother had always told her, and that was what really counted. Street smarts had saved her life on many occasions, but she yearned for the other kind of smarts—the kind that made you fit in and seem normal and get ahead in this world.

The bell rang, and Sadie looked up at the teacher. The tall, skinny woman barked out their assignment as the students began filing out the door like evacuees during a bomb threat. Sadie closed her books, loaded them back into her backpack, and followed the students out.

She went to her locker and got the books she would need for the last class of the day. Next to her, the three girls who'd been writing notes babbled about a party that Friday night.

"On South Beach," Crystal Lewis was saying. "My parents are letting me hire a DJ. Everybody'll be there."

Sadie knew that "everybody" didn't include her. The girl giving the party was the one who'd called her a tramp.

Not for the first time, Sadie wished Morgan had allowed her to home-school or work fulltime instead of enrolling here. She could have gotten a job in one of the souvenir shops on the island

and done just fine with the tourists and beach bums. Last summer, when she'd first come to Cape Refuge, she had worked at the *Cape Refuge Journal* and had been proud of the job she'd done. But the paper had closed, and Morgan had insisted on school.

Even the principal knew the story of how she'd shown up here and slept on the beach until Cade had forbidden her, and how she'd then slept in the boathouse that belonged to Hanover House, until Morgan had discovered her and brought her home. And the principal knew—like everyone else—that her mother still served time on drug charges.

She closed her locker and headed up the hall to her class, walking against the flow of rushing students, as if she alone had a class in the other direction. She always felt alone at school, even in a crowd. She sometimes went entire days without anyone in class acknowledging her.

Sighing, she slapped her fine hair back over her shoulder and heard a voice behind her.

"What class do you have next?"

She glanced back and saw Trevor Beal, the star linebacker for the Cape Refuge football team, whom many of those intercepted notes had been about.

"Biology," she said with a nervous, surprised smile. "I hate biology."

"Could be worse." He fell into step beside her. "Could be calculus. That's where I'm going."

She thought of the remedial math class they had put her in and knew that she would never make it through calculus. Not in a million years.

"Hey, listen, I'm going to a party Friday night on the beach. Crystal is giving it. You want to come?"

Sadie stopped in the hall and looked up at him. It was no wonder Crystal Lewis followed him around like a starving puppy. With his black, wavy hair, those movie-star blue eyes, and that athletic build, every girl in the school had tried to get his attention.

She didn't really want to be one of them. "I can't go to that party. I wasn't invited."

He grinned. "If you go as my date, you're invited, okay? Come on, it'll be fun."

She just stared at him. Was he making fun of her? Asking her on a dare? She glanced around, expecting to see a vicious crowd of giggling girls waiting nearby.

But no one watched.

The hall was emptying. The bell would ring any second.

"I don't think so, Trevor."

He looked shattered. "Why not?"

"Because . . ." She didn't want to confess her distrust of any- one here who was nice to her. If she was wrong, she'd seem piti- ful, a fate worse than being mocked.

"Come on, Sadie. I really want to get to know you."

She narrowed her eyes. "Why?"

"Why?" he repeated. "Have you looked in the mirror lately?"

Her defenses shattered, and she smiled. He meant it. He wasn't mocking.

She thought of Crystal, her nemesis who had coined the worst phrases about her. It was no secret that she'd had a crush on him all year. If she went out with him, Crystal would declare all-out war.

Sadie pushed her hair behind her ears, then flipped it back out and raked it back with her fingers. She started to say yes, that she would go as his date.

But then reality struck. She couldn't go to that girl's party and risk having her call her the "tramp daughter of a jailbird" out loud in front of everyone. She didn't want people whisper- ing about her, snubbing her, staring at her. What could she be thinking?

"I'd like to, Trevor. I really would, but I don't think I belong at Crystal's party. Maybe some other time." She started to walk away.

Trevor stepped in front of her. "Okay, then we can do some- thing else," he said. "I don't have to go to that party. We could go to Savannah and see a movie, maybe get a bite to eat."

Her eyebrows shot up and her eyes widened. It was too good to be true. "You'd miss the party?"

"Sure. There are millions of parties every weekend. Nothing special about this one." He pushed her hair back, sending a jolt through her. "Besides, it was just an excuse to get you to go out with me. I don't care anything about Crystal's party."

Her heart felt like a dove flapping at her rib cage, ready to soar. "I'd love to go," she said. "It sounds fun."

"Okay, I'll pick you up at six Friday night. Sound okay?"

She bit her bottom lip. "Yeah, sounds great. You know where I live?"

He grinned. "Everybody knows Hanover House."

She watched him lope off to his classroom. Quickly, she headed to her own, ducked inside, and sat at the back. Crystal and her cohorts clustered at the front, their sandaled, red-toenailed feet stretched out in front of them, their moussed hair perfect as it blew under the vent of the air conditioner.

Somehow she didn't feel quite so alone anymore. There was someone in this school who saw value in her. Someone substantial. Someone important.

Maybe things were about to change.

CHAPTER

18

Sadie found Morgan sitting at the desk in the little office off the kitchen. A Bible lay open in front of her, and next to it a stack of checks that had come from the donors who supported the house. On the floor behind her, little Seth slept soundly on his favorite blankie, his little mouth open. She knelt down beside him and gave him a gentle kiss.

"What you doing?" she asked Morgan in a low voice.

"Just posting these donor checks."

"Any news about Chief Cade?"

Morgan shook her head. "None. They're still looking for him." She put her pen down and reached for Sadie's hand. "How was your day, sweetie?"

Sadie grinned and bit her lip. "Good. Really, really good."

Morgan seemed to notice the excitement on Sadie's face and pulled her into the kitchen so they wouldn't wake Seth. "Okay, spill it. Something happened." She sat her down at the table and reached for a soda in the refrigerator.

"Something really unbelievable," Sadie said on the edge of a squeal.

Morgan set a plate of cookies down and joined Sadie at the table. "Come on, start talking."

Sadie giggled. Her life at Hanover House seemed like a fantasy, something she had dreamed of at night when she had lain in her bed and heard the sounds of Ozzy Osbourne music coming from her mother's living room, people cackling and doors slamming, and strangers intruding on her private space. She had dreamed of a home where she could go off to school rested and secure, then come home and have a snack waiting for her, someone to ask her how things had been and get excited when she had news. And now she had all that. She had no right to complain about a few smart-aleck girls at school treating her like trash.

"A guy asked me out for Friday night!"

Morgan's eyes reflected her delight. "Sadie, that's great!"

Sadie did a little dance in her seat. "He originally asked me to some party that Crystal Lewis was giving, but I told him no way I was going to one of her parties, not that she'd let me come, anyway."

Morgan touched her hand. "Honey, she'd love you if she got to know you."

"Well, she's not too interested in that. Anyway, I said no, so he's like, 'We don't have to go to the party. We can go to a movie. It was just an excuse to take you out.'" She stopped and covered her mouth and let out another muffled squeal.

Morgan laughed with her. "So who's the boy? Do I know him?"

"A senior named Trevor Beal. The star linebacker on the football team."

Morgan's face changed, and Sadie thought that if smiles could really crash, there'd be lip fallout all over the floor. "Oh. Him."

Sadie didn't like the sound of that. She set her cookie down. "What's the matter?"

Morgan got up and went to the counter. She got a wet sponge and began to wipe it. It was her way. Whenever something disturbed her, she wiped something. "Nothing. It's just that . . . I know his family. They're not very . . . reputable people."

Sadie sat back in her chair. "Well, I'm not very reputable, either, if you ask anybody at my school. What's the matter with them?"

Morgan stopped wiping and turned back to her. "Sadie, Trevor's family has been involved in criminal activities for years. A few years ago his father and uncles were indicted for drug trafficking. During the trial, their major witness wound up dead. No one could ever prove they'd had anything to do with it, but without that witness they couldn't get a conviction, so they got off scot-free. But not before a bunch of evidence came out about their family being one of the biggest suppliers of cocaine in the southeast."

"But Trevor's not a druggie. He's a nice person."

"No, none of them are druggies. They don't *take* drugs—they just sell them. And that's not just a rumor, Sadie—I've heard it from a number of the people we work with at the jail. The drug dealers get their supplies from this family. They're also big loan sharks around this area. And I can't prove it, but I think Trevor is one of the ones who goes around beating people up for not paying on time."

Sadie gaped at her. "No, he wouldn't do that. I mean, he's big and everything, but he wouldn't just beat people up over money."

Morgan sat back down and took her hands. "Sadie, a guy at our church was having financial problems and borrowed from them. He wound up in the hospital with two broken legs. He told the police that Trevor and some other guys did it, but they got off because they had some tight alibis."

"Then he couldn't have done it."

"But it was his own family that backed up his alibi, Sadie. They've been known to lie to protect their own before. They're scary people."

Sadie wanted to cry. Maybe Trevor *was* too good to be true. "Morgan, I'm telling you, he wouldn't do that. You're just listening to gossip. And I thought we were supposed to love everyone. Not just the ones whose parents are perfect."

"Sadie, I have prayed for that family. When Trevor's grandmother died, I took food over there. I've invited them to our church. I would love it if any one of them wanted to come. But dating one of them is another thing altogether."

"But he's the only one who's asked me out! And besides, Jesus hung out with the publicans and the prostitutes. Maybe Trevor's family are just the kind of people Jesus would have spent time with."

Morgan breathed a bitter laugh. "Honey, you don't know how many times I heard my sister say that to my parents, when she wanted to hang around with people who were getting her into trouble. The fact is, Jesus did come to seek and save the lost. But he didn't *leave* them lost. He told them to go and sin no more, and lots of them listened and did just that."

"Well, maybe I could do that for Trevor. Maybe I could lead him to Christ."

Morgan tipped her head and touched Sadie's chin. "Honey, that hardly ever happens in a dating relationship. What happens instead is that the unbeliever changes the believer."

"You don't have much faith in me." Blinking back tears, Sadie wadded her napkin and took it to the waste basket. "He's a good person, Morgan."

"Sadie, as long as I'm your guardian, it's my job to protect you." Morgan sighed. "I know you're excited about this boy asking you out, but I don't feel comfortable letting you go. Please understand. You're a great person, and there will be other guys."

Sadie felt as if the world had been pulled out from under her, just when she was getting her footing. "I was so excited . . . I've tried to make friends, but it hasn't happened. And then he came along." She started to cry and hated herself for it. "I've been there for months already, Morgan. Almost a whole school year. I'm older than everyone in my class. I'm a freak. Nobody's noticed what a great person I am. Nobody *cares* what a great person I am.

Nobody even *thinks* I'm a great person. They think I'm the tramp daughter of a jailbird."

Morgan looked as if she'd been slapped. "Did someone say that to you?"

"Yes! It's like some kind of nickname. I hate it there. I didn't want to go in the first place. But now something's happened that makes it bearable, and you're telling me you won't allow it?"

"Honey, like I said, you can be his friend. But you cannot go out with him."

"But you've told me that we're supposed to influence the world around us. Salt and light and all that. How can we be that if we avoid people who need it?"

Morgan was undaunted. "Sadie, we've been over this. You can be salt and light to someone without *dating* them!"

It was the closest she and Morgan had ever come to fighting, and Sadie hated it. But she wasn't ready to back down yet.

She heard Seth chattering in the office off the kitchen, then he appeared, sleepy-eyed and with the imprint of his blankie on one cheek. "Say-Say," he said and reached up for her. She picked him up and kissed his warm cheek. He saw her tears and touched her wet cheek.

"Here, let me have him." Morgan took the chubby baby. Sadie watched, crying silently, as Morgan poured some apple juice into his sippy cup and took him to his high chair.

When he was settled, Morgan reached for her hand and pulled her back to her chair.

Sadie sat down and looked dully at her.

"Sadie, I'm not trying to ruin your fun. I know how much this means to you."

"Morgan, please don't make me tell him no. I'll look like such a dork. It'll be one more rumor that'll go around about me."

Morgan inclined her head as if Sadie had made her point. "If he's the kind of guy who would start a rumor about you, then why do you say he's so decent? Sadie, you've got to quit worrying what people think of you. You've gotten this far in life without it."

"I've *always* cared what they think," she said. "I just didn't have any control over it before. When I was living in Atlanta with my mom and her boyfriends, I pretty much just rolled with the punches. People thought I was trash at school. And I knew I couldn't ever be anything better, so it didn't really matter." She watched as Seth bit into a cookie. "But now I'm different, Morgan. I'm with you, and things are better . . . and I feel like I could really be somebody if I just had a chance."

Morgan gazed into her eyes. "You are somebody, Sadie. You're somebody very special. That's why I feel so protective. That's why I don't want you dating Trevor Beal. There'll be other guys, Christian ones."

"And where will I meet them?" she asked. "Our church doesn't exactly have a youth group, since Seth and I are practically the only ones under twenty-five."

"Well, then we need to work on getting you some fellowship with other Christians your age. Maybe you could join a Christian club at school or start going to Bible study at one of the local churches that does have a youth group."

Sadie sighed. She wasn't getting through to her. Even the Christian kids at school shunned her. She had little hope of friendship with any of them. She pictured the Christian guys having conversations just like this with their parents, only about her. *I don't want you dating that girl. Haven't you heard about her mother?*

The doorbell rang, and welcoming the chance to end this dead-end conversation, she got up. "I'll get it."

As she went to the front door, she heard Morgan talking baby-talk to Seth, and his laughter filling the room. She opened the door.

A black woman who looked at least ten months pregnant stood there with a suitcase in her hand. "Hi," the woman said. "I'm looking for the Clearys—Morgan or Jonathan. Is this the right place?"

"Sure," Sadie said in a flat voice. "Come in. I'll get Morgan."

The woman waddled in and set her suitcase down. Sadie went back to the kitchen. "Somebody here for you. I'll clean Seth up."

Still sulking, she got a napkin and wet it and began to wipe the baby's face as Morgan rushed to meet her visitor.

Morgan noticed the suitcase first. "Hello, I'm Morgan," she said.

The woman stuck out her hand. "I'm Karen Miller. I knew your mama and daddy. I was in the jail when they used to come. I got out just a few weeks before they died. When I heard what happened to them, I cried my eyes out."

Morgan gave her a weak smile. "Thank you." She glanced at the suitcase again.

"You're as pretty as your mama said, Morgan. Your mama talked all the time about you and your sister."

Morgan didn't want to talk about her mother. "What brings you here, Karen?"

"Your mama and daddy wanted me to come live here after I got out of jail." She looked around at the room she stood in. "It's just like they described—antique tables, Victorian sofa, plants and baubles every which way you look. I should have come then, but I didn't. I went back to the old neighborhood and my boyfriend. I thought I could make it on my own, but it was hard, going back to all the same temptations. Crack dealers on every corner . . ." Her voice faded off. It was the kind of thing Morgan warned the prisoners about in her own jail ministry. Without a sound strategy, it was difficult for any of them to make it.

"I just kept remembering how your mama tried to convince me to come here. And then I found out the house was still running. I know I haven't filled out the application, and you don't know me from Adam, but I thought you might take me in, anyway. For the sake of my baby."

Morgan regarded the girl's swollen belly. She looked ready to give birth right now. She took the woman's hand. "Come sit down, Karen." She led her to the couch in the parlor. As the young woman got settled, Morgan checked her watch. Jonathan would be home soon. Maybe he could help her with this. They had agreed not to take in anyone who hadn't been through a stringent application process—those who proved they wanted to change their lives, who could commit to hours a day of Bible study, who were willing to get jobs and work and help with the chores. They wanted to do extensive interviews with them to make sure they were sincere in their desire to change, to screen out those who were violent or dishonest, or those who might pose a danger to Seth or Sadie or anyone else in the house.

But when they showed up at the door like this, with no place else to go, clearly in a bind . . .

"Karen, when is your baby due?"

"Any day now. And I couldn't let it be born at home." Tears sprang to Karen's eyes. "My baby's daddy is a dealer, and he gets mean. . . . It's no place for a baby . . . and it's no place for me. Your mama told us in jail, she said we had to have a plan for when we got out. That we couldn't make it on our own. I came up with my plan too late, but I don't know where else to go. I want to change, Morgan. I want to live a life like you have, one that's clean and good and Christian. God put it in my mind to come here. I know he did. I don't have money or a job or any plan past ringing your bell, but I didn't think you'd turn me away. I have Medicaid, so you don't have to worry about hospital bills, and I'll get a job as soon as I can after the baby comes."

Morgan's heart burst with compassion. Her mother wouldn't have turned her away, she knew, and neither would her father. Jonathan was a little more pragmatic, but even he would have been persuaded by the urgency of Karen's situation.

"I'm a Christian, Morgan. I found Christ in jail. I backslid real bad when I got out." She patted her stomach. "I shouldn't have, but I can't undo it now."

Morgan sighed. "I have to talk to my husband, Karen. If you can't stay here, we'll find another place for you."

There were homes for unwed mothers with no place to go, ministries that took in people like Karen. They would be better for her in the long run, with their parenting classes and their counseling, their day care, and their help finding jobs.

"I promise I won't send you back out into the streets," Morgan said.

The woman looked around. "I don't think there could be a better place than right here. It looks like a dream."

Morgan got up and grabbed the suitcase. "Come with me, and I'll show you a room where you can relax until Jonathan gets home."

The woman beamed through her tears as Morgan led her up the stairs.

CHAPTER

19

Voices yelled above and around him, and Cade squinted his eyes open. Paramedics ran his gurney down a hospital corridor, and Blair hurried beside him, sweating and panting with her blonde hair flapping into her face.

"Hang in there, Cade! We're going to help you."

He felt a jolt as they pushed him through double doors.

Then all at once he saw blue sky and an egret flying and felt the cool breeze in his hair, and he opened his eyes and was flying across the heavens, soaring and sailing through the blue, following his egret until it took a nose-dive and started down ... down ...

He woke with a shock.

There was no egret and no blue sky, no gurney and no hospital, no paramedics and no Blair.

Just Cade lying on the cold concrete floor, sticky in his own blood.

He'd been shot through the left calf, shattering bone and slicing out muscle, and the pain strangled him, nooselike, closing his throat and tearing a moan from deep within him. He forced himself to sit up, and winced at the pain spearing through his right ribs. He'd been shot there too.

Sweating with the pain, he tore his shirt open and stared down at the wound. The bullet had missed his rib, though it had blasted the flesh in its deadly path. It had not missed the bone in his leg, however. The bullet had gone right through him, shattering a hole in his tibia before exiting out the back.

He'd been going up the stairs . . . a gun in Ann Clark's ribs. So who had been at the top of the stairs? Who had shot him? And why hadn't they killed him?

He reached down to his bloody leg and ripped the fabric of his pants, so he could better see his wound. Carefully, he peeled it away from his blood-caked skin.

The sight of it made him dizzy, so he stopped a moment and looked up toward the vent that hummed and blew cold air into the room. He needed to get up. He needed to stop the slow bleed, and figure out a plan of escape.

He tried to rise up, but there was no way he could put weight on his leg.

With his good arm and leg, he managed to pull himself up. His head throbbed, and as he rose up to the mattress a wave of dizziness washed over him again. He grabbed the blanket and ripped off a strip, then used it as a bandage on his leg.

He didn't know what to do for his side.

Lying back, he tried to catch his breath. The only relief was the cool air blowing through that vent on the ceiling just above him.

But he couldn't lie here, wallowing in his weakness. He had to get away.

He knew the life was running out of him, and he didn't have much time left.

Sadie hadn't had the nerve yet to tell Trevor Beal that she couldn't go out with him. She'd tried talking Morgan into it, and when Jonathan came home, she had enlisted his help. But he was too preoccupied with Karen's appearance and Cade's *dis*appearance. Irritably, he'd told her no. She was not to go out with "that boy."

She had to tell him soon, but she hadn't seen him yet today, and she dreaded what he would think of her. How dare she judge him for his parents' reputation? *Do not judge, or you too will be judged.* She pushed through the crowd to her locker, rolled in her combination.

A locker two down from her slammed, making her jump, and she turned to see Crystal glaring at her.

"Is it true that you're going out with Trevor Beal?" the girl snapped at her.

Sadie looked from Crystal to the two friends who waited behind her, spearing her with hateful looks. She wasn't going to discuss this with them. Slamming her own locker, she turned and started away.

"I'm talking to you!" Crystal shouted. "I asked you a question."

Heads were turning, so she stopped and looked back. "Who I go out with is none of your business." She kept her voice low to keep from calling more attention to herself.

"The only reason he's interested in you is that he thinks you're easy. A tramp like you, living at Hanover House, of all places. He knows he can get you to do whatever he wants."

Sadie hadn't expected for Crystal to have a more hurtful comment than "tramp daughter of a jailbird" in her arsenal. *Don't react. Just turn and walk away.* Blinking back the tears threatening her, she turned and started up the hall.

"That's the only reason he'd go out with you," Crystal shouted. Others turned their heads, looking to see who she was referring to. Sadie lifted her chin in the air and held her lips tight.

She hurried into her biology class, tears in her eyes, but she would not cry in front of anyone who would tell that girl and her friends. She bit her lip and pulled out her biology book, opened it to the page they had studied for homework, got out her pen, and held it poised.

Crystal and her friends filed in like Nazis in a prison camp. The teacher sat at the front of the room, a sentinel who kept them quiet. But she couldn't stop the looks the girls shot her—hate-filled, venomous looks.

She kept her head down and her eyes on her book, and when the class finally ended, she dashed out of the room. Trevor Beal was waiting for her.

"So how's it going?" he asked, those blue eyes twinkling, oblivious.

She looked up at him. He *couldn't* be part of a criminal family. He looked so normal.

She shrugged and looked back over her shoulder. Crystal and Company were down the hall, watching with those piercing eyes, their faces twisted with contempt. "I'm okay, I guess."

"So have you thought about what movie you want to see Friday night?"

She drew in a deep breath and decided to get this over with. "Morgan and Jonathan told me I couldn't go."

His face changed, and his cheeks suddenly mottled red. "What do you mean they told you you couldn't? Why?"

"They just didn't approve. It's a long story." She hurried to her locker, knowing the girls were following behind. Pulling her backpack off, she started digging through it.

Trevor took it out of her hand. "Sadie, you're not going to do what they say, are you?"

"I'm sorry. I wanted to go, but I just can't."

He flung the backpack against the locker, startling her.

"It's because of my family, isn't it?" he said.

She looked away.

"Come on, Sadie. Those people you live with are so holier-than-thou that there's probably not a guy in this school they'd let you go out with. They think they're better than everybody. They're the moral police, that's what they are. And you're their prisoner."

"No, I'm not!" She picked her backpack up. "They care about me."

"Then they should let you go. Come on, I'm a nice guy. You shouldn't judge me on the basis of my family any more than I judge you on the basis of yours."

It was as if he had read her mind.

"Come on," he said, leaning toward her. "I want to take you out. I'm not going to drag you to some family dinner or any other place that you don't want to go. I just want to spend time with you. I want to get to know you. Is that wrong?"

She thought of what Crystal had said about his reasons for asking her out. "Are you sure that's all?" she asked. "Because there's talk that you had ulterior motives. So if you think that I'm easy or that—"

"Who told you *that?*" His words slashed across hers.

"It doesn't matter," she said. "It's just a rumor going around, that the only reason you asked me out is that you think I'm easy."

His hand hit the locker again. "Whoever said that is a stinking liar." He leaned down until his face was inches from hers, his blue eyes searching her face. "I don't want anything from you. Come on, Sadie. Give me a chance. I didn't think you'd let somebody's background or their family ruin your opinion of them. I thought you were different."

Sadie thought of Morgan and Jonathan. There had been no gray area in what they'd said to her. She was simply to obey. And why wouldn't she? They'd been nothing but good to her, and all their advice so far had been wise. They cared about her and Seth, worried about her well-being . . .

But they didn't understand.

She looked into Trevor Beal's blue eyes. His interest made her feel better about herself. She needed that, she thought. If Morgan and Jonathan understood how much, they wouldn't deprive her of this.

"Come on," he whispered. "I won't pick you up at Hanover House if that's a problem. We can meet somewhere and then go off quietly. Nobody has to know. You can tell everybody you broke the date with me, and then Morgan and Jonathan will never have to know. Who could it possibly hurt?"

Sadie closed her eyes and tried to think. "I don't have a car," she said. "I can't meet you anywhere."

"You can walk, can't you? You have feet." He wasn't going to give up easily. That fact sent a warm thrill rushing through her. "What about their boathouse? You could walk down to the boathouse, and I'll pick you up there. Nobody will ever have to know. We'll go to Savannah, eat, see a movie, come home. I'll drop you off a little distance from the house and you can go home."

"Where will I tell them I've been? They'll have to know I'm gone."

He considered that for a moment. "Tell them you're going to the Methodist dance. There really is one Friday night, no kidding. Tell them some girls invited you to come. They'll like that, won't they? They'll buy it."

She grinned. "You've done this before."

He shrugged. "Sue me for being creative."

She laughed then as the bell started to ring. Quickly she grabbed her book out of the locker and shoved it into her backpack. "I've got to go."

He blocked her way. "Not until you say yes."

She grinned up at him. "All right, yes."

"Great," he said. "So Friday night, the boathouse at six. We'll have a blast together. You'll see."

A chill shivered over her, but the thrill that rivaled it made the reservations flee from her mind. It wasn't her fault Morgan and Jonathan were being narrow-minded. She wasn't hurting anyone, after all. Pushing her doubts to the back of her mind, she hurried to her next class, knowing that nothing Crystal or her friends said to her could hurt her now.

CHAPTER

*B*lair's preoccupation with Cade's disappearance worried Morgan almost as much as Cade did. She had been camped in front of her computer for hours at a time, forgetting to open the library or closing it at odd hours of the day as she took off on a hunch that led nowhere. She hadn't been eating or sleeping, and her face was pale and distracted, her eyes full of things that only she could see. The scar on her face burned more brightly than usual.

"I want you to come to Hanover House for dinner tonight," Morgan had insisted when Blair finally answered her phone. "You need to be around people and get your mind off things."

"I don't want my mind off *things,*" Blair said. "Other people's minds are off *things,* and that's why no one's found Cade."

"Just come," Morgan said. "You have to eat, and maybe we can put our heads together and come up with something."

She had reluctantly agreed to come, but the moment she'd arrived, Morgan knew Blair would rather be any place but here. The house was crowded with the tenants who had just gotten home from work, the television in the den blared, and Seth cried intermittently as Morgan tried to prepare dinner.

Blair seethed past the den, where Karen, the pregnant woman Jonathan had reluctantly allowed to stay, sat watching a rerun of *Step by Step* at a volume so loud you could have heard it from the second floor.

"Blair," Morgan yelled over the volume, "I'd like for you to meet Karen. Karen, this is my sister . . ."

"Nice to meet you," Blair yelled, and turned with disgust to go into the kitchen. Morgan followed her in as Karen mumbled that it was nice to meet her too.

"Karen just showed up yesterday," Morgan said in a low voice when they were out of her earshot. "Mama and Pop led her to Christ when she was in jail. She isn't married, and she finally realized that she couldn't have her baby in the environment she was living in, so—"

"So she came here to get a free ride and leach off you for a while?"

Morgan glanced around, hoping no one had heard. Sadie sat at the table feeding Seth. She looked up and then hastily looked away. Morgan hoped she hadn't taken the comment wrong.

Out on the sunporch sat Mrs. Hern, rocking blankly. She was having a bad day, and her boss, Mr. Jenkins, had sent her home early from her job at Goodfellow's Grocery. The woman's Alzheimer's wasn't severe enough for a nursing home, but she couldn't live on her own or support herself. The donations that came to the home helped to subsidize her. Thankfully, she hadn't heard Blair's comment, and if she had, she'd have forgotten it so quickly that it would hardly have mattered.

Felicia, the fifty-year-old former bank robber, who was strong as an ox and worked for the town's sanitation department, was out in the backyard pulling weeds. It was one of the household chores on her list this week.

"Blair, keep your voice down, please," Morgan said. "I don't want the tenants to hear you say that kind of thing."

"I'm serious, Morgan. I thought you only took Christians who were committed to studying their Bible and stuff."

Morgan smirked at Blair. "Yes, that's true, although I can't imagine what difference it makes to you."

"I'm just saying that she wouldn't be walking around nine months pregnant and unmarried, if she'd really become a Christian in jail."

Morgan sighed. "She says she backslid. But who am I to judge where she is in her faith?"

"Who are you to judge?" Blair asked. "Are you kidding me? For safety's sake, you *have* to judge. Mama and Pop always judged. They wouldn't let anyone in here unless they were sure they were committed. The whole purpose of having this place is to help them get on their feet and get a good foundation in their faith."

Morgan stared at her sister and wondered if this defense of their work was the beginning of a softening in Blair's heart toward Christianity. It wasn't like her to talk about faith.

"I mean, I don't care whether she's a Christian or not," Blair went on, "since all that seems like nothing more than illusion anyway, but the fact is that it does sometimes change people's behavior. And the ones who come here and commit to changing usually do. I'm just saying that there may not be a commitment to changing her behavior if she's walking around pregnant and unmarried."

"I understand and agree with you, Blair. But the woman is in desperate need. She's going to have that baby any day. I'm trying to get her into one of the unwed mother homes, but until I do, she has to stay here."

Blair still didn't like it, and that fact shone clearly on her face. "Morgan, what are you going to do when she has that baby?"

"Bring it home, I guess," Morgan said.

"How in the world are you going to take care of two babies at once?"

"I won't be taking care of two babies, Blair. She'll be taking care of hers."

"And what if she doesn't? What if she just dumps him on you?"

"She won't." Putting an unmistakable period on the end of that sentence, Morgan went to the oven and pulled out the roast. Its scent wafted over the room.

"Smells good," Sadie said. "Doesn't it smell good, Seth?"

Blair finally noticed the girl at the table. "Oh, hi, Sadie."

"Hi, Blair."

Blair touched Seth's head and bent over to kiss his forehead.

"Any news about Cade?" Sadie asked, as if trying to help change the subject.

"No." Blair turned back to Morgan. "Look at you. You're working yourself to death with all these people to feed. It's a bed-and-breakfast, for heaven's sake. You're not obligated to cook supper for an army every night."

"I like cooking supper for them," Morgan said. "They've worked hard all day. Besides, it makes us feel more like a family."

"But you're not a family," Blair said. "Except for Sadie and Seth, these people are strangers living in your house."

Morgan drew in a deep breath and stirred the pot of beans on the stove. "Come on, Blair. Give it a rest, will you? Mama and Pop did this for years and it never bothered you."

"That's because it's who they were. But you don't have to be Mama's clone just because you feel the need to continue her work."

"I'm not continuing her work. I'm continuing *Christ's* work. End of story. Now will you please put ice in the glasses?"

Blair sighed and went to the cabinet. "Let's see. I don't think you have twenty-five glasses."

Morgan groaned. "There aren't twenty-five people, Blair. There's you, Jonathan, Sadie, Karen, Felicia, Mrs. Hern, Gus, and me. Seth has his cup. So that's eight."

"Eight," Blair said, pulling the glasses out. "That's almost a baseball team. An army. My twenty-eight-year-old sister is mother to an army."

"I'm not their mother," Morgan said. "What is wrong with you?"

Blair shook her head and jerked the ice drawer out of the freezer. "Nothing. I shouldn't have come. I don't feel like a party."

"It's not going to be a party," Morgan said. "After we eat, we can talk."

"Yeah, after we've spent a couple of hours doing KP."

Sadie wiped Seth's face and got up from the table. "I'll clean up after supper, Morgan."

Her voice was soft, hurt, and Morgan shot Blair a scathing look. Then she moved to kiss Sadie's cheek. "Thank you, sweetie. We'll all help. Don't mind her. She's just worried about Cade."

Blair didn't seem to appreciate the comment and began firing the ice cubes into the glasses. The front storm door slammed, and Morgan glanced through the living room and saw Jonathan coming in, flanked by Gus. They both looked filthy from the day's work.

Morgan crossed the house and kissed Jonathan. It didn't matter how dirty he looked or the way he smelled after a hot day of salt-water fishing with a boatload of tourists, the sight of him always made her heart jolt. "Go on up and shower. Supper's almost ready. Blair's here."

"Any news about Cade?"

"None yet." She looked up at the Jamaican man standing behind her husband. "Hey, Gus. How was your day?"

"Okay, Miss Morgan. Hot like hades."

Morgan noticed that Karen had suddenly turned the volume down on the television, and the *Step by Step* theme was now a distant melody rather than an amplified, heart-shaking aggravation.

Karen smiled up at Gus. He nodded at her. "You okay, Miss Karen?"

"I'm fine. How are you, Gus?"

"Dirty," he said. "I'll go take a shower now."

He bolted up the stairs, and Karen watched him go.

Morgan got an uneasy feeling.

From Jonathan's expression, she knew he was troubled too.

Jonathan pulled her through the kitchen, greeted Blair and Sadie, and kissed Seth on the top of his head. "Morgan, I need to talk to you in the office," he said in a low voice.

She followed him into the small room, and he dropped into the chair that used to be her father's.

"Did you see that look Karen gave Gus?"

"Yeah, I thought I saw something there."

"If Karen is interested in Gus," he said, "then it isn't good to have her staying in the house with him. Your parents were always very strict about dating among the tenants."

"I know," she said. Several times they had decided to make it an all male or all female house, but inevitably someone of the opposite sex came along who was desperate for help, and they hadn't had the heart to turn him away.

The few times that there had been attraction between male and female tenants, her father had found another home for one of them immediately.

"So if there's an attraction, we'll make one of them leave. But which one?"

Jonathan began taking off his shoes. "Gus has been here for almost a year. I don't think we should run him out."

"But Karen's in such need, and that poor baby . . ."

"Well, I doubt Gus would return the interest with her nine months' pregnant. But after the baby, it could be a real problem." He got up, hooking his dirty shoes with two fingers.

"I know," she said. "But I had really hoped we could keep her until after the baby comes."

He smiled down at her. "Tell the truth. You just really want a newborn baby in the house, don't you?"

"No, that's not it at all. Seth has filled my yearning for a baby."

"But a newborn." He pressed a kiss on her lips. "I know you, Morgan."

Something clanked in the kitchen. Morgan glanced out. Blair was almost slamming the glasses onto the table, and Sadie was putting the dishes out. "I have to finish supper," she said. "We'll talk about this later."

Jonathan grabbed her hand. She looked up at him. "Honey, we'll have a baby of our own. I know we will. It's just a matter of time."

How much more time? Morgan wanted to ask. They'd been trying for over a year. "I know," she said, though she didn't know at all. "Go upstairs and get cleaned up now. Supper's almost ready."

Jonathan crossed the kitchen in his sock feet and went upstairs to shower. Morgan went back into the kitchen and found that the table was set.

Sadie had managed to get Blair's mind off Karen and Cade and was chattering about Trevor Beal.

". . . Morgan and Jonathan said no. I understand why and everything. I was just so amazed that he asked."

Morgan tuned in to the conversation as she took the roast beef out of the oven. "You hear that, Blair?" she asked. "She was flattered. Like he's the only guy who wants to ask her out."

"Morgan's right, much as I hate to admit it," Blair said. "You're the kind of girl whose pictures men hang on their gym lockers."

Morgan shot her a look. "Blair!"

"I don't want them hanging my picture up," Sadie said. "I just want one to like me. And one does."

Morgan looked back over her shoulder. "Honey, I know you're disappointed. What did he say when you told him you couldn't go?"

Sadie turned back to Seth and wiped his face again, even though it didn't need it. "He tried to talk me into going anyway."

Morgan sighed. "I'm so sorry, Sadie. But another guy will come along soon. You'll see."

Sadie fell into silence as she folded the napkins and set them beside each plate.

After the prayer to bless the meal, it seemed as if the group gathered around the big round table erupted into football-stadium chatter with everyone talking at once—everyone, that is, except Blair, who brooded as she picked at her food.

Karen sat on one side of her, and Gus on the other, and they talked over her as if she wasn't there.

"When is the baby supposed to come?" the Jamaican asked Karen.

Blair leaned back so they could see across her. "I'm due Thursday," Karen said.

"You don't look that big."

"Well, thank you, Gus. I feel like the Goodyear blimp."

Blair tried to tune out their conversation and fixed on the one across the table between Morgan and Mrs. Hern.

"Mama called me today and told me she'd painted her house," the old woman said.

Blair knew her mother was dead, but she often relived past days. The house-painting story was one of her favorites. She'd probably repeat it five times before Blair left here tonight.

She glanced at Felicia, the big woman who practically inhaled her food. She ate like a linebacker. Blair hoped the donations this month were enough to cover her meals.

Seth chomped string beans and mashed potatoes and made an occasional squeal, but Sadie ate quietly, as if lost in her own little world.

The whole situation gave Blair a searing anger. Cade was suffering somewhere, maybe even dead, and life was going on just as it had before he left. She resented it and fought the urge to scream out that they needed to *do* something, that a friend could be dying, and no one cared.

"I was in there for three years, worked out on the road crew," Karen was saying to Gus. "Ate slop most days. Spent all the money I earned on commissary. Snickers and Milky Ways, potato chips and such. Gained about fifty pounds in there. I lost thirty of it when I got out, but then I had to go and get pregnant and gain it all back."

"You look fine to me," Gus said, and Blair shot him a look of pure disgust.

"Would you like to trade places with me?" she asked him loudly.

Silence fell over the table, and Morgan and Jonathan looked up at her.

"Uh, no, Miss Blair. I'm fine right here."

Karen seized the opportunity, though. "I'll trade."

Morgan stiffened. "No, everybody stay where they are, please."

Blair rolled her eyes and wondered when and if the conversation was going to come around to Cade.

"You'll never guess who came to see me at the dock this morning," Jonathan said, taking advantage of the lull in the conversation.

"Who?" Morgan asked.

"Morris Ambrose, Jerry Ann Shepp, Matt Pearl, and Gerald Madison."

Blair looked up. That was the same group who had urged her to run for mayor. "Don't tell me. They want you to run for mayor."

He smiled. "That's right."

Morgan put her hands over her mouth and started to laugh. "Really?"

Blair's eyes glowed. "Are you going to?"

He shrugged. "I don't know. It's kind of crazy, don't you think?"

Morgan grabbed his arm. "I don't think it's crazy at all. We need someone with integrity in that seat. Why *not* you?"

"Well, Sam Sullivan and Ben Jackson are both running, for one thing. I'm not the politician type. And it would cost money. Signs and whatnot. I'm just a fisherman."

"You are not *just* a fisherman," Morgan said. "You're a businessman. You own your fishing tour business *and* Hanover House. You're a part-time preacher too. You're more qualified than Sullivan or Jackson, and you're sure more honest than our former mayor."

He shrugged and cut a piece of roast. "I'll think about it," he said. "I'm not sure yet."

Blair set her fork down. "I think you should do it. Too bad we don't have a newspaper on the island anymore. You could get some free publicity through that."

Sadie laughed suddenly, and everyone looked at her. "If Jonathan was mayor, he would be Blair's boss, wouldn't he?"

Blair gave a half-grin. "Something like that."

"And Cade's boss too," Sadie added.

Blair's grin crashed, and Jonathan's faded. They all looked down at their food.

"Mama called me today to tell me she'd painted her house." Mrs. Hern's sweet voice rose out of the silence. "Lemon yellow. She said the shutters are white. I'm going to see it this weekend, I reckon."

Blair closed her eyes and fought the urge to scream at Mrs. Hern that her mother was dead, and there wasn't a house, lemon yellow or any other color.

But suddenly Karen yelped out and grabbed Blair's arm. "Whoa. This is some contraction!"

Morgan froze. "Is there anything I can do?"

Karen stared down at her food, her hand over her stomach, concentrating on the birth pang.

Blair stiffened. This was all they needed. Cade in trouble, and everyone's attention focused on this woman and her labor. And Karen clutching her like she had something to do with it.

Karen came out of the contraction and let go of Blair's arm. "Man, I didn't expect that. I thought it would come easier at first. My back's been hurting today, but I didn't think anything of it."

Morgan looked flustered. "Do you think it's labor?"

"I don't know," Karen said. "Guess we'll see."

Blair had had enough of the drama of this household. She scraped back her chair and got up. "I have to go." She took her plate to the sink, rinsed it out, then clattered it into the dishwasher. "Thanks for dinner."

Morgan looked distraught. "Don't go, Blair. We were going to talk afterward."

"You won't have time to talk," Blair said. "Let me know if it's a boy or a girl."

With that, she hurried out of the house and back to her car on the gravel driveway, wondering why the woman's contraction had revived the rage in her heart. It was because of Cade, she thought. He was somewhere in trouble, waiting for rescue, certain that of all the friends he had on Cape Refuge, someone would be able to help him.

But no one was giving it much thought because of crazy old ladies and pregnant ex-cons and the mayor's race and Sadie's love life . . .

She should be ashamed of herself for letting those things make her so angry, she thought. Where was her compassion? Her sense of decorum? Her mother would have given her a good tongue-lashing for having so little feeling for the people her sister loved.

But her mother wasn't here, and neither was Cade. So really, there was no one to be her best for. No one who cared whether she was a good, loving person or a bitter spinster. Morgan didn't have time to care.

Her heart swelled with missing Cade, and she remembered not so long ago how they'd sat in the church warehouse after her parents died, and she'd opened her heart to him about what the burn scars had done to her life. . . .

He had touched her scars with gentle fingertips and told her that she was the best looking woman on the island of Cape Refuge, and he didn't even see those scars anymore.

She had fallen apart at that and run out like a scared kid. But she'd never forgotten it.

Where are you, Cade?

The question ached through her heart as she made her way home.

CHAPTER

*J*oe McCormick had never applied for the job of police chief, and he didn't much want it. At twenty-eight, he was just settling into the job of detective. But since cops didn't seem to stay long in Cape Refuge before moving to Savannah to work for a larger force, he was the one with the most seniority and the greatest amount of training.

Even so, he'd never expected to have to step into Cade's shoes at a moment's notice.

He creaked back in Cade's chair and ran his hand over his bald head. It needed shaving, but he hadn't had a minute to put a razor to his face—or his head. The smooth top of his head, where he was naturally bald, contrasted against the dark stubble of the rest of his hair, making him look much older than his age.

Today he felt even older than that.

He clutched the phone to his ear, mentally rehearsing what he wished he could say to the person who'd put him on hold. You wouldn't think it would take an act of

Congress for an investigating officer to get forensics information. The medical examiner who'd examined Clark's body had sent the gunshot residue analysis to the crime lab on Sunday, and he still hadn't gotten the results. Until they knew if Clark had fired the gun on himself, it was difficult to proceed.

Finally, the music that Joe was sure had been designed to drive people insane stopped, and someone answered the phone. "Craig Haughton."

Joe sat up and leaned on the desk. "Yes, Craig, this is Joe McCormick of the Cape Refuge Police Department. I've been waiting almost a week for the results of the GSR test on William Clark. I need that information ASAP."

The man hesitated a moment, as if fumbling through his files. "Yeah, uh . . . I have his file here, but I'm gonna have to call you back."

"No, you don't." Joe had had enough. "I'm trying to conduct a police investigation here, and I need to know if the man's shooting was a suicide attempt or a homicide attempt! You people are supposed to be the forensics geniuses. Just tell me if the man had gunpowder stains on his fingers!"

Silence again, then finally, a loud sigh. "All right, Detective, just a minute." More fumbling. "Okay, the man did not have gunshot residue. Of course, this isn't conclusive. The rain or blood could have washed it off."

Joe leaned back hard in his chair. "All right, fax me that report, will you?"

The man agreed, and Joe hung up. Carefully, he read back over his notes and studied the photographs taken at Clark's car. The fact that Clark had no gunshot residue on his hands only corroborated the conclusions he'd already drawn. The gun had been fired from at least two feet away. From the position of the bloodstains, it appeared that Clark was resisting the shot, backing away, possibly opening the door.

His shirt had a trace of mud stains that hadn't been completely washed away by the rain, as if he'd fallen out on his back.

Those things, coupled with the angle of the bullet hole and, now, the lack of gunpowder residue on the dead man's fingers made Joe suspect that someone in the passenger seat had shot him, then left him for dead. But Clark had lived, and he had gotten up and stumbled through the woods to the busy street beyond them.

So it was a homicide. Someone had been with William Clark when he pulled his car into the woods. Someone had shot him, then vanished.

But who?

His wife?

The gun had been registered to William Clark. So someone had shot him with his own gun, and other than his and his wife's, there were no new prints on either the gun or the car.

Ann Clark was looking guiltier all the time.

And how did Cade fit into this? If the woman had tried to kill him, then the fact that Cade ran into him would not provoke an act of revenge.

But the man had spoken to Cade. He distinctly remembered Cade saying that in the press statement he'd made. He went to the door and called across the squad room, "Somebody get me the video of Cade's press conference the other night."

In a moment, J.J. Clyde loped in with the video. "Want me to pop it in?"

Joe nodded and stared down at his notes. J.J. put the video in and turned the set on.

Joe watched and listened through the statement. Nothing about the man speaking. Then someone asked a question.

"Chief Cade, did the impact kill him instantly?"

Cade shook his head. "No, it didn't. He was alive and speaking right after he was hit, and did make it to Candler Hospital in Savannah alive. He died shortly thereafter."

There it was. Joe stared at the television, running the facts through his mind. So the woman, who had heard the report that night, thought that her husband had spoken to Cade. Could she have wanted to get him out of the way before he identified the killer?

But that was crazy. He was a cop. Of course he would have identified the killer the moment the man told him. For Ann Clark to wait for the next morning, then do him some kind of harm, wouldn't even make sense.

"That it, Joe?" J.J. asked him. "Want me to play it again?"

Joe rubbed his mouth. "No, thanks. That's all I needed."

As J.J. headed out, Georgette, the woman who served as office clerk to the small operation, came in. "Here's your mail, Joe. I'm giving you all of Cade's too, in case there's anything important."

He took the stack of mail and started sorting through, as his mind still worked through the evidence.

And then he froze. In the return address corner on one of the envelopes, he saw the name "Matthew Cade," typed with no address.

He dropped it on his desk, pulled some tweezers out of Cade's drawer, and pulled the letter from its envelope. He grabbed a plastic evidence bag from another drawer and slipped it inside. It might have fingerprints, or some other evidence he could use. Slowly, he began to read through the plastic.

CHAPTER

*T*he phone was ringing when Blair got home from Hanover House, and she dove for it. "Hello?"

"Blair, Joe McCormick here."

Blair froze. His voice sounded grim, clipped.

"Do you have something on Cade?"

He was silent for a moment. "Can you come down to the station for a minute? I have something I need to show you. I just got off the phone with Jonathan. I want him to see too."

Blair didn't want to know, yet she forced herself to ask, "What is it, Joe?"

"Just come in, Blair. You're not going to believe this if you don't see it."

For a moment after she hung up, Blair just stared at a spot on her wall. If Cade was dead, would Joe have told her over the phone?

She tried not to panic, but forced herself to move and made it to the station in record time. Jonathan was just pulling in too. She jumped out of the car and crossed to her brother-in-law, who stalked across the parking lot with a grim look on his face. "Jonathan, what's going on? Have they found Cade?"

"He wouldn't say. But I have a bad feeling."

They burst into the station together and found Joe in Cade's office. He sat in Cade's executive chair, slouched back with his legs crossed, his shoulders hunched as he leaned on the armrests.

He looked up at them with weary eyes.

"What is it, Joe?" Blair demanded.

He pointed to a clear bag with a handwritten letter on his desk and turned it around so they could read it. "A letter from Cade. Don't touch it. It might have evidence."

"A letter from Cade?" Jonathan leaned over it, and Blair began to read.

> *Joe,*
>
> *Just wanted to touch base with you guys and let you know that I haven't dropped off the face of the earth. I was just a little depressed after the accident, so I decided to take some time off. The truth is, I'd been seeing a girl from Savannah, and we decided to get married.*
>
> *I know it sounds crazy, and I'm going to have a lot of explaining to do when I get back, but I've never been happier. Let everyone know that for me, will you?*
>
> *I'll call as soon as I know when I'm coming back. Meanwhile, I know Cape Refuge is in your good hands.*
>
> *Matt Cade*

Rage rose like lava inside her, and Blair backed away. "No way," she said. "There's no way. Cade did not write that."

Jonathan stared at the words. "It looks like his handwriting, Blair."

"It's not, though." She looked up at Jonathan as if he'd just betrayed his best friend. "Jonathan, you know Cade better than anybody. Would he just run off with some mystery girlfriend and get married? Is that even possible?"

He sighed. "I wouldn't think so. But at least it would mean he's alive."

She slammed both hands down on the desk. "Then why wouldn't he call?" she yelled. "Why would he write a stupid note like some kind of wimp? He killed a man just a few days ago. He wouldn't just run off and get married! Jonathan, why would he hide a girlfriend from you ... from us? It's not true, that's why!"

"I'm gonna have a handwriting expert analyze the letter, Blair," Joe said. "But I think it's his. I've seen Cade's handwriting a good bit. He has a funny way of making his *d*s. This is it. And his fingerprints are on it."

She couldn't catch her breath, so she sat down and studied the letter again. The paper shook in her hands. She read it over, looking for some sign, some clue, in the words. But there was nothing ... until ...

"His signature!" she said. "Since when has Cade gone by 'Matt'? I've never heard him refer to himself as Matt in his life! He goes by Cade, just Cade. Why would he sign 'Matt,' all of a sudden? Matthew, maybe. That's his official signature. But never 'Matt.'"

Jonathan looked over her shoulder. "She's right."

"Of course I'm right." She bent over the desk. "If someone was holding him, say Ann Clark, she might not know that he only went by 'Cade.' It would be his way of telling us that things about the letter weren't right or true. That he was being forced to write it."

"Maybe the girlfriend—er, wife—calls him Matt," Joe said. "That happens, you know. My brother went by Billy for twenty-five years, and all of a sudden he meets this girl, and he becomes 'Bill.'"

"It's not the same thing!" Blair said. "There are too many things that don't add up! This is a sign—a clue for us. He's letting us know."

"What, Blair?" Joe asked. "What is he letting us know?"

"I don't know," she said, her eyes beginning to sting. "That the letter isn't true. That he's not really married and irresponsible and reckless. That he's not really a different person than we all knew."

Her voice cracked, and she turned away. Could it be true? Could Cade be a different person, someone she thought she knew, but didn't really?

No, her mind couldn't adjust to the new picture. It couldn't be possible.

Tears pushed to her eyes, and she realized that at least the letter did put their fears to rest, that Cade's corpse didn't lie undiscovered in a swamp somewhere.

She looked up at Joe. He needed a shave, both on his face and his head. She knew he hadn't gotten much rest since this whole thing had started. He sighed. "I guess I wanted to believe that Cade's disappearance wasn't connected to Clark's death. That all I had to figure out was who shot him before he walked out in front of Cade's car."

"Shot him? I thought it was suicide."

"Nope, couldn't have been. No gunpowder stains on Clark's fingers, and the gun was fired from a couple of feet away, in the direction of the passenger seat. There was definitely someone in that car with him. But if you're right and Cade didn't mean anything in this note, then what would the shooter have to do with Cade?"

Blair needed to think. She got up, paced back and forth across the room. She looked back at Jonathan, saw that his eyes were fixed on a spot on the back wall, as if he could reach an answer if he stared hard enough.

"Who knows, Joe?" Blair asked. "But I'll guarantee you the shooter *knows* what happened to Cade. If you were going to skip town and get married, would you go park your truck at Cricket's? No. Even if it was some spontaneous crazy last-minute idea, you'd take a minute to take your truck home and leave some food out for your cat. And he was *seen* with Ann Clark!"

"Yep," Joe said. "She's my number one suspect."

Blair backed up against the door's casing. "So are you going to arrest her?"

Joe stiffened. "Not yet. I have some work to do yet, Blair. It doesn't pay to go arresting people before you have enough evidence. I'm going to start with this letter."

"What about fingerprints in the car?"

"Well, her fingerprints were in the car, all right, but that's to be expected. She was his wife. She would have been in that car all the time."

"What about the gun? Were her fingerprints on it?"

"Yes. But again, she was his wife and they owned it."

She looked at Jonathan, saw the deep lines of worry around his eyes. "That woman knows where Cade is. She knows who shot her husband. And they're not going to do anything."

"We are going to do something, Blair," Joe said. "Just not your way and not in your time. We're going to go by the book and get this right."

"Meanwhile, Cade's life is in jeopardy," Jonathan said quietly.

Joe tipped his head. "You think I don't realize that?"

Blair pointed at the letter. "I need a copy of this."

"No, Blair, you can't have one."

"Joe, please. I just want a copy to take home. I won't give it to anybody. You know you can trust me."

He looked up into her face. "Why do you want it, Blair?"

She sighed and looked down at the page. "I don't know. But sometimes if I have something in front of me, I'll get ideas. I might notice something. I just want it so I can look back at it if something comes to me."

He groaned and took the letter into the squad room to the copier, made her the copy. "I don't know why I'm doing this. But Cade put a lot of stock in your brains, so maybe I ought to, too."

She took the copy out of the machine. "Thank you, Joe."

"Yeah, no problem." He shot Jonathan a look. "I'm not making one for you."

Jonathan just nodded. "I'll look at hers if I need to see it again."

Joe stalked back into Cade's office, and Blair looked around at the other cops sitting at their desks, staring up at her. They were practically kids, most of them. How could they be expected to solve a murder and find their missing chief?

She headed for her car, and Jonathan came out behind her. "You okay, Blair?"

She turned back to him. "Yeah. You?"

"He's alive," Jonathan said. "Don't forget that. He's not dead somewhere. He's alive and well enough to write."

"Yeah, I'll try to hold onto that." She stopped at her car and realized she was going to shatter. Any minute now, she'd fly into a million pieces. "I'm telling you, he's in serious trouble. We have to help him, Jonathan."

"I know," he said. "I agree with you. But Joe is our best bet for finding him. Don't give up on him yet."

But as Blair drove home, she realized she *had* all but given up on Joe and Jonathan and anyone else who was looking for Cade. His life was, quite possibly, on the line. And she was the only one she could trust to find him.

When she got home, Blair crossed the street to the Bull River and stood on the rock wall, looking out at the water. Any moment now, they would get a phone call. There would be a body lying in the woods, and they would discover that Cade was dead, after all, murdered like her parents.

She sat down on the grass and looked up at the dark sky and the angry constellations above her head. Times like these she desperately needed to believe in something. But a belief system wasn't something you concocted just when you were in need. God wouldn't exist just because she forced herself to believe, any more than Cade would be all right just because she wanted him to be.

Believing in God had to do with a system of convictions, deep faith, things that her parents and her sister and Jonathan had, things that had never come easily to Blair.

She was tired, bone-weary, for she hadn't slept well in days, not since Cade had disappeared. She couldn't think, couldn't eat, for thinking of him somewhere helpless and wounded, praying to the God he believed in that some rescue was imminent. But they were failing him, everyone who loved him and cared for him. Everyone who would hear about that stupid letter and believe it . . .

Tears rolled down her face, and she wiped them away, then got up to walk some more. She had been by his house to check on Oswald at least three times a day. Joe had sealed up the place so evidence couldn't be disturbed, so she hadn't been able to go back in. But it was clear he hadn't been home. His truck still sat at Cricket's as if waiting for its owner to return. Somewhere there had to be a clue, a puzzle piece, that would lead them to wherever he was, but she couldn't help believing that Ann Clark held the mystery to it all.

She walked back to her house, but instead of going in, she got back in the car and pulled out of the gravel driveway. As if her car knew exactly where to go, it headed across the bridge to Tybee Island and up toward Savannah. She navigated her way through the town and back to Washington Square. Her heart pounded with urgent certainty as she stopped directly across the park from Ann Clark's house.

The old Victorian home had an eerie look at night, like a Halloween screen-saver with its haunted windows blinking on and off. Light shone from these windows, stark white in some, a yellow flicker dancing against the curtain in others. The drapes were closed, but Blair watched them for shadows walking by—Ann Clark's or even Cade's.

What if he was there, just on the other side of that wall? What was keeping him from escaping?

Was he bound in some way? Injured? Had she taken him somewhere else?

Or was he honeymooning with his secret bride who called him Matt?

She chased that renegade thought out of her mind. No, Cade was in trouble.

She would find him, no matter what it cost her.

CHAPTER

*M*organ woke during the night and saw that Jonathan wasn't sleeping. He lay on his back with his hands behind his head, staring up at the ceiling.

"Can't sleep?" she asked him softly.

He shook his head. "I just don't know what to do."

Morgan sat up and turned on the lamp. It lit the small room in a yellow glow, illuminating the pictures they'd hung of Seth and Sadie, a painting Mrs. Hern had done, and a tapestry wall hanging over their bed that Morgan had made herself.

Even though her parents had been gone for several months now, she hadn't had the heart to move into their room. It still sat just as they'd left it on the morning of their death.

But nights like tonight, she wished they had a sitting area with a Bible on the table, rather than a twelve-by-twelve room that could barely contain a bed, dresser, and chest of drawers.

Her shadow moved across the wall as she lay back down and snuggled up to her husband. "You can't do anything, Jonathan," she said. "You just have to wait, let the police do their job."

"He's my best friend," he said, as if that heightened his own responsibility. "What would he do if I was missing?"

"That's different. He's a cop. You're not."

"I don't know what I was thinking, considering a campaign for mayor. I'm completely inadequate. That letter was a cry for help, and here I am in bed." He threw back his covers and sat up.

Morgan got up on her knees and began massaging his shoulders. "You can pray for him, Jonathan. That might be all you can do."

"I've been praying all night."

"Then stop thinking you're not doing anything. God knows where Cade is." She kissed his neck, pressed her face beside his. "And I think you should run for mayor. If you weren't a good candidate, they wouldn't have asked you."

A knock on their door startled them both, and Morgan let him go.

"What now?" Jonathan asked. "It's the middle of the night."

"Maybe it's Karen."

Jonathan went barefoot to the door, wearing his T-shirt and a pair of gym shorts. Morgan got up and pulled on her robe.

Karen stood leaning against the casing, her face covered in sweat and her hand over the lower part of her belly. "I know it's after three, but I think I better go to the hospital."

Morgan crossed the room. "How far apart are the contractions?"

"Five minutes. And they're hard, Morgan."

"Well, then, we'll go. Let us throw some clothes on."

They quickly got dressed and told Sadie they were leaving. Then Jonathan carried Karen's suitcase to the car as Morgan helped her get in. In the grips of a contraction, Karen couldn't get the seat belt on. Morgan slipped into the backseat with her and hooked it. "Hurry, Jonathan!"

Morgan held Karen's hand. "Don't tense up, honey. Try to relax. Breathe."

Jonathan pulled away from Hanover House, quiet as Karen went through that contraction. When she came out of it, they all breathed a collective sigh of relief.

"Hold tight, Karen," he said. "We'll be there soon."

It was almost dawn when Karen's labor began to reverse itself. After hours of contractions as close as three minutes apart, their severity began to decrease and slowed to every ten minutes. Exhausted, Karen lay on her side, watching the monitor for the signs of the next contraction.

Morgan sat like a rag doll in the chair next to the bed, staring into space with eyes red from lack of sleep. Her head had begun to throb, and at this pace the road ahead of them looked long.

Jonathan had fallen asleep in a chair across the room, his head back against the wall and his jaw slack.

"Maybe it's a false alarm," Karen said in a voice raspy from groaning. "I'm sorry, Morgan. Really, I am."

"Don't apologize. It isn't your fault." Morgan got up and went to the door, looked out in the hallway for the nurse. "And we're not going home until they can assure me you're not in labor. How long's it been now?"

Karen checked the clock. "Fifteen minutes since the last one. And it was too mild to speak of. It's tapering off. I can't believe it. After all that."

Morgan tried to muster a smile. "Wonder if that says anything about the baby's personality."

"Oh, I know my baby's personality," Karen said. "This baby's a survivor."

The statement came out with such conviction that Jonathan woke. "A survivor?" Morgan asked. "Why do you say that?"

"Because of what we been through." Karen slid off the bed, stood up with her hand on her back.

Morgan's mind was too foggy to follow her. "What have you been through?"

"With my baby's daddy," she said. "See, he had another baby a few weeks ago, with one of his other girls."

Morgan's eyes met Jonathan's. "He has another girlfriend?"

She breathed a bitter laugh. "Not just one. But this one, she was pregnant, and she had her baby three weeks ago. That baby's wishing it'd never been born."

While she spoke, Karen paced the length of the bed, stretching the IV tube with her as she did. "She left her baby with him while she went to work. Went back too early, but she had to make a living, you know? He took this week-old baby with him on his drug deals. Somebody somewhere hurt that baby. When she got it back that night, the little thing had a seizure. She got him to the hospital . . . but it was too late. He had a cracked skull, and his brain was swelling. . . ."

A strange sense of anger and injustice soared up inside Morgan's chest. Here she and Jonathan were, so far unable to conceive a child, yet people that careless and irresponsible could have as many as they wanted. "Karen, that's awful," she managed to say.

Karen's eyes filled with tears. "Poor baby's not but three weeks old. And then Jeffrey, that's my baby's daddy, he came to me all mad and upset, breaking things and kicking furniture over, scaring me to death. And I knew I had to get out of there if this baby was gonna be all right. I had to get out of that place, away from him."

Morgan crossed the room and put her arms around the girl. "I'm glad you came to us," she whispered.

Jonathan stayed where he was, but Morgan saw that he, too, was moved. He leaned forward, elbows on knees, his serious eyes fixed on Karen.

"I haven't always lived like this," Karen said. "I was brought up better than to hang with crack dealers. I was walking the straight and narrow until I got with the wrong man. He got me started on crack myself, and next thing I know, I'm hanging with dealers and walking the streets so I can pay for my habit. I got nobody to blame but myself, but I want you to know that I haven't always been like this."

"And you're clean now, Karen," Morgan whispered. "That's what matters."

"That's right. I been clean since I was arrested. Haven't used once since I got out of jail. But it's been hard, when everybody around me was using, and it was like they wanted me to fail, like they wanted to see me back hooked, so I could be just as miserable and ruined as they are. It was just a matter of time if I stayed there, Morgan. Just a matter of time."

"You're right," Morgan said. "That's what we always warn the inmates we work with. We always tell you that you have to remove yourself from that environment."

Karen looked down at her huge, swollen belly. "I want to be a good mama, Morgan. Like you with Seth. I want to raise my baby to be smart and healthy and never to run around with anybody who'll lead him wrong. I want to raise him to think for himself. I want him to know God, Morgan. I've prayed so many times for that."

Morgan's eyes misted over, and she smiled down at Jonathan. He was smiling back. "I think your prayers are going to be answered, Karen," she said.

Jonathan agreed. "Karen, I know that God sees a willing, obedient heart when he looks at you. I know he sees that you're trying."

Karen hugged Morgan, and the baby kicked. Morgan jumped back. "He kicked me!"

Karen started to laugh, and Morgan pressed her hands over her stomach and waited for more movement. "Come here, Jonathan. You've got to feel this!"

Jonathan had a grin on his face as he came and touched Karen's abdomen. As if on cue, the baby stomped.

Laughter renewed their strength.

When the nurse came in, she smiled with them. "Glad you're all in a good mood, because the doctor told me to send you home."

Karen's smile crashed. "You mean I'll have to go through all this again?"

"I'm sorry," the nurse said. "But you don't want to stay here if it's not real labor." She started to remove the IV.

"Seems like I'm going to be the first woman in history to carry the baby the rest of her life."

The nurse laughed. "They all think that, but it can't be that much longer."

Within the hour, the paperwork had been filled out releasing her. They rode home in sleepy silence, just as the sun began to rise.

Morgan couldn't wait to lie down, but she knew that the tenants would expect breakfast soon. Jonathan had tours booked on his boat, so he wouldn't have the luxury of catching up on his sleep. When Karen had gone up to her room, Jonathan stopped Morgan from going into the kitchen. "Tell you what. I'm going to get a few boxes of donuts. It'll be a treat for everybody, and you won't have to cook."

"Good," she said. "No argument here."

She went up the stairs as he left the house and peeked into Seth's room. Sadie was already with him, changing his diaper as he sucked on a bottle. "Hey, Sadie." Morgan went to kiss her forehead. The girl's hair was tousled, and she still wore her gown. "Seth got you up?"

"That's okay," Sadie said. "Have you been at the hospital all night?"

Morgan bent over Seth and blew a raspberry on his stomach. He squealed with giggles. "Almost all night."

"What did she have?"

Morgan picked Seth up and grinned back at Sadie. "Nothing yet. False alarm."

Sadie gasped. "All that for nothing?"

"It wasn't Karen's fault. She really was having contractions. They just stopped. That happens sometimes, I understand." She kissed Seth, and he closed his little arms around her neck and hugged back in a way that sent her heart into meltdown.

"You go get ready for school, Sadie. I'll take over with Seth."

Sadie stood there a moment, raking her hand through her tangled hair. "Morgan, I need to ask you something."

"Yeah? What?"

"Tomorrow night there's a dance at the Methodist church. Do you think I could go?"

Morgan smiled. "That sounds like fun. Who with?"

"Some girls from school. I don't know them very well, but they invited me. Sharon Zeal and Beth Walker."

Morgan tried to place them, but couldn't. "I guess that would be all right."

Sadie looked a little uncertain. "Okay. Good. I'll go then."

"See? I told you you'd make friends."

Sadie didn't answer her as she left the room. Morgan decided she was just a little groggy. She sat down in the rocker and gave the bottle back to the baby, as a sense of peace fell over her.

Things would work out for Sadie, Seth was happy and healthy, and Karen's baby would be born into a safe and loving environment.

If only they could find Cade, all would be right with the world.

CHAPTER

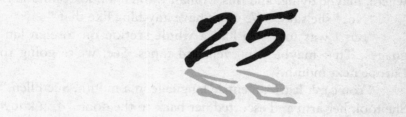

*B*lair wasn't surprised when she got the phone call from Joe McCormick at the library the next day.

"Blair, our handwriting expert has confirmed that it was Cade's writing, all right."

Blair picked up her copy. It was dog-eared and wrinkled, for she'd read it so many times, wadded it up, and bitterly thrown it away, then dug it back out of the trash to read it again. "Big surprise, huh?"

"Not to me. But I thought you'd want to know. And we weren't able to get any other fingerprints or fibers from the letter, so it didn't provide any clues."

After thanking him for the information, Blair hung up and let out a frustrated yell that shook the small library. What good was it to know he'd written this letter full of lies if it didn't help them find him?

The front door opened, and anger surged through her. Who would come in here at a time like this? She didn't have time to show them where she kept the cookbooks and help them find a recipe for Mud Bottom Pie.

Storming across the wood floor, she saw that it was Sue Ellen Jargis. "Hey, Blair," she said. "I was just looking for something that would teach me how to speak Italian. You got anything like that?"

Rage erupted inside her. Cade was in trouble, suffering somewhere, maybe dying, and this woman wanted a book on Italian?

"No," she said. "We don't have anything like that."

"But I was told you had a whole section on foreign languages. That maybe you even had tapes. See, we're going to Europe next month."

"You can't learn an entire language in a month, Sue Ellen." She took her arm and escorted her back to the door. "You know what? I just remembered that I need to close early today. Maybe if you come back tomorrow I can help you."

"Closing early?" Sue Ellen stopped at the door, resisting Blair's efforts to evict her. "Well, why? The hours on the door clearly say you're open until six."

"Emergency," Blair said. "Really, I have to close." She got her out the door, then started to close it behind her. "You have a nice day now."

Before the woman could object, she locked the door and leaned against it.

Ann Clark, she thought. Ann Clark was the key to the whole thing. The police might need evidence, probable cause, motive, warrants. But she didn't.

Cade might not have time for red tape.

She hurried back to the office and got the letter again, folded it, and shoved it into her jeans pocket.

She had to get out of this place and think. She had to make a plan.

She got her keys and locked the library behind her.

Outside, she saw the sun glaring down on the water, and she longed to see Cade kayaking by, his tanned skin soaking up the rays of the rising sun. There were days when she'd sat on the shore and watched him without his knowing and dreamed stupid dreams befitting of an adolescent.

But Cade wasn't here, and those stupid dreams left her with a sense of loss so great that her heart felt too weak to contain it. She'd dealt with many things in her life—pain, humiliation, rejection, deceit. But of them all, loss was the hardest to bear. And this particular loss—the might-have-been kind—pierced so deeply within her that she knew no place to turn for relief.

What if Morgan was right, and Cade had harbored interest in her? What if there really was one man on this earth who could see past her scars? Wouldn't it be the height of cruelty for him to be snatched away?

She was selfish, she told herself. This wasn't about her. Cade's vanishing was a tragedy for him, regardless of what it did to her.

She thought of Oswald, probably standing sentinel over his empty bowls, waiting for his master to come home and put the world back on its axis.

For now, she was the only one who would do that for the cat, even if she couldn't do it for Cade or herself.

She drove to Cade's house and went around to the backyard.

Oswald began grumbling and croaking to her in his clipped, agitated meows. "I know, Lee Harvey," she said as she filled his bowls. "The service is lousy around here, huh?" While he ate, she sat down on the patio chair and looked around at the yard. Maybe she'd borrow Jonathan's mower and come cut it tomorrow.

Hugging herself, she scanned the crepe myrtles that weren't yet in bloom, the azalea bushes that were, and the hodgepodge of untended and unidentifiable plants that grew in his yard.

How would anyone expect them to think he was bringing a bride back here with no preparation at all? He would have called someone to come and cut the grass, at least. He would have put up his mud-caked boots that sat in one of the chairs. He would have weeded the garden.

But what if she was giving Cade more credit than he deserved?

What if the letter was true?

She pulled the letter out of her pocket and stared down at it again. The possibility that it was, indeed, true had hung in the back of her mind since she'd first seen it, a distant thought that she dared not entertain. What if Cade did have a secret girlfriend and had run off to marry her to counter his depression? A spontaneous act like that wouldn't have provided for a mowed lawn or a fed cat.

Was Cade even capable of such a thing?

He was a man, wasn't he? She'd had lots of experience with men, though not the kind that most of the women she knew had. Her experience consisted of brush-offs and snubs because of the scars on her face. Men who were attracted to one side of her face while being repulsed by the other.

She had long ago begun to believe that there was something different about Cade. He was not the womanizer that so many of his cohorts were. He wasn't what she called a serial dater. He seemed too serious to spend time with a woman if he couldn't consider her for a wife.

There had been times lately when, like Morgan, she had sensed his affection for her. He'd called her beautiful, asked her to abandon her plan to leave the island, behaved as if he cared. But even then, some part of her knew that he would never consider her seriously. Their worldviews were too different. They didn't have the same core values, the same deep-seated faith.

But the signs were still there. Was she so deluded that she'd manufactured them in her mind?

Maybe there *had* been another woman all along, one he kept secret. He was a private man and wouldn't have wanted his life to be examined under everyone else's microscope.

And it would mean that he was alive and not in danger. Wouldn't it make her feel better to know that?

No, she thought. Somehow, the very idea of that made her want to put Cape Refuge in her rearview mirror and never think of it again.

But the alternative, if the letter was a fake or if he'd been forced to write it, meant that he was suffering, his life in someone else's hands.

It all came down to what she believed about Cade.

She rubbed her unadorned eyes and combed her fingers through her hair, trying to sort out all she knew about him.

He was kind and wise and diligent and thoughtful. His compassion for William Clark would not have allowed him to blow things off and elope. She knew that for a fact. Wasn't that why he'd been reading about bloodguilt and the cities of refuge?

If it turned out she was wrong in proclaiming the letter a fraud, then she'd just have to look like a fool. But if she was right, she had to save Cade's life.

First, she had to use all her resources to learn everything she could find on Ann and William Clark. Then she could decide how to proceed.

She didn't really care what it cost her.

That night, as Sadie prepared to go and
meet Trevor, guilt almost unraveled her. But it was too
late. The plans had been made, and she had to go. If Morgan had been her age, she would have understood. She
might have done exactly the same thing if her parents had
been unreasonable.

She stood in front of the mirror and tried to see herself from Trevor's eyes.

Have you looked in the mirror lately?

She had inherited her mother's blonde hair and big
eyes. She could see that fragile look she'd always seen in
her mother—that look that invited men to rescue her.
They had rescued her with the drugs of her choice, then
turned on her under the strain of those choices.

Sadie hoped her own fragile look didn't attract the
same kinds of men.

Was Trevor like the many men who'd come in and
out of her mother's life? Wild, dangerous, reckless?

No. She turned from the mirror and banished that thought. Trevor was not like Morgan and Jonathan said. He was decent, sweet . . .

. . . and looked like he belonged in Hollywood.

It would all turn out fine, and Morgan and Jonathan would never know she'd lied.

Seth had already been bathed and was dressed in his pajamas, taking his bedtime bottle as Morgan rocked him. For so long, Sadie had served as his surrogate mother, and it had been a heavy burden. What a miracle that Morgan had stepped into that role, and now he had two surrogate parents who delighted in him, leaving Sadie to enjoy him as a sister and not his sole protector.

She left them thinking she was walking to the Methodist church for the dance, but instead walked toward the boathouse that Morgan and Jonathan kept for the tenants of Hanover House. It was the place she had discovered months ago when she was a scared runaway with a broken arm. It had been a comfortable place to rest and hide. It had also been a place of terror where bullets had been fired and people had been killed. But now it was a place of redemption, she thought, where Trevor Beal would meet her, and things in her life would begin to turn around.

When she walked up the long dirt road toward the Bull River that fed into the Atlantic, she saw him leaning there against the wooden structure, his arms folded and his feet crossed at the ankles. He looked like one of those renegade guys in a prime-time television show, with his dark hair and his blue eyes and that knowing grin on his face. Her face flushed with pleasure at the sight of him.

"So, you came," he said, pushing off from the wall. "I was afraid you wouldn't."

She smiled. "Me? Why wouldn't I?"

He put his arm around her shoulders and kissed her on the lips, startling her. She hadn't expected that. She had kissed guys before back in Atlanta, greasy motorcycle types with tattoos on their arms and no familiarity with shampoo bottles or soap. They'd been some of the ones who came and went from her house when Jack was manufacturing his crystal meth and raking in the bucks as he made it available. She'd never had a guy kiss her in a chaste way that suggested he had nothing further in mind.

"You look awesome," he said, his face near hers. "Absolutely awesome."

She started to tell him he did too, but her throat seemed to tighten. Taking her hand, he pulled her to his car—a black Firebird that she had often watched driving away from school.

He helped her in. "So you're okay with this?"

She looked up at him, and her fears fled. His eyes were so crystal clear, so honest. "I think I am," she said, "only I feel pretty crummy about lying to them. I told them I was going to the Methodist dance."

"So we'll go." He went around the car and got behind the wheel. "I'll drop you off at the door and you can step inside, buy a ticket if you want to, walk through. Hang out for a minute. Then you can say you were really there."

She thought about that for a moment. That would make her feel less like a liar. "That might help. But I can't be seen there with you."

"I'll wait in the car, and then we'll go out to eat. There's a new restaurant in Savannah that I've been wanting to try. I've heard a lot about it." His voice was a lazy rumble that made her heart flip into a triple-time cadence.

"But we could be seen there too. I really don't want to make Morgan and Jonathan mad. Maybe we ought to stay here, just sit out in the boathouse and look at the water and talk."

Those eyes. She watched them laugh as if he loved the idea. "Sounds good to me. Just the two of us, alone."

She looked away quickly. Maybe that was a mistake—to be alone with him. "Or maybe we could get a hot dog on the beach and go for a walk. Not a date, so I wouldn't really be lying that much."

"And don't forget that Crystal's having her party tonight. We could still go if you wanted."

She laughed bitterly. "Yeah, like I'd really want to go to that."

"All right," he said, "but first things first. We need to eat, and I don't want to buy you a hotdog. You'll think I'm cheap."

Cheap? In his brand-new Firebird that made her feel like Somebody?

"Come on," he said. "We'll go into Savannah and eat at this little place, and we won't call it a date. It'll be just two friends interviewing each other."

"Interviewing?" she asked.

"Yeah. You used to work for the paper, right? Just pretend you're interviewing me and I'm interviewing you."

"We're playing games with words," she said. "Trying to make me feel better about telling lies to people I love."

"Well, we're playing games with words whether we sit at the beach or go out to eat. You're on a date with me, Sadie. Face it. You lied to Morgan and Jonathan, but it was for a good reason."

She didn't like the reality of that, but she wasn't about to back out now. "Okay, let's go eat."

"Then when we get back it'll be getting dark and I'll drop you by the dance. You can go in and make your little appearance and come back to the car. Then we'll go sit on the beach and talk. By then it'll be too dark and nobody will recognize us."

It sounded good to her, so she tried to relax as he started the car and pulled away from the boathouse.

They sat over mozzarella sticks and hamburgers, and Sadie listened to funny stories about Trevor's charades with his teachers in school.

Finally he took her back to Cape Refuge, to the Methodist church. She ran in and paid for a ticket, walked around the rec hall and heard the band, saw the people dancing and having fun, and quickly headed back out to his car.

He drove them to a public parking lot on the side of the beach, and they walked across the sand and sat on a blanket he'd brought, watching the waves hit against the shore. Not too far away they could see the firelight of Crystal's party. The music made its way all the way up to where they were, and she heard the sounds of laughter and people having fun. She looked in that direction and wondered if Trevor wished he were there.

"I heard that Crystal's parents let her have alcohol at her parties," Sadie said.

"Oh, sure," Trevor said. "They're real laid-back. They don't get all hung up over the stuff most parents do."

She didn't know what to think about that. Were Morgan and Jonathan "hung up"? Her own mother sure hadn't been.

"What about yours?" she asked. "Do they let you drink?"

"They let me do what I want," he said. "They trust me."

Somehow she had expected him to say that, and as she turned it over in her mind, it seemed reasonable and healthy.

He put his arm around her so naturally that it was as if they'd been going out for a very long time. It made her feel as if she belonged to someone, as if she had worth and value, as if she wasn't the school outcast whom everyone wanted to avoid.

"So when do you have to be home?"

"Ten. That's when the dance is over."

"All right." He looked over at the party still going on. The music drifted up on the wind.

"You're going to go to the party, aren't you?" she asked.

He shrugged. "Well, why shouldn't I? I mean if you're not going to be with me, I've got to have something to do."

She knew he was right. She couldn't expect him to go home and moon over her. She supposed it was fine. She just hoped word didn't get around that he had been out with her earlier tonight. She hoped she could trust him to keep the secret.

As he walked her back toward Hanover House, she realized how much she dreaded the secret she was keeping. The more people knew about it, the more likely she would be to get into trouble. She didn't want Morgan and Jonathan to be disappointed in her.

He held her hand as they walked back, and finally he stopped across from Hanover House and kissed her on the lips. This time it was a slow, mournful kiss, a kiss that said good-bye ... but not for long.

"Say you'll go out with me again," he said.

"When?"

"Tomorrow night."

Sighing, she looked up at her house. "I don't think I can come up with another lie for tomorrow night. I'm going to get caught."

He pulled her closer. "It'll be okay," he said. "Just tell them you're going for a walk along the beach. Some friends of mine are having another party tomorrow night. Don't worry, Crystal won't be there. It's mostly friends I know from my boating club. For the most part they're college-aged, so you probably won't even know them."

"I don't know," she said. "The more people that see me with you . . ."

"What do you think, they're going to call Morgan up and say, 'Oh, by the way, I saw Sadie out with Trevor last night'? These are the kind of people who mind their own business."

He tipped her chin up and kissed her again, and she melted in it, washed in a tide of protection, propriety, possession. She liked the way that felt.

"All right," she whispered. "I'll meet you out at the South Beach Pier at eight. How's that sound?"

"Eight? That's too late."

"It has to be late," she said. "I'll tell them that I'm going to my room to read and that I'm turning in early, and then I'll sneak out when they're not looking and I'll meet you, okay?"

He chuckled. "I kind of like this clandestine stuff. Makes me feel real decadent."

Decadent wasn't something she'd ever wanted to be, but she dismissed that thought. "I probably can't stay long. I don't want to make any noise coming back in, and the later I get there, the more locked up everything will be. They have rules."

"All right," he said. "So we'll do whatever you have to do to keep from getting caught. I'll see you tomorrow night."

Sadie floated back into the house. Morgan waited in the den, hemming a skirt that she had on her lap. She had made it for Sadie to wear to church. "Hey," she said as she came in.

"Hey, there!" Morgan sounded oblivious. "How was the dance?"

Sadie had trouble looking her in the eye. "Fine."

"Did you like the band?"

"It was okay."

Morgan stared at her for a moment, and her smile faded. She got up and came to face her, and Sadie wondered if she could see the deceit on her face. "Honey, what's wrong? Did something happen?"

Sadie forced a smile. "No, really. It was fun. I'm just tired."

Morgan looked skeptical. "Then you'll go back to the next one?"

"Maybe." She started up the stairs. "Is Seth asleep?"

"Yeah, I put him to bed a couple of hours ago."

Sadie stood there awkwardly, knowing that she had guilt written all over her face. "I think I'll go on to bed then," she said.

"Okay, goodnight, honey."

"Goodnight." She didn't look back at the worried expression on Morgan's face as she hurried to her room.

CHAPTER

27

Cade woke, still locked in the tiny room, with the pain of his bullet wounds radiating through his body. His sheets reeked with the smell of blood, and cold air blew from the vent over his bed. He shivered and tried to sit up.

She had taken out the toilet lid and the commode seat, so he couldn't use them as weapons. He sat up, wincing at the stabbing pain in his side. Slowly, he slid his legs off the edge of his bed. His broken left leg was swollen and bloody, and as he brought it to the floor, the pain exploded.

He imagined his body splitting apart into a million directions, then falling like shrapnel to the concrete floor. He fell back onto the thin mattress.

He was going to die here.

From the foggy depths of his brain he groped for Scripture, something to cling to like a hand, something to remind him that he could make it. He had memorized much Scripture in his life. Wayne Owens had seen to that.

"O Lord, do not . . . do not rebuke me . . . in your anger . . . or discipline me in your wrath. Be merciful to me, Lord, for I am faint; O Lord, . . . heal me, for my bones are in agony. My soul is in anguish."

He had learned that passage from Psalm 6 when he'd made it his business to memorize as many psalms as he could. He'd never expected to need it so much. Every morning, he had met Wayne at Cricket's, and over coffee he would recite the Scripture he'd memorized the day before. Wayne had committed to learning the same passages, and they had recited them together, their eyes transfixed on each other.

Oh, how he missed Wayne.

"How long, O Lord, how long?" His throat was raspy, hoarse, almost too weak to be heard. "Turn, O Lord, and deliver me . . . save me because of your unfailing love. No one remembers you when he is dead. Who praises you from the grave?"

He had often wondered if David understood about heaven, that there was a place of joy and peace where our hearts would overflow. If he had, would he have written those words?

Yes, maybe, Cade thought. Maybe from the depths of his own danger, he had only seen death as being a dreaded end. Cade understood that.

"I am worn out from groaning; all night long I flood my bed with weeping and drench my couch with tears. My eyes grow weak with sorrow; they fail because of all my foes."

Yes, he had foes, though he didn't know what they wanted with him. Whether they would murder him in revenge for the life he had taken, or use him for some other evil intention, he didn't know.

"Away from me, all you who do evil, . . . for the Lord has heard my weeping. . . . The Lord has heard my cry for mercy; . . . the Lord accepts my prayer."

Peace calmed him in the midst of his pain, and he knew that God heard the Scripture he prayed aloud.

"All my enemies will be ashamed and dismayed; . . . they will turn back in sudden disgrace."

Let it be so, Lord, his mind cried out. *Please turn them back in sudden disgrace.*

He wondered who was looking for him. He pictured Blair sitting at her computer day and night, pulling up databases and searching for answers—the armchair detective who should have been a cop herself. Would this be more reason for her to never acknowledge God? Would this be yet more evidence that no one sat on a sovereign throne, governing the universe?

That thought filled him with more despair than his own imprisonment.

He closed his eyes and wondered if she'd seen that sham of a letter he'd been forced to write. Did she believe he'd been hiding some secret girlfriend?

Surely not. Too much had passed between them. She must know that she was the woman he'd been waiting for. Even though he'd never said it, never even acted on it ... she must know.

He had long ago resolved in his heart not to break God's heart by marrying an unbeliever. That wasn't the kind of life he wanted for himself. How could he become one with a woman whose philosophies and life goals were so radically different from his own?

That meant that he remained a bachelor, biding his time and praying for God to change Blair's heart. So far it hadn't happened. The wait had been long.

But she must sense his feelings for her, and in his heart, he sensed hers too. She wouldn't believe he'd eloped, would she? She'd never buy that.

But if she did have doubts, there was always his signature to clue her in. Blair knew he never went by Matt.

Please, Lord, don't let her believe that letter.

He heard a scraping sound and knew that Ann was coming again. The bookshelves were being moved, the door unlocked. He lay there, defenseless, knowing that he could never make a run for it now.

She came in cautiously, checking to make sure he hadn't found some kind of weapon to waylay her before she could get to him. He wished ... oh, he wished ...

"I brought you some water," she said, handing him that two-liter bottle again. It was drugged, he knew. If he drank it, he could be out for days.

"Thank you," he whispered. He set it down on the concrete floor next to the bed.

"Drink it now," she said.

He shook his head. "I'm going to throw up. I'll drink it later."

"You need food."

He could tell from her tone that she had no intentions of bringing him any. Not now.

He looked up at her. "Mrs. Clark, I need a doctor. I've lost a lot of blood, and the bullet shattered the bone in my leg . . ."

"No doctor," she said. "That doesn't fit into my plan."

"So what is your plan?" He gritted the words through his clenched teeth. "What are you holding me for? Ransom?"

She laughed then. "One ransom note and they'd be on me in thirty seconds. No, not ransom. I doubt if anyone in Cape Refuge would pay it anyway. They all believe you ran off with a woman. It's all over the news. They're not even looking for you anymore."

Now he really did feel like he was going to throw up. "Then what do you plan to do with me?"

"I plan to kill you." Her tone was matter-of-fact. "But not yet. You're still of some use to me."

She was crazy or evil, or both.

"I didn't kill your husband on purpose. And he was shot first. Maybe you shot him."

Her face was stone cold. "He shot himself."

"I don't think so, judging by where I am right now." He caught his breath, shivered at the pain. He watched with a chill as she left him there on his bloody sheets, locked the door, and scraped the bookshelves back in front of the door.

He forced himself up on his good leg. Pain shot through him as he grabbed the water bottle, unscrewed the top, and dumped its contents into the toilet. Then he put the empty bottle in the tank, where the clean water flowed in, and filled it up. Desperately, he drank a third of it.

Then he hopped back to his bed, his nerve endings screaming out with each jolt, and fell back onto his rancid sheets.

CHAPTER

A yellow lamp burned in Blair's office, casting threatening shadows on the walls and ceiling. She checked the clock—2:00 A.M. She'd been at this for hours and had come up with little information. She'd learned that William Clark was a contract lawyer who worked independently. He had no police record and had led an uneventful life up until the day he stepped out in front of Cade's car.

And she'd found next to nothing about Ann.

She sat back in her chair and rubbed her aching forehead. Regardless of her spotless record, Ann Clark knew something about Cade. He could be somewhere in that house. There had to be a bomb shelter the police hadn't seen, a tornado room, something somewhere that they hadn't run across.

The Clarks didn't own any property other than the house at Washington Square. The woman could have him in some vacant structure that she didn't own, of course. A warehouse somewhere or an empty house, or maybe that of a friend who was helping her.

She got up and walked out of the office into the library lit only by a small recessed bulb near the door. The smell of dusty books permeated the room, and her heels clicked on the hardwood floor as she paced, trying to make some sense of it all. What did she have?

Ann Clark had probably been angry about her husband's death and might have sought revenge. It was clear that she had met with Cade on the morning of his disappearance, that he'd gotten into her car, and that he'd never been seen again since.

But that still didn't tell her where he was.

Her stomach sank as if it contained concrete, and her breathing seemed labored and short. The thought that Cade was dead, lying somewhere undiscovered, shot through her. Quickly she shook it away. She couldn't think that way. He had only been gone a few days. He was a strong man, tough and capable, not prone to being bested by a hundred-ten-pound woman.

She went back in and turned off the computer and the lights, locked the door and walked across to her own home. Before going in, she stood out and looked across the street to the water glistening under the moonlight, stars sprinkling without number across its black expanse. Tears came to her eyes, and her heart swelled with emotion. And in her despair, she did something she had rarely done before.

"God, I don't know if you're even there," she whispered, "and if you are, I know you don't have any reason to answer anything *I* ask. But Cade's one of yours. You didn't save my parents, and I don't know why. But save him. Save him, please, if you're really there."

A strong wind blew up from the water, sweeping her hair back from her face and whispering through the leaves on the trees above her. She wiped a tear from her face and felt the hard scaly skin of her burn scars under her fingertips.

It reminded her again of that day Cade had touched her scars, after she'd called God a divine terrorist who enjoyed wreaking havoc on people's lives. Her anger about her scars and the secrets surrounding them had come out that day. Cade had looked at her with puzzlement on his face. Touching her scars with his gentle fingertips, he'd whispered, "I don't even see them anymore."

No one had ever been that intimate with her. Even her parents had avoided touching the scars she was so sensitive about. No one else would have dared do what Cade had done that day. In a lot of ways he had rescued her then, pulled her out of the pit of despair, given her a reason to stay in Cape Refuge and a reason to think she had some value to the people who lived here. She wished she could return the favor now and pull him out of whatever pit he was in.

"Don't let him be dead," she whispered out loud. "Please don't let him be dead."

When she finally went into her house and got ready for bed, she knew she was in for another night of lying awake and filing through the possibilities, dozing off and dreaming of some great Avenger chasing Cade down the road to the City of Refuge.

In her dream, he was overtaken, and left to die outside the city walls, only inches from the gate.

CHAPTER

29

*T*he lies came more easily Saturday night.

Sadie waited until Seth was bathed and put to bed, the dishes were clean in the kitchen, and all her responsibilities were done. Then she excused herself to go and read herself to sleep. She was very tired, she said. Though Morgan had looked at her with confusion and a little suspicion, she thought she had pulled it off.

She had finally sneaked out the front door, while everyone else was in the kitchen, and headed across the street to the beach and down toward the place where Trevor had told her to meet him.

The sun had set, and the sky at twilight billowed with lavender clouds, waiting for dark. God's handiwork, Sadie thought. Just like she was God's handiwork, inscribed on the palm of his hand.

Guilt surged through her again.

What kind of ungrateful daughter was she, to take the goodness God had shown her through Morgan and Jonathan and throw it back in his face?

She almost turned back, but then she saw him, elbows braced on the rail of the pier, wind teasing through his hair. He was watching her approach with a smile on his face. All thoughts of turning back fled from her mind as he came back down the pier and met her on the sand.

"Hey, gorgeous," he said.

She smiled. "Hey. Am I late?"

"Not too." He kissed her, melting the residue of her guilt. She pulled back, looked up at him, and decided that any trouble this brought her was worth it.

"Come on." He took her hand and pulled her across the sand. "The party doesn't start until after nine," he said. "But we can head on over."

Their shoulders bumped together. "I'm a little nervous."

"Why? A girl like you? You've been to parties before."

She shrugged. "Yeah, but I'm not the same person I was back in Atlanta. And I haven't really been to any in Cape Refuge." The warm breeze flirted with her hair. "I wish we could just skip it."

"But then you wouldn't meet my friends. Come on, Sadie, you can do it. I want to show you off a little."

The idea that anyone considered her something to show off flattered her, and she felt pink warmth climbing her cheeks. He swept her hair behind her ear. Something like an electric shock went through her, jolting her heart. How did that work? she wondered. How could his simple touch make her heart skip beats?

"So you said these aren't your friends from school?" she asked. "Where do you know them from?"

"Here and there," he said. "But some of them are from school. You know how it is. Most of the parties on the island start out with a small list and wind up full of crashers, so there's no telling who might come."

She pictured the kinds of parties her mother used to have. They'd been much the same way. "So they're a real party crowd, huh? Are there any Christians?"

He laughed. "I don't know. If they are, they don't talk about it."

That would be a no, she thought. She slowed her step and looked up at him. "What about you? Do you believe in God?"

He shrugged. "I think there's something up there. I'm not sure what."

She frowned and tried to process that. "What about the Bible? Do you believe in that?"

He laughed again, as if he thought she was cute. "How can I? I'm not going to let some ancient book dictate how I live. No, I don't believe in it. I have my own truth."

For a moment, Sadie walked quietly beside him, battling those guilt feelings ambushing her again. "But Jonathan says that the Bible is the living, active Word of God. How can you know God if you don't know his Word?"

He grinned again. "I don't believe it *is* his word, if he's even there. If there's really a God, he would have more respect for us than to set us up a list of rules. He would want us to be happy and to do what we think is right."

"My mother did what she thought was right, and she let all our lives get messed up. Her boyfriend, Jack, did what he felt was right, and he nearly killed me."

"Come on, Sadie. You don't think they really thought those things were right, do you?"

Darkness was fading over the night sky. "But see, that's the thing. If they don't believe in any system of right or wrong, then who's to say those things were wrong. *I* might think they were wrong, and *you* might think they were wrong. But *they* didn't. They did what they thought was okay . . . for them. But the things that made them happy—drugs and parties and stuff—weren't good for my little brother or me. People need a clear-cut system of right and wrong. And we can't just decide that as we go along."

Even as she spoke, she recognized the hypocrisy in her words. Wasn't that what she was doing? Justifying her sins and making it up as she went along?

Her spirits sank again. He seemed to sense that and stopped walking. Turning her to face him, he whispered, "You're cute when you talk religion."

Before she could muster a retort, he kissed her, a long, dis-
arming kiss that made her forget that guilt again.

When it was time, they walked up the beach until they came
to the condo where a party was in progress. Loud music spilled
out onto the beach behind it. A bonfire raged in the middle of the
sand, and people danced together on one side of it and sat in clus-
ters around the other side. It looked harmless enough.

In the golden light of the bonfire, Trevor introduced her to a
few of his friends, then left her alone to go get her a drink. She
stood awkwardly among his friends, trying to look accessible and
not nervous.

"What in the world are *you* doing here?"

The voice chilled her, and she swung around and saw Crystal Lewis. Her heart crashed.

She lifted her chin. "I came with Trevor."

"Trevor?" The girl's lips curled in contempt. "I thought you
said you weren't going out with him."

"I changed my mind." Sadie started to walk away, but the
girl grabbed her arm.

"He only wants one thing from you and you know it. Everybody on Cape Refuge has heard about where you came from and
what you were like in Atlanta."

"You don't know anything about me," Sadie said.

"Well, we know that a person who grew up with a mother
in prison and a stepfather with a crystal meth lab sure doesn't have
lily-white morals. And there you live in the Hanover House with
a bunch of ex-cons."

Sadie jerked out of her grasp and started to walk around the
fire to get away from her, but Crystal followed.

"You don't have any right to be here, you know. Nobody
wants you here. Trevor, maybe, but we both know what *he* wants.
If you don't deliver, you're going to wind up all by yourself anyway. And if you do deliver, it's going to be all over town because
everybody is going to know."

Sadie saw Trevor heading toward her, so she met him
halfway. Crystal saw him, too, and fell away.

He brought her a drink. "You okay?"

"You told me Crystal wouldn't be here," she said. "You told me this wouldn't be the friends from school."

"Well, I told you that lots of people crash. Why? What did she say to you?"

"Nothing." She took a drink from the yellow paper cup he'd given her. It had a sweet citrus taste with a bit of a bite. "What is this?"

"Punch. You like it?"

She took another drink. "Yeah, it's not bad."

"Good," he said. "It's some of Brian's special concoction."

She wanted to cry. "It's not alcoholic, is it?"

His grin told her that it was, but he pulled her close again and put his mouth close to hers. "What if it was? You can handle it, Sadie. You're a big girl."

She started to pour the drink out onto the sand, but then she saw Crystal sitting in the firelight, muttering to her friends. They were all watching him hold her.

She didn't want them to see her acting like a prude, so she drank it, telling herself she wouldn't have any more after this one.

But with each gulp of the sweet liquid, her inhibitions fell. She stopped caring what Crystal and her friends thought of her, and she relaxed and danced with Trevor. Not nearly as tense as she'd been earlier, she actually started getting to know his friends and having fun with them. He brought her another drink, and another, and finally she lost count and just surrendered herself to its numbing power.

She would draw the line when she needed to, she thought. But not now. Not yet.

CHAPTER

*T*he sound of knocking cut into Morgan's sleep. Groggy, she sat up and looked through the darkness, hoping it had been a dream.

The knocking came again.

"Tell me no one's knocking at our door," Jonathan muttered.

"I'll get it." Morgan slipped out of bed and cracked the door open. Light from the hall spilled in.

Karen stood there with a distraught look on her face.

"Karen, are you all right?"

"I'm sorry to wake you up again, Morgan, but my water broke. And I'm having labor pains again. I called the doctor and he said I need to get to the hospital."

Morgan's brain came to full attention. "Okay, then we need to hurry." She flicked on the light, and Jonathan threw his arm over his eyes. "Jonathan, wake up! Karen's in labor."

"I heard." He got out of bed, looking disheveled and disoriented. "Just let me get dressed."

"Is your bag still packed from the other night?" Morgan asked her.

"Yeah, packed and ready to go."

"Okay. We'll be ready in five minutes and we'll head out."

Morgan ran back into her room and got dressed. "Will you drive us, Jonathan? It's one in the morning."

"Sure." He still wasn't awake enough. She wished they had time to make a pot of coffee. "Wake Sadie up to let her know where we'll be. Just in case we're not home by morning."

Morgan buttoned the last button on her shirt and raced out of the room. She got to Sadie's room, knocked lightly so she wouldn't disturb the other tenants. When there was no answer, she opened the door and leaned inside. "Sadie? Honey, wake up a minute. I have to talk to you."

There was no answer, so Morgan opened the door farther. The lamplight from the hall spilled in, revealing a bed that hadn't been slept in. Sadie wasn't here.

She went back to her own room and found Jonathan brushing his teeth. "Jonathan, Sadie isn't in her room. She hasn't slept in her bed. It's still made up."

"What?" He spat out the toothpaste. "Well, go look downstairs. Maybe she couldn't sleep and is reading or something."

Morgan dashed downstairs and looked in the kitchen. No sign of Sadie. When she wasn't in the parlor or the den, either, she started to get worried.

Karen had already brought her suitcase down and was waiting in the parlor.

"Karen, how long have you been up?"

"I never went to bed," she admitted. "I was having pains, so I just stayed up. I been down here watching TV since you went to bed."

"Have you seen Sadie? Did she come down for anything?"

"No, I haven't seen her at all. I figured she was sleeping."

Jonathan came down the stairs, and Morgan looked up at him. "She's not here, Jonathan. *Where is she?* It's one o'clock in the morning!"

Jonathan looked over her shoulder to Karen. "I don't know, but we'd better hurry."

Morgan turned back to Karen and saw her doubled over with a contraction, and she remembered the urgency of their mission. She ran to the woman's side and stroked her back. "Okay, honey. We're going." She turned back to Jonathan. "Jonathan, someone has to stay here and look for Sadie. I'll go to the hospital, and you call the police or something. She couldn't have just vanished! Something's happened to her."

He followed them to the door. "Do you think she could have snuck out?"

"No way," Morgan said. "That's not like her. She wouldn't have gone out without telling us."

Trying to keep her heart from giving in to the sudden terror that had overtaken her, she walked Karen out to the car. Jonathan followed, scanning the beach across the street for some sign of Sadie.

"Don't worry, Morgan. I'll find her."

"You have to, Jonathan. She could be in danger, like Cade." Tears came to her eyes, and she hugged him quickly. "Oh, Jonathan, find her."

She heard Karen moaning in the passenger seat and quickly ran to the driver's side. As she pulled out of the driveway, she saw Jonathan standing on the front porch, trying to decide what to do.

CHAPTER

*J*ust after one in the morning, Trevor suggested they leave the party and walk a little way down the beach to be alone. It sounded good to Sadie, even though she found she couldn't walk in a straight line. He seemed to enjoy steadying her.

She had never laughed so much in her life.

When they'd gotten far enough away from the crowd, he sat down in the sand and pulled her down next to him. She lay back and pillowed her head in the sand.

"You've had fun tonight, haven't you?" he asked her with a grin.

"Yeah, I did." Her words slurred, amusing her. "I love your friends. They're great."

He lay on his side in the sand and looked down at her. "So are you."

"Yeah?" she asked, grinning up at him.

"Yeah." He leaned over and kissed her, long and hard and hungry, and she felt him moving closer, his hands groping where they shouldn't. . . .

Despite her buzz, an alarm went off in her mind.

But she didn't want to heed it. She wanted to let him kiss her just the way he was, wanted to feel that she belonged just a little while longer . . .

Sliding her arms around him, she surrendered fully to that kiss . . .

CHAPTER

Vonathan called the police department as soon as Morgan was gone. Jim Henry answered.

"Jim, this is Jonathan Cleary. I have an emergency. Our foster daughter, Sadie, has disappeared."

"Disappeared?" Jim sounded irritated. "What do you mean by 'disappeared'?"

"I mean that she went up to her room to read and go to bed around eight o'clock tonight, and just now we checked and she hadn't even slept in her bed."

"Well, that goin' to bed at eight business shoulda been your first clue. How old is she? Sixteen?"

"Seventeen."

He breathed out a laugh, and Jonathan knew he wasn't taking this seriously. "Jonathan, I know you ain't been doin' this parenting thing that long, but when a seventeen-year-old goes to bed at eight o'clock, you can bet they got somethin' up their sleeve. She ain't disappeared. She's just gone out. You mark my word. She'll come home."

Appalled at the man's dismissive attitude, Jonathan gritted his teeth. "Do I have to call Joe at home, Jim? Because my best friend is missing right now and no one can find him. Now my daughter vanishes. There's a pattern here, man. Sadie would not just sneak out!"

"Hey, you don't have to get all huffy now. First time my nephew snuck out my brother felt the same way, Jonathan, but I'm telling you, she's probably at that party down at the McRae Condominiums. I been gettin' complaint calls from neighbors all night. Went over there myself to check things out, and the place was crawlin' with teenagers. I tried to break it up and get them to turn down the music, but you know how that goes."

Jonathan clutched the phone to his ear. "Sadie wouldn't go there."

"Think again, brother. You'll see. Just give it a little time, and she'll get herself home."

"And what if she doesn't?" he yelled again. "What if she's been kidnapped, too?"

"Any sign of breaking and entering in your house, Jonathan?"

"Well, I haven't looked, really."

"Broke windows? Locks?"

"No, I don't think so."

"Any sign of a struggle?" Jim asked.

Jonathan wanted to ram his fist through the phone. Then they'd have signs of a struggle, all right. "Look, if you're not going to do anything then I'm going down to that party. If she's there, I'll find her!"

"Yeah, that's a good idea. You let me know, you hear?"

Jonathan threw the phone down.

CHAPTER

*T*hat alarm kept clanging in Sadie's head as Trevor's kiss grew deeper. His hands roamed, and she tried to get hold of them and stop them. But he slipped them free and groped some more.

Breaking free of the kiss, she rolled away from him and got up on her knees. "I have to go."

Trevor looked stricken. "Why? Nobody even knows you're gone. It's not like you have a curfew."

"I just have to go." She wobbled to her feet and straightened her blouse.

"Aw, man, I didn't think you were some prude who'd tease me and then turn to ice."

She looked down at him. "Ice? Just because I won't do what you want? And I didn't tease you."

"Right." He got up and dusted the sand off of himself. "Just forget it."

"I will." On the edge of tears, she started walking away from him. He didn't follow.

The ocean whispered against the shore, reminding her that she was small, insignificant, against the world that seemed to converge against her. She remembered another time that she had been on the beach at night, utterly alone. She had been injured and had fled from home. With no place to stay and not a soul here who knew her name, she had slept on this very beach.

That old loneliness welled up inside her again, and she started to cry as she headed home. She should never have come out tonight. She shouldn't have gone to the party. She shouldn't have gotten drunk.

What had she been about to do?

The question resounded through her mind, blustering up on a wind of paranoia. She had damaged her relationship with Morgan, with Jonathan, with God.

She heard Crystal's voice, cold and condemning, as she'd accused Trevor of wanting only one thing from Sadie. And there she'd been, almost willing to give it to him.

She managed to make her way to the part of the beach across from Hanover House, stumbled across the street, and got up to the porch. Realizing that her gait was still unsteady, she took a slow quiet step up, then tripped over the last step and fell face-down on the porch. Putting her finger to her mouth and shushing herself, she got up and fumbled with the front door lock, got it to open, then stepped inside.

Jonathan stood just inside the door, gaping down at her. "Sadie!"

The light came on, shining overhead like a beacon glaring in her eyes. "I . . . I was just out for a walk."

"At one-thirty in the morning?" Jonathan's voice wobbled with anger. "Sadie, where have you been? I called the police, I was so worried about you. I was just about to come out looking for you."

She backed against the wall to steady herself, and Jonathan took her shoulders and stared into her face. "Sadie, you've been drinking."

"No. I wou'nt do that." She wished her words would come out the way she intended them to.

His face was blurry. "I smell it, Sadie. Were you out with that boy?"

Sadie stiffened and tried to pull herself together. She couldn't fade now. She had to convince Jonathan she'd done nothing wrong. "What boy?"

"Trevor Beal. Sadie, were you with him?"

She searched her mind for an answer that would satisfy him, but her brain wasn't operating the way she needed. "I was with a lot of people." There, that ought to do it. She started to the stairs. "I have to go to bed now." Grabbing the banister, she started up.

"Sadie, don't walk away from me when I'm talking to you." She'd never heard his voice that angry before, so she turned back around and sat down on the step. "I asked you where you'd been."

"On the beach," she said. "Thasall, Jonathan. I think I'm gonna be sick. Can we talk about this in the morning?"

Jonathan sighed, and she hoped that meant that he was going to back off and give her a break. He came up the stairs, took her arm, and helped her the rest of the way up. When they reached the second floor, Sadie broke free of him and stumbled into the bathroom, locked it behind her, then bent over the toilet and wretched. Still nauseated, she sat on the floor and waited for it to pass.

*B*y the time they got to the hospital, Karen's contractions were three minutes apart. There was no question about it. The baby was going to come tonight.

As the nurses prepped Karen and hooked her up to the IV and monitors, Morgan took a moment to find a pay phone in the hall. She called home, and Jonathan answered on the second ring.

"Jonathan, have you found her yet?"

"She's home," he said.

Morgan almost collapsed in relief. "Thank goodness. Where was she?"

A moment of silence followed. "She snuck out, Morgan. She was with Trevor Beal."

Morgan's heart plunged. For a moment, she couldn't speak. "Are you sure, Jonathan?"

"Oh, yeah. I heard it from the horse's mouth. Slurred, though it was."

Morgan froze. Was there really more? Not just the sneaking out? "What do you mean 'slurred'?"

"She'd been drinking, Morgan," he said. "She came home drunk."

Morgan backed against the wall and put her hand over her face as she clutched the phone to her ear. "Are you sure?"

"Yes. She could hardly walk, and she reeked of it."

"She knows what chemical abuse and alcohol have done to her family. Why would she do such a thing?"

"We'll have to wait until morning to ask her," he said. "She's not in any shape to discuss it right now."

One of the nurses came out of Karen's room, just up the hall. She had to get in there. "Honey, are you all right?" Morgan asked.

"I just feel like the recipient of a one-two punch right in the gut. But yeah, I'm fine. You be fine too, okay?"

She sighed. "I've got to go. Karen needs me."

She hung up the phone and pressed her forehead against it. Not Sadie. She hadn't rebelled like that. There had to be an explanation. Finally, she went back to Karen's room. The woman lay on her side, her eyes closed as she suffered through another of her contractions. A nurse stood by her, monitoring the strength of it.

"How's she doing?" Morgan asked.

The nurse glanced back at her. "She's already dilated six centimeters, so she's pretty far along. I don't think this is going to take very long. It's too late for an epidural, I'm afraid."

She watched as the numbers on the monitor went down, and Karen began to relax out of her coil. Morgan stepped up to her side and pushed her hair back from her face. "You're gonna be okay, Karen. It's gonna be all right."

Karen looked as if she braced herself for the pain about to come again.

Morgan made herself comfortable on the chair beside Karen's bed, and trying to keep her mind off of Sadie, prepared for a long night.

Not much later, the nurses declared that Karen had dilated enough to go into the delivery room, and the doctor was called.

"Don't leave me," Karen said, squeezing her hand. "I'm scared."

"There's nothing to be scared of." Morgan stroked Karen's damp forehead. "You're participating in a miracle. Soon you'll meet your child."

"Come with me, Morgan. Please, I need somebody with me."

A sense of excitement jolted up inside her at the idea. She would love to see a little baby coming into the world.

"Is it all right?" she asked the nurses who were moving her to a gurney.

"Sure," she said. "You can be her coach."

"I don't know how to coach. I haven't had classes or anything."

"Honey, you just hold her hand and remind her to breathe."

They went into the antiseptic room, bright with fluorescent lights and cold as winter. Morgan wished they could warm it up and lower the lights for the child.

The doctor got there within minutes. After one quick examination, he declared that it was time for Karen to push.

Karen squeezed her eyes shut and clamped her hand on Morgan's, groaning with the effort.

Morgan hung on, wishing there was something more that she could do. She wondered how it would be when she was in Karen's place. Would Jonathan know what to do? Would he want to videotape? Capture the first breath of their child?

She yearned to have the opportunity to find out.

"The baby's crowning," the doctor said as Karen came out of the contraction. "Just a few more minutes."

Karen fell back on her pillow, trying to catch her breath.

"A couple more pushes and we'll be home free."

They adjusted the mirror over the delivery table so that Karen and Morgan could see.

Then the contraction came, and Karen rose up, gritting her teeth and bearing down. Morgan watched the mirror.

The head emerged, covered with wet, black curly hair. "It's coming!" she cried. "Come on, Karen. Keep pushing."

She watched its little shoulders emerge, then its tiny purple body.

Karen gave a final groan as the baby came fully into the world. Then she fell back and began to weep as she caught her first glimpse. "My baby!"

The doctor turned it over, and Morgan saw that it was a boy, and his face was the most beautiful sight she'd ever seen. She burst into tears.

"Oh, Karen, it's a boy. He's so beautiful."

As the doctor suctioned his mouth, the baby began to scream.

Morgan wept as they wiped him off, wrapped him up, and handed him to Karen. The woman took him like a precious gift and brought him close. Morgan touched his tiny little foot as his mother introduced herself.

"Hey, there, Emory," she said in a soft, weepy voice. "Oh, you're a precious thing. Look at you."

Emory. Morgan hadn't thought before to ask Karen if she had a name. She wiped her eyes and breathed in a sob. "He looks like an Emory."

Karen smiled up at her. "Emory, I want you to meet your aunt Morgan." She handed the baby to her.

Carefully, Morgan gathered him into her arms and looked down into eyes that seemed to understand everything he saw. Every maternal hormone she possessed fired within her. She started to laugh through her tears.

What a miracle. What a joy. What a privilege to have witnessed this.

Lord, let it be me sometime soon.

When they had taken away the baby and put Karen back in her room, Morgan's exhaustion caught up with her.

"You go home now, Morgan," Karen said. "It's Sunday and you have church and all. You need to get some rest. I'll be fine here."

Morgan didn't want to leave. What if they brought the baby in, and she had another chance to hold him?

Then she realized that it wasn't her child. Karen needed time alone with her baby. "Are you sure?"

"Sure, I'm sure," she said. "I'll probably sleep until they bring him to me, and then I've requested that they let me keep him in here with me all day."

"Oh." The word came out softly, and she thought that was what she would have done, too. She would have wanted the baby close, so she could be the one meeting all his needs. "Are you sure you're up to that?"

"If I'm not, I can change my mind, but I want my baby with me. They said it was my call."

Morgan didn't blame her. She got up and found her purse. Every bone in her body seemed to weigh twice its usual weight. The night they'd been here for the false alarm had exhausted her enough, and she'd never quite caught up. Now she felt too weary to even walk to the car.

But it had been well worth it. She kissed Karen on the forehead. "You rest now, and I'll come back this afternoon. Call if you need anything."

As she drove home, she realized that motherhood was one of the greatest blessings of all. She hoped Karen realized it.

Why hadn't God chosen to bless her that way?

As quickly as she'd asked the question, she kicked herself. He *had* blessed her, with Seth and Sadie. But she hadn't been a very good steward of that blessing, if Sadie had come home drunk this morning. She didn't blame God for not trusting her with a baby of her own.

She tried to think like a good mother. There were going to have to be consequences. Sadie needed to understand exactly what she'd done. But how? What would good parents do to teach a teenager to stay on the right path?

When she reached Hanover House, she found Jonathan already up with Seth, feeding him in the kitchen. Jonathan had already had his shower, and wore his pressed black "preacher" trousers with a white T-shirt.

"What did she have?" he asked with a smile.

"It was a boy," she said. "A beautiful boy. Eight pounds. In perfect health." She dropped her purse on the table and smiled at her husband. "Oh, Jonathan, you should have seen it. The birth was such a miracle, and that beautiful little body slid out, and those arms and legs were kicking and moving, and he let out this scream that told us he was healthy and whole . . ."

He took her hand and pulled her down next to him. "I'm glad you got to see it."

Tears welled in her eyes, and her throat seemed to close up.

"How's Karen?" he asked.

"Exhausted."

"Like you?"

"I think she's a little tireder than I am." She reached for Seth. "Come here, you." He laughed and reached back, and she pulled him out of the high chair, wiped his face, and kissed his plump cheek. "You hear anything from Sadie this morning?"

"Nope. I'm sure she's zonked out. I was trying to decide whether to wake her up for church."

"Oh, yes," Morgan said. "She's definitely getting up for church."

"Well, she's not going to be in any mood to worship."

"I don't care," Morgan said. "She needs to understand that we go to church in this family. We arrange our Saturday nights so that we'll be in good shape to worship on Sunday morning. And if she chooses to do what she did last night, she'll pay for it in the morning. But we're not letting her off the hook for church."

"Okay," he said. "I'm with you. So you're going too?"

She wilted with Seth in her lap, and propped her chin on his little head. "I have to if I'm making her. I'll sleep later." She settled her tired eyes on him. "Jonathan, how did this happen?"

"I don't know." He slid his chair back and took Seth's breakfast bowl to the sink. "I've thought about it all night. Maybe it's just the power of peer pressure. Or loneliness. Maybe we should have let her home-school. Maybe we need to try to understand her side before we start disciplining her for it."

Morgan got up, Seth on her hip, and poured some orange juice into his cup. "I don't even know how to discipline her. She's seventeen years old. She comes from a background of parties day and night, strangers in and out of her house, druggies, alcoholics. I don't know why she'd want even a taste of that for herself. I'm so mad at her."

"Me too," Jonathan said, "but these are the perils of parenthood. It's gonna be okay. We'll survive it just like every other parent of a teenager."

Morgan finished feeding Seth as Jonathan got ready for church. Then she headed up the stairs and went to Sadie's door.

The girl lay sound asleep in the middle of her bed, her covers all twisted around her, and one of her pillows on the floor. Her mouth hung open and saliva pooled on the sheet beneath her.

Morgan stood there looking at the girl who seemed so young and so innocent, and she remembered finding her hiding in the boathouse. She had seemed so small and vulnerable then, with her broken arm and her big, frightened eyes.

She'd been through so much since then. The strength of character she'd already shown Morgan and Jonathan couldn't be overridden by one night of teenage rebellion. Still, her behavior couldn't be overlooked.

She set Seth down on the bed next to his sister, pushed her hair gently back from her face. "Wake up, Sadie. It's time to get up for church."

Sadie stirred, and Seth began to pat on her bottom, trying to wake her up. She turned over and squinted her eyes open, saw Seth and smiled. "Hey, Bud," she said. "What are you doing here?"

He laughed aloud and crawled up to her face, planted a kiss on her cheek. Sadie seemed to remember the night before, and she sat up in bed and squinted up at Morgan. "I thought you were at the hospital."

"Karen had her baby," Morgan said. "It was a boy."

"Great. Everything okay?"

"Yeah," Morgan said. "She's resting, so I decided to come home for a little while."

Sadie rubbed her eyes, shoved her hair back from her face. "Morgan, I'm so sorry about last night."

Seth slid off the bed and toddled to Sadie's dresser.

Sighing, Morgan pulled a chair out from under her desk and sat down facing her. "What happened, Sadie? Talk to me."

Sadie got up and directed Seth to the blocks she kept on her closet floor. "Trevor just asked me to meet him on the beach, and we went for a walk. It wasn't going to be any big deal. But his friends were having a party, and we went to it, and when we got there Crystal Lewis told me he was only with me for one reason, and I got so tense and upset . . . then he brought me this drink. I was embarrassed to throw it out in front of these people who already hated me, so I drank it. I didn't intend to drink anymore after that, Morgan. I was just going to have that one, and then I was going to find some excuse to leave and go home." She started to cry. "I don't know what happened. That first drink relaxed me so much that I didn't remember what I'd planned to do. When he brought me a second one, I drank it, too. And then there was a third . . ." She wiped the tears from her face. "I lost count after that."

"Sadie, do you understand now why we didn't want you going out with that boy?"

"Not really," Sadie said. "He's nice. He likes me, and he's the only one who does. He's kind of like the gatekeeper, you know? I can make friends through him, and finally become a part of the people on this island."

"You *are* a part of the people on this island. You're a part of our family."

Sadie sat down next to Seth on the floor. "I know, Morgan. But that's not enough. I need friends my own age."

Morgan shook her head. "But Sadie, when a guy inspires you to lie to your parents and sneak out and get drunk, he's not good for you. And I'm not so sure that Crystal wasn't right about what he wanted."

"He's not like that." But Sadie's denial was weak. "Man, my head hurts. I'm just like my mom. Nursing a hangover and apologizing about the night before . . ."

"You're not like that," Morgan said. "This was a one-time thing. I'll fix you some breakfast and give you some aspirin or something. But you *are* going to church. We're not going to tolerate having you party on Saturday night and then be in no shape to worship the next day. That's not how it works around here."

"I know."

Morgan took Seth downstairs and, fighting her aching fatigue, began cooking the eggs and bacon she normally cooked on Sunday mornings. After a few minutes, Sadie came down and took her seat at the table.

Jonathan came in and gave her a look. "So how do you feel?"

She shrugged. "Head's killing me."

He sat down beside her. "Sadie, who was at that party last night?"

"Nobody you know."

"How can you say that?" he asked. "I've lived on this island for most of my life. I know everybody here. Were they kids from your school?"

"A few."

"College kids?" Jonathan asked.

"I don't know how old they were."

Morgan shot Jonathan a look. "But they were drinking and they served alcohol to a minor?" he asked.

"They didn't *serve* it to me," she said. "It was just punch. I didn't know—"

"You didn't know it was alcoholic?" Jonathan asked.

"Well, okay, I did know, but—"

Morgan moved the frying pan from the stove. "Sadie, I don't know what to do. I'm new at having a teenager in the house. I don't know whether I'm supposed to ground you or what."

Sadie just looked up at her miserably. "Ground me from what? I never go anywhere."

Morgan knew she had a point.

"I want to do something effective, honey. I want to make sure that you don't make mistakes that will ruin your life. Sadie, you're stronger than that. You have more character. This is not what I'd expect of the girl who got away from Jack Dent and took care of herself on the beach for days with a broken arm."

Sadie sat back in her chair. Morgan saw the pain in her face, and her heart ached for her. She couldn't seem to work up any anger toward her.

Morgan came to the table and leaned over her. "Sadie, I have high hopes for you. I want you to go to college, do something with your life. I pray every night that someday you'll meet a wonderful godly man who will be your husband, that you'll have a family of your own, and that all the things in your past will be redeemed. I pray that for you. But if you start down this path, Sadie, none of that is going to happen."

Sadie started to cry again. "It's not a path. I'm not on a path, Morgan. I just made some mistakes last night. I won't do it again."

Morgan hugged her. When she let her go, she sat down next to her.

Sadie had trouble looking at her. "I'm so ashamed. I never thought I'd do something so stupid. It's like throwing all the good things you've done for me back in your faces, and I didn't mean to do that. I really didn't."

"You don't owe us anything," Jonathan said. "Nothing at all. We took you in because we love you. And we expect you to obey us because you love us."

"It was just one night," Sadie said. "I really won't do it again."

Morgan wiped the tears off of the girl's wet cheek. Then she did what her mother would have done. She got up from the table and, with her spatula, dipped out some scrambled eggs and a couple of pieces of bacon and put them on a plate for Sadie. "Here. Eat this. It'll make you feel better."

"I don't know if I can eat." Sadie looked up at Jonathan. "Are you going to ground me?"

"Honey, I don't know what we're going to do," Jonathan said. "I need some time to pray about this, whether to ground you or take away privileges or what. But just know that whatever comes is because we love you."

"I know." She stared down at her plate and finally pushed it away. "I'll eat something later." She got up and started back up the stairs. "I have to get dressed for church. I'll be down in a minute."

Morgan watched her retreat up the stairs. Finally, she turned back to her husband. "Jonathan, what are we going to do?"

"I don't know. Maybe it's just a phase. Maybe it won't happen again." He got up and pulled her close. "You look so tired. Why don't you stay home from church?"

She sighed. "I thought about it. But I just feel like I need to worship this morning. With Cade missing, and Sadie . . . I'll sleep later before I go back to the hospital."

As Morgan went to get Seth and herself ready for church, she prayed that this thing with Sadie was an end, and not a beginning.

CHAPTER

35

Cade emerged from a shallow sleep. His throat felt on fire again, so he reached for the empty bottle beside him and looked over at the toilet tank. If he could just get there again, relieve himself, take clean water from the tank . . .

He moved his legs over the side of the bed, gritting his teeth against the pain. Without putting his weight on his wounded leg, he stood up. He managed to make his way over, groaning with the pain incited by each movement. He relieved himself, flushed, then dunked the bottle into the tank of clean water and drank some of it.

He leaned against the wall and looked around the room. There must be something he could use to overpower Ann Clark the next time she came in. But it wasn't just her he was dealing with. There was someone else, someone he hadn't seen, the one who had shot him from the top of the stairs. Even if he bested Ann, he'd have to contend with that other person if he tried to get away.

This time they'd kill him for sure.

He couldn't imagine why they hadn't finished the job by now. She had already stated her intention to kill him. But he still had a use to her, she'd said. He was their scapegoat, but for what?

He made his way back to the bed and dropped down on it, exhausted from the short journey across the room. Carefully, he set his leg back on the bed. She hadn't changed his sheets. They were still bloody and smelled of decay.

"Help me, Lord," he whispered. "Please help me."

He had to find something he could use as a weapon. He couldn't just lie here and do nothing. He looked around the room and saw the bare beams against the tar paper in the wall. Maybe he would be able to break one of the beams free. He began to hit on the one closest to his bed with the heel of his hand, trying to loosen it, but it didn't budge, and each effort shot pain through his side, cutting each nerve ending like a scalpel, making him want to scream out in agony. But he had to think . . . he had to stay focused.

He began to quote Psalm 6 again, praying God's Word back to him and trusting from the depth of his heart that the Lord had heard.

CHAPTER

*B*lair yawned as she crossed the Islands Expressway back onto Tybee Island. She had spent the night staked out in her car down from Ann Clark's house but hadn't seen anything that gave her clues about Cade's whereabouts.

Instead of going home when she reached Cape Refuge, she went to Cricket's and pulled into the space next to Cade's truck. It had been parked here for six days now. *Six days!* Where in the world was he?

She got out of the car, opened the passenger door, and slipped into the driver's seat. On the passenger seat she saw a box of breath mints, a small New Testament, and a couple of ATM slips. A windbreaker hung on the hook behind her head. She unhooked it and brought it to her nose, breathing in his scent. It smelled like wind and sea air and the soap he used.

She sat in his driver's seat, clutching the jacket to her chest and staring out the window to the activity on the dock.

Behind her, she heard the singing from the warehouse church her parents had led for years and where Jonathan and Morgan were now presiding, since they hadn't been able to find a permanent preacher. The parking lot was full.

The chorus of "Be Thou My Vision" floated over the wind. It had been one of her mother's favorites. She'd sung it herself dozens of times as a child, sitting on the front pew in that very building with her father preaching and her mother playing piano. Around her, she had always been aware of the misfits and outcasts, those who'd come in from the sea and those who were just passing through. . . .

But it wasn't just those who had no place to go who came to church in that little warehouse. Islanders who could have gone to church anywhere came to worship there and considered it their church home.

Cade was among them. If he were here today, he'd be in that building, sitting on his favorite pew, raising his hands to the Lord he believed in, and worshiping with his whole heart and soul.

She hung his jacket back up and got out of the truck. The breeze blew through her hair as the song continued, and she thought about the prayer she'd breathed the other night in her yard. The prayer for Cade. If there was a God to hear it, she didn't know why he'd pay any heed to her, not when she'd been so blatantly defiant about her parents' religion. She had grown to hate the church and, somewhere during her college years, had decided to stop going.

Now she would give anything to be within those walls, singing that song led by her mother and soaking up the wisdom her father imparted.

That was never to be again.

But the longing was still there, to go into that building where she'd spent so many Sundays of her childhood. She felt that yearning to sit among those people who believed in a God who answered prayers. Maybe if she did, she could get them to understand the urgency of praying for Cade. Maybe then something would break and he would be found.

But she couldn't go in there. It would be hypocrisy, sitting in a church pretending to worship when you didn't believe a word of what you were hearing or singing. Instead, she turned to Cricket's. How many times had she gravitated here on Sunday morning only to sit inside the dirty little restaurant and listen to the music pouring from the windows of the building next door?

She could do it again today, but she didn't want to. She wanted to go to the church.

Maybe she did believe . . . just a little.

Quietly, she crossed the boardwalk and made her way around to the front of the building. Her parents' murder came back to her, their blood on the floor, their bodies lying there while the police investigated the scene.

She stood at the front door before going in, put her hand over her chest, and tried to breathe deeply. There were good memories here too. Mostly good ones, if the truth were known. And if Morgan and Jonathan had been able to clean up the stains of their parents' murder and come back to this building to worship each week, then she should be able to do the same.

The song ended and she waited a moment. She heard Jonathan's voice and knew he must be praying. Then the piano started up again, and they started to sing "The Old Rugged Cross." Finally, she opened the door and stepped inside.

The building was full, nothing like she remembered. From somewhere Jonathan had gotten extra pews and had put them in four rows of five pews each. He'd moved the pulpit that her father used to stand behind, and now it was more in the center of the room. Morgan sat at the piano playing the songs that they had known since they were children. Sadie sat on the second row, holding Seth.

Jonathan had had the room air-conditioned, and Blair suspected that was why so many of the sailors coming in from the sea filed in here. It probably had nothing to do with worship, she thought. They were just trying to get cool. To her, it seemed like manipulation.

She slipped into a back pew, hoping to be unnoticed, but the moment the song ended and they sat down, Jonathan met her eyes. She saw him look over at Morgan, and Morgan's face erupted into a smile.

Don't get your hopes up, Blair told them with her eyes. *I'm not here to convert.*

But she wasn't sure why she had come. She couldn't have explained it if she had tried, but as Jonathan began to preach she felt an overpowering sense of nostalgia. She would have never figured him for a preacher, yet he had learned well from her father.

She closed her eyes, and tears pinched through her eyelashes at the memory of her parents filling up this room, their spirits and souls so big that everyone who came in felt as if they'd been hugged—whether they really had or not. Oh, she missed those hugs.

She swallowed and looked around at the faces of those who had meant so much to her family. Cade should be here, she thought, sitting on that second row in the middle. He might have gotten up to lead a prayer or pass the plate for the offering.

Jonathan read from the parable about the shepherd leaving his ninety-nine sheep to look for the one. She wondered if God would do that for Cade—or if Jonathan considered *her* the one lost sheep in this group. As her mind worked on the implications of that story, Jonathan closed out the sermon. He led the group in a prayer for Cade's safety, for his health, for him to be found, or for him to return from wherever he'd been. She found hope in that. There was supposed to be power in the prayers of groups. Her parents had quoted the two-or-more Scripture so many times.

Maybe she didn't have to rely on her own meager prayers to reach the ears of God if he really did exist. Maybe he would hear the prayers of these righteous people and deliver Cade from wherever he was.

When the sermon ended, Morgan led them in "Love Lifted Me." Blair didn't sing along. Instead, she slipped out of her pew and out the front door. She could still hear the voices singing the song as she went to her car.

CHAPTER

*W*hile everyone napped after church, Jonathan paced in the office, a million frustrations whirling through his mind. Another day—and Cade was still missing.

Why wasn't there an all-out hunt for him?

He decided to go to the police station and see what was being done. Then he could decide how he could be involved.

He found Joe sitting at Cade's desk, poring over lab reports, looking even more exhausted than Morgan. "Hey," Jonathan said. "Got a minute?"

Joe nodded and rubbed his eyes. "Come on in."

Jonathan dropped down into the chair across from the desk and set his elbows on his knees. "It's been six days, Joe. What are you doing about Cade?"

"Everything I know to do." Joe leaned back in the chair. "I decided to turn his house into a crime scene. We searched it last night, but I don't think it turned up any leads. Today I'm going to have his truck moved from Cricket's so we can search it more thoroughly."

"Can't you do a full search of Ann Clark's house?"

"I wish. But I've still got to have more evidence to establish probable cause. I've finally got the Savannah Police Department looking for Cade too, but it's taken a few days to convince everybody he's really disappeared. And the letter didn't help. People who don't know him are inclined to think it's real." He rocked forward and set his jaw on his fist.

Jonathan let out a long sigh and shook his head. "What can I do, Joe? I feel like I'm letting him down, just sitting here doing nothing."

"Let the police do it, Jonathan. We have the resources and the training."

"Come on," Jonathan said. "You may be trained, but half the force is under twenty-five. They don't have the experience to solve something like this."

"It's not just us. Cops in other jurisdictions are looking, Jonathan. He's one of our own. We're not going to let it rest."

Jonathan looked down between his feet and stared at a spot on the floor. It was going to take an act of his will to leave it in their hands, he thought. He didn't know if he could do that.

Looking back up, he said, "There's one other thing I wanted to talk to you about."

"Yeah? What?"

"Last night, Sadie, my foster daughter, went to a party on the beach. Mostly teenagers, but alcohol was served. I thought there was a statute against that. I thought we weren't allowed to have parties on the beach after dark. And I want to know why no one was arrested for serving alcohol to a minor. Jim Henry told me last night that he'd been over there, but nothing was done."

Joe looked as if he had more important things to talk about. "Jonathan, I don't know anything about them serving alcohol to minors. We do have statutes, but they're not real enforceable."

"Why not?" Jonathan demanded. "All you have to do is have an officer patrol the beach. It's not that hard."

"It's harder when people have parties in their condos, and they spill out onto the beach. There's not a lot we can do about that. And I don't know, Jim might not have realized there was alcohol there."

"He *told* me there was. Why didn't he break up the party, slap them with fines, take them to jail?"

"Look, I'm sorry your foster daughter got involved in that, but don't dump it on us. We have a lot going on. The last thing I needed last night was a jail full of drunken teenagers and a lot of screaming parents."

Jonathan felt his ears growing hot. He stiffened and looked across the desk. "So you're telling me that you let it go because you don't want the hassle?"

"Hey, I didn't ask to be in charge, Jonathan. I didn't set policy. Alone, I can barely handle the murder investigation and Cade's disappearance, but you want me hovering over the night shift to make sure they crack down on every kid with a beer?"

"So who could change policy and see that you enforce the laws? The mayor?"

Joe moaned. "You know we don't have a mayor."

"No, but we're voting in June. Would you listen to *him?*"

"I'd have to," he said. "He'd be my boss."

"I thought so." Jonathan got to his feet. "Well, we'll just have to see what we can do about that."

When Jonathan got back in his car, he sat behind the wheel, tapping his hand angrily as he looked across the street to the beach where Sadie had gotten drunk last night. Maybe he really should run for mayor. Maybe then he could make sure that the laws already on the books were enforced. If he was mayor, maybe he could make them clean up the beaches so that they were a safer place for families.

As he pulled out of the parking lot and back on to Ocean Boulevard, he began to feel a growing sense of purpose. Had God called him to run for mayor? Was it something he was supposed to do?

He wouldn't tell Morgan until he'd made up his mind for sure. There was still time to talk God out of it.

CHAPTER

38

*M*organ woke from her nap midafternoon but still felt weary and unrested. She made herself get up, determined to get back to the hospital to check on Karen and the baby.

She went downstairs and found Sadie sitting outside on the back lawn, watching Seth climbing on his plastic jungle gym.

Sadie looked a little more like herself now. The hangover must have worn off, and there was a little more color to her face. Morgan pushed through the back screen door.

"Sadie, thanks for watching Seth while I slept. It was a long night."

She smiled up at her but still had trouble meeting her eyes. "I didn't watch him the whole time," she said. "He slept most of the time."

"Good. Then you got some rest too?"

"Yeah, I did."

Morgan went to Seth and picked him up, deposited him on his little slide, and watched him go down. Seth hit the dirt, then got on his knees, and crawled through the little tunnel. They could hear him laughing inside.

"I'm going back to the hospital," Morgan said. "I want to check on Karen and see how the baby's doing."

Sadie looked up at her. "Can I go with you, Morgan?"

Morgan was glad she wanted to. "Sure. I'll get Jonathan to keep Seth."

Sadie got up, and her trademark smile cut across her face. "I love tiny little babies."

"Me too," Morgan said. "You really should see him. He's so sweet. Curly black hair and this full-of-himself voice. It felt so good to hold him. I wish I'd gotten Seth when he was newborn."

Sadie's smile faded, and she gazed toward her brother. "Boy, I do too."

"I can't wait to bring them home. A newborn in the house."

"Do you think she'll let me hold him today?" Sadie asked.

"I'm sure she will."

CHAPTER

39

Karen couldn't have been happier. There had never been a time in her life when she'd felt such intense love for another human being. She had already managed to nurse without a hitch, and Emory lay cradled in her arms now, sleeping contentedly. His hair was still curly, hours after his birth, and his skin was the most beautiful shade of ebony she had ever seen. Softly, she kissed his plump little cheek.

When a knock sounded on her door, she looked up, hoping to see Morgan. But it was only a nurse. "Hello, Mrs. Miller?"

Keeping her voice low, Karen said, "Yes?"

The woman came farther into the room. "I'm afraid I need to take the baby for a few minutes. The pediatrician is on the floor, and he likes for the babies to be in the nursery so he can examine them."

She didn't want to let him go. "Can't he come in here?"

"No, I'm sorry. But don't worry. I'll bring him right back in just a few minutes."

Sighing, she kissed him again, then handed him to the nurse. The woman's long brown hair almost swept into his face. Karen thought of telling her to tie it back, that it might carry germs.

"Say bye-bye to Mommy," the woman said, then grinned back at Karen. "Get some rest."

Karen nodded and watched them leave. Laying her head back on her pillow, she checked her watch, and hoped that the doctor wouldn't take long.

But a half hour passed, and the nurse didn't come back. Finally, she pressed the buzzer.

"Yes?" a nurse called from the station.

"I was wondering if the doctor was finished with the babies yet. I expected to have mine brought back by now."

There was a long pause. "Isn't your baby in your room with you?"

Karen's chest tightened. "No. A nurse came and took him. She never brought him back!"

She waited for a reply, but none came. Frustrated, she pressed the button again.

Her door flung open and two nurses came in. The alarm on their faces was unmistakable. "Miss Miller, are you sure a nurse took your baby?"

"Positive. She said the doctor was on the floor. . . ."

"Miss Miller, the doctor hasn't been here this morning. None of our nurses told you that."

She stared at them for a moment. "What are you saying? She came right in here and took my baby—"

One of the nurses dashed out of the room. "I'll call the police!"

"The police?" Suddenly it was all clear to Karen. Her baby had been kidnapped, just like those other babies she'd heard about on the news. "No. She was a nurse. She had on a nurse's uniform!"

"Miss Miller, your baby isn't in the nursery. Please—describe the woman to me."

A sense of horror settled over Karen.

Her baby was gone.

CHAPTER

There was a commotion in the hall when Morgan and Sadie reached Karen's floor. Several police officers stood among a cluster of nurses, as if taking statements.

"What's going on?" Sadie whispered.

Morgan shook her head. "Maybe Karen will know."

She got to Karen's door and heard wailing from the other side. Without knocking, she pushed the door open.

Karen was on her bare feet, still in her hospital gown, and two men stood with her. It was clear that she had been weeping. She turned as Morgan came in. "Oh, Morgan, thank God you're here!"

Morgan crossed the room and embraced the woman. "Karen, what is it?"

"My baby! She took my baby."

"Who did?"

"Some woman who looked like a nurse, only no one here knows her! I waited and waited for her to bring him back, and when I asked about it, nobody knew who she was. She had a thirty-minute head start out of the building. They have video of her just walking out with my baby!"

Morgan felt the blood draining from her face. She looked at the two men.

"I'm Detective Hull, Savannah Police Department," one of them said. "This is Officer Coleman."

Morgan introduced herself. "You don't think it's that kidnapper, do you? The one who's taken all those other babies?"

"It looks like it."

"They have to find him!" Karen wailed. "Please, you need to go look for them. She's probably still in her car. Do one of those Amber Alert things, so people will know."

Detective Hull looked as if he was one step ahead of her. "Ma'am, we're putting out an alert as we speak, and we have roadblocks being set up. They're going to be looking for a white woman in green scrubs with long brown hair."

"She was small," Karen said, "not as tall as me, and that long brown hair. If they set up roadblocks they'll see my baby, won't they? How many day-old babies are there out there?" She swung around to Morgan. "He's just a few hours old, Morgan. What if he's not all right?"

Morgan looked back at Sadie. She stood back at the door, listening in horror. Her face was white.

Morgan knew she was remembering her own baby brother, in the grips of evil.

The memory of five other kidnapped babies reeled through Morgan's mind. One in Hilton Head, others in Pensacola and Mobile, the most recent from St. Joseph's here in Savannah.

"We've also called in the FBI," Hull said. "Since the babies have been taken from three different states, they're taking over the case."

"Have they found any of them?" Karen demanded. "Even one?"

"Not yet, ma'am. All of the babies are still missing. But this might just be the case that helps us find the rest of them."

CHAPTER

*J*onathan came as soon as he'd heard about the baby's kidnapping. When the FBI had finished "sweeping" the hospital and questioning Karen, Jonathan realized there was nothing more he could do. Dismally, he left Morgan with Karen and drove Sadie home.

Sadie was quiet as he drove, her silence broken only by sniffs.

First Cade and now Karen's baby. And all that following the murder of his in-laws just a few months ago. It was as if the world tipped off its axis. . . .

Sadie got a tissue out of the box sitting on the seat and blew her nose. "Jonathan, I'm so sorry I gave you guys more to worry about last night. It all seems so stupid with so many desperate things going on."

"It's okay, Sadie. We'll get over it, as long as it doesn't happen again."

She wiped her face. "That poor little baby. It's just like when Jack had Seth."

"Maybe not." It was starting to rain, and rivulets of water streamed down his windshield. He turned his wipers on. "I was just trying to think why a person would kidnap a little baby like that. Maybe it wasn't a violent thing, like when an older child gets kidnapped. Maybe it's somebody who's just desperate to have a child of their own. . . ."

Sadie looked at him hopefully. "Somebody like you and Morgan?"

He frowned. Did everyone realize how much he and Morgan wanted a baby? He hadn't told more than a couple of people. "Maybe someone like us, only more desperate."

"That makes me feel a little better," Sadie whispered.

He glanced at her. "Why?"

"Because maybe it's somebody nice. Not somebody like Jack. Maybe it's somebody who loves babies, who'll take care of him. Maybe they won't hurt him, and he'll be found in one piece."

He drove in silence for a while, making her hope into a quiet prayer.

Sadie hadn't been home more than an hour when the phone rang. She answered it quickly, hoping it was news about the baby. "Hanover House."

"Sadie? Good. It's you. I didn't want to get you in trouble."

She recognized Trevor's voice and looked around to see if she would be heard. No one was in the kitchen, and Jonathan sat out on the sunporch with Seth. She pulled the phone cord into the office.

"Trevor?"

"I was going to hang up if anyone else answered."

She drew in a deep breath. "You shouldn't have called. I shouldn't even be talking to you."

"Well, I was worried about you. I just heard about that baby being kidnapped. The news said that the mother lived at Hanover House."

"Yeah. It's Karen, the new tenant."

"I figured you were all freaked out and everything. I wanted to call and see if you were okay."

She raked her hair back from her face and tried to force away those warm fuzzy feelings he always invoked. "I'm fine. But I can't talk. I have to go."

"No, don't do that," he said. "Come on, Sadie. We had something good going between us."

She swallowed and checked the kitchen again. "Look, Trevor, I got caught when I got home last night. I was drunk. I lied to them and deceived them, and then I got drunk. That's not the kind of person I want to be."

"I can understand that."

She thought of the way he'd groped her out on the beach, Crystal's predictions coming true. "I'm so embarrassed by everything that happened—"

"What happened?" he asked. "Nothing happened."

"Something happened, all right. I wasn't so drunk that I don't remember that. Crystal Lewis said you were only with me for one thing. And you pretty much proved her point."

"What did *I* do?"

"What did you do?" she repeated. She looked out and saw Jonathan pushing through the screen door with Seth on his hip, walking out into the yard. "Let's just say you got a little too aggressive."

"Oh, that," he said, and she heard a chuckle in his voice. "Sadie, I was drunk too. I won't judge you for what you did drunk, if you won't judge me."

That stopped her. She leaned back against the wall, wondering if she was, indeed, being judgmental. She hated that and didn't want to be accused of it.

It was true. He had been drunk. And didn't everyone act out of character when they'd been drinking?

"Look," he said, "if it means that much to you, I'll promise to be nothing but a perfect gentleman from now on. And no more alcohol when I'm with you."

She wanted to believe him, but Morgan's and Jonathan's voices kept playing through her mind. "Why do you even want to go out with me when you could have any girl in the school you want? It doesn't even make sense."

She could hear in his voice that that pleased him. "It's you I want, Sadie. Are you so down on yourself that you can't believe someone would want you?"

"I'm just not your usual type."

He laughed. "That's a good thing. I'm raising my standards, okay? You're the smartest and the best looking and the most interesting."

Those didn't sound like Crystal Lewis's reasons. Maybe he was being straight with her.

"Come on," he said. "Go out with me again. I promise not to take you to any wild parties. I promise. I just want to spend time with you. And you know you need to talk, after all this with the baby."

Confusion settled into her heart. She had promised Jonathan and Morgan that she wouldn't drink again, and she intended to keep that promise. But what would it hurt just to spend a little more time with him?

"I don't want to let Morgan and Jonathan down again. They've made it clear that they don't want me with you."

"So it won't be a date. You'll just go for a walk along the beach and run into me. We'll get a Coke somewhere. It doesn't have to be a big deal. I want to hear about the kidnapping. We'll just talk."

Sadie looked out the door and saw that Jonathan was still in the yard. "I don't know, Trevor. I'm just not sure it's worth all the trouble I could get into."

"Sadie, you're going to have to decide if I'm worth it."

That was just it, she thought. She hadn't decided that.

"When you do, I'll be waiting. Just call me, and I'll meet you anywhere you say."

She listened to him hang up and kept holding the phone to her ear as the dial tone clicked on.

As she hung up, she made her decision. She wasn't going to let Morgan and Jonathan down again, whether Trevor was worth it or not.

CHAPTER

*T*he tenants of Hanover House waited in the living room as Morgan brought Karen home the next day. Silence hung over the room, much like the silence after the days of Thelma and Wayne's murder.

Karen hadn't wanted to leave the hospital. She had fought to stay until her baby was found, as if part of her believed that Emory lay hidden somewhere within that building and would forever be out of her grasp if she left that place.

Several FBI agents had turned their parlor into a communications center, in case the kidnappers made contact. They sat in there now, talking silently as they prepared for any call that might come.

Sadie had made tea and pulled Karen into the kitchen. Gus, Felicia, and Mrs. Hern followed her in, all of them looking as if they wanted to help but didn't know how. Sadie poured her a cup, then hugged the forlorn mother. "Karen, I'm so sorry. I know what it's like to worry about a little baby being in trouble. It's an awful feeling."

Karen nodded silently and wiped her red eyes. "I just don't understand why anybody would want my baby. Why *my* baby? Why not somebody else's? There were so many of them there. Why did they choose my room to come into?"

Morgan had already asked that question. "She seems to be targeting single moms. Maybe it's because there's no dad in the room to stop them."

Karen couldn't drink her tea. She looked weak and bent over, her face gaunt and unhealthy. She hadn't eaten at all since the baby disappeared. Morgan had spent the night at the hospital with her last night, but neither of them had slept.

"Honey, why don't you go up and lie down? Jonathan took your suitcase up."

Karen nodded weakly. "I just want to be alone for a while. You'll call me if anything happens?"

"Of course."

She watched her go up the stairs, then turned back to Gus and Felicia, Mrs. Hern and Sadie.

"What can we do, Miss Morgan?" Felicia asked her.

"Pray," Morgan said. "She's a wreck, and who could blame her?" She sank into a chair, and dropped her face into her hands. "Who ever would have thought we'd have two people close to us missing like this? It's just unbelievable."

And as Morgan started to cry, the tenants who were used to receiving Morgan's comfort did their best to comfort her.

CHAPTER

43

*C*ade shivered with fever when Ann Clark came back to him. He'd heard voices from the vent for the last several hours—a man and a woman embroiled in an argument, and a baby's incessant crying. Part of the time he thought he might be dreaming, but now as the sound of the scraping bookshelves pulled him from his sleep, he came fully awake and knew it was real.

The door opened and Ann came in. She had food again—a burger and fries this time—and a Walgreen's bag.

She took one look at him. "You're getting sick. I don't want you to die of those wounds. I have other plans for your death."

He swallowed and sat up. His leg had swollen and was still bloody and black with bruises, and bone stuck through the skin.

She pulled some bandage material and a bottle of alcohol out of the bag.

"Do you have antibiotics?" he asked.

"No," she said. "This'll have to do."

She pulled back the cloth that Cade had already ripped on his pants leg and cringed at the sight of his wound.

She opened the rubbing alcohol and poured it over his leg, letting it run down onto the bloody sheets.

He arched his back with the pain but lay as still as he could, knowing he needed it. She began to clean the dried, congealed blood, then wrapped a bandage around his leg. It was a haphazard job, but it was better than nothing.

He heard the baby crying through the vent again. So did she, and she stopped wrapping and looked up. He saw surprise on her face, as if she hadn't realized sound would carry down here.

"How old is your baby?" he asked.

She looked stunned. "What baby?"

"The baby I keep hearing. I know it must be very painful to lose your husband when your baby is so young."

"That's the television," she said. "I don't have any children."

She kept working, finished wrapping his calf, then moved to the wound on his side and peeled back the cloth.

He could shove her back, try to escape again, but he knew for certain that the mystery person was still in the house, that he would shoot him again from the top of the stairs, that this time he would kill him without a thought. Besides, he couldn't step on his leg, much less run.

The alcohol stung, but he prayed that it would help the wound. He lay still as she taped the bandage to his bloody side.

"I have to change your sheets," she said. "Get up."

He moved with great effort, but managed to pull up and stand on his good leg. She pulled the sheets off his bed, then backed out of the room, her eyes on him, and grabbed a set of clean sheets she had left in the outer part of the basement.

He felt dizzy, nauseated, as he leaned against the wall.

The room smelled less rank now. He was grateful for that.

When she was finished, she stepped back to the door.

"Thank you," he said.

She didn't meet his eyes. "Eat your dinner."

She left him alone then, locked in his vault, and he heard those bookshelves being pushed back in front of the door.

He sat down, propped his leg back up on the mattress, and ate the first meal he'd had in days.

CHAPTER

The parlor at Hanover House had quickly been transformed into command central, from which FBI agents working on the kidnapping case had come and gone since yesterday. They prepared to record any ransom calls that might come in, and each time the phone rang, recording equipment launched and tracing began.

It seemed to Morgan that the whole focus of their lives had shifted to the missing baby. She tried to go about her daily duties without getting in the agents' way, but it was difficult to keep the house running smoothly.

Seth was on edge, fussy and nervous from the extra traffic in the house, so she tried to keep him upstairs with her as much as she could. She had finally rocked him to sleep and put him down for a nap, when she heard Karen sobbing from her room just down the hall.

Her heart swelled and her throat tightened. She remembered that grief well.

She thought of knocking on Karen's door and trying to comfort her, but the woman had rebuffed her efforts earlier. Inconsolable, she'd told her she just needed to be alone.

The sound of that unquenchable grief was too much to bear, so she went to the closed door of her parents' room, and stepped inside.

The room remained as they'd left it a few months ago, except that her parents' smells had faded. But the quilt folded at the foot of their bed still spoke of love and warmth. She went to her father's side of the bed and ran her hand across the comforter where the mattress dipped.

What would her parents say about all this tragedy?

Their own murder, Cade's disappearance, and now this baby being snatched out of its mother's arms.

It was too much. She curled up on the bed and pulled the quilt up to cover her.

Fresh tears began to seize her, and she let her grief climb to its peak inside her, then spill over onto her parents' comforter.

So many tears had been shed in this very place in the last few months.

She wondered what her parents would say or do about this missing baby and the grieving woman in her room.

She needed to talk to Blair. She needed to tell her about the baby. She needed to cry on her sister's shoulder.

Her parents' phone still sat on the bed table. Still crying, she picked it up and dialed Blair's number. It rang four times, then her voice mail kicked in. "Blair, call me. I have some more bad news. Karen's baby was kidnapped. Please call!"

Where was she? Hadn't she heard about the missing baby on the news yet? Why hadn't she called?

Fear and worry welled up inside her as she hung up. Had she gone back to Savannah to watch Ann Clark's house again? The danger in that, if Ann indeed had something to do with Cade, struck her.

What if something happened to Blair next? What if the phone rang and it was more police with more bad news. . . .

The idea of that sent her over the edge, and she wilted and sobbed into the quilt clutched in her hands.

A light knock sounded on the door, and it opened. Jonathan stepped inside. "Honey, are you all right?"

She nodded and pressed the quilt against her mouth. "She's not home. I tried to call her. . . ."

He came to her side. "Who's not?"

"Blair. Where is she?"

"She's okay. You don't have to worry about her."

"I need to talk to her!" Her voice broke off at its highest pitch. He sat down and pulled her against him.

She clutched his shoulder with one hand and his shirt with the other, and wept like an abandoned child against his chest. He held her quietly as she cried.

"That little baby. That poor little baby. I watched him coming, Jonathan, his little wet head and his scrunched up little shoulders. And he was all purple, and he let out this yell. And I got to hold him. . . ."

"He'll be okay. You'll see."

"But what if he's not? And what if Cade's not? What if they both wind up like Mama and Pop? And where is Blair?"

"Blair is fine. She's a big girl. And we just have to trust that God knows where that baby is, and he knows where Cade is. They're in his hands. We can't do anything for them except pray, and that's plenty. And we can support Karen and be there for her through this."

"She's already had such a hard life. Why her? Why this baby?"

"We'll never know that." He stroked her hair and lay down next to her.

"It's just one more reproach against Hanover House," she said. "People will say that nothing good ever happens to the people here."

He stroked her arm. "I thought maybe I could deter that. I thought I might go to the city council meeting tonight. I was going to skip it this once because of the kidnapping, but I realized that I need to be there more than ever. They'll talk about Cade for sure, and probably something will come up about the baby and Hanover House. I just want to be there. Would you be okay if I went?"

"Sure, go ahead." She pulled a tissue out of the box on her mother's bed table. It was almost empty. She didn't want it to run out.

Dabbing at her nose, she said, "I'll be okay in a minute. I just needed to have a little nervous breakdown. Nothing serious." Getting up, she blew her nose. Jonathan stood and pulled her back into his arms.

"We'll get through all this too, Morgan," he whispered. "We're strong."

She knew it was true, though her fears seemed to have banished whatever strength she had left.

CHAPTER

45

*B*lair didn't check her messages when she got home that morning. She'd been at Washington Square all night, sitting in her car and watching the lights in Ann Clark's house. She had walked around the block to get closer to the house without trespassing, and had lingered on a park bench across the street.

But she had seen nothing. It was as if the woman never came out. She hated to leave this morning, for fear that the woman did go out during the day. But she'd feared falling asleep in her car and calling attention to herself.

She saw the message light blinking on her voice mail, but didn't feel like listening to people calling to ask why the library wasn't open. Instead, she clicked through her caller ID for the police department's number.

But Joe hadn't called her, so he must not have any information about Cade.

She went to her bedroom and shed her clothes, put on a big T-shirt, and climbed into her bed. Her body sank into the mattress, but her mind would not relax.

How could she sleep when Cade was in trouble?

She lay there with her eyes open, and saw her father's Bible lying on her bed table.

She had planned to do more research about the cities of refuge, but she had almost forgotten it as her search for Cade had occupied her mind.

But it was her last link to him. That morning he'd disappeared, he had read of those cities. He'd been consumed with guilt over the man he had killed, and it was clear that he'd longed for a place where his guilt could be justified.

Wearily, she gave up the idea of sleep and sat up. Grabbing the Bible, she turned back to Numbers 35. Her eyes scanned the passage again, and she paid careful attention to the distinctions God had made between murder and unintentional killing.

Beside that passage, her father had written, "Matthew 5:21–22."

She turned to Matthew, and found those verses in red. Jesus had spoken them.

> *You have heard that it was said to the people long ago, "Do not murder, and anyone who murders will be subject to judgment." But I tell you that anyone who is angry with his brother will be subject to judgment. Again, anyone who says to his brother, "Raca," is answerable to the Sanhedrin. But anyone who says, "You fool!" will be in danger of the fire of hell.*

She sat back, staring at those words. This was why she couldn't buy into her parents' theology. How could Jesus assign equal punishment to murderers and those who called someone a fool?

That didn't even make sense. Was Jesus saying that if we were angry with someone, we were like killers? That we were *all* manslayers?

If her anger and hatred toward those who got in her way made her a killer, then Blair would be on death row.

Beside that verse, her father had written, "1 Peter 5:8."

She turned there, and found the verse.

Be self-controlled and alert. Your enemy the devil prowls around like a roaring lion looking for someone to devour.

She frowned and set the Bible down. Why had her father gone from the cities of refuge, to Jesus's words about murder being a heart thing, to the devil waiting to devour?

Her father had left the clues. It was her job to put them together.

She thought of her own anger and hatred and bitterness, feelings that heaped blood-guilt upon her. It was a heavy burden. Who could honestly not hate? Who could not get angry?

By Christ's standards, everyone carried around a heavy load of bloodguilt. Satan was roaming around, trying to catch one of them outside the city walls, hoping to devour them.

But if hatred and anger were the equivalent of killing, and if Satan was like the Avenger, then what was the City of Refuge?

None of it really made much sense. Yet it had been important enough to her father to have it marked up in his Bible. And it had been vital to Cade, who'd been studying it that morning.

Had Ann Clark become Cade's Avenger? And if so, where could Cade run for refuge? Was there any hope for him?

Frustrated, she closed the Bible and got back under her covers. She wouldn't think of those mythical cities again. There weren't answers there. Only more questions, and as hard as she tried to make all the dots connect, they were not going to lead her to Cade.

CHAPTER

46

*T*he weekly City Council meeting was not usually well attended, unless there was a controversy of some sort brewing. Jonathan tried to make every meeting just to ensure that the Council didn't pull anything underhanded. Just months ago they had tried to shut down Hanover House, until evidence surfaced that the mayor had ulterior motives.

Though the members were duly elected by the people of Cape Refuge, Jonathan often wondered if any thought had gone into their placement or if voters simply marked the name of their cousin or neighbor or anyone whose name they recognized, just so they could say they'd voted. Character didn't seem to play a role.

The small city hall stood on Ocean Boulevard across from the beach. Jonathan pulled his car onto the gravel parking lot. The meeting was already in session, so Jonathan went in and slipped into one of the middle rows. The members droned on about whether to put a stop sign at River Road and Third Street.

Jonathan tapped his foot nervously, wishing they'd move ahead.

"Next on the agenda," Art Russell said, "is the matter of the beach cams that Chief Cade has asked to have put up all over the beach." He fanned himself with a paper fan with the face of one of the mayoral candidates on it, and looked around the room. "I see that Cade isn't back from his honeymoon yet, so he isn't here to argue his case."

Jonathan almost leaped out of his shoes. Had they heard about the letter? Did they really believe it?

Doug Shepherd propped his chin like he might fall off to sleep. "If he don't care enough to come to the meeting and tell us why he thinks we need these, Art, then I say we go ahead and vote on it."

Sarah Williford weighed in. "We can put it off till next time. Wouldn't hurt anything."

"But the plain simple truth is that we don't have the money in the budget for no security cameras on the beach," Art said. "And I don't see why we need them, anyway."

Jonathan could see where this was going. They would vote against it tonight, ending any discussion, and when Cade got back he'd find his proposal dead in the water.

"Does anybody have any discussion on this?" Art asked.

Jonathan got up. "I do, Art."

"Step to the microphone, please, Jonathan."

Jonathan knew the mike wasn't necessary when there were no more than a dozen or so people in the room, the Council included. But he stepped up to it, nonetheless.

"First, I'd like to say that I don't know how you people found out about the letter that allegedly came from Cade, but I can tell you that not even the police are taking it seriously. Cade is not on his honeymoon."

"You're entitled to your opinion," Art said. "Now, if that's all—"

"No, it's not all," Jonathan cut in. "Most of you probably know about our tenant whose baby was kidnapped Sunday."

Sarah perked up. "Yes, Jonathan. Have they come any closer to finding it?"

"No," he said. "But one of the strongest pieces of evidence they have is the video of the woman leaving with the baby. There were cameras in the hall, the elevators, and at each door. If they find her, that video will help convict her."

Sarah looked fascinated, as though she'd just been given insider information on the juiciest piece of gossip in town. "Can they see her face in the video?"

Jonathan didn't see any point in feeding her morbid curiosity. "I can't really talk about the case beyond that, Sarah. My point in bringing it up is that cameras on the beaches would be a big deterrent to crime and would help get convictions. They'd help police to enforce the laws already on the books."

"What laws?" Art asked.

Jonathan cleared his throat. "Laws, for instance, about parties on the beaches at night."

"But it's communism, Jonathan," Morris Ambrose, the lone conservative, said. "We don't need to put Big Brother cameras all over this island, infringing on people's privacy."

"Why not?" Jonathan asked. "We have them in hospitals, convenience stores, banks, grocery stores. A lot of towns have them at red lights. They work in cutting down crime."

"Jonathan, we understand your concern for your foster daughter," Doug said. "But just because Sadie got drunk Saturday night don't mean the whole island should be videotaped twenty-four–seven."

Jonathan grabbed the microphone and shot Doug a killer look. "The City Council is not supposed to be a breeding ground for gossip, Doug, and if you want to make one more comment about Sadie, you and I can step outside—"

"All right!" Art hammered the gavel. "Thank you, Jonathan." It was meant to dismiss him, but he kept standing there.

"I guess we will go ahead and vote. We seem to have our minds made up."

"You can't do that." Jonathan's angry voice cut across the room.

The council members looked up at him. "Why not?" Sarah asked.

"Because Cade isn't here. As police chief of this town, he should have the right to make his case."

"He gave up his rights when he skipped town," Doug piped in. "He should have thought about them beach cams before he run off."

"He didn't run off!" Jonathan bit the words out. "That letter was clearly written under coercion. Anyone who knows Cade knows that he would never rush off and get married like that. He would have put a lot of thought and prayer into getting married, and he would have wanted his fiancée to know his friends. He wouldn't have hidden her."

"We'd expect you to think that," Sarah said. "Being his best friend and all. But most everybody believes that Cade is off on his honeymoon, and any day now he'll be back with his new wife. But his whims shouldn't control this body. So if you'll sit down, Jonathan, we're going to go ahead and vote."

Jonathan sat down, gritting his teeth, as every one of the members voted no. He hoped Cade would appreciate his feeble effort to defend the cause. He knew Cade probably had specific crime statistics, stories of crimes that could have been avoided with greater security on the beaches, other towns' success rates.

"Next up," Art said, "is that we have to name an interim police chief in Cade's absence."

"I say we name a permanent chief," Sarah said. "We don't need somebody as irresponsible as that boy running the police force on Cape Refuge."

"Well," Art said, "I think we can deal with that at some point in the future, but for right now, do I hear a motion that we appoint Joe to run things? He's the second-in-command and is already filling in. We'd just be making it official."

"So moved," Doug said.

"Second," Sarah added.

"Any discussion?"

Jonathan got up again. "I have something to say, Art."

Art sighed. "What is it now, Jonathan?"

"First of all, I'd like to point out that Cade hasn't even been gone more than a few days, and if I'm not mistaken, he did have some personal leave that he'd accrued. Except for a couple of days here and there when we've gone diving down in the Keys, Cade hasn't had a real vacation since he took the job. So there's no reason to get all in an uproar over his absence."

"Thank you for your comment," Art said with clear condescension. "Sit down, Jonathan."

His face burned. "No, I'm not finished. I wanted to point out that without a mayor you don't really have the right to make any decisions regarding the chief of police. When the new mayor is elected, *he* will decide who the chief is going to be. So unless you want a real fight, I suggest that you give Cade a chance to be found before you go naming interim chiefs!"

Dismissing him again, Art looked at the other members. "On whether or not to appoint Joe as interim chief, all in favor?"

Everyone on the council said "aye," and none was opposed.

Jonathan sank back down. These people couldn't be reasoned with.

"Next on the agenda," Sarah said. "Sue Ellen Jargis has a complaint about the library."

Jonathan rolled his eyes and watched as Sue Ellen headed for the microphone. Dressed in some kind of designer garb, she seemed to wear every piece in her jewelry box draped around her neck or wrist, or jangling from her ears.

She cleared her throat. "Ladies and gentlemen of the city council," she said in a saccharine voice. "I feel it is my duty to let you know that our town's library is being neglected and mismanaged. I went in there last Friday in the middle of the day, looking for some Italian tapes. My husband and I are going there next month—to Italy, I mean. More specifically, to Rome, Milan, and Vienna."

Jonathan smirked. "Uh, Sue Ellen, Vienna's in Austria, not Italy."

She could have murdered him with her look. "Of course it is. I meant to say Venice. I certainly know the difference between Venice and Vienna." She softened her tone and turned back to the microphone. "Anyway, as I was saying, I went looking for tapes, and Blair Owens practically threw me out the door, telling me she was closing early, even though the sign on the door said that her hours are nine to six. I came back the next day *and* the next, and both times the library was closed."

"Give me a break!" Jonathan said, coming to his feet again. "Sue Ellen, you know darn well that Blair is preoccupied with Cade's disappearance. Everyone on this island ought to be!"

The woman wouldn't be daunted. "Furthermore," she said, talking over him. "Gray Foster, a college student who uses the library a lot, told me she's left him there alone while she traipses off to who-knows-where.

"Now I think that if the city of Cape Refuge is paying Blair Owens to run the library, she should be expected to keep it open at regular hours. I think that woman needs to be fired for neglect and rude treatment of its patrons."

Jonathan had lost his temper at city council meetings before, but until now, he'd never wanted to hurt anyone. "Blair has never given anyone a reason to question her handling of the library before! Not once!"

Art sat back in his expensive chair and crossed one hairy leg over the other. "Very interesting. We appreciate your bringing this to our attention, Sue Ellen. And Jonathan, we appreciate your defense of your sister-in-law. We'll take this matter under advisement."

Jonathan sank back down. "Whatever that means."

When the meeting was over, he stalked back out to his truck and sat behind the wheel as the council members came out. Sarah Williford threw one flip-flopped foot over her Harley and cranked it up, letting the deafening roar of the motor pollute the peace of the town. Morris got into his Jaguar and pulled out. Doug and

Art had ridden together in Doug's pickup. They laughed about stopping by Cricket's for a beer before going home.

Oh, how the town needed a decent mayor, he thought. And so far the mayoral candidates were nothing but more of the same. Nothing would change if either of them got elected.

But if Jonathan were elected . . .

He started dreaming about the changes he would make, the commonsense approach he would use to matters that came up on the city council's agenda. Maybe he could set a new tone, absent the greed and lack of compassion characteristic of these people now.

As he started his truck and headed back to Hanover House, Jonathan made up his mind. He might not win, but he was going to give it a good run for his money.

He only wished the town had a newspaper so he could get the word out.

*M*organ tried again to call Blair after Jonathan came home from the city council meeting, but there was still no answer.

When her voice mail answered again, Morgan tried to keep her voice level.

"Blair, where are you? By now you must have heard about Karen's baby being kidnapped, and you haven't called. I'm starting to think that you've vanished too. Come on, Blair, help me out here. I need to hear from you."

When she hadn't yet heard from Blair by midnight, she and Jonathan drove to her house. Her car was not out front.

"Okay, that's a good sign," Jonathan said. "When Cade disappeared he left his truck. If Blair took her car, then chances are nothing's happened to her."

Morgan wasn't convinced. "I still want to go in."

They used Morgan's key to unlock the door and cautiously stepped inside.

The living room was dark, a breeding place for shadows. The pale yellow walls did little to brighten the place. Morgan turned on the light and looked around. The room had always looked much more feminine than anyone would have expected of Blair. Morgan and her mother had helped her decorate a couple of years ago, but the choices had been Blair's.

She looked around and saw that some of the sofa cushions were on the floor, as if Blair might have lain down on the couch.

She pictured her sister sitting up late, terrors about Cade at war in her mind.

Jonathan passed her and went into the kitchen. "It's a mess in here," he said. "If she's been home she's been in a hurry."

Morgan stepped into the kitchen and saw a few dishes and cereal boxes sitting out on the counter. Blair had never been the most domestic one in the family, but she did at least do her dishes.

Jonathan left her there and went into the bedroom. "Bed's not made."

Morgan walked back through the living room to Blair's bedroom. She had slept here herself a number of times, mostly after her parents died, when Jonathan was wrongly imprisoned. Even in her grief, Blair had kept it relatively neat, but tonight a week's worth of clothes hung over a chair and several pairs of discarded socks lay on the floor.

"Okay, here we go." Jonathan picked up her alarm clock and pushed the "wake" button. "She must have been home at some point today, because it was set to go off at 2:00 P.M. Looks like it went off and was reset for tomorrow."

"Are you sure?"

"Yeah. If she hadn't turned it off, it would still be buzzing. Now it's set for 2:00 P.M. tomorrow."

Morgan took the clock. "What is she doing?"

Jonathan shook his head. "You don't think she's been staking out the Clark house all night, do you?"

Morgan looked at him. "I'd be willing to bet that's exactly what she's doing."

"Well, at least there's no sign that she's in trouble." He glanced at the Bible that lay on her pillow. "Look at that. Blair has a Bible?"

Morgan picked it up. "It's Pop's. I gave it to her. She was interested in the cities of refuge."

Jonathan nodded. "Because of what Cade's Bible was open to. Well, looks like she's been reading it. Maybe it'll do her some good."

Morgan set the Bible back down and looked around for anymore clues.

"Let's go home," Jonathan said. "Leave her a note telling her we've been here, and threaten her life if she doesn't call you the minute she comes in."

Morgan left her a scathing note, then wearily, they locked the door and went back to the pickup. As they drove home, she wished she'd found something more conclusive. She wanted to talk to Blair, needed to hear her voice.

Silently she prayed that she hadn't met the same fate as Cade and the baby.

C H A P T E R

*M*organ lay awake for most of the night and got up with Seth at six in the morning. When the phone rang at eight, she ran to the parlor, where Agent Tavist sat with his recording equipment. He gave the signal, and she picked it up.

"Hello?"

"It's me." Blair's voice was hoarse with fatigue.

Relief washed like warm honey through Morgan's body. She motioned to the agent that it was okay. No kidnapper.

"Blair, where have you been?"

"Looking for Cade."

"Are you crazy?"

"Morgan, what's this about the baby?"

Morgan sighed and glanced at the agent. He was still taping. "He was kidnapped right out of her arms in the hospital, Blair. Don't you listen to the news?"

"Kidnapped? How?"

"A woman impersonating a nurse told Karen the doctor was on the floor and needed to see the baby."

Silence hung between them for a moment. "What is going on?" Blair said finally. "Morgan, I'm so sorry I haven't called. How is Karen?"

"As well as can be expected." She wanted to tell her about the FBI agent and the recording equipment, but it didn't seem like the right thing to do.

"Morgan, are you all right?"

Morgan breathed a laugh. "You know me."

She could tell Blair was crying now. "The two of us are a real pair," Blair said. Silence again, then, "If only Cade were here. I'll bet he could find that baby."

Morgan rubbed her eyes. "Blair, Jonathan went to the City Council meeting last night, and there was a complaint about you."

"What kind of complaint?"

"Sue Ellen Jargis complained that you've been closing the library. You're going to lose your job if you don't watch it."

"Don't worry about it. There's nobody else on this island qualified to run it." She sighed. "I don't want to talk about it right now."

"Okay," Morgan said. "Go get some sleep."

Blair didn't move to hang up. "Morgan?"

"Yeah?"

Another pause, then, "Do you think that Cade ran off and got married?"

Morgan tried to focus her thoughts. "No, Blair. I don't think that."

"Good," she whispered. "I don't either."

Morgan wasn't sure if she heard doubt in Blair's voice. "Blair, please don't kill yourself trying to rescue Cade. I'm worried about you getting into trouble yourself. Getting hurt, maybe killed. If you're right and Ann Clark had something to do with his disappearance, she could be a very dangerous woman."

"I hear you," Blair said.

"And you need to eat. Why don't you come over here for supper?"

"Can't."

Morgan frowned. "You're going to go back to Savannah again?"

"Don't worry about it, Morgan. You do what you have to do to find the baby, and I'll do what I have to do to find Cade."

Morgan didn't like the way that sounded. Tears stung her eyes, and she twisted her face and tried to control her voice. "Be careful, Blair."

"I will."

When Morgan hung up, she stared down at the phone and wept into her hand. "Lord, help us."

"Amen." She looked up and saw Karen standing in the doorway, her eyes swollen and her arms crossed over her fleshy stomach.

Morgan went to her and pulled her into her arms, and Karen fell apart again. "I handed my baby over to a maniac," she whispered. "I let her walk away with him."

Morgan didn't know how to assuage that guilt, so she just clung to her as they both wept out their grief.

CHAPTER

*T*he phone woke Blair up, and she pulled herself out of the fog of her sleep and squinted at the clock. Twelve o'clock . . . midnight? No, noon.

She grabbed the phone up. "Hello?"

"Blair, this is Sarah Williford."

Blair fell back onto her pillow. What did the city councilwoman want?

"I can't believe I finally got you on the phone. Where in the world have you been? I've left messages—"

"What is it, Sarah? Cut to the chase."

Sarah paused, as if making note of Blair's abruptness. "We've had some complaints about you keeping the library closed, Blair."

Blair thought of hanging up the phone, but decided that wouldn't be prudent. She sat up in bed, clutching the phone to her ear. It was time to get up anyway. She'd slept for four hours, and that was enough. She had to get back to the Clark house. "Yeah? And?"

"And I wondered if you intend to open the library today?"

"Wasn't planning on it, Sarah."

Sarah gave an indignant grunt. "And may I ask why?"

Blair stiffened. "Sarah, how many times have I done this in the years since I've been running it?"

"Well, I don't know, Blair, but you've done it a lot lately. What am I supposed to tell people who are complaining? We pay you to work there so that people can have access to it. If you're not going to do that, then we're going to have to make other arrangements."

Blair got up then. "You can't fire me, Sarah. You don't have the authority. The mayor has to fire me, and last I looked, we don't have one."

"Think again, Blair. The City Council has the authority to make decisions about the running of this town during the mayor's absence. And I should tell you that we do have an alternative. The Cape Refuge Ladies' Auxiliary has expressed interest in taking on the library as one of their projects. They could run it on shifts, if it comes to that."

Blair thought of ripping the cord out of the wall and flinging the phone across the room. "The Ladies' Auxiliary? So you think they could do a better job?"

"They would keep it open during its regular hours! I don't see what else they'd have to do. The place practically runs itself."

Now Blair was fully awake, and nuclear rage shot through her head. "You know what, Sarah? I think you should do that."

"Do what?"

"Let the Ladies' Auxiliary run it. Because I quit."

Sarah's silence screamed over the line. "Blair, I do suggest that you think this over."

"No," Blair said in a dramatic voice. "Far be it from me to stand in your way when you have a better option. Let the Ladies' Auxiliary run it. I'm sure they'll do a bang-up job."

"Blair, is this about Cade?"

Now Blair was speechless. "What?"

"Is this all about Cade? Jonathan said that you were distracted trying to find him. I don't know why you can't accept, like everyone else, that he's married and on his honeymoon. You're going to feel foolish when he comes back with his new bride, and you've up and quit your job so that you can spend your time obsessing over him."

Trembling now, Blair clutched the phone to her ear and leaned over, as if looking into the woman's face. "And you're going to feel foolish when he's found dead, and we learn that his life could have been saved if someone had done something!"

"Blair, you're not being rational."

"I'm so rational, Sarah, that I'm going over there right now and clean my stuff out of the library. And you better send one of your ladies over right away, because I'm leaving that pup open! Nice talking to you!" With that, she slammed the phone down, then picked it up and slammed it again.

Furiously, she got dressed, then stormed next door to clean her things out of the building that had been like her home for the last four years.

CHAPTER

*S*ue Ellen Jargis showed up to "take over" the library just as Blair got the last of her personal things out. Adrenaline had enabled her to do it in record time. Lugging a box of floppy disks and programs that she'd bought herself, Blair bolted past her. "Knock yourself out, Sue Ellen. The key to the building is on the desk. Stay open as long as you want."

Sue Ellen made some kind of protest, but Blair didn't wait to hear it. She marched across the gravel parking lot and threw the boxes just inside her front door. She didn't go in herself, just slammed it and headed to her car.

Spinning out of the gravel, she headed for Hanover House.

She found Jonathan and Morgan sitting on the front porch with Seth.

Flinging her door shut, she cut across the yard. "Jonathan, run for mayor. We need someone reasonable running this town."

Jonathan got up. "Blair, what's wrong?"

"I lost my job, that's what!"

"Blair!" Morgan handed Seth to Jonathan. "They fired you?"

"No! They made me mad enough to quit!"

She came up the four porch steps and stood seething in front of them. "The Ladies' Auxiliary is taking over. Sue Ellen Jargis is there as we speak, showing everyone how easy it is to run the library since there's nothing much you have to do. It practically runs itself, according to Sarah Williford. They're going to run it in shifts. Can you believe that?"

Morgan looked exhausted. "Blair, you shouldn't have quit. You should have waited until your head is clearer."

Blair ignored her and turned to Jonathan. "So what's it gonna be, Jonathan? Are you going to run for mayor and rescue this town before the City Council flushes it right down the toilet?"

"Thinking about it," Jonathan said. "But without a newspaper in town, it's hard to get my issues out. I don't have much money for signs and bumper stickers and whatnot. I need a forum."

"You've got me," Blair said, slapping her chest. "I'll personally go door to door for you, giving every citizen of Cape Refuge an earful."

"Why don't *you* run?" Morgan asked wearily. "Wouldn't you love to be the boss of your tormenters? You were asked, weren't you?"

"Yeah, I was asked. But I'm not the type. I'm not photogenic, and everybody knows that politics is eighty percent cosmetic and twenty percent brains. Jonathan has a much better shot."

Jonathan looked at her like he didn't quite know how to take that.

"I'm one of the least popular residents on the island," she went on. "No, Jonathan has a much better shot."

"And when are you going to go door to door, Blair?" Morgan asked. "You'd have to give up your new career as private detective."

"I'd work it in," Blair said. "Don't you worry about that. So, Jonathan, what do you say?"

Jonathan leaned against the post and studied her for a minute. "I'll make a deal with you, now that you're unemployed."

"What?" she asked.

"You start the newspaper back up, and I'll run."

Blair took a step back. "The newspaper? No way. I'd have to buy it from the previous owner. I wouldn't give her one red cent."

"Then start one up on your own. You could do it, Blair."

"With what money?" she asked. "Talk about irrational. I have some savings but not enough to buy all the computers, photography equipment, and printing presses I would need."

"You could get a loan."

Blair almost laughed. Then her bitter amusement faded, and she stared at her brother-in-law. "You're serious about this, aren't you?"

"Yes, I am," he said. "We desperately need a newspaper, and frankly, if I spent a whole day listing possible candidates to run it, I couldn't think of anyone who'd be better at it than you."

For the first time in a long time, Blair found herself speechless.

Morgan filled in the silence. "He's right, Blair. Maybe losing the librarian job is a blessing in disguise. Maybe the Lord's opening another door for you."

"I think it's more likely that *Jonathan* is opening a door for me. Or kicking it down, would be more accurate."

Jonathan's eyes twinkled with the possibilities. "You do it, Blair, and I'll run for mayor," he said. "I'm not asking for special treatment, either. You could cover all the candidates. But as it stands right now, the one with the most signs up wins. Give us a place to air our convictions."

As much as she hated to admit it, Blair was catching his vision. "I could also cover Cade's disappearance and make people understand that he's in trouble. Put to rest all those insane ideas about him being on his honeymoon."

"You could!" Morgan's eyes rounded. "That would do more good than sitting in your car all night."

Blair started pacing, working out the details in her mind. "And I could cover Karen's baby. Maybe help the FBI get some leads. Being part of the media could give me access to things I can't have access to now."

Morgan started to smile. "Do it, Blair. I think you should do it."

Blair looked out across the street, to the beach beyond it. "Who am I kidding? I don't even own a computer now. I have zilch to start with."

"Don't give up before you try," Jonathan said. "Wouldn't you love to show the City Council and the Ladies' Auxiliary that they haven't bested you?"

That did it. "Yes, I would." She turned back to him, grinning. "I'll look into it."

"When?"

"Tomorrow," she said.

Morgan grabbed her arm. "How about today?"

"Can't. I have to be somewhere."

Morgan groaned. "Washington Park. Blair—"

Blair didn't want to hear it. "I have to go," she said. "Thanks for the idea, Jonathan."

"I'm ready when you are," he said.

Her mind reeled with possibilities as she pulled out of the driveway.

CHAPTER

51

*A*gain, the night had been long. Blair sat across the park from Ann Clark's house, watching every light in every window. The woman never seemed to leave the house. Not once had she seen her car back out of the driveway. She stayed inside that place as if it were a fortress that hid her darkest secrets.

Blair was more certain than ever that it did.

She hated to go home for rest, but as the sun grew higher in the morning sky, she realized that it wouldn't pay to sit here until she fell asleep and have someone notice her. Besides, she doubted the woman would do anything suspicious in broad daylight.

She drove home, fatigue aching through her body. As she pulled into the gravel parking area she shared with the library, she noticed Sue Ellen's car there already, along with a couple of others.

For a moment she sat in her car, staring at that library door. How dare they? She hoped the pages fell out of all the books, that the tapes broke, that the microfiche jammed. She hoped no one on the island brought back another book and that they never collected another dime for their budget.

Anger revived her as she cut across the gravel and went into her house. The phone was ringing, so she picked it up.

"Hello?"

"Yeah. Blair, hi. This is Jason Wheater down at the Island Bank."

She tossed her bag on the table and sank into a chair. "Uh-huh."

"Jonathan called me and said you were interested in buying the *Cape Refuge Journal.*"

Her eyebrows shot up. "He did, did he?"

"Yes. I told him that we recently foreclosed on all the equipment and the building. We own it now. We're about ready to auction it off, but we'd rather sell it."

Blair rubbed her eyes. She couldn't think. "Look, Jason, it's not a real good time, with Cade missing and all. I haven't slept."

"I understand," Jason said. "But if we had a newspaper on this island, maybe it would help to locate Cade. Heaven knows the *Savannah Morning News* isn't talking enough about it, except to cast aspersions on Cade."

The man had done his homework. He knew which buttons to push. "Truth is, Jason, I haven't really given it all that much thought."

"Well, why don't you meet me over there this morning and I can take you through it? You could see what you'd be getting, and maybe we can make a deal. We'd even be willing to do some financing, Blair. We know you're good for it. And you'd probably have a built-in subscription base, so we know there'd be some income."

Blair sighed. She really didn't want to deal with this now, but Jason was right. If she started the paper back up, maybe somebody would read something and come up with a lead that could help them get to Cade. And she had to make a living somehow. Even if Sarah Williford begged her, she had too much pride to take the library back.

Research was her first love. But she could do that from a newspaper office and actually turn her knowledge into something productive for everyone. What could it hurt to look?

"All right, Jason," she said, "I'll meet you over there at four this afternoon."

"Good deal," he said. "I'll see you there."

Blair got a few hours' sleep, then went over to Hanover House before her meeting with Jason Wheater.

There had been no productive leads on the missing baby, and the parlor still looked like a cockpit, with recorders and telephones and tracing equipment piled on one of her mother's antique tables.

Blair went to the kitchen, and saw Morgan on the back porch playing with Seth.

Morgan heard her and looked in through the window. She motioned for Blair to come out. Blair pushed through the door and dropped into a rocker.

Morgan regarded her for a moment. "You look awful."

"Thanks."

"No, really. You look worse than you did after Mama and Pop died. I'm worried about you."

"Then stop it."

"Blair, you're not going to do Cade any good if you don't take care of yourself."

Close to tears again, Blair got up and went to the screen door. Peering out, she said, "Who cares if I take care of myself? I can sleep when he's found." She turned back. "Any word about the baby?"

"None," Morgan said. "Nobody's getting much sleep these days."

She put Seth into his Flintstone mobile, and he used his feet to pull himself along.

Blair went to sit back down. "I know Ann Clark knows where Cade is," she said, knowing she was changing the subject, but unable to help herself. "I know that as sure as I've ever known anything in my life."

"Has she done anything that you've seen? Had visitors? Gone anywhere?"

Blair shrugged. "Nothing yet."

Morgan got up as Seth hit the wall, and turned him back around. "Want some tea? I could use some."

"No, I didn't come over here for tea. I actually came over to ask you if you'd go to the newspaper with me. Jonathan got Jason Wheater to call me. He wants to make a deal."

Morgan grinned. "So you're going?"

"I thought I would. It's gone into foreclosure," she said. "The building, the equipment, everything. The bank owns it now, and they're trying to get rid of it. They've offered to finance it and everything."

Morgan's face changed. "Blair, that's amazing. You're the only one I know who can quit her job in a fit of rage and not suffer for it."

"It's not a done deal yet. I'm meeting him at four. Wanna come?"

Morgan started to laugh. "Sure, I'll come with you."

She heard the inside door closing and Sadie tromping through the house. "Morgan, I'm home!"

"Out here, Sadie," Morgan called.

Blair looked up as Sadie came to the door. "Hi, Blair."

Blair lifted her hand in a silent wave.

Morgan pulled Sadie out. "Sadie, you'll never guess what Blair's doing this afternoon."

"What?"

"She's meeting a banker about buying the *Cape Refuge Journal*."

Sadie sucked in a sharp breath and stared down at Blair. "You're kidding!"

Blair gave her a weak grin. "Nope."

"Oh, my gosh. Can I go with you? I can show you where everything is. I worked there long enough to get real familiar with the place. I can even show you how to use the equipment."

Blair grinned. "That'd be real nice, Sadie. I could use your experience."

Morgan started into the house. "Let me go change Seth's diaper, and I'll get ready to go. I'll just bring him with us."

Sadie kept staring at Blair, as if it was too good to be true. "Oh, Blair, if you buy the newspaper can I work for you, please? I was a real good employee for Nancy. I can do a good job. I promise."

Blair got to her feet. She'd never been so tired in her life. "I thought Morgan didn't want you to work, Sadie. I thought she wanted you to concentrate on your school."

"But I can do both. I really can. I don't think she'll mind if it's you. And school will be out for the summer in just a few weeks."

"Well, I will need somebody," Blair said, "and it sure couldn't hurt to have somebody who knows the ropes working there, at least part time."

Sadie punched the air and laughed. "Maybe if I work there, Morgan won't make me go back to school next year. I could work for you and home-school at night—"

"Whoa," Blair said. "I haven't even bought the place, and you're dreaming about quitting school?"

"Not quitting. Home-schooling. The ones my age are seniors now. The kids in my class all hate me. This town isn't very forgiving, you know."

"Forgiving?" Blair asked. "What in the world do they have to forgive you for?"

Sadie's delight faded. "My past," she said. "Everybody knows where I came from, what my mother's done, how I was raised. I'll never escape it, no matter where I go."

Blair looked out across the yard. Morgan had done a good job of keeping the flower beds intact, keeping the weeds out, keeping everything growing and beautiful the way her mother had done it. She'd thought she'd done miracles with Sadie too.

But she understood the girl's insecurities. She'd had much the same experience in school because of her scars.

"You know, my parents came here years ago, and they had a lot of baggage too," she said, "a lot of history, a lot of guilt in their lives. Some of that guilt had to do with me."

Sadie nodded. She'd heard the whole story months before.

"But the town came to love them. They did good things, helped a lot of people." Her voice broke off. "They'll love you too, Sadie. They will. One of these days you'll be so at home here that you'll never be able to leave."

"Like you?" Sadie asked.

Blair shrugged. "Truth is, I had every intention of being out of here by now, but things keep making me stay." Her voice trailed off, and she stared at those flowers and thought of Cade.

"And if you buy the paper," Sadie said, "then you'll be obligated to stay, won't you?"

Blair thought about that for a moment. It might be a good reason not to buy the paper. She wasn't sure she wanted to be that committed to staying in town indefinitely, especially if Cade wasn't here.

She got up, feeling a little dizzy. "Well, I guess I'd better get going. You ready?"

"Oh, yeah," Sadie said. "I'm ready, all right."

CHAPTER

*B*lair told Jason Wheater that she'd have to give it some more thought. While everything looked intact and seemed to be in working order, she just wasn't sure that buying the paper was what she wanted to do. As Sadie had pointed out, it would give her roots here like a ball and chain, tying her ankle to this island, keeping her from ever escaping.

And escape might be just what she needed.

On the other hand, if she bought the paper, she could have it up and running within a few days, and she could use it to turn the town's attention to Cade. Jason indicated that he'd have no problem getting the bank to finance her loan. If she wanted it, he could have the paperwork ready within a day.

Until she decided, she would proceed as she had been, staking out Ann Clark's house since no one else would.

That night, as darkness settled in, she drove back to Washington Square in Savannah and watched the lights in the Clark house flicker on and off from room to room.

She had sat here night after night for days and had still not seen a thing. No one had come or gone from this place. Ann Clark hadn't left at all.

Discouraged, she had almost decided to go on home and admit that, perhaps, she was wrong about the woman.

But then something changed.

In one of those windows flickering with light—like several carefully placed candles—she saw Ann Clark's silhouette in the curtain.

She wasn't alone.

The silhouette of a man stood facing her for the briefest of moments, then he walked out of the window's frame.

Blair's heart seemed to stop. She hadn't seen anyone arrive at Ann's home. There were no cars in the driveway. Could that be Cade? She got out of her car and rushed across Washington Park, her eyes locked on that window.

There he was again, the same silhouette in that window. The shape of his face did not look like Cade's, and he was shorter, only six or seven inches taller than Ann's five-feet-two. Cade was taller—at least six-feet-two. This man's nose was bigger, his chin more prominent, his hair longer.

So who was it? She hadn't seen anyone come or go from this house.

She crossed the rest of the park, not taking her eyes from that window. Someone rode by on a bicycle, a car passed, she heard voices on the other side of the park.

She crossed the street to Ann's driveway. Did she dare go to that window to peer in and see who the man was? The curtains were closed. She doubted she could even get a look.

Instead, she went up the driveway that turned behind the house and looked in the garage window. Ann's car still sat there.

She pulled back from the window and looked around the yard.

Then she saw it. A motorcycle, parked next to the garage. She put her hand on it, felt that it was warm.

How had anyone ridden this in without her seeing them?

She looked around, wishing she had a flashlight. There were trees separating the Clark house from the house behind her. On another side, between a fence and a hedge, separating her house from the one next to her, she saw a small driveway. There it was, another way out and another way in. She stole across the yard and started down that driveway. It cut between two houses and came out on the adjacent street.

No wonder she hadn't seen Ann or anyone else coming and going.

She checked the motorcycle, saw that it had no tag. Who was on it? She had to know.

Slowly, she walked toward that window where she could still see the shadows of a man and a woman. . . .

CHAPTER

53

*M*organ checked the address she'd hastily jotted down and turned onto the block where Washington Square sat. She had tried to call Blair tonight, hoping she was home figuring out how she could buy the paper. But once again, she had not answered, and Morgan had little doubt where she was.

A sense of dark foreboding had fallen over her at the thought of her sister trying to be a hero. She had to go talk her out of one more night spent in her car, she decided. She had to convince her that her mission was insane.

Knowing that Jonathan would never let her go after Blair, she told him only that she was going to talk to her. He assumed she meant at Blair's house. If he'd known she was circling the block now, looking for Ann Clark's house and Blair's car, he would have thrown his body in front of her car to stop her.

But someone had to look out for Blair.

She found the address and slowed in front of it. There were lights on in the Clark house, clearly indicating that the woman was home.

But Blair's car was nowhere to be seen. She drove around the block, making the square. Maybe Blair wasn't here. Maybe she had gone to a movie or shopping in the mall. Maybe she had been here and left.

But as she turned the corner, her heart plunged. There was Blair's car, strategically parked where she'd have a direct view through the park to Ann Clark's front door.

She pulled in behind it, and as her headlights shone through it, she realized Blair wasn't in it.

Morgan threw her car into park. Where was she? She cut her engine off, got out quickly, and ran to look in Blair's window.

The car was empty. She looked around, hoping to find her sister on a park bench, but Blair was nowhere in sight.

The Clark house. She had to be there.

Swallowing back her fear, Morgan crossed the park, her eyes straining to see through the darkness. Quietly she reached the sidewalk directly across from the house. She scanned the property for any sign of life.

Finally, she saw her, standing just under a window, peering up over the rim.

Someone was going to see her and call the police—or worse! Morgan crossed the yard and bolted toward her sister.

"Blair, what are you doing?" The question came out in a loud whisper.

Blair caught her breath and spun around. "Morgan! You scared me to death!" she whispered harshly. "What are you, crazy?"

Morgan grabbed her hand and led her off of the property and away from the house as fast as she could. Blair came like a child caught misbehaving. When they were on the other side of the park, Morgan finally stopped.

"I've always thought you were a little cracked, Blair," she said, trying to catch her breath, "but now I know it for sure."

"I'm not cracked," Blair said. "Cade is in that house."

Morgan shoved her hair back from her perspiring face. "Did you see him when you were peaking in the window?"

"No," she said, "I didn't see anything. But that doesn't mean he's not there."

"Blair, you're not thinking clearly. You're breaking the law! You can't trespass on people's property and look in their windows, no matter what you think is going on inside!"

"There was a man in there with her, Morgan! I saw his shadow in the curtain. He drove a motorcycle through a back driveway."

Morgan wanted to shake her. "Blair, I don't want to see you get arrested, and I don't want you killed. You're playing with fire here, and you have to stop it. Let the authorities handle it."

"The authorities are doing zilch," Blair said. "Cade is in trouble and nobody cares, nobody but me."

"You're wrong about that."

"Oh, am I? Then you tell me why the police haven't torn this house apart brick by brick looking for Cade? He's in there somewhere. It's a no-brainer. While they're dancing around probable cause, I'm doing something!"

Morgan started to cry. Blair couldn't be reasoned with. Malnutrition and lack of sleep had caught up with her. "Come home, Blair. Please leave this place and come home. You're scaring me to death."

"Oh, stop crying! This isn't about you, Morgan."

"I know it's not about me," she said. "I just feel like I've lost control of everything in my life. Cade, Karen's baby, Sadie, you. You're all in danger, and I have no control."

"You never had control over me in the first place," Blair said, "so get over it. And calm down about Sadie. She hasn't done anything all that awful. She's just being a kid, and she's going to be all right."

"That's beside the point." She straightened and wiped her face. "My sister has been trespassing on private property and stalking a woman who may have nothing to do with Cade's disappearance at all. You're going to wind up in jail, Blair. I want you to come home now."

Blair turned back to the house as if something might have changed since she'd walked away. "I can't go, Morgan. Something's happening in there."

Morgan had had enough. "Blair, don't make me report you to the police myself. I'd rather have you locked up safely than know you're risking your life here."

Blair glared at her. "You wouldn't dare."

"Try me," Morgan said. "I'll drive straight to the police station."

It was clear that Blair knew she meant it. "Morgan, you're bullying me."

"Whatever it takes." Morgan pointed to Blair's car like a mother who'd had enough. "In the car, Blair. I'll follow you home."

When Blair hesitated, Morgan said, "Now!"

Grunting out her frustration, Blair got into her car and slammed the door. Morgan waited as she started the car, then she got into her own. Blair pulled away from the curb, and Morgan followed.

As she followed Blair back down Highway 80 to Tybee Island, she cried out to God. "Blair doesn't have the power to save Cade, Lord. And I don't have the power to save Emory. And Jonathan and I don't have the strength to save Sadie, either. You're our only hope. Please intervene here. Please let all of them be all right."

She wept into her hand as Blair headed for Cape Refuge. "And let Blair be all right too. Lord, she needs to see your power. Please don't let Satan win this battle."

She followed Blair back to her front door, then watched her go in. Wiping her tears, she drove back to Hanover House. But as she went back in, she knew that Blair wouldn't stay home. She'd be back at the Clark house within the hour.

CHAPTER

*T*he phone call that came to Hanover House on Thursday morning silenced the household. As she'd done each time it had rung since the baby's disappearance, Morgan picked up the cordless phone and ran into the parlor. Agent Tavist had started his equipment rolling, and he held his arm up in the air, making her wait for a signal.

The phone rang a second time, and Morgan glanced at the Caller ID. There was no name on the screen, just a number.

"It's a cell phone," Tavist said.

It rang a third time and his arm came down. He pointed at her to answer.

"Hello?"

"Put the mother on the phone." The voice had an eerie, split quality, as if someone spoke through a disguising device.

Morgan froze. Her eyes met Tavist's, and he motioned for her to get Karen.

The kidnapper! She turned back to the stairs. *The kidnapper was on the phone!*

She grabbed the banister. "Karen!" she screamed at the top of her lungs. "Karen, telephone! *Hurry!*"

Karen, who had not come out of her room yet this morning, bolted down the stairs, a look of stark terror on her face. "Is it about my baby?"

"I think so!" Morgan thrust the phone at her, then pressed her face close to Karen's so she could hear the call.

"Hello?" Karen's voice trembled with anticipation.

"Leave fifty thousand dollars in locker number 36 at the Trailways Bus Station."

Karen clutched the phone. "When will I get my baby back?"

"Leave the money by 4:00 P.M. tomorrow, and if it's all there, we'll contact you about where you can find him."

The agent gestured for her to keep him talking. "How do I know you'll do what you say?" Karen asked into the phone. "How do I even know my baby is still alive?"

But the phone clicked, and the dial tone hummed behind it.

Karen began to wail, and Morgan took her in her arms and looked at the agent who was still on his phone. "Did you trace it?"

He took off his headphones and looked up at her.

"Did you?"

"Oh, yeah. We traced it, all right. We have SPD on their way to the site right now."

Karen's face blossomed with hope. "Oh, Morgan, they might find my baby!"

But something in the agent's eyes gave Morgan pause. "Maybe so," she said, putting her arm around the woman. "We just have to wait."

They sat huddled together on a love seat in the parlor, their eyes on Tavist as he talked to other field agents. Finally, he finished the call and turned back to them. "Okay, here's what we've got. The phone call was made near the Laurel Grove Cemetery. Police found the phone, but the caller was gone."

Morgan stood up. "So whose phone was it?"

Tavist cleared his throat and looked at his equipment again. Finally, he turned back to her. "Police Chief Matthew Cade."

The world seemed to freeze, and Morgan couldn't move. Her throat constricted, her heart stuttered. . . . "No way in the world," she said. "Not in a million years."

Karen didn't care who it was. "Are they going after him? Are they going to arrest him? They have to find my baby!"

Cade. It couldn't be Cade.

Morgan grabbed the phone. Blair. She needed to talk to Blair.

"Who are you calling?" he asked.

"My sister!"

He shook his head. "We need to keep this quiet."

"Please," she said. "I'll just tell her to come over."

He finally agreed, so she dialed Blair's number. Thankfully, she was home.

"Hello?"

"Blair, get over here. It's important. There's something you need to hear."

Silence, then, "He's not dead. Don't tell me he's dead."

"No, that's not it. Something else. Just come over here, Blair."

Morgan hung up. She needed Jonathan, but he was out on the Atlantic with a boat full of fishermen.

Cade's phone? It couldn't be!

Beside her, Karen began to pace. "The ransom. I have to get fifty thousand dollars. I have to pay them so I can get my baby."

Morgan's mind raced frantically. It couldn't be Cade.

Karen kept ranting. "The bus station, he said. Tomorrow by four, locker 36. I have to do it!"

Morgan heard Blair's car on the gravel, heard her slamming her door. She kept holding Karen as Blair bolted into the house.

"What is it?"

Morgan got up. "Blair, we got a ransom call about the baby. It was from Cade's cell phone."

Blair blinked at her. "*What?*"

"I heard the voice," Morgan said. "They were using some kind of disguising device, so the voice was indiscernible."

Blair turned to the busy agent. "I want you to tell me something." Her voice quivered with emotion. "You're a cop. If you decided to commit some horrendous crime, would you really be so stupid as to make a ransom call on your cell phone?"

"I wouldn't. But people don't think."

She gritted her teeth. "Cade would think! It proves that it's not him. Someone is using his cell phone! Don't you see?" She went to his chair and braced her hands on his armrests. "Someone had him write that letter so we wouldn't look for him, and now they're setting him up for kidnapping!"

She rose up and shoved her fingers through her hair. Her scars flamed with excitement. "We never even considered that there was a connection. But there is! If we can find the baby, maybe we can find Cade."

The agent didn't give any indication whether he agreed with Blair's deduction or not. He just got back on the phone.

Frustrated and fearing further smearing of Cade's name, Blair went into the kitchen and called Joe McCormick. He showed up at Hanover House just a few minutes later.

He got a briefing by the agent, then joined Morgan and Blair in the kitchen. "I'm with you, Blair. I don't believe that Cade has anything to do with that kidnapping. Someone used his cell phone, then left it for us to find."

Blair's eyes were frantic as she moved closer to Joe. "Ann Clark is still the key. Maybe she's the one who stole the baby. They didn't have to keep him alive to use his phone. He could already be dead!"

The agent got off the phone and came into the kitchen. "We have an all-points-bulletin out on Chief Matthew Cade, and they're getting a warrant for his arrest."

"A warrant for him, but not for Ann Clark?" Blair shouted. "That's absurd!"

But Morgan saw it another way. "No, it's good," she said. "Blair, at least there will be an all-out hunt for him."

"What about the fifty thousand dollars?" Karen asked. "They demanded that. Said they would give me my baby back if I left it."

Tavist shook his head. "I'm sorry, Miss Miller, but there aren't any lockers at the bus station anymore."

"What? Yes, there are. I've seen them!"

"They took them out after the September eleventh attacks. There was too much risk of someone planting a bomb in them. No, the caller knew that."

Blair gave a bitter laugh. "That call wasn't about ransom at all, but just a way of setting Cade up."

The cop didn't answer. "If they call back, Miss Miller, you demand some proof that they even have the baby, and that he's alive."

Karen moaned and fell against Morgan. "But they already told me what to do. My baby needs me!"

Morgan tried her hardest to comfort the inconsolable mother.

But the look in Blair's eyes frightened her even more than the call itself. She was going to do something stupid, and Morgan knew she couldn't stop her.

CHAPTER

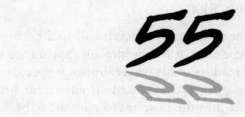

*T*he FBI considered Cade a criminal to be caught now, not a missing person who needed to be found. At least, that was the way it appeared to Blair. She sincerely hoped she was wrong.

But at least they had more than Cape Refuge's tiny police force searching for him. With the feds on the hunt, they would surely be able to find him soon.

When she arrived back at Ann Clark's block that night, Blair half-hoped to see a crowd of FBI agents surrounding the place, searching it like the crime scene that it was.

But no one was there. Ann Clark was still free to do as she pleased.

This time Blair parked on the street where the back driveway came out and watched for anyone to come or go.

No one did.

She wondered if Cade and the baby could be in the same place.

She sat there for another grueling night, fighting sleep and hunger. Early the next morning, when the paperboy began delivering the newspapers to the driveways surrounding the park, Blair borrowed one and unrolled it. The headline stopped her heart.

SEARCH ON FOR POLICE CHIEF: ALLEGED INVOLVEMENT IN KIDNAPPING RING.

The reporter told that a ransom call had been made from Cade's cell phone and that his sudden disappearance two weeks ago had spurred rumors of his whereabouts. It speculated that his credentials as a cop may have made it easier for him to get a female accomplice into the hospital to take the baby.

Furious, she rolled up the newspaper and threw it back on the driveway she'd taken it from, then headed back to Cape Refuge.

That was it, she thought. She was going to buy the *Cape Refuge Journal* if it took every dime she had. She'd call Jason Wheater tonight and tell him she would offer all of her savings as a down payment. He would draw up the papers as soon as possible, and she could have it up and running in record time. For the life of her, she would counter every allegation the *Savannah Morning News* had made about Cade today, and she would show the inconsistencies in the case and draw attention to the questions that still plagued her about his disappearance.

It might be the only hope Cade had left.

CHAPTER

*C*haos reigned at Hanover House as they waited for the phone to ring again. Though the FBI seemed convinced that the caller had known there weren't lockers at the Trailways station, Karen still hoped that the kidnapper had made a mistake and would call back to correct it.

While they waited, Morgan tried to comfort Karen, but it was almost impossible.

The sound of Karen's anguish all night had been a terrible thing to hear, and Morgan had spent most of the night in earnest prayer. The pall continued to hang over the house as morning gave way to afternoon, and a quivering sense of anticipation preoccupied them all.

In the parlor, the agents worked, taking calls and coordinating the search for Emory and Cade. Nervous and somber at the accusations being leveled against his best friend, Jonathan paced the kitchen with his hands in his pockets.

"I have to get that money and do what they say," Karen cried. "Lockers or not, I have to be there with that money!"

Morgan leaned against the cabinet, trying to think. Gus and Felicia sat on either side of Karen, like allies against the world that conspired against her.

"You all right, Miss Morgan?" Gus's bass voice cut through her thoughts.

"I'm fine, Gus."

"I been thinking," he said. "What if I go with Miss Karen to make the drop? I could protect her from anybody out to hurt her."

Morgan met Jonathan's impatient eyes. "Gus, there are no lockers," Jonathan said, "and we don't have the money. There's not going to be a drop."

"All's we need to do is stand there with a duffel bag, mon. Maybe they'll come."

Karen slapped her hand on the table. "It's something, Morgan. Something more than we're doing now." She looked at her watch. "They said four. It's two-thirty now!"

Felicia put her plump arm around Karen's shoulders. "Miss Morgan, don't you think you could raise the money with some phone calls to church members? I know fifty thousand is a lot, but for the life of a baby . . ."

Morgan had a crick in her neck, and her shoulder muscles felt as if they'd been tied in knots. The "maybes" and "ifs" were starting to make her crazy. "Thanks, Felicia. I'm sure the FBI is considering everything."

"I don't know why you think that," Gus said in a low voice. "They haven't done nothing for Cade, mon. And now they think he did it."

Morgan knew Gus was right.

Tavist came to the kitchen, leaned in. "Miss Miller, can you come in here, please?"

Karen sprang up and grabbed Morgan and Jonathan's hands. "Come with me."

They both followed her into the parlor, where four agents sat around a table. Tavist lowered his voice so the others wouldn't hear. "Miss Miller, we've decided to stake out the Trailways Station in case the kidnappers show up."

"Yes!" Karen turned and started out of the room. "I'll go get ready!"

"Wait." Tavist's voice turned her back. "You're not going."

"But they told *me* to come!" she shouted. "They said for me to bring the money!"

"But you can't make the drop without the lockers. We're just going to have agents watching for them."

"Watching for who? You don't even know what they look like!"

"We know what Matthew Cade looks like, and the woman who took the baby was a white woman of about five-feet-two."

Jonathan snapped. "If you're looking for Cade, Tavist, then you're going to miss the real kidnapper! Cade is not involved!"

"Whoever is involved, our agents are trained. They know what to look for."

"You can't do this!" Karen cried. "I have to be there if they bring my baby."

"Miss Miller, they're not going to wheel a stroller in there and swap with you. Trust us. We have experience with this kind of thing."

Karen wouldn't hear any of it. "But if they don't see me, they might kill my baby. We have to do what they say."

Tavist stepped toward her. "Miss Miller, I know this is hard for you. But what we're doing is in the best interest of the baby. If you hope to get him back, you need to let us call the shots."

As Karen wilted against Morgan, Seth toddled in, and Sadie ran in behind him. "Sorry, Morgan. I'm trying to keep him out of the way."

Morgan had forgotten the girl was home. Early this morning, when Sadie would have gone to school, she'd convinced Morgan to let her stay home to help with Seth while the decisions were being made. Morgan had been so distracted she'd agreed.

Letting Karen go, Morgan picked Seth up and kissed him. "It's okay, Sadie. We need a distraction."

Sadie stood in the doorway and looked at Karen as if the sight of her tears hurt her as well.

"They're risking Emory," Karen said. "By not doing it the way they said, they're risking his life."

"They're trying to save it," Morgan said quietly.

"He'll be all right, Karen," Sadie whispered. "God took care of Seth. He'll take care of Emory."

"Babies are hurt and killed all the time, Sadie," Karen snapped. "It's a horrible world. Their daddies take them to terrible places, where people hurt them. They're left in hot cars. They're neglected and left to cry for hours and hours and hours. If they survive being babies, they're hurt when they're older."

Morgan shot Sadie a stricken look, then touched Karen's hand. "Karen, I know things are bad right now. But you can't give up hope. And when things are out of your control, you have to realize that there's ultimately only one person who is in control. And that's God."

"Then where was he when Emory was taken?" Her voice broke off and she covered her mouth and wailed. "I've prayed and prayed and prayed. You said prayer works, and I believed you."

Sadie watched her now, waiting for her answer, as if she too needed to hear why it seemed God had not acted.

"Prayer does work. God answers, Karen. You'll see. He could be protecting that baby from harm while he's with strangers. He could be working it out so that the police find the kidnappers. He could be doing a number of things that we can't see."

Karen looked at her skeptically. So did Sadie.

"And even if God doesn't save Emory, we still have to trust him, because he's still good."

Sadie looked as disappointed in her answer as Karen did. "I think I'll go for a walk, if it's all right."

Morgan nodded. "I don't blame you for wanting to get out of here. Go ahead."

Sadie looked close to tears as she went to the door. Morgan wanted to run after her and make sure she was all right.

But the crisis had not yet passed. She would see about Sadie a little bit later.

CHAPTER

*T*ension hung in the air at Hanover House, and Sadie was glad to escape it. She crossed the street to the beach and walked the shoreline. The ocean was gentle today, and the sky a cloudless, solid blue. One would never know that people had vanished, babies had been stolen, and good people might really be evil.

She didn't know what to think about Cade now. Did he have it in him to do these kinds of things?

He was the first one she'd met on the island, the one who had taken her to the doctor and paid, himself, to have her arm set. He was the one who'd tried to get Seth out of Jack Dent's home.

If you couldn't trust him, who could you trust?

Morgan and Jonathan were certain he was victim and not perpetrator, but Sadie wasn't so sure.

She needed to talk to someone who wasn't involved in these tragedies, but every call in or out of the home was being recorded. There was a pay phone on the South

Beach Pier. She thought of calling Trevor—her only real friend—just to talk.

What could a simple phone call hurt?

She checked her watch as she reached the phone. By now, he was probably home from school. Quickly, she thumbed through the phone book for his number.

Inserting her coins, she dialed. Her heart pounded as she waited for him to answer.

"Hello?"

"Trevor? This is Sadie."

"Sadie!" The pleasure in his voice was unmistakable. "Where were you today?"

"Some stuff was going on at Hanover House. Listen, I'm pretty freaked out about Cade and the kidnapping and everything. You want to meet somewhere to talk?"

"Sure," he said. "Tell me where."

"Well, I'm at the South Beach Pier right now. How soon can you come?"

"Give me ten minutes."

Sadie hung up, gratified that he would come so quickly. She walked out to the pier, took her shoes off, and sat on the side.

Evil was everywhere, she supposed. Though she hated to admit it, even Hanover House wasn't immune.

She leaned her forehead against the pier's railing and looked out at the water billowing beneath her. Another storm was headed this way, and the waves rushed the shore with mad urgency, mirroring the restlessness in her soul.

"Wow, you look really bummed."

She looked up. Trevor stood there in a pair of shorts and a Miller Lite T-shirt. "Hey. You made it fast."

He sat down next to her. "I was anxious to see you."

She couldn't be sucked in by his charm. Not this time. "This is not a date," she said. "I'm not lying to anyone about anything. I just needed someone to talk to."

"I'm your man. What's wrong?"

She crossed her arms on the rail and rested her chin on them. "I'm just . . . confused. Wondering if all the things Morgan and Jonathan say are right."

"They're not," he said. "I can tell you that right now."

Sadie knew better than to dismiss them that easily. She thought of Morgan's deep faith in the power of prayer and knew she couldn't talk this out with Trevor. He wouldn't be objective. So she sidestepped it.

"I was just thinking a lot about why some babies are born into perfect, loving homes and others are born into dangerous, evil homes with mean parents. Or why good people who would make great parents sometimes can't have kids."

She knew the argument Jonathan would make about a fallen world giving birth to evil. About Satan being the "prince of this world" and doing as much harm as he could to the most innocent.

"If you ask me," Trevor said, "it all boils down to luck."

Sadie shook her head. "You can't really believe that."

"Sure I do," Trevor said. "And the truth is, some people make their own luck. Like my dad, for instance. He's a self-made man. He doesn't wait for things to happen. He goes out and makes them happen."

Morgan's warnings about Trevor's family chimed through her mind. "But how do other people fit into that? I mean, if it's all luck, and you make your own luck, but you can't control their behavior. . . ."

"Oh, we can control their behavior, all right." He started to laugh.

Sadie looked at him. Was he talking about beating people up when they paid their loans late? "How?" she asked. "How do you control it?"

"You set examples. You give consequences."

"What kind of consequences?"

He grinned and regarded her for a moment. "What are you asking?"

She decided that she had to know the truth. "Trevor, I heard that you work for your father, beating up people who are late with their loans. Is that true?"

He grinned. "Now, do I look like a mean guy?"

"No," she said. "But you are big. You could do that if you wanted."

"Hey, my job in my father's business is to make sure people keep their end of the bargains they make. That's all. Sometimes a little intimidation is required."

She tried to think it through. Intimidation was not the same as violence, was it? And it was a business thing, not meanness. It didn't mean he was not a decent person.

He nuzzled her neck, trying to illicit a smile. "You have terrible ideas about me and my family, don't you?"

"No, I don't. I haven't believed all those rumors."

"You sure? Because it isn't fair, you know."

"I know."

"Then I want you to do something for me. I want you to meet my folks."

Sadie stiffened. "I can't."

"No, just hear me out. I want you to come with me to a wedding. You can meet my folks and find out they're all right."

"A wedding?" she asked. "Who's getting married?"

"A cousin of mine," he said. "And I hate weddings, but I have to go. It won't be so painful if you're there."

Sadie just looked at him. "I don't know. A wedding's a pretty public thing. If I went, Morgan and Jonathan would be sure to find out."

"So go ahead and tell them you're going to a wedding. She lives in Savannah, so they won't know her. Tell them you met her back when you worked for the paper. If they hear we were together, they'll just think we ran into each other."

Sadie knew that Morgan and Jonathan would never want her there. And she had promised not to lie again.

"Come on," he said. "What could happen at a wedding?"

"I'm not afraid to go to a wedding with you," she said. "I just don't want to lie again."

"You gotta admit, the Clearys are not thinking clearly right now. And you're seventeen, Sadie. At some point you've got to start making decisions for yourself."

She sighed. "When is it?"

"Saturday night."

She looked into the wind as it slapped across the water. It lifted her hair from her shoulders and sent it flying around her face. This storm might even be worse than the last one.

His arms slid around her, and he nuzzled her neck again. "Come on, Sadie. Say yes."

It felt so good to have him hold her like that. Morgan and Jonathan were so wrong about him. "I guess I could go."

"All right!" he said. "You've made my day!"

And she could tell he meant it.

Later, as she walked back down the beach and across the street to Hanover House, she told herself that she wasn't really doing anything wrong. She was just going to watch decent people unite themselves in marriage—and she would meet Trevor's family.

What could it hurt, after all?

CHAPTER

58

*C*ade had been drugged again. He didn't know how, since he hadn't drunk the water she'd brought him in days. She must have figured it out and hidden the drug in his food.

Now each of his limbs seemed to weigh a ton, and he couldn't tell how long he'd been out.

Forcing himself, he came to a sitting position, carefully slid his swollen, mangled leg off the side of the bed. Pain racked through him.

Taking his weight with the good leg, he managed to stand. Slowly, he made his way to the toilet and relieved himself.

He went back to the bed, dropped back down. The sheets were clean for the first time in days. She must have come in while he slept and changed his bed. The sick-sweet smell of dried blood was thankfully gone. But his bandages had not been changed, and blood stained them.

His head ached from the original gash that had begun to heal, and the drug's fog blurred his vision and muddled his thoughts.

He pulled himself back up to examine his wounds. His leg had swollen to twice its original size, and blood seeped through his bandage. His side felt raw and infected, and every breath sent pain ripping through him.

He lay there for a while, staring at that vent over his bed. *I'm still here, Lord. You haven't forgotten me, have you?*

God's silence screamed through his heart and settled like panic on his psyche. There had to be a way out. He was a cop, for Pete's sake. How could he let this happen to him?

After a while, he heard the scraping outside the door and knew that Ann Clark had come to check on him. He closed his eyes and pretended to sleep.

He heard her come close to his bed, felt her checking his leg. As she prodded the wound, he forced himself not to react with the pain.

He could grab her, he thought. If she checked the wound on his side, he could grab her wrist, twist it behind her back, and find the gun she always kept in her pocket.

He lay still as she unwound the bandage and then wrapped it again.

Closer, he thought. *Move closer.*

As if obeying him, she moved to his rib cage. Carefully, she lifted his wrist to move his arm.

Cade clamped hers instead. She screamed as he lunged up, twisting her around. Balancing on his one good leg, he got her hand behind her back and groped for her gun.

It was in her pocket, so he plunged his hand in and pulled it out.

"We're gonna do it different this time," he said, breathing hard with the effort of holding her still. "You're going to help me get up those stairs, and you and I are going to be so close that any bullet meant for me will have to take you with it." He shoved the gun into her waist. "Now let's go."

He leaned on her, using her body to keep from stepping on his shattereed leg, but the effort still caused agony. He managed to get her to the door that led out into the basement.

He stopped there a moment, looked toward the stairs. If someone else was in the house, he waited at the top of those stairs as he had before.

"You shoot me," he yelled, "and she goes too!"

They had no sooner stepped through the door, when something hit him from the side. He hit the floor.

Someone was on him, wrestling his hands back, grabbing his hair. "Want to try that again, pal?"

It was a man's voice, slightly familiar.

Pain cracked though his forehead as the man rammed his head into the concrete, once, twice . . .

Light faded into darkness, and Cade gave up hope.

CHAPTER

Someone had to get into that house. As Blair sat on the road behind Ann Clark's property, near the hidden driveway, she decided it would have to be her. So she'd break the law. So she could do jail time for this. It was a small price to pay for saving Cade's life.

Besides, she didn't intend to get caught.

She had worn black for her mission, in hopes of merging into the shadows. As she got out of her car and stole up the driveway, it occurred to her that she should have had something on her head. Her blonde hair was too stark a contrast against the darkness.

The moonlight was brighter than she would have liked, so she stayed close to the trees as she made her way between the houses.

The house on her left was lit up as if on display, and through the window she saw a mother working in the kitchen, her child at the computer in his room.

The house on the other side of the driveway lay dark, but as she stole past it, she thought she heard a door closing. Maybe someone had let his cat out.

Ann Clark's house came into view, and she looked to see if the motorcycle was there. Not tonight. That was good, she thought. If Ann didn't have company, it might be easier for Blair to get inside.

Her heart whammed against her chest wall as she made her way to one of the lighted windows. Slowly, carefully, she rose up to peer inside.

She saw the parlor where she and Joe had sat that day, breaking the news to her about her husband and listening to her lie through her teeth.

No one was there. The window from the room next door flickered, and she moved to it. The curtains were pulled shut, but there was a slit down the center that she was able to see through.

She caught her breath at the sight of Ann Clark sitting at that table, eating a meal and watching the television just beyond it.

Perfect, Blair thought. She could go in on the other side of the house, counting on the noise of the television to keep Ann from hearing. Surely she could find a window or door unlocked. If not, she was prepared to break the glass.

She ran around the house, to the farthest end from the parlor and dining room. The windows were all covered with screens, so she couldn't check the locks without first removing one of the screens.

But she had to do it.

Her hands shook as she pulled her key chain out of her pocket and slid one key under the screen. She wedged it out, got her fingers underneath it and started to slide it out of its brace.

As soon as she had it pulled out enough, she tested the window. It wouldn't budge.

She snapped the screen back into place, then tried the next one. This one was more stubborn and resisted as she tried to pull it out. It rattled as she worked it loose.

The light flew on, and Blair hit the ground.

Ann had heard her. She would call the police.

Blair headed for the trees near the driveway, made her way along the side of it, cut across the neighbor's yard . . .

She heard a siren, and wondered if they could really be coming for her so quickly. She tried to make it to her car.

But it was too late. The headlights of the flashing squad car found her. The car skidded to a halt, and the door swung open. "Freeze!"

She turned and raised her hands, staring at the blaring lights. "Don't shoot," she said weakly.

"That's her, Officer," a man said from the shadows of the neighbor's house. "I saw her sneaking around in my yard."

One of the officers came toward her, threw her across the hood of her car. Her cheekbone slammed against the metal, and she stiffened as hands began to pat her down, looking for a weapon. "I can explain," she said. "I'm a friend of Police Chief Matthew Cade's. I had reason to believe—"

"You have the right to remain silent." The officer's sharp voice cut through her words.

"You're arresting me?" One of the officers kept her face pressed to that hood, and she found it hard to talk. "I told you I could explain!"

But no one was interested in her explanation.

She felt handcuffs snapping on her wrists, and she tried to straighten. "I didn't do anything!"

They pulled her up, and she looked at the man who'd accused her. He stood in the dark yard, wearing nothing but a pair of gym shorts and a T-shirt. It was the yard where she'd heard the door close. He must have seen her stealing down the driveway.

That meant that Ann hadn't called the police. Maybe she hadn't heard Blair's attempt to break in. Maybe she didn't know.

The officer walked her to the backseat of the squad car. "Please. Once you hear what I was doing, you'll understand. If you'll just listen to me."

They shoved her in, then slammed the door shut. She sat back on the seat, hating herself for getting caught. By now, she might have gotten into the house, found Cade, and exposed Ann for what she was.

She looked through the window, saw the neighbors from the lit up house standing on their front lawn. Thankfully, Ann wasn't among them. Maybe she didn't know.

She leaned back on the seat as the car started to move, and wondered how in the world she was going to break this news to Morgan.

CHAPTER

60

*T*he distant, faint sound of a siren startled Cade, and he sat up in bed. Had they figured out he was here? Were they raiding the place even now?

He tried to stand, the shattering pain in his head and leg shooting fireworks through his nerve endings. Dragging it, he pulled himself to the door. With all the strength left in him, he banged on it. "I'm in here! Please ... can anybody hear me? Behind the bookshelves! Please ..."

No one came. Sweat dripped in his eyes as he frantically looked around. If they were upstairs with her and weren't looking for him ...

He banged again. "Hello! Please ... can anybody hear me? This is Matthew Cade! They have me locked in the basement...."

They were coming! He heard urgent scraping, the door being unlocked....

Ann Clark opened the door and leveled her gun on him. "What are you doing?"

Cade almost collapsed. "I heard something . . . the police . . ."

"That wasn't here, you fool," she said. "Get back on the bed."

She waited with that gun as he lowered to the mattress.

"I think one of the neighbors must have had a break-in. Nice try, though. Too bad there was no one here to hear it."

It was too cruel. He was sure they had come. "Mrs. Clark, please. My leg is shattered and badly infected, my head is killing me—"

"Your problems are no concern of mine."

He wasn't ready to give up. "You know they're looking for me," he said. "Somebody's going to come looking. You're not going to get away with this."

"I already have," she said. "You underestimate me." She backed through the door and started to close it. "By the way, they *are* looking for you. You're wanted for kidnapping. You and your new wife."

She closed the door back, and he heard that scraping of the bookshelves again. Kidnapping? Wife? She must mean the letter he'd written. Had they really believed it? And the kidnapping . . . *he* was the one who'd been kidnapped.

Had they pinned some kind of crime on him? Was that why they were holding him?

Disheartened and dejected, he fell back onto the bed, shivering and fighting the crushing pain. He was going to die here, he thought, and no one would be able to help him.

It seemed as if even God had forgotten him.

CHAPTER

*T*he telephone rang near midnight. Morgan bolted upright in bed and lunged for it.

Jonathan caught her hand. "Tavist," he said.

It rang again, and she grabbed her robe and dashed out into the hall.

Karen was already on the stairs. "I'll get it!"

Morgan hurried down as Karen answered. "Hello?" She was breathless, hoarse. Her expression crashed, and she thrust it to Morgan. "It's not them. It's for you."

Morgan took the phone. "It's midnight. Who is it?"

Tears in her eyes, Karen started back up the stairs. "It's your sister."

Morgan frowned and put the phone to her ear. "Blair, do you know what time it is?"

"I'm in trouble." Blair's words were muffled, as if she didn't want to be overheard. "Morgan, you've got to come."

"What?" Morgan asked. "Blair, where are you?"

"I've been arrested, Morgan."

"You've *what?*" She turned to Tavist. He was still taping, but he looked up at her and mouthed "police station."

"You're in *jail?*" She yelled the word out, and Jonathan came hurrying down.

"Who's in jail?"

"Blair!" she said. "What have you done? Tell me you didn't break into that house."

Blair grunted. "I got arrested for trespassing."

Morgan brought her hand to her throat. She would kill her. She would just kill her. "I warned you, Blair. I told you this would happen! What has gotten into you?"

"Could we discuss this later?" Blair asked, her voice strained. "Right now, I could really use your help."

Morgan realized she was trembling. "Blair, are you all right?"

"I'm fine," she said. "Just a little frustrated."

Morgan knew that frustration. "Which jail?"

"Precinct Three on Victory Drive."

Morgan sighed. "I'll hurry, Blair."

Blair breathed a laugh. "Take your time. I'm not going anywhere."

CHAPTER

62

*B*lair was in no mood to play games with these officers. They had treated her like a common criminal, ignoring her explanations and protests. She'd had enough.

"If you jerks would do your job," she told the arresting officer, "then I wouldn't have had to be out there doing what I was doing. I was trying to save Police Chief Cade of Cape Refuge."

The cop shot her a look. "The one wanted for kidnapping?"

She sprang out of her chair. "He is not a kidnapper! He's been set up, and he's in trouble!"

"What do you have to do with Chief Cade?"

"I'm a good friend of his," she said, throwing her chin up. "If you want to check on me, you can call Detective McCormick who's running the Cape Refuge PD. Anybody there can vouch for me. I'm a decent citizen who's worried about my friend."

"That doesn't give you the right to go prowling through people's yards."

"If you would do it, I wouldn't have to. That's what I'm trying to tell you!"

The cop laughed and shook his head, and went back to typing up his report.

Blair wanted to go for his throat. "You people are amazing! Unbelievable. You're a police department. Don't you care that a crime's being committed?"

"Yes, I do," the man said. "That's why I'm about to lock you behind bars."

She groaned. "Lock me up then, I don't care. But go back there and search her house. I'm telling you, if you want to find him—whether you think he's the kidnapper or not—you'll find him in that house."

"Ma'am, Ann Clark is not a suspect. And that case is in the hands of the FBI now."

She realized she wasn't getting anywhere with him, so she tried to calm down. "But you can still arrest people. You can search houses if you have reason to believe that someone's life is in danger." When the cop kept hunting and pecking at the typewriter, she leaned across the desk and grabbed his wrist. He glared at her.

"Look," she said in a lower voice as she stared into his face. "I know that you don't know Cade or what kind of man he is. But he doesn't have it in him to kidnap a baby. He also doesn't have it in him to run off and get married secretly. He left his car parked at the restaurant he ate at the morning of his disappearance. He hasn't been home since." Her voice broke, but she had him. He was listening, for what that was worth. "He's a good, decent man with a heart. He wouldn't make his friends suffer this way."

"Maybe. Maybe not. Maybe you don't know him as well as you thought you did. People get under stress and they snap."

She slapped her hand on the desk. "He did not snap!"

"Blair."

She turned to see Morgan and Jonathan. Jonathan looked as if he'd just rolled out of bed, and Morgan's curly mane of brown hair had not been brushed. Smudged mascara underlined her eyes.

Blair got up and hugged her. From the way Morgan clung to her, one would think she faced thirty years. "Morgan, meet Officer Gray, who thinks that crimes being committed under the FBI's jurisdiction are no longer of any concern at all to the police department."

Morgan squeezed Blair's arm to silence her. Blair hated that. "Uh, Officer, I'm Morgan Cleary, and this is my husband, Jonathan. Blair has been under a lot of stress, and sometimes she says things—"

The man shot a look at Blair. "Sit down, lady."

Blair had made up her mind to keep standing, but Morgan pulled her down beside her. Since she had the checkbook, Blair acquiesced.

"He's still there, Morgan," she said. "In that house. To know he's there and not be able to do anything—"

"What's her bail?" Morgan cut in.

"None set yet," he said, still typing. "She's going to have to spend the night here and see if the judge sets bail in her arraignment tomorrow."

"No way!" Blair sprang up again. "I am *not* spending the night here."

He grinned. "Think again."

Blair gaped up at Jonathan. "Do something!"

"What?" he asked. "You broke the law and got arrested, just like Morgan told you you would. What do you want us to do?"

"I want you to talk some sense into them. Get me out of here!"

Morgan started to cry. "Blair, you can't throw yourself headlong into jeopardy, then expect me to fix everything for you. I'll bail you out tomorrow. But short of breaking you out of jail, I don't know what else to do."

Blair wasn't going to break down and blubber like some kind of frightened kid, in front of this cop and his buddies. "Okay, then let's get this show on the road. You're locking me up? Do it now. I'm ready for bed."

Morgan's face twisted, and she cupped her hand over her mouth. "Blair, don't make it worse. Come on, please cooperate."

"Hey, I'm cooperating," she bit out. "I'll fill out the forms for him if he wants me to. I'm not afraid of a jail cell."

Officer Gray couldn't stop grinning as he led her out of the squad room.

CHAPTER

*B*y the time they got Blair processed and transferred to the Chatham County Correctional Facility several hours had passed and morning had begun to dawn. Enduring the indignities they put her through, she donned the orange jumpsuit they gave her and surrendered all her personal items.

She would miss her appointment with Jason Wheater this morning to sign all the papers making the newspaper hers. She wondered if the banker would change his mind when they learned she'd been arrested.

She followed a deputy onto the elevator, and they got off on the third floor. Her parents had often talked of the Bible studies they did in this very place, and some of the "graduates" had wound up as tenants at Hanover House. Morgan and Jonathan came twice a week now. She hoped their efforts had done some good and that she wouldn't run into any angry inmates withdrawing from their drugs of choice, wanting to kill anyone who was handy.

They stopped at a room right outside the elevator and handed her a thin mattress, sheets, a blanket, and a bag of government-issued personal items. She stood there with the stack that almost covered her face. "I'm not going to be here long enough to need these."

But the deputy had heard that before. He led her to Pod 312—a circular room with doors to eight cells around it.

She went into the pod with the small metal table in the center of it and considered the pay phone on the wall. She'd been told she could make collect calls, and she thought of calling Morgan or Joe McCormick or Jason Wheater . . . or a lawyer. Would any of them take her collect call from jail?

She shivered in the cold and wondered why they wasted tax-payers' money refrigerating this place. She was glad she'd taken the blanket. Even if she wasn't spending the night, she needed to keep warm.

A voice blared out over the intercom speaker. "Get up, girls. Five A.M. Out of bed!"

Her heart sank. She wasn't ready to meet her cell mates.

She went into her own cell and dropped her mattress on the metal bed frame. She piled the folded blanket and sheets on top of it and set the bag down.

"Who are you?" She turned and saw a woman with pink spiked hair peering in.

Blair refused to cower. Crossing her arms, she walked toward the girl. "I'm Blair Owens." She thought of telling her that she was in here for killing a former cell mate who'd given her a hard time, but she wasn't sure she could pull it off. "And you are?"

"Brandy," the woman said.

Blair reached out to shake her hand, but the girl didn't respond. Blair dropped her hand and went back to her bag. "Don't get used to me, Brandy. I won't be here long. Probably only a couple of hours."

"Yeah, that's what I said two weeks ago." The girl was staring at her scars, so Blair turned away and started putting on her sheets.

"You been in a fire?"

Bristling, Blair looked back at her doorway. Even in a jail cell her disfigurement stood out. "Not lately."

"Then what's wrong with your face?"

Blair didn't need to ask why she was here. Jail was the only safe place for a woman with such social skills. "My scars are none of your business."

The woman enjoyed that. "Oh, you got an attitude, huh? You think you're somebody?"

Blair went to her door and slammed it shut, right in the woman's face. Fortunately, it locked from the inside.

The woman banged on her door, cursed at her, and Blair began to realize her reaction may have been ill-advised. When she did go out to use the bathroom or eat, the woman would likely ambush her. Watching the door, she sat down Indian-style on her bed and waited for the powers-that-be to come for her before she had to meet the rest of her neighbors.

As she sat there, she felt a surge of shame. If it had been Morgan in here, or her mother or father, they would have used the opportunity to minister to these women. They would have seen them as people with souls, needy, impoverished women who'd been dealt bad cards in life and needed a helping hand to get them back on track. Blair just saw them as a threat. The truth was, she feared them, but she wouldn't admit it, not to anyone. She hated admitting it to herself.

Wouldn't Cade have had a good laugh out of this? Blair Owens sitting in jail for trespassing. And if she'd gotten into that house, she'd be in here for breaking and entering. Yeah, he may have enjoyed the irony in it, but he'd be there to get her out. She had no doubt about that.

Morgan, on the other hand, was probably ranting and raving, waxing eloquent to Jonathan about how irresponsible and compulsive Blair was. But Blair couldn't understand why Jonathan and Morgan weren't trying to break into the Clark house to find Cade themselves, no matter the cost. She leaned back on the concrete wall and looked at the ceiling.

"Please let him be alive," she whispered to whatever Force was listening. "Please don't let anything happen to him." But she feared her plea fell on deaf ears—or no ears at all.

The judge released her that morning on a thousand dollars' bond, which Morgan withdrew from Blair's savings account.

"I hope you're happy with yourself," she told Blair as she waited for her personal items. "Now you're unemployed with a prison record, and the money you would have used to buy the paper is down a thousand dollars."

"It doesn't matter. I'm still buying it. Jason will understand that I got in trouble looking for Cade."

When she'd gotten her things, Morgan walked Blair out to her car. She and Jonathan had retrieved it late last night from the scene of the crime. Blair got in and sat behind the wheel.

"Are you going home?" Morgan asked. "Or are you heading back over to Ann Clark's so they can lock you up again?"

Blair looked up at her with dull, weary eyes. "You're not very supportive, you know that?"

Morgan shook her head. "How can I be supportive of you when you're breaking the law? Blair, next time you could get yourself killed."

"Then you do admit that Ann Clark is dangerous?"

"I don't *know* if she's dangerous," Morgan said. "All I know is you've got to stop this!"

Blair looked at a small chip on her windshield. "I've got to figure out a way to get in there that's not illegal." She looked up at her sister. "Help me, Morgan. I'm desperate to get in that house. I know he's in there, and I just have this feeling that if we don't hurry—"

"Oh, my gosh. You aren't seriously trying to make me an accomplice to your madness!"

"No, I'm not. You're not criminal material." She looked at Morgan carefully. "But I was thinking, sitting in that cell this morning. Maybe we could get Ann Clark to invite us in."

Morgan closed her eyes. "I can't believe you're saying this."

"Just listen! Mrs. Clark didn't see me last night. I don't think she knew anything was going on. So ... suppose we bring her dinner, a casserole or something, and just tell her that we were from the church in Cape Refuge, and we'd heard about her husband and just wanted to come and minister to her?"

Morgan opened her eyes and leveled them on her sister. "Go on."

Blair grinned. "I knew the casserole part would get you. Most people wouldn't turn you away if you come bearing food. And we could be kind of pushy. I mean, if she tries to take the food at the door, we could insist that we get our dishes back. We could go in and start transferring the food into her dishes. If things go well, maybe I could somehow slip away and look around."

"What if she realizes what we're doing? She could get violent or something."

"I could bring my gun," Blair said. "Just in case."

Morgan gasped. "I'm *not* helping if you take a gun. I mean it. Are you hearing me?"

"Fine! I won't. So you'll do it?"

Morgan blew out her frustration. "I have to go with you, or I'm going to be visiting you in jail every Saturday for the next few years. Or at the cemetery."

"We could find him," Blair said. "It could work!"

Morgan looked sick. "All I'm saying is we'll get into the house. What we see after that is up to God. He's just going to have to reveal stuff to us. But I'm not getting you in there so you can play cops and robbers."

Blair grinned. "So when do we do this dastardly deed?"

Morgan rolled her eyes. "I don't know," she said. "Not tonight. We have to rest. We have to think and plan."

"Cade may not *have* another night," Blair said.

Morgan sighed. "Well, I can't tell Jonathan what I'm doing. He'll never let me go."

"So you're going to lie to him?" Blair asked hopefully.

Morgan shook her head. "Yeah, like the wonderful Proverbs 31 woman that I am. I hate that you put me in this position, Blair!"

"It's to save someone's life," Blair whispered. "You know it is. Jonathan will understand."

"I sure hope so." Morgan blew out a long, weary breath. "All right, Blair. We'll go tonight."

CHAPTER

64

*M*organ was exhausted by the time she got the casseroles made. All day, she'd dealt with Karen's swings from despair to rage at the plight of her baby. The FBI had been staking out the bus station since yesterday, but nothing had happened and the kidnapper had not called back. And having the FBI agent there twenty-four/seven was beginning to drain her, as well.

It had begun to rain around noon, so Jonathan had to cut his fishing tour short. He came home early and helped with Seth as Morgan cooked.

"So who is it you're going to see?" he asked as she set the casseroles into a box for her car.

"I don't think you've met her." Morgan couldn't look him in the eye. "She's new on the island, and Blair and I just thought we'd go by and say hello and take her something to eat."

"You know, you could let Melba take this one. You've got a lot going on. It's not like someone's going to think less of you for missing one newcomer."

"I just want her to feel welcome. And the truth is, I need the distraction." She hated lying to him. Several times today she had thought of coming clean and asking Jonathan to come with them. But Ann Clark was more likely to buy their story if it was just two women.

She hoped God and Jonathan would forgive her when the truth came out.

"I've already bathed Seth," she said, "so he should be ready for bed in a couple of hours. All you have to do is feed him. And Sadie's going out tonight. She's going to a wedding."

Jonathan frowned. "What wedding?"

"Some girl she met when she worked at the paper. I told her she could take my car. I'll ride with Blair."

He got an apple from a bowl on the counter and turned it over in his hand like a baseball.

"You know, we never did ground her," he said. "We should have done something."

Morgan sighed. "A lot's been going on. I haven't had time to think about it. She has so few friends, though. I thought it was nice that she was invited."

He nodded and looked through the kitchen door. The agents were switching shifts, and Tavist was leaving. Morgan was sick of having these people in her house, and they were no closer to finding the baby than they had been the day he was born.

As Morgan waited for Blair on the porch, she prayed that God would forgive her for failing to submit to her husband and lying to him through her teeth. She didn't know what she'd been thinking to agree to such a scheme. It was desperation, she thought, to keep Blair from breaking out a window or shooting her way in. And it might be the only way they were going to find Cade.

But her own deception wasn't so far removed from Sadie's scheme the other night. She hated herself for going along with this.

When Blair pulled into the driveway, Morgan saw that she looked like the perfect church lady. She had worn a dress for the occasion and pulled her hair back in a bun. The scars on her face flamed redder than usual. She got out and took the casseroles, arranged them on the backseat.

"Where's your gun?" Morgan whispered.

"In my house."

Morgan grabbed Blair's purse off the seat and dug through it.

Blair smirked. "Are you going to frisk me, too?"

Morgan wasn't amused. "Should I?"

Laughing, Blair got back into the car. "I swear, Morgan, I left the gun in the house. We're flying without a net. Now, come on."

Morgan got into the car.

"What did Jonathan say?" Blair asked.

Morgan stared straight ahead. "Nothing. He trusts his wife. He thinks I'm going to welcome a new neighbor to Cape Refuge. I can't believe I lied to him."

"Good story, though."

Blair was silent as they crossed the bridge to Tybee Island, then wound their way around the island and up Highway 80 to Savannah. Quiet hung between them as they got to Ann Clark's house and pulled into the driveway.

"All right, Blair, we're going to get in that house, but I want you to promise me you're not going to do anything heroic or dangerous. Do you promise me that? Can I have your word?"

Blair just stared at the door to the house. "I'm not going to do anything dangerous. I'm just going to try to find Cade."

"Blair, I need your word that you're not going to do anything stupid. I'll never forgive you if you get me killed."

"I'm not, okay?" Blair opened the door and got out of the car. Sighing, Morgan got out the casseroles. Blair came around and took one of them.

"So, how do we act?" Blair asked in a low voice. "Bouncy and happy?"

"Just like Mom used to do," Morgan said. "We have to act genuinely friendly and concerned or she's never going to let us in."

"Okay," Blair said. "I can do this."

They walked up to the front steps of the house, rang the doorbell. There was no sound within, none at all.

"She's got to be home," Blair whispered. "She hardly ever leaves." With her elbow she pressed the doorbell again and waited, then finally balanced the casserole on one arm and banged on the front door.

"She's not here," Morgan said finally.

Blair waited another few moments and finally realized that Morgan was right. Either the woman was in there, refusing to answer, or she really wasn't here. She couldn't believe she hadn't been here to follow her.

"Here." She handed Morgan her casserole, weighing her down.

"Where are you going?" Morgan asked.

"Just down the driveway to see if her car is here."

"You can't trespass again, Blair," Morgan whispered harshly. "You'll be locked up forever. If the neighbors see you—"

But Blair kept going. "I just want to see if her car is home."

Morgan headed back to the car, arms laden down with hot casseroles. She managed to get them back in the box without spilling them and watched as Blair walked down to the back of the house and peered into the garage. Finally she shook her head and came back.

"She's really not here. Wouldn't you know it?"

"Then we'll just have to try again later."

Blair groaned and looked back at the house. "It's a great time to go in. If I could just find an open window . . ."

Morgan grabbed her sister. "Blair, so help me, I will throw myself in front of a moving vehicle to stop you. You're not going to do that tonight."

As she pulled out of the driveway, Blair wondered at the wisdom of involving her sister.

CHAPTER

65

*T*he wedding of Trevor's cousin was held at the home of his father's sister, in a terraced English garden that looked like something befitting royalty. Sadie sat through it, holding Trevor's hand and feeling a sense of euphoria that he would want her here with him.

She didn't know anyone here, so her fears that Morgan and Jonathan would find out faded from her mind not long after the wedding began. Only one face in the crowd looked slightly familiar, and she couldn't quite place it.

The small woman had come in alone, and an usher had seated her near some of the family, whom she greeted as if they were close friends.

Where had Sadie seen her before?

She watched the woman as the ceremony began, racking her brain for a name. When it did not come to her, she leaned over to Trevor.

"Who's that woman over there?" she asked.

Trevor shrugged. "Don't know. I think she's a friend of my father's, but I don't know her name."

Sadie tried to forget about her, but her mind couldn't seem to let it go. She thought of finding her at the reception and asking her who she was, but then she feared that she might be a friend of Morgan's. She couldn't risk letting word get back to them.

The reception was set up on the other side of the house, in another garden area. Before sitting down, Trevor took her around to introduce her to some of his family.

She felt like an honored guest, someone of worth, as they hugged her and welcomed her here. This wasn't a crime family, she thought. They were decent, loving people. Morgan and Jonathan were wrong about them.

She felt giddy as she took her place at their table. But he didn't sit down. His eyes were on a man a few yards away, hobbling toward him on crutches. Trevor seemed to change as he approached. A hard look came over his face. "Smart of you to come," he told the man.

The man's hand trembled as he reached out to shake. Trevor took it coldly, staring into his eyes.

"I wouldn't have missed it," the man said. "And I brought the check. Your father has it."

"So you're not as stupid as I thought," Trevor said.

Had she heard right? Had Trevor really said that? She looked up at his hard face, then at the man's. He was clearly intimidated.

"I won't be late again." The man's voice trembled.

"Smart man."

The man crutched away, and as Trevor sat down, a chill fell over her. Had Trevor had anything to do with that man's injury?

She looked over at him, afraid to ask. "How did he get hurt?"

"He got in a fight," Trevor said. "Don't worry about it."

She stared at him for a moment. "He wasn't . . . late for a loan, was he?"

He picked up his glass and brought it to his lips. He said nothing, but the look in his eyes silenced her.

The music started, and she looked down at her plate. A man with a broken leg, obviously afraid of Trevor....

Maybe Morgan was right, after all.

She watched the bride and groom dance the first dance, but her mind raced with images. Trevor cornering the man, beating him until his bones broke. Would he have used his fists or some kind of weapon?

She started to get dizzy, and beads of sweat broke out on her temples.

Trevor noticed. "Are you okay?"

"Uh, yes." She slid her chair back on the grass. "I just need ... where is the rest room?"

He pointed to the house. "Sure you're okay?"

"Yes. I'll be right back." She took her handbag and started up to the house, but she saw some of the servants inside, and she didn't want to talk to them.

Instead, she walked back to the other garden, where the ceremony had been held. The chairs were still set up, the flowers still beautifully placed.

She saw a path that led from the rose-covered arbor deeper into the garden, so she headed for it, trying to breathe deeply and calm down.

So a man had a broken leg. She was overreacting. She had no evidence that Trevor had anything to do with it—only her suspicions. Then again, he knew what she was thinking, and he hadn't denied it.

She smelled the scent of jasmine as she followed the path, her mind racing. There was nothing wrong with this family. They were nice, decent people, and Trevor was good.

But he had admitted to her that intimidation was sometimes required to make people pay their loans.

She imagined him swinging a bat at the hunkering man, teaching him a lesson about paying his debts.

She felt sick. She couldn't go back yet. She needed a moment to breathe ... to think ...

She turned on the path and stopped suddenly.

A man and a woman stood kissing in a grove of trees. Their lips broke off, and she saw the woman she had recognized earlier. "Ann, we've got to stop this," the man whispered. "Someone could see us."

Sadie caught her breath. *Ann?*

Then suddenly, it all came back to her. The DMV photo Blair had of Ann Clark. She had seen it when Blair showed it to Jonathan.

But who was the man?

She backed away, but her foot broke a twig, and the pair turned and saw her.

"Uh . . . excuse me. I was just getting some air . . ."

She saw the man's face. It looked familiar too, but for the life of her, she couldn't place it.

She turned and started away and made her way back to the reception. Trevor looked up at her as she reached the table.

She could hardly breathe, and her hands shook as she groped for her chair.

"You look like you just saw a ghost," Trevor said. "Are you okay?"

"No. I'm sick, Trevor. I need to go home."

"Sick? Just like that?"

"Just like that. You stay. I've got Morgan's car. But I have to get home."

He walked her to her car in silence, as if he didn't believe her story, but she couldn't worry about that now.

As she drove home, her mind raced through the night's images. What was Ann Clark doing with another man, so soon after her husband's death?

Did it mean something, or was it all just coincidence?

And how could she not tell Morgan? It could be important information. But if she told her, she'd have to reveal the fact that she had disobeyed and deceived them again. She'd have to come clean.

If she didn't tell them, they would go on thinking she was repentant and trustworthy. But Cade's life, and Emory's, might depend on her telling them. It might matter to the investigation if, indeed, Ann was involved in Cade's disappearance.

By the time she reached Hanover House, she was in tears. But she had made up her mind.

Morgan and Blair were inside at the kitchen table when she went in. Morgan looked up at her. "Sadie, you're home early. How was the wedding?"

"I lied to you." The confession came quickly, leaving no room for backing down. "The wedding was Trevor Beal's cousin's. I was his date."

Morgan looked as if she'd been slapped. Slowly, she came to her feet. "Sadie—"

"You can do what you want to me later," Sadie said as tears began to roll down her cheeks. "Throw me out, whatever. I deserve it. But the reason I'm telling you is that Ann Clark was there."

Blair sprang up. "Ann Clark?"

"Yes. I didn't recognize her at first. But then I stumbled on her in the garden, kissing a man. And it came to me who she was."

Blair came toward her. "Who was the man, Sadie? Did you know him?"

"No, I don't know him, but I've seen him somewhere before. I don't know where. I've tried to remember."

Morgan still looked shell-shocked. "Could you ask Trevor or someone who was there?"

"No, because no one else saw them together. They were hidden. I heard him call her Ann. He said, 'Ann, we've got to stop this. Someone could see us.'"

Tears rimmed Morgan's eyes. "Did they see you?"

"Yes," she said. "But I just acted like it was no big deal. And it was dark. They probably couldn't see me that well."

Blair's face was tight, and her scars darkened. "Okay, so now we know that Ann Clark has ties to the Beal family and that she's not exactly grieving over her dearly departed husband. If she's involved in this kidnapping scheme, then it's possible that they are too. We have to tell McCormick. We have to tell Tavist."

But Morgan was still staring at Sadie with those tear-filled eyes. "Why did you lie to us again, Sadie?"

Sadie had never hated herself so much. "I don't know. I liked him so much, but Morgan, I think you were right about him. There was a man there with a broken leg, who'd been late paying a loan. I think Trevor had something to do with his injury. I'm so sorry I didn't listen. I don't know what's wrong with me. I know better, but I just follow my emotions like some airheaded idiot. I don't blame you if you want me to leave."

"Leave?" Morgan asked. "Sadie, we're not going to make you leave. You're not a tenant. You're family."

Sadie wanted to die. "But I betrayed you, not just once, Morgan. I did it over and over."

Blair stepped between them. "Can we do this woe-is-me stuff later? We've got a crisis here. And for heaven's sake, Morgan, she did tell us the truth. If she hadn't, we wouldn't have known about Ann Clark. She did the right thing, even if it started out wrong."

Morgan sighed, and pulled Sadie into a hug. "Blair's right. Right now we've got to decide what to do with this information. We have to tell Agent Tavist and Joe."

An hour later, they had informed law enforcement of the information Sadie had brought home, but it seemed to make no difference.

"Even if Ann Clark was having an affair before her husband died, it doesn't prove that she has anything to do with her husband's death, Cade's disappearance, or the infant kidnappings," Tavist said.

Blair wanted to explode. "Are you telling me that her connection to the biggest crime family in the southeast is not important information?"

"That's not what I'm saying. It may play out later, but right now it gets us no closer to finding either one of them."

Law enforcement was going to be of no help at all in this, Blair finally realized. No, she would have to do this herself.

As Morgan walked her out to her car, Blair turned back to her. "I'm going back there tomorrow night. I'm going to get in that house, with or without the casseroles."

She'd expected Morgan to balk and throw a fit, but instead, her sister just nodded. "Pick me up at six. I'll have them ready."

CHAPTER

I'm scared." Morgan muttered the words as she got one of the casseroles out of the backseat. She had pictured them doing this at night, but at almost seven in the evening, darkness had not yet fallen.

Blair got the other one. "Stop shaking! She'll get suspicious."

Morgan looked up at the house. "Aren't you scared?"

"Scared for Cade," Blair said. "Just think about him."

Blair had spent the day choreographing their moves. She'd decided that the parlor just inside the front door didn't give her the access she might need to the house. If they got into the kitchen, she knew that Morgan could distract the woman while Blair went farther in.

Morgan followed her to the side door.

"Ready?" Blair whispered.

"I guess so," Morgan said.

"Remember," Blair said. "We're happy southern church ladies. In other words, be yourself."

Blair rang and then held her breath as they waited for the woman. She heard footsteps and saw the curtain being pulled back slightly as Ann Clark peered out to see who was there.

Blair and Morgan smiled like Welcome Wagon ladies.

Slowly, the woman unbolted the lock and cracked the door open. "Yes?"

Blair put on her best Georgia voice. "Mrs. Clark, I don't know if you remember me, but I was here a few days ago when we notified you of your husband's death. Blair Owens?"

Ann stiffened. "Uh-huh."

"This is my sister, Morgan." Morgan's face was white, but she managed to smile.

"Hello, Mrs. Clark," Morgan said. "You've just been on our minds so much lately, that we wanted to come by and offer you a little comfort in your time of grief." She raised the dish. "We brought casseroles."

"They're a little hot," Blair said. "Can we come in and set them down?"

Ann opened the door farther but blocked the entrance. "I'll take them."

She took Blair's from her and set it on the counter next to her, then reached for Morgan's.

Morgan surrendered it willingly and gave Blair a look that said, *What now?*

Blair grabbed the screen and pushed her way in. "Mrs. Clark, I hate to ask this. I hope it doesn't sound rude, but we were hoping we could transfer the food into some of your dishes, because we need ours back."

Ann gaped at her. "The fact is that I'm in the middle of something right now, and I don't have time for company."

"Oh, you go right ahead with what you were doing," Blair said. "We'll take care of everything."

As they'd rehearsed, Morgan came in behind her and went straight to the cabinets. Opening one, she said, "Where do you keep the casserole dishes, Hon? We'll need one about the same size, since I don't want the casserole to look like mush. It's chicken spaghetti, very good, if I do say so myself. And it freezes well. You might want a dish that you can freeze."

Clearly annoyed, Ann opened the right cabinet and pulled out two casserole dishes. "Here."

Blair slipped behind her, and headed into the hall. "May I use your rest room?"

Ann swung around. "I told you, I'm in the middle of something. I'd rather you—"

Something crashed, and Blair looked back. Morgan had dropped Ann's casserole dish, and the glass was all over the floor.

"Oh, Mrs. Clark!" Morgan cried. "I'm so sorry. You must think we're the rudest things, coming in here like this and breaking your dish. I'll just clean every bit of this up. . . ."

Blair seized the opportunity and took off down the hall, looking in each room for some sign of Cade. She saw a closed door and thought it might be the basement. Quickly, she opened it, flicked on the light and started down the stairs.

She heard Ann shouting at her from the kitchen, and Morgan fussing over the broken glass . . .

She looked around, saw the small basement area. There were no doors down here, only pipes and a furnace, and a set of bookshelves against one wall.

The concrete floor in front of one set of the shelves looked scraped, as if the shelves had been repeatedly pulled away.

She wondered what was behind them.

"Miss Owens, the bathroom is not down here!"

Ann Clark stood halfway down the stairs, her eyes aflame, as if she knew what was happening. "I don't want your casseroles. Get out of my house now before I call the police!"

Blair started back up the stairs. "I was just looking for the bathroom."

"You don't know a bathroom from a basement?" Ann said. "Get out of my house."

Blair thought of running for the bookshelves, knocking them over, seeing if there was a door behind them. She tried to think it through.

Then Morgan appeared at the top of the stairs. "Blair, you heard her. We have to go. Now!"

"All right, I'm sorry." Blair started back up the stairs. "I didn't mean to be rude. I've just had a kidney infection, and when I have to go, I have to go, if you know what I mean. I was kind of in a hurry."

She passed Ann on the stairs, felt the murderous hatred in her eyes. She hurried to the kitchen.

Morgan went back to the pile of glass on the floor. "Mrs. Clark, do you have a broom and dustpan anywhere?"

"I'll clean it up," Ann bit out. "I want you both out of my house."

Morgan opened the door. "Look, just keep our dishes. I'm so sorry to be so rude."

Blair hung back, but Morgan grabbed her hand and pulled her out. Ann slammed the door behind them.

Blair swung around. "Morgan, I was there!" she whispered. "Why couldn't you distract her a little longer?"

"She was going to stop you, Blair! I feared for your life! Besides, I had what we needed."

As she spoke, Morgan got into the car. Blair jumped in next to her. "What do you mean, 'what we need'?"

Morgan pulled a ball of gauze out of her pocket. "This. I found it in the trash when I was throwing away some of the glass."

Blair caught her breath and took it from her. A bloody bandage.

"It's Cade's blood, Morgan." Blair hadn't expected the tears that pushed to her eyes. "He may be dead."

"They don't bandage dead people," Morgan said. "But I'm afraid she'll know I took it."

Blair tried to think as she pulled out of the driveway. "She might do something drastic, like moving him. I can't take that chance. We have to watch her and follow her if she leaves. And somehow I have to get back in that house. I think there might be a door in the basement behind the bookshelves. I have to move them and see—"

"No!" Morgan shouted. "Blair, you can't go off half-cocked and start breaking into people's houses, *especially* if they're criminals. We're taking this to the FBI. Maybe if they can confirm that it's his blood, they'll realize that they've been wrong."

"They won't!" Blair said. "They think he's the criminal! If he's not dead already, she could kill him before those Keystone Cops get stirred up enough to do anything about it."

"Blair, so help me, you are not doing this yourself. We'll head for the nearest police precinct for safety and notify Tavist from there."

"Tavist," Blair said bitterly. "You don't seriously think he'll do anything!"

"Blair, so help me, you drive to the police station now or I'll turn you in. I'll tell them what you're planning. At least if they arrest you you'll be safer in jail than breaking into Ann Clark's house."

Blair hit the steering wheel with the heel of her hand. "Morgan, it'll be a waste of time. We don't have time to waste!"

"Do it!" Morgan yelled. "Blair, I mean what I say. Drive to the police station right now!"

"All right," Blair shouted. "But Cade's life is in *your* hands. You'd better be right about this."

CHAPTER

The police station was just as it had been the night of Blair's arrest. She found Officer Gray—who had arrested her—sitting behind his desk, eating pizza from a greasy box.

She made a beeline toward him, and Morgan followed.

"I need to use your phone to call Agent Tavist with the FBI," she said when she reached his desk.

He looked up at her. "What?"

"It's me. Blair Owens, the one you arrested the other night. I was in Ann Clark's house tonight, and we found a bloody bandage. I have reason to believe that it's Chief Matthew Cade's blood. I need to notify the FBI."

He set his pizza slice back in the box and closed it. "Are you confessing to breaking and entering?"

"No!" Blair shouted. "Ann was there. She let us in. Please, I need to use the phone."

He shoved his phone across his desk, and as Blair dialed Hanover House, he got up and headed to the back.

She got Tavist on the phone, told him what had happened. He seemed more worried about what he called her "interference in the investigation" than he did with the bandage. He told her to wait there, while he consulted with his superiors.

Blair hung up and looked at her sister. "I hope you're happy. They're probably not going to do anything. She's probably doing something drastic as we speak!"

"Calm down, Blair. They're not going to ignore this."

Officer Gray came back, followed by a man dressed in a tweed sport coat with a dark T-shirt under it. He crossed the room and shook their hands.

"Ladies, I'm Detective Hull."

Morgan nodded. "I met you at the hospital when the baby was kidnapped."

He stared at her for a moment, as recognition dawned. "Yes, now I remember. You're Miss Miller's friend." He shoved his hands into his pockets. "I just got a call from Agent Tavist, ladies. He wants me to take a statement from you and take a look at that bandage."

Finally, they were getting somewhere. Blair withdrew the bandage from her pocket, and handed it to him.

She would have expected him to handle it with gloves or something, but he took it in two fingers. "Come back to my office," he said. "You can wait for Tavist there and fill me in on how you got this."

Blair and Morgan followed him quickly, assessing the man from the top of his tousled, too-long hair, to the deck shoes he wore without socks. When they got to his office, he went in, dropped into his chair, and lit up a cigarette. "Have a seat," he said.

Blair sat down, and Morgan hesitated, then picked up a wadded coffee cup that lay in her chair. She set it gently on his desk.

"Sorry about that."

Morgan sat down.

He frowned down at the bandage and leaned forward, blew out a stream of smoke.

"Don't you want to bag that or something?" Blair asked. "Seems like your smoke could compromise the evidence."

Cigarette hanging from his mouth, he pulled an evidence bag out of his desk and dropped the bandage in. "So why were you in the Clark house again?"

"We took her some casseroles," Blair said. "She invited us in. My sister broke a dish and was cleaning it up, and that was in the trash can. It's Cade's blood, Detective Hull. I know it is. All you need is to prove it's his, and you'll have probable cause to do a thorough search of her house."

"It doesn't work that way. We can't test it without his own blood samples."

"Look, I'm not stupid," Blair bit out. "I know how DNA works. You could go to his house and get a hair off of his comb. Besides that, he's probably had blood tests, drug tests, and all sorts of stuff for the police department. There must be medical records. You have to start somewhere."

Hull looked down at the bandage soaked with blood. "Of course we'll do those things."

His noncommital attitude sent her over the edge. "What is wrong with you people?"

Morgan sighed. "Blair, calm down."

"It's like you're afraid you're going to solve a crime or something. I don't get it. I thought police officers were supposed to be real sensitive when it came to violence against their own, but you don't even care."

"I do care," he said, "but I was with Detective McCormick the day he questioned her. There's no one being hidden in that house!"

Blair slammed her hand on his desk. "Are you going to do anything or not? Because if you're not, I'll do it myself."

Hull leaned forward, pinning her with his eyes. "And what exactly are you going to do?"

Blair evaded the question. "I know where she's holding Cade. There are bookshelves in that basement, and they look like they've been moved back and forth to hide something behind them."

He took the cigarette out of his mouth and squinted at her through the smoke. "I went in that basement myself. Your chief is not there."

"Are you blind?" Blair yelled. "Did you see the arching scrape marks on the concrete?"

Morgan touched Blair's arm to calm her, but Blair jerked it away.

Hull got up. "Look, I have to check on something. Stay here for a minute. I'll be right back." He took the bandage and headed back into the squad room.

Blair wanted to erupt. "Morgan, we tried it your way. These people are idiots! They're not going to do anything!"

Morgan sighed. "Blair, you have a way of rubbing people the wrong way, putting them instantly on the defensive. Haven't you ever heard that you attract more flies with honey?"

"I don't *have* any honey," Blair bit out, "and I don't have time to attract flies. Cade could be dying."

"Just calm down. We've done what we're supposed to do, and I know that the bandage is going to be enough to get them to act."

"Well, you have more faith in them than I do." Blair got up and looked out into the squad room. Hull was on the phone.

She had to get out of here, she thought. She had to get back there and move those bookshelves. She never should have listened to Morgan. She should have taken her gun with her and forced Ann to lead her to him.

Well, she didn't have her gun, but she could get back in that house somehow and go down into that basement. . . .

She looked around. "Where's the bathroom in this place?"

Morgan shrugged. "You're the one who was locked up here the other day. I don't know."

"I'm going to go find it," Blair said. "I'll be right back."

But instead of finding the bathroom, Blair looked instead for a side exit. Hull was still deep in conversation, so he didn't see her as she slipped out.

She hurried toward her car before Morgan could figure out what she'd done. Cade was in that house, and she was going to get to him tonight if it absolutely killed her.

CHAPTER

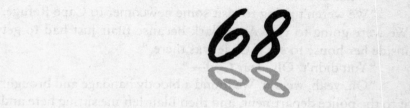

68

*F*ifteen minutes passed before Morgan realized that Blair had left the station. She ran out to the parking lot, and saw that Blair's car was gone. Morgan screamed out her rage, then rushed back inside.

"She's gone," she told Hull, "and I know right where she is. She's gone back to Ann Clark's house to handle this by herself!"

Hull was listening now. "She wouldn't be that stupid."

"Oh, yes, she would," Morgan screamed back. "Please! You guys have got to get over there and do something. She's going to get herself killed!"

Hull sprang into action and rushed out. Morgan sat there a moment as fear gripped her.

She needed help. She needed Jonathan.

She picked up Hull's phone and dialed Hanover House. It rang three times, and she knew one of the agents was giving them the signal to answer.

"Hello?"

"Jonathan, I need you."

He paused. "Morgan, what's going on? Why did Blair call Tavist?"

She started to cry. "I'm in Savannah. I'm no better than Sadie. I lied to you, Jonathan, right through my teeth. Not once but twice."

"What about?"

"We weren't going to visit some newcomer to Cape Refuge. We were going to visit Ann Clark because Blair just had to get inside her house to see if Cade was there."

"You didn't. Oh, dear God—"

"Oh, yeah, we did. We found a bloody bandage and brought it to the police department, and then Blair left me sitting here and went right back there by herself. Jonathan, she's going to break back into that woman's house!"

He was breathing heavy. "Morgan, which precinct?"

"Three, on Victory Drive."

"Stay right there. Don't move until I get there. Do you hear me?"

Morgan knew she couldn't talk him out of that. "Hurry, Jonathan."

"Morgan, I'll be there as soon as possible. But don't you leave there!"

"I hear you," she said. "I'll be right here."

CHAPTER

*D*arkness had fallen over the city by the time Blair got back to Ann Clark's house. She had not left. Her car was still in the garage, and Blair could see her through the kitchen window, pacing and ranting into the phone.

She hurried to the window she'd tried to break into last night and saw that the screen was still crooked. No one had noticed it.

She worked it loose, careful not to scrape. Then she tried the window.

It slid up.

She froze. Could she do this? Could she climb in without being heard?

Did she have a choice?

Any minute now, Morgan would notice she was gone. The police would come and stop her, further alerting that woman. She had to hurry.

She pushed the window open a few more inches, then managed to pull herself in. The room was dark, but in the lamplight from the hallway, she could see that it was a library. Law books lined the shelves, and a big wooden desk sat in the middle of the room.

She stood silently in the dark, listening for the sound of Ann Clark's voice.

"I can't move him alone! Even if I drug him, it'll take some time for it to take effect, and I can't carry him!"

Blair shuddered. He was here, all right, and she hadn't come a moment too soon.

She tiptoed to the doorway and stopped.

Ann Clark was coming up the hall.

Blair stepped back into the shadows and waited. She heard a door opening, feet going down basement stairs.

Blair stole out of the room and tiptoed to the cellar door. Sweat beaded across her lip as she peered down.

She couldn't see Ann, but she heard a scraping sound.

Slowly, she stepped down the stairs. Ann was pushing the bookshelf away, and just as Blair suspected, there was a door behind it. She watched the woman open the locked door, heard her talking to someone.

A man replied.

Her heart almost leaped from her chest. Cade! He was alive!

She searched around for a weapon that she could use against the woman. Hurrying back up and into the hall, she reached for a vase that sat on a table.

Her trembling hand slipped. The vase toppled over and crashed.

"Who's there?" she heard the woman cry.

"Cade!" Blair screamed. She picked up the broken glass and held it like a weapon. "Cade! Can you hear me?"

She heard his voice, muffled and weak.

A bullet fired past her head, and she dove to the side. Rolling into another room, she searched for something, anything, that she could use.

She found a fireplace tool leaning against a dusty hearth and wielded it like a sword.

She heard the woman searching for her, going from room to room.

Blair knew she would come here next. She held the tool above her head, waited for her to come through the door . . .

Ann was still holding the gun in both hands, her arms stiff as she came through the door. Blair swung the tool and knocked the gun out of her hand.

The woman screamed, and Blair dove for the gun. Before she reached it Ann was on her back, desperately trying to choke her as she reached. . . .

CHAPTER

$\mathcal{J}$onathan flew behind Agent Tavist's car to Savannah, then detoured to the Third Precinct to pick up Morgan. He ran inside and found her, pacing in front of the glass doors and crying hysterically.

He threw his arms around her.

"I'm so sorry, Jonathan! So sorry!"

"Let's go," he said. He pulled her back out to his truck, and they took off for Ann Clark's house, hoping to stop Blair before she got herself killed.

71

*F*rom his bed, Cade heard Blair's voice
screaming out his name.

Ann had left the door open as she'd dashed out of his
room. He heard crashing glass, breaking furniture, Blair's
screams ripping through the house.

Cade pulled himself off the bed and lunged for the
door. Pain exploded through his body, but he got out into
the bigger basement room.

He heard another crash, Ann's cursing, Blair's frantic voice—

He fell at the bottom of the stairs. Sweat covered his
face and neck, and he gritted his teeth against the pain. He
pulled himself up one step after another, only able to use
his good leg.

"Please, Lord, help me," he whispered. "Don't let
anything happen to her."

One by one he made his way up the steps, pain bolt-
ing through him with each shove of his body upward. He
got to the top of the stairs and looked up the hall. Broken

things and toppled furniture bore witness to what he had just heard, and he heard more scuffling in a room just off the hallway. Holding onto the wall and gritting his teeth in pain, he managed to drag himself along.

He heard a siren outside, saw headlights through the windows, but he didn't have time to wait for the cops. He reached the doorway.

Ann Clark was on top of Blair, choking the life out of her. Blair's scars were purple, and her eyes were bulging. He saw the gun lying on the floor where Ann had dropped it just out of either of their reach. He kept his eyes on it, moving toward it as pain sliced through his nerve endings, shards of bone piercing tissue and muscle. . . .

He was going to black out. He turned and saw Blair losing the fight.

The gun still lay there. He got himself over it, grabbed it. . . .

They were too close together—and his hands weren't steady. The danger of hitting Blair was too great. But Ann's hands clutched Blair's throat.

His finger closed over the trigger, and he fired.

Ann Clark fell away.

CHAPTER

*B*lair screamed as the force of the bullet threw Ann off her. Trying to catch her breath, she twisted and saw Cade leaning in the doorway with the gun in his hand.

"Cade!"

She started to sob at the sight of him. Getting up, she went toward him. He had a two-week growth of beard, and his skin was deathly gray. His pant leg had been cut off at the knee, and she saw his mangled leg with its blood-soaked bandage.

He fell toward her, and she caught him. "Cade!" She'd heard sirens outside. Where were the police? "Help! Somebody help me!"

She heard the kitchen door crashing open as she fell with him, trying to buffer his landing. "Help him!" she cried as they came into view. "He's wounded!"

Paramedics pulled Cade away, and Blair scooted back against the wall, watching, helpless, as they tried to bring him back around. Others ran for Ann Clark, who lay bleeding on her floor.

Blair shivered and rubbed her neck where Ann's fingers had dug into her skin.

"She's dead," one of them said.

Blair looked through her tears at the woman who had done so much evil. If Cade hadn't shot her exactly when he did, Blair would be dead.

She crawled toward him, touched his face. "Can you hear me, Cade?" she asked through her tears.

His eyes fluttered back open, and he focused up at her. "I hear you."

She caught her breath. "Cade . . ."

"Are you okay?" His voice was hoarse, raspy. "Did she hurt you?"

The question undid her. "No, it's you who's hurt."

Her tears dropped onto his face, pooled in his stubble.

"Leg's shattered," Cade told her. "Bullet wound. Another one on my right side."

The paramedics were already on it.

"Baby," he said. "Where's the baby?"

She frowned. "What baby?"

"She has a baby. We can't leave it."

Blair looked up and saw Tavist standing in the doorway. "He said she had a baby in the house."

Tavist frowned and looked down at Cade. "Did you see it?"

"No, I heard it crying," he said. "She denied it, but I know what I heard. And she had an accomplice. He's the one who shot me."

But there was no baby in the house.

When they had him on the gurney, she followed them out into the night. Morgan burst through the crowd forming around the house and pulled Blair into a crushing embrace. "He's alive," Blair wept against her hair. "He's alive!"

"So are you."

Morgan held her and wept as they loaded him into the ambulance.

CHAPTER

*B*lair felt a lump the size of Kentucky in her throat as she stood in front of the hospital's bathroom mirror, trying to put herself back together. For the past several hours, half of Cape Refuge had waited with her as Cade's surgery lingered on.

Because of the severity of his wounds, he had been taken straight to the operating room when the paramedics brought him in. A metal rod was inserted into his marrow cavity to repair the shattered bone in his tibia. Because it was set internally, a cast was not needed, only bandages dressing the wound.

He was awake now, and Joe had come to tell her that he was asking for her.

But she couldn't let him see her like this. The bruises had surfaced on her neck from where Ann Clark had choked her. Her throat burned and her voice was hoarse. But it was a small price to pay. Her eyes were so tired they looked sunken in, and scratches marred the good side of her face.

Thankfully, Morgan had makeup in her purse and, sensing her insecurity, had thrust the bag at Blair.

She smeared powder over the scratches, then applied a pale pink lipstick, tapped a few dots of it onto her good cheek. Then she dug through Morgan's bag until she found her mascara and some eye shadow.

She did the best she could, given her fatigue, her injuries, and of course, her scars.

But it wasn't good enough.

She stared at her reflection and slowly brought her hand up to cover the right side. Looking at only half of her face, she could almost think herself pretty. But the other side was what mattered most.

Who was she kidding?

Feeling like a fool for trying, she dropped Morgan's makeup back into her bag and walked out into the hall.

Taking in a deep breath, she went to his door, knocked lightly, and pushed inside.

He was lying in bed with his leg elevated, and as she walked toward him, he smiled.

"Hey," she said.

Cade held out a hand for her. "There's my hero lady."

Blair took his hand. His beard was gone, and the sight of him almost brought tears to her eyes. She stood awkwardly beside his bed, making sure the scar side of her face was away from him. "So how are you feeling?"

"Blessed," he said. "The Lord delivered me. And I know you don't believe, Blair, but he used you to do it."

She couldn't seem to comment on that. If she got too vulnerable, she would fall apart completely.

He reached up and touched the bruises on her neck. "She almost killed you," he whispered. His hand lingered there. "Are you sure you're okay?"

She couldn't stop the tears rimming her eyes. "Better than you."

He smiled. "I thought about you a lot while I was in there," he said. "I worried about you."

She breathed a laugh. "Worried about me? Why?"

"Because I thought this would make you even firmer in your resolve not to believe in God."

She just stared at him for a moment. "You were being held captive in a basement with gunshot wounds, waiting for them to kill you . . . and you worried about whether I would ever believe in God?"

He took her hand then and brought it to his heart. "That's right. You're in much more danger because of that than I've ever been, Blair."

She turned away for a moment because she felt too raw, standing here looking at him. She got the chair that was pushed against the window and slid it next to his bed. Slowly she sat down.

"I took care of Oswald for you." She knew it was obvious, but she had to change the subject. "He sends his love."

He grinned. "Bet he's mad."

"He'll get over it."

"Did you go in?"

She nodded. "A couple of times. I saw your Bible. You'd been reading about the cities of refuge, like you were one of those manslayers and you needed an escape from the dead man's Avenger."

He groaned. "I think God led me to that passage that morning kind of as a way of preparing me for what I was about to go through. He wanted to remind me where my refuge was."

"Only you never made it to the city. The Avenger overtook you."

Cade pulled himself up on his elbow and looked into her face. "Actually, I had already made it to the real city of refuge," he said. "And the Avenger *didn't* overtake me."

She frowned and shook her head. "I don't know what you mean."

"I mean that Christ is my refuge, Blair. He was there for me the whole time, protecting me and watching out for me. When I'm in him, the Avenger can't touch me."

"But Ann Clark did touch you. She and her accomplice shot you, Cade. You almost died."

"But I didn't die, because God didn't let you rest until you found me. And even if they had killed me, Blair, I still would have had that refuge in Christ. Evil might be able to destroy my body and change my life, but it can never destroy my soul. Can you understand that, Blair?"

She understood more than she wanted him to know, but she couldn't make herself answer.

"I want you to understand about that refuge, Blair," he said. "You have enough Avengers chasing you. I'd love to see joy in your eyes."

She swallowed the emotion tightening her throat. "You may not believe this, Cade, but I prayed for you."

A poignant smile lit up his face. "You did?"

"I did," she whispered. "And it appears that my prayer was answered."

"What do you know."

She met his eyes, wishing her heart didn't feel so raw and vulnerable. But he seemed vulnerable, too, as he looked back at her.

Hoping to get the subject on safer ground, she said, "Did you know I quit my job?"

His smile faded. "No, Blair. Why?"

"Long story," she said.

He stared at her for a moment. "You're not leaving town, are you?"

"No, I . . . I'm staying, for a while at least. Actually, I'm buying the *Cape Refuge Journal.*"

He caught his breath. "Blair, that's great! You'll be perfect for that. I couldn't think of a better job for you."

"And in my first issue, I'm going to focus on Ann Clark's accomplice. He's still out there, Cade. We have to find him."

"Not 'we,' Blair. The FBI and the police. You've risked your life enough. I want you to stay out of it."

"But Karen's baby is still missing, and that person must know where he is."

"We're going to find him," Cade said. "Trust me on this. That man is not going to get away with what he did to me. And that baby and all the other babies will be found."

"May I quote you in that first issue?"

"Feel free."

She could see he was getting tired, so she got up. "There are others who want to see you. Joe's waiting outside. I guess I should go."

He reached out then and caught her hand. "Thank you for not giving up, Blair."

She smiled. "How could I?"

He reached up and touched her face—the smooth, soft side. His eyes lingered on hers, and she knew what those sappy poets with their love images meant when they talked about hearts melting. . . .

She was like them, helpless in her connection to him.

The thought made her angry. Who did she think she was? Some bikini-clad beauty-pageant queen? Cade could get any woman he wanted. How dare she fantasize that he would want her?

"You never believed that marriage story, did you, Blair?" he asked.

"No, I didn't believe it."

"Good. Because that never would have happened."

She left him there, and went out into the hall. Morgan and Jonathan stood near his door, and as Blair came out, Morgan reached out to hug her. "Is he all right?"

"Perfect," she said. She knew if she stood here, she would fall apart right in front of everyone. "I have to go. I need to be alone. If anyone needs me, I'll be in the chapel."

Morgan's face changed. "Sure, okay."

Blair hoped she could make it to the room before her tears overcame her.

CHAPTER

The chapel was dark except for four electric candles burning on a table at the front of the room, flanking an open Bible. Six small pews filled the room, three on each side of a narrow aisle. Blair slipped into one of the back pews and sat there quietly, staring straight ahead.

"Thank you," she whispered out loud. "I owe you one. I just wanted to tell you that."

She closed her eyes as her tears came forth, dripped off her chin, and wet the front of her shirt.

Where did they come from? Was it gratitude or relief? Or was it the raw, unfettered hope that left her so vulnerable and frightened?

He had looked in her eyes, touched her, and confessed to thinking about her while he was held. . . .

It was too much. The hope birthed by those facts was cruel, painful.

She pulled her feet up to the pew and buried her face in her knees, weeping out all the weariness and dread that had ridden her for the last few days.

What was she to do with these feelings?

Hugging her knees, she looked up at the front of the room again. "I know I've really imposed lately," she whispered. "It's not like you have nothing better to do. But I'm really out on a limb here, thinking these thoughts about Cade and knowing I'll probably be shot down like all the other times in my life. I don't want . . . to want."

She saw a box of Kleenex someone had slipped under the pew in front of her, so she grabbed a tissue out and blew her nose. Drawing in a deep breath, she went on.

"You answered that other prayer, even though I didn't deserve it. If you wouldn't mind helping me out with this, I'd really appreciate it. Whether it's to make me stop caring so much or work it so it comes out the way I wish. . . ."

The very utterance of that desire sent a shiver of fear through her, greater even than the fear when she'd gone in through Ann Clark's window.

"Stupid," she whispered. "I'm so stupid." What could Cade ever see in her?

Maybe he just sensed her own inane feelings and didn't want to hurt her. That would be just like Cade. Being gentle and sweet to keep from making her feel like an idiot.

But had she been obvious about her feelings? Had she even known for sure what her feelings *were?* Denial *was* her middle name, after all. Maybe it wasn't as obvious as she thought.

She grabbed another tissue and blew into it, then another and wiped her face. She had to stop this. Somehow she had to pull herself together.

She thought of what Cade had said to her about her own Avengers and the refuge he thought she needed. Was she just another potential convert, or were his frequent attempts to share his faith the greatest acts of love he knew?

She pictured herself running, running, away from her own Avengers—away from the secrets that had caused her scars, the bitterness that had taken root and grown within her, the grief over her parents' murders, the loneliness and anger.

She saw herself running from those who would destroy her, racing down that smooth road that would take her quickly to safety. She pictured herself reaching that gate where salvation waited. She lingered outside it, wanting that sweet peace the city walls would provide but fearful of crossing that threshold.

Cade had lived within those walls, even though he'd been trapped in the confines of a basement room. He'd called Christ his refuge, and he *had* been rescued.

But her parents had also lived in Christ, and they had suffered a violent end. She believed what Morgan had said all those months ago, about Christ being there to greet them the moment they closed their eyes. They had lived their life in a city called Refuge, and now their home was Refuge, itself.

What peace there must be in knowing that whether you live or die, the Avenger could not overtake you.

"Jesus, I long for that peace," she whispered on a sob. "I'm so tired of running."

She closed her eyes, covered her face, and pictured herself reaching that gate. She raised her hand to knock, preparing to make her case. . . .

But the door flew open, and she stepped inside . . .

And fell into the arms of Refuge Himself.

CHAPTER

CHAPTER

Blair kept her decision to herself. She had been in church enough as a child to know that a public profession was important, but she couldn't do that just yet. How could she trust her own faith? What if this was just a knee-jerk reaction born of her emotional state? What if it didn't hold up under pressure? What if she simply wanted to believe, but didn't really?

She would sort through it all later when things quieted down. But for now she had a paper to write. Jason Wheater had come to the hospital earlier with a briefcase full of papers for her to sign, making the newspaper hers. She had the keys to the building now and didn't intend to waste a moment. There was a kidnapper and a killer still at large. And that baby needed to be found.

She came back to the crowd of friends in the waiting room and located Sadie across the room with Morgan.

Cutting through, she tapped Sadie's shoulder. The girl turned around.

"Sadie, I need your help. Jason gave me the keys to the newspaper office tonight, and I want us to start working."

Sadie caught her breath. "Really?"

Morgan frowned. "But Sadie has school tomorrow. I don't want her up late. And, Blair, you need to rest."

"There's plenty of time for that later," Blair said. "We're going to need to work through the night to get the first issue out. She'll have to miss one day of school because I'll need her tomorrow too."

Sadie's face glowed. "Oh, please, Morgan. Let me do it!"

Morgan sighed. "Okay. I guess one day won't hurt. You take care of her, Blair."

Energized and full of new purpose, Blair led Sadie out of the hospital, ready to right the wrongs done against Cade by finally getting the truth out.

*B*lair and Sadie worked until morning writing the story, with sidebars about the accomplice still at large and the possible connection this person had to the kidnappings of babies across the south.

Blair placed Ann's DMV photo on the front page.

Sadie came up behind her. "I can't believe I was so close to her at that wedding, and all the time she was holding Cade captive. I wonder if the man I saw her with was the accomplice."

Blair nodded. "My guess is that he is. I'm including his description. I'm hoping someone will read it and remember seeing him with her."

She got Sadie busy hunting down articles about the other missing babies, while Blair wrote about the lies perpetrated against Cade while he'd been held.

It was daylight by the time they had most of their first issue laid out, but they still needed a few things.

"We need some quotes from people who were involved in the case, and a few more pictures," Blair said. "I want to interview that detective who walked through Ann's house with Joe. I want to see him squirm when I ask him how he feels knowing he overlooked the clues that Cade was there."

"You think he'll even talk to you?" Sadie asked.

"He'll talk, even if it's to say he won't talk. And you're going to get a picture of him doing it. Then we'll get back here and get this puppy printed and have it on every driveway in town by this afternoon."

It had started to rain, reminding her of that day over two weeks ago when all of this had started. Her windshield wipers swiped across her windshield, making it hard to drive. Exhausted, but driven, Blair and Sadie drove to the Savannah Precinct as the first shift was getting under way.

The sergeant at the front desk was making coffee, and he looked up as he poured the water in. "Help you?"

"I'm Blair Owens," she said, shaking her umbrella out. "I need to speak to Detective Hull, please."

The sergeant pointed to the back. "He's around the corner there."

Blair looked back at Sadie, who carried the digital camera. "Okay, now you take pictures as I'm talking to him. I want his ragged head right on the front page, with a caption that says what a prince of a cop he is."

"I'm on it," Sadie said. "Photojournalist-slash-newspaper-woman."

"Don't say anything. Just let me do all the talking." She spotted him standing at the coffeepot. "There he is now. Just hang back a minute until I get him engaged. Try to get the front of his face." Locking her eyes on the man who had failed so miserably to help Cade's case, Blair headed toward him.

Sadie hung back a few steps behind Blair and watched as she approached the man. She could only see him from behind, but something about him was familiar.

Then he turned, and she knew where she'd seen him before.

The wedding. He'd been the man with Ann Clark, holding her as if they were lovers!

She quickly brought the camera to her face to cover it and began flashing pictures.

Her heart hammered as she heard Blair asking him if he had any comments on why he failed to find Cade when he'd done the original search of Ann Clark's house.

"If I recall, one of Cape Refuge's finest was also searching the house. Why don't you ask him?" he said.

"I have," Blair said. "He told us that you were the one who searched the basement. I can't imagine why you wouldn't have seen the scrape marks on the concrete floor in front of the bookcase. I was there myself, and it was very clear that the shelves had been moved because something was behind them. Why would a trained detective fail to notice that?"

Sadie turned away and pretended to be adjusting her camera. Her hands trembled so badly that she almost dropped it.

What did this mean? If this man was the detective who searched Ann's house, it was no wonder they hadn't found Cade. He must have known. He must have been helping her.

And he had seemed familiar at the wedding because she had seen him before, in Karen's hospital room after the kidnapping.

She couldn't stand here and take the chance of his seeing and recognizing her, so she took off for the exit door. Stepping outside, she waited for Blair just under the overhang. Lightning bolted nearby and thunder cracked behind it.

Panic sent her mind racing. The accomplice was a cop! And if he saw her face, he would remember that she'd seen them.

Frightened, she dashed out into the rain and got into Blair's Volvo.

After a moment, Blair came out, looking for her. "Sadie, what's wrong with you? I asked you to take pictures."

"Blair, it's him!"

Blair got in and stared at her. "Him who?"

"The accomplice. The one I saw Ann Clark with. He's the one!"

"Detective Hull? Are you sure?"

"Positive. Blair, he's the one. He was working with her, helping her, and that's why he didn't find Cade that day."

Blair looked back at the door, and for a moment Sadie feared she would go back in. Then she started the engine and pulled out of her space.

"Okay, we're going to the hospital. We're going to tell Cade and the FBI. If Detective Hull is who we think he is, he's about to have a big surprise."

CHAPTER

77

Joe McCormick sat in Cade's room when Blair reached the hospital. She burst in without knocking, Sadie on her heels. "Cade, you're not going to believe this!"

Cade sat up. "What, Blair?"

She stood over him, breathless. "We know who the accomplice was. Tell them, Sadie."

Cade regarded the girl, who looked as if she'd been up all night. "I went to a wedding with Trevor Beal . . . it was his cousin's—"

"Skip ahead," Blair blurted. "He doesn't care about the cousin."

Sadie tried again. "Ann Clark was there. I stumbled on her in the garden. She was with a man, kissing him."

Cade frowned. "Who was it?"

Blair took over. "She didn't know him. But just now, Sadie and I went to Savannah Police Precinct Three to interview Detective Hull for the paper. And the minute Sadie saw him she recognized him."

Cade's mouth fell open, and he looked at Joe. "Hull?"

Joe took a step toward Sadie. "Are you absolutely sure?"

"Positive. They didn't come to the wedding together, but they snuck away together."

Cade's face looked stricken as he stared at Blair. "No way. Hull's too good a detective to do something so stupid."

But Joe didn't seem so sure. He got up and ran his hand over his just-shaved head. "He was the one who searched the basement when we walked through the house, Cade. He made sure I would search the upstairs. If I'd gone down there, I would have seen the scrape marks and looked behind the bookcase. Any cop would have."

The color was draining from Cade's face. "So he missed it. It doesn't mean he was involved."

Blair's eyes flashed with conviction. "Cade, last night when we found your bloody bandage in the trash, we took it to the police. Hull kept it, then stalled like crazy. He was probably calling her, warning her to get you out of there. I heard her on the phone when I broke in. She was saying she couldn't move you herself, even if she drugged you."

Cade shook his head. "You don't know that she was talking to him."

Joe started pacing. "I wondered how Ann got your unlisted home number. A cop could have gotten it for her. And when the first baby was taken from here in Savannah, Hull was the one in charge of the case. He could have been destroying evidence as he pretended to search for it."

"You're jumping to conclusions! So he was having an affair with Ann, that doesn't mean he's guilty of murder and kidnapping!"

Blair gaped at him. "Cade, if Ann was involved in the kidnapping, then he was too. He may even be the one who shot her husband, if she didn't do it herself."

Cade stared down at his bandaged leg. "This can't be. No cop would have shot me."

"A crooked cop might, Cade!" Blair bent down, her face close to his. "Cade, add things up! If he is involved, then maybe he has the baby."

Cade sat for a moment, his eyes transfixed with possibilities. Finally, he threw back the covers. "I've got to get out of here. I've got to tell the FBI. I want to be there when they question him."

"Cade, you can't leave," Blair said. "Your leg . . ."

He gritted his teeth as he moved his leg to the floor. "I'm fine," he grunted. "Just get me some crutches."

"But you need the IV," Blair said. "The antibiotics. . . . Cade, just talk to the FBI on the phone and let them handle it."

"No," he said. "This is personal, Blair. I'm not a spectator in this. Sadie, will you go find someone who can get me a pair of crutches? Tell them I'm leaving. I'll sign whatever I need to, but I'm outta here."

As Sadie left the room, Blair stood in front of him. "Cade, you're the only witness to these crimes. Hull—or whoever Ann's accomplice was—still wants you dead."

Cade wasn't listening. "I'll go straight to the FBI, Blair. I'm not going to compromise the investigation. But I can't stand back on the sidelines and watch. And if Hull was involved, I have to know for sure."

CHAPTER

78

*S*he's following us, Cade." Joe muttered the statement with dread. "That woman never quits."

Cade looked out Joe's back window. The rain hadn't slowed Blair any. She drove so close behind them that he feared she'd skid and hit them at the next red light. He sighed and turned back around. "Let her follow. They won't let her anywhere close to the house."

They had found out that Agent Tavist was at Ann Clark's house, directing the search for evidence that would lead them to any accomplices and, hopefully, to the babies. He had called ahead and told Tavist he was coming and that he had some information. Tavist had left word that the agents were to let him in.

Joe couldn't get much closer to the house than Blair could since so many cars blocked the driveway. "Just stay here and I'll go in," Cade said.

Joe gave him a worried look. "Sure you can walk on those things in the rain?"

Cade wasn't sure, but he was going to give it his best shot. "I'll be fine." Carefully, he pulled his leg out of the car and pulled himself up on the crutches. There was no way he could carry an umbrella, and he knew the rain would soak his bandages. He would just have to hurry.

Blair got out of her car when she saw him emerge. "Cade, you need help. You could slip."

"I'm okay, Blair. Just wait in the car."

An agent came forward with an umbrella and held it over him as he hobbled up the porch and into the house. He got in and stood on the entrance mat, waiting for Tavist.

The man came through the house and shook Cade's hand. "Good to see you up, Cade. After last night, I didn't expect to see you out of bed for a while."

Cade looked around at the house where he had been held. "I have some information that may or may not be helpful." He told the agent about Hull's involvement with Ann Clark, and Joe's suspicions about his part in the investigation.

"I don't know what it all means," Cade said. "I've known Hull for a long time. I've trusted him. I find it hard to believe he'd be involved in something so criminal. But it has to be looked into."

Tavist drew his eyebrows together and looked down at his feet. "We found some hair on the sheets of her bed. Brown curly hair, doesn't belong to her or her husband."

"Hull has brown curly hair," Cade said. "Shouldn't be hard to compare."

"We've also found plenty of evidence linking her to the kidnappings. She had papers in a safe in her closet with the name of a prominent lawyer in town—Jasper Beal."

Cade gaped at him. The wedding Sadie had gone to. Hadn't it been for one of the Beals? He knew the family well and had investigated them on a number of occasions. Jasper was the only lawyer, and he lived in Savannah.

"Do you think he was the accomplice?"

"Could be. We have a warrant out for his arrest."

Cade couldn't explain the relief he felt. "So if he's the accomplice, then maybe Hull is innocent."

Tavist shook his head. "There may have been more than one accomplice," he said. "We've investigated Beal and his brother on a number of other cases. Typically, he lets others do the dirty work and keeps his distance."

"It was his daughter's wedding where Ann Clark and Hull were seen."

Tavist nodded. "We think he may have been selling the babies to desperate couples who wanted to adopt. There were five substantial deposits into Ann Clark's bank account the last few weeks. Could have been payoffs for delivery of the babies."

Cade drew his eyebrows together. "Five? But there were six. What about the Miller baby?"

Tavist shook his head. "Maybe it hadn't been placed yet."

"Then where is it?"

Tavist looked up at him. "We don't know."

Cade closed his eyes and tried to put it all together. Ann kidnapping the babies, Hull helping her cover the crimes, Beal placing the babies . . .

Was it even possible?

He looked around him at this house where he'd been held like some kind of caged animal. Had Hull stalked through it, scheming to use his name and his handwriting and his cell phone . . . ? Planning his death after the world was sure he'd committed those crimes?

Tavist touched his shoulder. "Go home, Cade. You've earned your rest. Let us do our job. We'll handle it."

Cade studied the man's face. *Would* he handle it? Or would he take too long compiling evidence before he even approached Hull?

He crutched his way back outside. It was still raining, and the morning sky gloomed gray and angry. He stood in the downpour for a moment, his mind racing through his options.

What if Hull wasn't guilty, after all? What if Sadie had made a mistake?

And even if she'd been right, wasn't it possible that Ann Clark had used him to get information about the investigations? Could it be that he was just a pawn too?

Or was Cade simply in denial?

He took one deliberate step after another, holding his bandaged leg up. The bandage was soaked, and he saw that blood was seeping through. It needed to be elevated, but not now.

Cade went to the car and dropped onto the passenger seat, carefully pulled the leg in. It was swelling within the dressings, and pain pulsed through it.

Joe looked over at him. "What's the story?"

Cade stared at the windshield for a moment. "They've found a lot of evidence, but nothing linking her to Hull yet."

Joe tapped on his steering wheel. "They will. Give them time."

"That baby may not have time."

Joe looked over at him. "So now you believe Hull was involved?"

"I still don't know." In the side mirror, he saw Blair getting out of her car, throwing her umbrella up, and hurrying toward his window.

He rolled it down when she reached it.

"What did he say?" she asked. "Does he believe Hull's involved?"

"He doesn't know," Cade said. "But I told him what you told me."

"So are you going back to the hospital?"

Cade looked up at her for a long moment. The truth was, he didn't want to go back. He wanted to go find Hull and look him in the eye.

But Blair couldn't know that.

"Yeah, we're going back," he said. "But you might want to stick around here for a while. They've found some things that do connect Ann to the kidnappings. Just wait and they'll probably make a statement soon."

That satisfied Blair, and he watched as she got back into her car. She would be safe here, he thought, and it would keep her out of trouble for a while.

Joe started the car and backed away from the blockade. "So we're going to the hospital?"

Cade shook his head. "No. I want to go see Hull."

Joe got the car turned around. "You're kidding, right?"

"No. I'm still not sure he did it, Joe. I just want to talk to him."

He picked up Joe's cell phone that lay on the seat and dialed the number of the Cape Refuge Police Department. Georgette, the office clerk, answered on the first ring.

"Hey, Georgette. Cade, here."

Georgette caught her breath. "Oh, Chief Cade, it's so good to hear your voice! We've been so worried about you! How are you feeling?"

"I'm good. Look, would you put Billy Caldwell on the phone for me, please?"

A moment passed and Billy came to the phone. "Hey, Chief! Good to hear from you."

"Yeah, you too. Look, Caldwell, I need your help. I need for you to find out if Detective Hull of Precinct Three in Savannah is on duty today. I need to get in touch with him."

"Sure. Want him to call you if I reach him?"

"No. In fact, I don't want you to reach him. Just find out if he's working, and I'll take it from there. Call me back on McCormick's phone."

He hung up and looked out the window, waiting for Billy to call back.

Joe shook his head. "Cade, you need to let the FBI do this. If you approach him knowing what you know, you may give him a heads-up that the feds are on to him."

"I won't," he said. "Just a friendly visit, that's all. I'm an angry victim who wants to put all the pieces of this thing together. He has some of those pieces, since he worked on the kidnappings *and* questioned Ann Clark with you."

The phone rang and Cade flipped it open. "Yeah?"

"He's not on duty right now, Chief."

Cade sat silent for a moment. What now? If he couldn't just drop into the police precinct to talk to him, he'd have to go to his house.

But would Hull suspect they were onto him?

"Do me another favor, Caldwell. Find his address for me. I'll hold."

He waited as Caldwell went to his computer and started the search.

Joe looked troubled as he navigated his way through traffic. "Cade, you can't seriously be considering going to his house."

Cade's jaw muscles tightened. "I want to see inside his house. Just look around, that's all."

"The feds'll do that."

Cade sat there for a moment, staring through the windshield. "Whoever was working with Ann Clark dragged me into that house and shoved me, unconscious, down the stairs. He conspired with her to plant evidence that I was involved in the kidnappings. He shot me twice when I tried to escape. He slammed my head into concrete." Cade's voice trembled with the last words. "I have to know if he's the one."

"You will know. Just wait."

Cade leaned his head back on the seat. Joe was driving toward the hospital, but Cade decided it didn't matter. He could make him turn around as soon as he made up his mind.

He thought of Hull, if he was guilty, hearing that there was a warrant out for Jasper Beal's arrest. Wouldn't he realize then that the jig was up? That there was no way he'd get away with placing the Miller baby? Wouldn't he see that baby as too much of a liability and want to get rid of it?

Then again, this whole thing could just be a deadend. Sadie thought she had seen him with Ann Clark, but everyone knew that teenage girls sometimes overdramatize things. Maybe she just *thought* it was Hull. That should be easy to find out. All they needed was the guest list from the wedding. If Hull was on it, then Cade would believe it.

Caldwell came back to the phone and gave him the rural address out on Highway 16.

As Cade hung up, he glanced over at Joe. "Turn the car around, Joe. We're going to Highway 16."

Joe groaned. "Cade, this is a mistake. If he's the one, we need to approach him with backup. We need to go by the book. We need a warrant."

"I'm not approaching him as a killer. I'm approaching him as a cop. I just want to talk to him."

Joe was silent as he turned the car around, and Cade stared out the window.

Joe was right. Cade didn't have any business showing up there like this, when the FBI was on the case. He could be jeopardizing the investigation. He could even get himself killed.

Was he going for the sake of that baby or for the sake of his own satisfaction?

Conviction pressed down on him, aching through him with the same intensity as his leg.

But he just wanted to look the man in the eye. He would know. If he saw him and talked with him about the case, he'd be able to tell if he had something to hide.

Hull was probably not even involved, and Cade would see it as soon as he looked the man in the face.

"You don't have to go with me, Joe. I don't blame you if you don't want to be a part of this."

Joe kept driving. "If you're going, I'm going, Cade. I can't let you do this alone."

CHAPTER

79

*H*ull lived out in a rural area off of Highway 16, outside the city limits east of Savannah, in a house that they almost missed because it was so hard to spot from the road.

"Secluded," Joe said as he pulled onto the man's dirt driveway. "He could do almost anything out here and no one would see him." He glanced at Cade. "Give me the plan."

Cade leaned his head back on the seat. The pain in his leg was wearing him down. "First we get him thinking we're just his colleagues paying a professional visit. When his guard's down, I've got some questions for him."

Joe pulled up the muddy driveway, his wipers arching back and forth across the windshield. Cade set his hands on the dash and peered through the wet glass as the back of the house came into view.

It was an old restored farmhouse that sat on the edge of a small lake, its front facing the water. As they approached, Cade made note of the doors and windows.

The back door opened on a small porch, and there were six windows, all of them shut against the rain. As they followed the dirt driveway around the house, he saw a side door.

They pulled up to the front of the house. A motorcycle was parked under a tree, a blue tarp thrown over it, protecting it from the rain. Next to it sat Hull's Taurus.

Cade got his crutches from the backseat and got out, wincing as he moved across the yard. He almost wished he had a cast to protect his leg from bumps. But with the internal splint, there had been no need for one. It was swelling now, and the bandage had grown too tight. Gritting back the pain, he made his way across the porch. He stood there a moment before ringing the bell.

What was he doing? He shouldn't be here, facing down his tormentor, if indeed that was what Hull was. He didn't even have a weapon. He needed backup, in case Hull figured him out and made a run for it. He needed to wait for the FBI to act.

But he had to look Hull in the eye.

Joe came up on the porch and stood next to him.

"Gonna ring the bell or kick the door in?"

Cade didn't find that amusing.

"Cade, are you sure you want to do this?"

Cade pushed the doorbell. He heard a television inside. He was watching a ball game . . .

But there was something else . . . another sound . . .

A baby crying.

Cade shot Joe a look. "You hear that?"

"Yeah. A baby." Joe reached for his gun, and Cade nodded. Drawing it, Joe stepped to the side of the door. Cade took the other side, in case Hull came out firing.

The door came open, and Joe raised his weapon. Hull jumped back. "Whoa, man! Hold on! What's this about?"

"I came to talk to you, Hull," Cade said. "But when I heard that baby crying, I decided that talking wasn't necessary." He moved close to Hull and began to pat him down. A pistol was holstered on his belt. Cade pulled it out.

"Come on, man. My sister's here with her kid."

Cade turned the gun on Hull. "How about we go into the house and meet your sister, Hull?"

Hull stared at him. "Look, I don't know what this is about, but, man, you've been under a lot of pressure. Probably on painkillers." He shot Joe a beseeching look. "Man, I don't recommend you go along with this."

"In the house, Hull," Joe said, pushing him back inside.

Clutching that gun, Cade hobbled in behind them.

Hull backed across the living room, deftly avoiding the furniture in his way. "Don't shoot," he said, holding his hands up. "You don't want to kill a brother."

Cade looked around at the mess in the place. It reeked of cigarette smoke, and ashtrays overflowed with butts. Beer bottles and plates with dried food adorned the coffee table.

He saw a closed door and knew the baby was beyond it. "That door," Cade said, motioning with his gun. "Open it slowly. One false move, it'll be your last."

Hull opened the door, and in one swift motion, grabbed up the infant seat sitting on a table just inside the door. The tiny black infant's screams pitched an octave higher.

Hull held the seat like a bucket, clutching its handle as the child squirmed and kicked, unfastened. If he tipped it enough, Cade saw, the baby would spill out.

"Put the baby down, Hull," Cade said.

But Hull kept moving into the room, knowing they wouldn't shoot with the baby so close to him.

Then Hull grabbed a gun out of the carrier and aimed it at Cade.

Sweat dripped into Cade's eyes. One crutch fell, and he put his foot down to steady himself. Pain exploded through him, blurring his vision and loosening his grip on the gun he held.

The child's high-pitched screams pierced through the room.

Cade bent down, grabbed his crutch back up, and propped it under his arm. His hand shook as he took aim again.

"Put the baby down, Hull. Put him down, now!"

Hull laughed. "You thought you could beat me, didn't you, Cade? You thought you could hobble in here and save the day."

"Give me the baby, Hull, and you can make a run for it. All I want is the baby."

"Are you kidding me?" Hull's face reflected his strain at the situation he was in. He held the car seat at his side, swinging it back and forth. "This baby is my way out. Remember, they still think you might have been involved, Cade. I'll let them think I found the baby, that you were running with it."

Joe stepped toward him, his gun aimed for Hull's forehead.

"Come one step closer, Joe, and I'll blow your head off," Hull said.

Joe stopped, but kept his gun on him.

"Take me, instead," Cade said. "Give Joe the baby, and I'll go with you. That's what you want, isn't it? Just a hostage?"

But Hull wasn't buying. He backed his way to a door that led out the bedroom onto the back porch. He managed to open it and stepped outside, still swinging the seat. "Stay back," he said, "or I'll kill it."

Cade held his fire, and Joe did the same. Hull took off through the rain, running toward the Taurus. He started the car and sped down the muddy driveway.

Joe shot out into the rain, firing at Hull's tires, but the car sped out of sight. Moving as fast as he could manage, Cade crutched back out to Joe's car and jumped in, jarring his leg as he did. Choking back his agony, he closed the door. Joe took off, radioing an all-points-bulletin for Hull's car. Within seconds, every officer in the area knew that Hull was fleeing with the baby.

But Hull had a radio of his own. "This is Detective Hull," he screamed into the radio. "I am in possession of an African American infant that looks to be a few days old. I found the baby in a warehouse on Highway 16. I am in hot pursuit of a Cape Refuge police car believed to be occupied by Police Chief Matthew Cade and Detective Joe McCormick, both of whom I believe to be connected with these kidnappings."

Cade heard the transmission and grabbed the radio from Joe. "Negative," Cade yelled. "Detective Hull is not pursuing us, we're pursuing *him* southbound down Highway 16. We found the baby in Hull's home at 353 Highway 16. He is armed and threatening to kill the infant. We need backup ASAP."

The car in front of them slowed, and Cade raised his gun.

Suddenly the Taurus made a U-turn. Joe slammed on his brakes and turned around, but Hull's car took a side street and disappeared.

Joe turned down the street. The Taurus was nowhere in sight. "Where'd he go?" Joe yelled.

Suddenly, a bullet fired through the back window.

"He's behind us!" Joe said.

Cade ducked as another bullet fired. He had claimed to be pursuing them, and now he had made it so.

Cade grabbed the radio and told them where they had turned. "We are under fire. Suspect is armed and dangerous and still in possession of the baby!"

They heard sirens turning up the street, coming after them, but it still looked as if Hull was chasing them.

"Cut him off," Cade shouted. "When he stops, I'll fire."

Joe slammed on his brakes. Hull swerved and came around him. Cade tried to take aim, but as long as that car was moving, he couldn't take Hull out. The baby's life was at stake.

Joe followed him, the convoy of police cars right behind them. "Shoot out his tires, Cade!"

Cade fired, but the Taurus was too far ahead of them, zigzagging from lane to lane, out of bullet range.

Other Savannah police began to fall in behind them.

Cade heard another transmission from one of the Savannah cops. "Hull, do you have that baby with you?"

"Yes, I do," Hull said.

"Then pull over immediately. Do you hear me, Hull? Pull your car off the road now."

"Can't do that," Hull radioed back. "I will not put this baby in harm's way."

"Where are you taking it?"

"To safety," he said.

Cade grabbed the mike again. "Hull, prove you're innocent. If you want to bring the baby to safety, pull over now and turn him over."

The radio crackled again, and he heard another voice. "This is FBI Agent Tavist. It's Hull you're after. Do you read me? It's Hull you want, not Cade!"

Suddenly there was a burst of radio exchanges among other officers. Hull made a turn and flew to the Interstate.

"Where is he going?" Joe asked. "He can't possibly think there's an escape."

"He realizes they're not buying his story," Cade said. "Maybe he's headed to the airport."

But then Hull turned on to Chatham Parkway and headed toward the Savannah River.

"He's going to try to get away on the water," Cade shouted.

They followed, sirens blaring and lights flashing, as Hull led them to a dock where two dozen boats were parked on slips out on the water.

He abandoned his car and got out, holding that car seat in one hand and waving his gun in the other. Rain pummeled down on them.

All of the cars came to a halt in a semicircle around him.

Cade got out. "Leave the baby, Hull! You can go, but leave the baby. Just set him down and run."

Panicked, Hull kept holding the screaming baby and, with his gun poised, backed his way down a pier.

He looked from side to side, trying to find a boat he could step into. But none was close enough.

Instead, he ducked into a shed at the end of the pier. Through the window, he began shooting, holding his colleagues at bay.

CHAPTER

*B*lair stood in the rain at the Clark house, trying to get a statement from one of the agents who had been searching Ann Clark's house, when the call came over his radio that there was a standoff at the Riverside Pier on the Savannah River and that Detective Hull was holding a baby hostage.

Her heart plunged, and she knew that Cade would be right in the thick of it.

As the agent ran to confer with his colleagues, Blair jumped in her car. Sadie, who had fallen asleep in her seat, jumped awake at the slamming door.

"What is it, Blair?"

"There's a standoff at the River. Hull has the baby."

Sadie straightened. "We're going there?"

"I am. But I'll drop you off at the Wendy's near the dock. I swore to Morgan I'd take care of you."

"Why are you going? You can't help. You should stay away too, Blair."

"I think Cade's there." It was all the reason she needed.

When they reached the Wendy's, Sadie started to get out. "Go in there and pray while you're waiting," she said. "Don't stop until I get back."

Sadie gave her a surprised look. "I sure will. Be careful, Blair."

Sadie got out of the car, and Blair sped away.

At Hanover House, the agents manning the phones had flown into a flurry of activity, but they weren't talking about what was going on. But when the local television station broke into programming to alert the public about the high speed chase that had taken place down the interstate, and the stand-off on the river that had something to do with one of the kidnapped babies, Karen sprang off the couch.

"My baby!" she cried. "They found my baby!"

Morgan stared down at the television. One of the agents stepped into the room, and Morgan looked up at him. "Is it true?"

"Looks like it," he said. "A black infant just a few days old."

"We've got to go there!" Karen shouted. She turned to the agent. "Please, will you take us? We'll stay back until it's safe, but I want to be there for my baby!"

The agent went to confer with his colleague, then came back into the room. "Let's go," he said.

CHAPTER

*N*eedles of rain slanted down, thunder cracking and lightning flashing, as if God had had enough.

Hull was still in the building, firing at anything that came near.

The FBI had arrived, and Tavist had taken over. But they were getting nowhere.

Cade sat inside Joe's car, struggling against the agony of his leg. But it was the pain of his own regret that almost did him in.

He never should have gone to Hull's house. If he'd waited for the FBI, they would have surrounded the place before Hull even knew they were there. They might have surprised him and subdued him before he could further endanger the child.

He watched from his car as the agents tried negotiating with Hull through a bullhorn. But the only response from Hull was the occasional gunshot firing from the window.

Someone had to risk going in there to talk to him. But with Hull firing out at anyone who tried, it had become impossible.

Unless . . .

As an idea dawned in Cade's mind, he got his crutches and got out of the car. Making his way through the storm, he got to Agent Tavist's car.

The man was in a huddle with several other agents.

"I want to go in."

Tavist turned around and looked at him. "That's absurd. He'll kill you before you get within thirty feet of him. Our sniper team is on its way. We're going to try to take him through the window."

"I could distract him," Cade said. "We could let him know I'm coming, injured and unarmed. I'm not a threat with these crutches."

Tavist stared at him for a moment. "You could be killed just like that, Cade. It's not worth it."

Rain dripped into Cade's eyes as he looked back at that shed. "It is to me."

Tavist turned back to his men, and Cade waited as they discussed the plan. He heard a van pull up and turned to see a dozen special agents filing out with their rifles.

If they tried to take him out from this distance, they could miss and hit the baby. If he could get in there, maybe he could protect him.

Finally, Agent Tavist turned back around. "Cade, are you sure you want to do this?"

"I'm sure," Cade said.

"All right. We can try it. We'll send you as our negotiator, but all we really want is for you to distract him while our agents move in. If you can, try to stand close to the baby. If we can see you, we won't fire in that direction."

Cade was ready.

Tavist brought the bullhorn to his mouth. Cade hoped Hull could hear him through the storm.

"Detective Hull," Tavist called to him. "We'd like to send someone in to talk to you. Chief Cade is not a threat. He's unarmed. He just wants to hear your demands."

For a moment there was no answer, then finally, Hull yelled out. "Tell him to take off his shirt so I can see if he's armed."

Cade didn't waste a moment. He hobbled on his crutches out in front of the police cars and FBI agents. The rain had already drenched him, but it pounded so hard that he hoped Hull could see him clearly enough. He stood at the end of the pier and, balancing on his crutches, peeled his shirt off and dropped it.

He hoped Hull could see that he had nothing on him, except a bandage over his ribs. His wet sweatpants were plastered to his skin. Anything hidden there would be obvious.

"I'm coming, Hull," Cade said. "We okay with that?"

When there was no answer, he started to move. Slowly, he crutched his way down the pier, one step after another, waiting, almost expecting, for Hull to shoot him dead and finish the job he started in Ann Clark's basement. But he kept going, one step at a time.

Lord, help me do this.

He reached the door of the building. "I'm coming in, Hull," he said. "I just want to talk."

The door came slightly open, and Cade pushed through.

Hull grabbed him and patted him down, each touch of his bandage sending rivets of pain shooting through him.

Satisfied, Hull pulled him in and slammed the door. The old shed smelled of dirt and dead fish, and there was no light except for what little came through the window.

Hull stood in front of him, his gun pointing at him. "Give me your crutches," he said.

Cade balanced on his good leg and handed him the crutches.

The baby seat sat on a shelf behind him. The baby had stopped crying and seemed to be sleeping.

"Start talking," Hull said.

"I came to listen." Cade checked Hull's distance from the window. He wasn't close enough. They would never be able to see him.

"Tell us what you want," Cade said. "The feds are in a negotiating mood."

Hull was sweating, and Cade recognized the terror on his face. He had to show him a way out of this.

"So far, there are no murder charges. We figure Ann killed her husband. And if the babies are found unharmed, then it'll even look better for you."

"The babies were never in danger," Hull said. "Not until you came along, trying to be the hero. Every one of the babies has been adopted out, and this one would have gone to its home tomorrow if you hadn't come along and destroyed everything."

Cade couldn't help the bitter contempt twisting his face. So it was all about money. Kill a man, abduct a cop, rip newborns from their families. He wondered how much they made on each one.

"We had a great setup," Hull said. "Until William went off the deep end. Ann tried to kill him to keep him from talking. You finished the job."

"So," Cade said, "you're not responsible for anyone's death. Get a good lawyer and you could beat this, Hull."

From the corner of his eye, he watched the window. Somehow, he had to get near the baby. "Let me see the baby," he said. "I want to make sure he's still alive."

Hull shook his head. "He's finally sleeping. I can't stand that screaming."

"I won't wake him up," he said. "I can move over there, if you'll give me just one crutch. They want me to let them know if he's okay."

Hull looked out the window, as if weighing Cade's words. Cade saw the confusion on his face.

"If I tell them he's alive, they'll relax a little," Cade said. "Everybody's on edge until they know that. They're liable to do anything."

Hull stared at him for a moment. Finally, he picked the baby carrier up and gave Cade a look. "See? Alive, even though I'm sick to death of it." He set the baby on the floor between them. "And frankly, Chief, I'm sick to death of you too. If I'm going to prison, I might as well make it worth it."

As he spoke, he raised his gun and aimed it between Cade's eyes.

CHAPTER

Blair pulled into the outer parking lot of the dock where the standoff was taking place. Through her frantically sweeping windshield wipers, she could see the police cars lined up like vicious dogs waiting to attack. Armed officers used their vehicles as barricades as they kept their weapons trained on that building just off the pier, waiting to fire when told.

At the back of the crowd, she saw Joe McCormick pacing back and forth, and she knew without a doubt that Cade was here too.

She got out of her car, leaving her umbrella behind, and ran up to the barricade.

"Ma'am, you can't come any closer," a cop told her.

"I need to speak to Detective McCormick," she said. "The bald guy over there."

The cop went to get him, and Joe hurried over. "Blair, what are you doing here?"

She ignored the question. "Joe, where's Cade?"

Joe looked back toward the pier, though it wasn't visible from where they stood. Finally, he ducked under the barricade and got closer to her. "He's in that shed with Hull and the baby. They sent him in as a negotiator."

Thunder cracked like a gunshot, startling her. Had he said what she thought he said? That Cade was in danger again?

She lunged at him, fists flying. "Why did you let him go? He can't even walk! What's the matter with you?"

Joe caught her fists. "I couldn't stop him, Blair."

"After everything that happened!" she railed. "Hull's going to kill him anyway. Why didn't you just shoot him yourself?"

She collapsed with her hands over her face, wailing out her fear and rage. Finally, Joe reached out for her, straightened her up, and put his arm around her. "Come on, Blair. Let's go back to your car, get you out of this rain."

She didn't care about the rain or the thunder or the gunfire. But she didn't have the strength to fight him.

He walked her back, opened the door, and she got in.

"Wait here," he said. "I'll let you know what's happening."

He closed the door, and she buried her face in her arms on the steering wheel, groaning out her anguished hopelessness.

And then she remembered God. She rose up, sobbing, and looked through that wet windshield to the angry sky above her. She believed that he was there, watching over Cade as he'd done when he was in that basement, fighting for his life. He was Cade's refuge. And he was hers too.

"Don't let him die," she whispered. "Please, God, protect him one more time."

Thunder rumbled, and she touched her windshield, as if reaching through to him. "Please, Jesus." It was real, her belief in the one true God. The one to whom she could run when the Avenger hunted her down. When this was over, no matter how it ended, she would profess his name.

She would make a lousy Christian, she thought. A blackeye to all of Christendom. A huge scar on the face of the church.

But Christ had a thing for scars.

Her crying settled, and her sense of helplessness faded. She was not helpless. She could pray.

It was the most she could do for Cade.

CHAPTER

"Nobody has to die." Cade stared into the barrel of that pistol, aiming dead center. "Give me your demands."

"I demand to see you dead."

Cade swallowed. "If you pull that trigger, they'll be on you so fast you won't have time to squeeze it again."

"It'd be worth it," Hull said, "just to see you lying in a bloody heap on this floor."

Cade's eyes locked with his, and he knew in his heart that Hull meant it, that he could kill him in a second without a thought, then go to prison for the rest of his life and think every day of that time that it was worth it.

Suddenly, he saw movement at the window behind Hull. Someone was there.

Cade was close to Hull, and any bullet meant for him could take Cade's head off too.

Hull must have heard movement, and he turned to the window and fired out. The baby began to scream.

Cade grabbed the baby carrier and hit the floor.

Another gunshot . . .

And Hull collapsed.

A moment of stark silence followed, and Cade lay there, his body protecting the baby.

The door flew open, and an agent burst in, still holding the gun that had killed the detective.

Cade pulled himself up, biting back his pain. His hands trembled as he scooped the baby out of his seat and brought it to his shoulder. "Shhh," he said. "You're okay. It's gonna be all right."

He grabbed one of the crutches that Hull had taken from him and put it under his right arm, and cradling the baby in his left, he started out of the building. Pain tortured him with each jolt, draining his strength. He stopped and leaned against the building. The baby was getting wet, so he dropped his crutch and bent over him, trying to shield the child from the rain.

And then he heard a woman screaming . . .

He searched the crowd through the rain and saw a black woman he'd never seen before, with Morgan behind her, running between the cars, forcing her way out into the parking lot toward him, making her way to the pier.

No one stopped her as she came toward him, running, screaming, "My baby, my baby!"

When she reached him, he handed her the baby. Dizziness swept over him, and he thought he might pass out. He wobbled and tried to steady himself.

He closed his eyes, heard voices screaming, yelling, feet running toward him . . .

"Cade, you stupid, reckless idiot! What were you thinking?"

It was Blair's voice, pulling him from his pain. He opened his eyes, and she ran into his arms.

Police surrounded Karen and whisked her off, while others went to the building where Hull lay dead.

Blair began to weep, her body racking with anguish that seemed greater than his. He reached down for her face, tipped her chin up, and pressed his forehead against hers.

"Thank you, Jesus," she whispered. "Oh, thank you, Lord."

It sounded like a prayer. Cade let her words register in his mind, and he pulled back for a moment and gazed down at her. She was more beautiful than he'd ever seen her, with the rain soaking her hair and tears reddening her eyes, and those scars flaming against her pale, smooth skin.

With both hands, he framed her face—the side with the dried-out, crusted-over burn scars, and the soft, silky side—both of which he loved.

Slowly, he lowered his lips to hers and kissed her in the way that he had wanted to for so many years. His heart burst with the joy of it, as she seemed to melt to his touch.

All around them, chaos reigned. Radios crackled, thunder boomed, people yelled and ran past them. But Cade didn't hear any of it. All he knew was the taste and feel of Blair Owens as she surrendered to that same joy.

AFTERWORD

*T*here are times when I read a passage of Scripture, and it goes right over my head. Later, the Lord will direct me to the same passage again, and it's as if one verse is framed in neon and takes on a whole new meaning that applies so perfectly to my life at that moment. I guess that's why we're told that "the word of God is living and active. Sharper than any double-edged sword . . ." (Hebrews 4:12).

Recently, that happened to me as I was reading Psalm 84. In the NASB translation, Psalm 84:5 says, "How blessed is the man whose strength is in Thee; In whose heart are the highways to Zion!"

I had been studying about the cities of refuge, and what they mean to us as Christians, so this verse took on special meaning.

And I asked myself if the highways to Zion are in my heart. Do all of my roads take me to Christ? Do all my desires, all my thoughts, all my emotions, all my intentions, point me to him? Have I put obstacles in my own way, roadblocks that make me stumble? Are there potholes I haven't repaired? Do I have detours that take me off that road?

I was further intrigued by the thought that the Lord didn't say that the fastest one to Zion wins or that I had to move down that highway in a certain type of vehicle or that my journey would be compared with anyone else's.

He simply blesses us if our hearts have the highways that take us to him!

I contemplated that for a while, and joyfully understood that the moment I surrendered my life to Christ, those highways were in my heart, already smooth and paved, and all of them took me to Christ. It is my job to keep them clear and well-maintained, to make sure they're not compromised by obstacles or unexpected pitfalls. It's my job to stay on that road. And if I ever do take a detour, with heartfelt repentance I can turn that road back to the highway.

Don't we serve a remarkable Lord, that he would bless us just for looking toward him? That the journey itself is blessed.

My prayer for each of my readers is that you will have the highways to Zion in your heart, and that every single road in your life will move you closer to almighty God, who helps us on our journey and waits with open arms when we arrive!

About the Author

*T*erri Blackstock is an award-winning novelist who has written for several major publishers including Harper-Collins, Dell, Harlequin, and Silhouette. Published under two pseudonyms, her books have sold over 3.5 million copies worldwide.

With her success in secular publishing at its peak, Blackstock had what she calls "a spiritual awakening." A Christian since the age of fourteen, she realized she had not been using her gift as God intended. It was at that point that she recommitted her life to Christ, gave up her secular career, and made the decision to write only books that would point her readers to him.

"I wanted to be able to tell the truth in my stories," she said, "and not just be politically correct. It doesn't matter how many readers I have if I can't tell them what I know about the roots of their problems and the solutions that have literally saved my own life."

Her books are about flawed Christians in crisis and God's provisions for their mistakes and wrong choices. She claims to be extremely qualified to write such books, since she's had years of personal experience.

A native of nowhere, since she was raised in the Air Force, Blackstock makes Mississippi her home. She and her husband are the parents of three children—a blended family which she considers one more of God's provisions.

CAPE REFUGE

By Terri Blackstock

Mystery and suspense combine in this first book of an exciting new 4-book series by best-selling author Terri Blackstock.

Thelma and Wayne Owens run a bed and breakfast in Cape Refuge, Georgia. They minister to the seamen on the nearby docks and prisoners just out of nearby jails, holding services in an old warehouse and taking many of the "down-and-outers" into their home. They have two daughters: the dutiful Morgan who is married to Jonathan, a fisherman, and helps them out at the B & B, and Blair, the still-single town librarian, who would be beautiful if it weren't for the serious scar on the side of her face.

After a heated, public argument with his in-laws, Jonathan discovers Thelma and Wayne murdered in the warehouse where they held their church services. Considered the prime suspect, Jonathan is arrested. Grief-stricken, Morgan and Blair launch their own investigation to help Matthew Cade, the town's young police chief, find the real killer. Shady characters and a raft of suspects keep the plot twisting and the suspense building as we learn not only who murdered Thelma and Wayne, but also the secrets about their family's past and the true reason for Blair's disfigurement.

Softcover: 0-310-23592-8

Pick up a copy today at your favorite bookstore!

ZONDERVAN™

GRAND RAPIDS, MICHIGAN 49530 USA

WWW.ZONDERVAN.COM

Emerald Windows

By Terri Blackstock

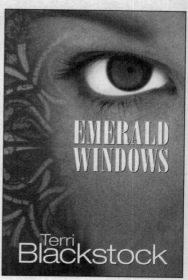

Ten years ago, devastated by an ugly scandal, Brooke Martin fled the small town of Hayden to pursue a career as a stained-glass artist. Now Brooke has returned on business to discover that some things never change. Her spotted reputation remains. Tongues still wag. And that makes what should be her dream assignment tough.

Brooke has been hired to design new stained-glass windows at Hayden Bible Church. The job is a career windfall. But Nick Marcello is overseeing the project, and some in the church think Nick and Brooke's relationship is not entirely professional—and as before, there is no convincing those people otherwise.

In the face of mounting rumors, the two set out to produce the masterpiece Nick has conceived: a brilliant set of windows displaying God's covenants in the Bible. For Brooke, it is more than a project—it is a journey toward faith. But opposition is heating up. A vicious battle of words and will is about to tax Brooke's commitment to the limit. Only this time, she is determined not to run.

Softcover: 0-310-22807-7

Pick up a copy today at your favorite bookstore!

ZONDERVAN™

GRAND RAPIDS, MICHIGAN 49530 USA

WWW.ZONDERVAN.COM

terri blackstock

seaside

A Novella

Seaside

Terri Blackstock

Seaside is a novella of the heart—poignant, gentle, true, offering an eloquent reminder that life is too precious a gift to be unwrapped in haste.

Sarah Rivers has it all: successful husband, healthy kids, beautiful home, meaningful church work.

Corinne, Sarah's sister, struggles to get by. From Web site development to jewelry sales, none of the pies she has her thumb stuck in contains a plum worth pulling.

No wonder Corinne envies Sarah. What she doesn't know is how jealous Sarah is of her. And what neither of them realizes is how their frantic drive for achievement is speeding them headlong past the things that matter most in life.

So when their mother, Maggie, purchases plane tickets for them to join her in a vacation on the Gulf of Mexico, they almost decline the offer. But circumstances force the issue, and the sisters soon find themselves first thrown together, then ultimately *drawn* together, in one memorable week in a cabin called "Seaside."

As Maggie, a professional photographer, sets out to capture on film the faces and moods of her daughters, more than film develops. A picture emerges of possibilities that come only by slowing down and savoring the simple treasures of the moment. It takes a mother's love and honesty to teach her two daughters a wiser, uncluttered way of life—one that can bring peace to their hearts and healing to their relationship. And though the lesson comes on wings of grief, the sadness is tempered with faith, restoration, and a joy that comes from the hand of God.

Hardcover: 0-310-23318-6

Pick up a copy today at your favorite bookstore!

ZONDERVAN™

GRAND RAPIDS, MICHIGAN 49530 USA

WWW.ZONDERVAN.COM

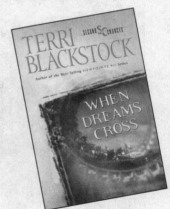

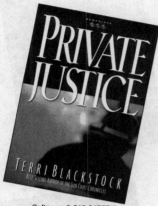
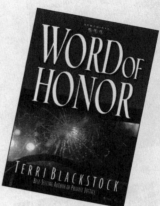
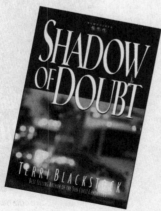
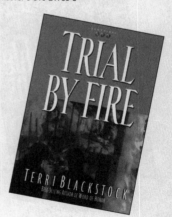

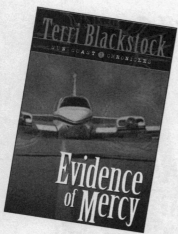
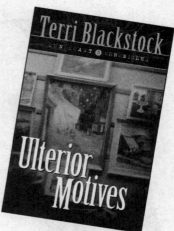

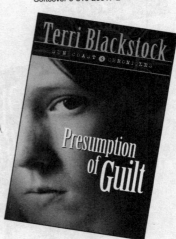

We want to hear from you. Please send your comments about this book to us in care of zreview@zondervan.com. Thank you.

GRAND RAPIDS, MICHIGAN 49530 USA

WWW.ZONDERVAN.COM